The Likely Resolutions of Oliver Clock

The Likely Resolutions of Oliver Clock

JANE RILEY

LAKE UNION
PUBLISHING

Published by Lake Union Publishing, Seattle

www.apub.com

Amazon, the Amazon logo, and Lake Union Publishing are trademarks of Amazon.com, Inc., or its affiliates.

ISBN-13: 9781542008143
ISBN-10: 154200814X

Cover design and illustration by Leo Nickolls Design

Printed in the United States of America

To Mum and Dad.

PART ONE

I must eat less cake.
I must stop watching infomercials.
I must take up a hobby – making model aeroplanes, perhaps?
I must go to the movies once a month, even if it means going on my own.
I must find love.
Can I find love?

The Yellow Notebook

They say old habits die hard, which is true, but I also think that new habits are born easily when you live on your own. Like talking to yourself. Ordering pantry items in alphabetical order. Storing balled-up socks in colour-coordinated rows in a drawer. Buying microwave meals for one when you should be cooking from scratch, because you really do love to cook. And fantasising – writing lists of things you'd like to do, imagining a life that isn't yours, all from the comfort of your sofa.

Mine are rather like New Year's resolutions. Except I make them at any time of the year, whenever I think my life needs reviving – jotting them down in a yellow, dog-eared notebook I've had for ages. It's an enjoyable way to spend an evening when you have little else to do and no one to share your time with. It's also a pleasant way to unwind from my job as a funeral director.

I was on the sofa with a red wine and mediocre microwave chicken cacciatore, fantasising again. I put my unfinished meal on the floor and picked up the notebook, turned to a new page and began to write.

Thou shalt not grow too large to fit comfortably into a standard-size coffin: I must start exercising.

I don't know why I adopted old-fashioned vernacular but I liked its authoritative tone, which I'd not used before. There was something arresting about addressing imaginary masses of people, even if I was the only addressee. It gave me a sense of hopefulness that maybe this time I might actually get off the sofa and carry out some of my desires. *Thou shalt be messy: I must refrain from excessive tidiness.*

I kicked a shoe out of place. Stared at its haphazard placement and sideways slant, out of whack with its partner. I knew the sight of it shouldn't make me break out into a sweat but it was a start.

Thou shalt broaden your social life: I must make friends with people other than those who have passed on.

The nature of my vocation, being on call day and night, made it difficult to have meaningful encounters with anyone else. And as for meeting potential dates, well, that was proving more difficult as time went on and my previously single friends were preoccupied with getting married and having children. You see, if you boiled it down as if deglazing a pan, what I really yearned for was a partner. And love. Ideally both at the same time.

I chewed the end of the pen and wondered with horror if my only option was to sign up to a dating site. *Quelle horreur*, as Mum would say. Yet if I did, how would I describe myself? Bachelor, thirty-nine years old, walking fit (at best), with excess podge and a slight slouch. Has a kind heart and is a good listener. Considers himself a gourmand (tonight's microwave meal notwithstanding, as well as the six others I have in my fridge). In his job people may be dying to see him but what he's looking for is a like-minded – living – female to bring love into his life.

Sigh.

The truth was, I had my eye on somebody already and had done for a long time. If only Marie knew that she was the like-minded living female I dreamed of enlivening my life. I suppose there was only one way to make it happen.

Thou shalt find a way to ask Marie out.

Marie may be married, but hadn't she said only a few weeks ago that she was unhappy? The idea of me asking her out was so outrageous it made me laugh. Not just a chuckle but uncontrollably, stupidly, unable to stop. A socked foot left the ground, then both feet were airborne as I fell back against the sofa in glee, rejoicing at the audacity of my latest resolution.

'Happy New Year,' I said out loud, even though it was a humid February evening, as I pondered the extraordinary notion of going on a date with the woman I had admired from a distance for fourteen years.

Then I put my feet back on the floor, picked up the television remote, turned on the TV and switched channels. Nothing took my fancy. I left it on a documentary about stars and galaxies with the sound on mute. Yet, as I drank the rest of the wine, I couldn't stop thinking about Marie. My mind clicked and whirred like the old ceiling fan above me, as if deciding whether to slow down or speed up. It was an apt analogy. Do I or don't I? Hold off or dive right in? Slow down or speed up?

Undying Love

The next morning I drove to work at the same time I always did (eight o'clock) and arrived at the same time I always did (twelve minutes past eight), parked in the small car park behind our building where there were four spaces reserved for Clock & Son Funeral Home, and went inside. I unlocked the front door, swung the 'closed' sign to 'open' and stepped on to the footpath to take a minute to survey the outside world, as I always liked to do – to remind myself for a brief moment of the beauty of life in the inner city, in contrast to the death behind the cloistered walls of my business.

I breathed in the reassuring smells of petrol fumes and roasted coffee, as the nose-to-tail rush of morning traffic eased to a comfortable road-rage-free rhythm along King Street. Clouds formed judder bars across the sky. The wind whipped everything around me into new shapes. I nodded to pedestrians walking past but they seemed unaware I was even there. I didn't mind. I'm not one to draw attention to myself and have learned the art of listening – a necessary trait in my line of work.

I went back inside and headed to the morgue to check on our latest client, whom our embalmer, Roger Dewfield, finished sprucing yesterday. Anne Mulligan lay snug in one of our solid oak coffins, nestled in white satin lining. I smoothed out her jacket to remove the creases, tugged at the corners of her collar and tucked a strand of hair back into place. You would never have known that the cause of death was anaphylactic shock from a bee sting while lawn-mowing. How serene she now looked. Gone were the signs of bee-stung fear and facial swelling. Her head was just so, muscles fully relaxed, lips a gentle smile, skin smooth and creamy. Her face was heart-shaped – chin on the pointy side – with almond eyes and a caring mien.

I know it sounds silly but I like chatting to cadavers. If I'm honest, it eases my loneliness and there are times when it helps make things clearer. Helps sort the dross from the vaguely sensible thoughts clattering around my mind like loose Smarties in a nearly empty box. I had gone to bed with Marie and resolution number four on my mind, and woken up with it, and her, still there. It followed me into the shower, sprung out at me from my underwear drawer and plopped on to my toast as if it had morphed into marmalade. Was this going to be the one resolution that shadowed me until I acted upon it, poking my bottom and tapping my shoulder like an annoying toddler?

You see, in our last conversation together, Marie had hinted at unhappiness in her marriage, which got me wondering. Was she really, truly unhappy or had it been a throwaway comment that meant nothing more than that her husband's habit of leaving half a banana on the kitchen bench at breakfast irritated her? Or perhaps he left used clothes in a mound on the bedroom floor, which would be most distressing if it was on a regular basis?

Marie was Clock & Son's preferred florist and had been ever since she started her business, Alchemy Flowers, fourteen years ago at age twenty-four. She reminded me of Cleopatra then, and still does, with her black hair, striking eyes rimmed with kohl and skin like porcelain. She had short no-nonsense nails and long, slender fingers with the occasional thorn-prick. At the time she was in between boyfriends; I was dating no one. Four months later, she started dating Henry and they married about two years after that. Four months! For most people that would be plenty of time in which to act upon their feelings. Me? I did nothing. Just imagine where I might be now, had I plucked a petal or two of courage. Ugh, it didn't bear thinking about. I even remember when she brought in her first bouquet: a beautifully symmetrical arrangement of brightly coloured flowers that was de rigueur for the early noughties. And she was punctual, just like me. When we last met – at a café on the main road, an easy walk between our two businesses – it was to discuss the arrangements for the funeral of the president of the Cactus and Succulent Society.

'The client wants the entire coffin covered in cacti and succulents,' I explained, 'plus large living sculptures of the president's initials using the same plants. Not your usual pastel-coloured bouquet.'

Marie nodded and took notes, unperturbed by sculpting cacti into letters.

'You've only got a few days,' I added.

'Don't look so worried, Oliver. I like a challenge,' she said. 'Better a challenging flower arrangement than a challenging husband.'

She may have laughed but when I looked her in the eye, she glanced away. That's when I started wondering: what did she mean and how unhappy was she? If it was to do with her marriage, then I have to say I had never warmed to Henry. I had assumed his brusque, rather arrogant manner hid a softer side that only those close to him saw. Yet, what if there was no softer side and Marie had had enough? So I asked, 'Everything alright?'

'Oh, you know . . .' she said, waving the words away.

'If you want to talk, I'm happy to lend an ear.'

'Thanks, Oliver. It's just . . . well, sometimes . . .'

I was going to probe further but her phone rang and the opportunity got sucked out of the window and churned in the back of the rubbish truck that was lumbering off down the road. It wasn't mentioned again but I couldn't stop thinking about it.

Could I be the one to bring happiness back into her life?

I glanced at Anne, checked my watch. Jean didn't usually come in until nine so I had time. Anne looked amenable to a practice run and if I pretended she was Marie . . .

'So, you see,' I said, walking around to the end of the coffin to face Anne, 'I was wondering . . .'

No, far too dithery. I moved away from Anne and did a circuit of the room.

'Hey,' I said casually, 'how about we have a drink sometime?'

No. We often had a drink after work and it was never anything other than a drink after work.

What about: 'Look, I don't want to be presumptuous but you know how you said you weren't happy? With Henry and all that? Well, maybe, you know, I could . . . we could . . .' I gave a European-style shrug with an open-palmed gesture to show how relaxed I was about whether she said yes or not, and that I had plenty of other women I could ask out if she declined. Ha! Then I caught sight of my pantomime pose freeze-framed in the antique mirror at the end of the room. Idiot. I shoved my hands in my trouser pockets and headed back towards Anne.

Or, I could tell her outright that I loved her. Announce it like it was mine to own.

'I love you, Marie. I love you and that's all there is to it.'

Or perhaps: 'Leave Henry. Be with me!' I practised again, with emphasis on the words 'leave' and 'me'.

I was Romeo. Figaro. Or was it Don Giovanni? I was the dashing suitor who would save Marie from her terrible marriage and abominable husband and be a far better partner than anyone else could possibly be. My right hand came out of a pocket – I couldn't help myself. 'Oh yes, Marie, I love you.' But my hand clonked the lid of the open coffin. Made me yelp – twice – and dented my knuckles. A red blotch spread across my skin, moved like running dye. I gripped my hand tightly in case it might fall off and thought, *I might have to go to hospital.*

'What are you doing?'

I turned around. Jean, our long-serving administrator, stood in the doorway behind me.

Taken aback, I said the first thing that came to me. 'You're early.'

As always, her hair was hairspray-set and a brooch fixed to her left lapel. Today, it was a silver cut-out of a bicycle. Not the usual type of jewellery for a woman of her age, but Jean was a woman who surprised every so often.

'Are you alright?' she asked.

I tried to smile but feared it was more of a grimace. 'Bloody coffins,' I said.

'It's just, Mr Mulligan is here. Waiting outside.'

I nodded. Jean left. I let go of my hand and pushed aside thoughts of proclaiming love and kinship till death do us part to Marie, and got on with the day.

The Folder of Systematic Funeral Protocol, Page Three

After Mr Mulligan left, a Ms Castor arrived, then a Mr and Mrs Robertson. I asked them all the same set of questions, based on those my father devised as part of his Folder of Systematic Funeral Protocol in 1977, following his own inheritance of Clock & Son. *What are your names? Who is the deceased? What is their relation to you? How did they die? Do they wish to be buried or cremated? Would you like the twenty-pound-a-head afternoon tea option or the fifty-pound? Asparagus sandwiches or mini quiches?* The list went on. It even included sample phrases of condolence I suspected came from the insides of Hallmark cards. They were to be regurgitated, as Dad once told me, 'when you can't think of the right thing to say'.

I followed it to the letter when I first took over the business, only to find that saying the right things came naturally. Having read the Folder so many times, I realised I had memorised every greeting card message and soothing word of consolation it contained. They rolled off my tongue as smoothly as floor dirt with my newly purchased microfibre cleaning slippers. Not only that, but I was able to sense what to say, when. Dad's folder of advice became the springboard from which I could tap into my own innate empathy and compassion to help soothe the souls of my clients.

After the Robertsons, I had just enough time to eat the leftover 'sympathy' biscuits – the flavour of which changed each week, according to what whetted Jean's appetite or, if Mum was buying, whatever happened to be on sale – and check my emails before a body was wheeled in at four, followed by a nursing home call-out at six. I was thrilled to have cheered the wife of a dentist who would have been familiar with the mouths of most in the local community by suggesting we hand out dental floss with every order of service and offering Marie's idea of featuring flowers in varying shades of white. It was another routine day.

A week later and I still couldn't stop thinking about Marie and how on earth I was going to proceed with my dilemma. But my desire to pursue her was having unsavoury side effects: I could feel a rise in blood pressure and had butterflies in my stomach. It was not only distracting but unsettling. As I often craved a quick fix of chocolate in times of distress, I bought a Mars bar on my way to work one day. I saved it to eat in the back room, on my own, leaning against the embalming table, enjoying the quietude of the place. At lunchtime, when I was certain no one else was around and the room was free from Roger and his handiwork, I scurried to my place of respite. I unwrapped the bar and took a mouthful. I closed my eyes to savour the taste. I don't know how many Mars bars I've eaten over the years but every time I do they make me drool. It's the rich caramel, high sugar content and the chewiness which slows down your eating. The perfect antidote to a stressful situation.

'Oliver?'

My eyes snapped open. A dribble of chocolate-flavoured saliva slid down the side of my mouth. Mum stood in the doorway. I pondered whether to pretend I was inspecting the embalming room because of Roger's recent laxness in tidiness and care, having recently left an apple core nestled into the wig of a ninety-seven-year-old lady, or offer her a bite. Mum got in before me.

'There's a man here to see you,' she said.

'Mr Muir?'

'He apologises for being early.'

'Of course.' Except I still had half the bar to go.

'And next time, buy one for me,' Mum said, and tapped the corner of her mouth to indicate the unseemly Mars bar residue on mine. I wrapped the rest of the chocolate in a paper towel, put it in my pocket and snapped myself into professional mode.

Mr Muir's wife had died suddenly from a heart attack at her local gym. She was only sixty-five. Fit but stressed, by all accounts, due to a high-pressure job as a lawyer and a family history of heart disease. The poor woman had the figure of a forty-year-old but the heart of an obese eighty-year-old. I met him in reception, shook his hand and ushered him into my office.

'Can we get you a tea or coffee, Mr Muir?' I said.

'It's Richard. You don't need to be formal with me. And for God's sake, don't call my wife "the deceased", if you were going to. She's Shirley. Dead or not dead.'

'Of course, Richard,' I said, according to page three of Father's Folder of Systematic Funeral Protocol, whereby you do whatever the client wants within the official parameters of the industry and the law.

'I'll have tea,' he added.

I called Jean to request two teas and a plate of biscuits. I especially liked the macadamia shortbread she had 'splashed out' on the other day. I smiled at Richard and wished, despite the man's cough, that I could give him a hug. But page two of the Folder insisted you never give a man or woman you didn't know a hug or kiss or any personal affection. Classic Andrew Clock. Yet I wondered if there were times when a hug wouldn't have gone amiss and that, contrary to my father's views, it would be greatly appreciated. As I was assessing whether Richard was a hug-loving man, he slapped a handwritten list on my desk.

'Now,' he said. 'I've decided on refreshments.' He pushed the piece of paper towards me. 'But what I can't decide on is the photo for the service handout. Personally, I like this one of her when we first met. It's grainy and in black and white but that's the woman I'm married to. She's not changed. Not really.' He hoicked and sniffed. Perhaps he wasn't the hugging type. 'Then I thought it could be this one, taken a week after she retired when we went on a trip to Italy. She came alive when we travelled. Such a free spirit. Or then there's this one. It's more recent. How most people will remember her, I suppose.' He fanned them out on the table before me, the sides of his mouth drooping.

'Why don't you have all three?' I suggested. Richard scratched his beard; I watched his brain whirr and click. 'I know it's difficult making decisions at a time like this. That's why it's best to take the decision out of the decision.' (That was my line, not Dad's, and while it may have sounded like real-estate jargon, the phrase always pleased me and I wished I had thought of it in time for it to appear in the Folder.) Occasionally I would veer off-Folder to stamp my own mark on things; it was nothing too outrageous but, still, I didn't let Mum know in case she disapproved.

'Why choose one if you like them all?' I continued. 'We could place them together on the front page or your favourite on the front and the other two inside. In fact, you can have as many as you like. Have you got any more?'

Richard nodded, his face as gloomy as a Monday morning. I opened the top drawer of my desk and took out a folder of service handouts. 'You see, there's no end of options.' I smiled because a smile always lifts a mood, even if only a fraction.

Richard fiddled with the booklets but didn't look like he was studying them at all. 'How do you do this, day in, day out?' he said. 'It's shit, isn't it?'

'It may not be for everyone but it's very satisfying. My job – *our* job,' I said, gesturing to Jean, who had arrived with the refreshments, 'is to try and make it easier for those who are left behind, to ease the . . . shitty-ness.'

'But grief? Every day. I bet no one comes in happy. Or if they did, they wouldn't let on.'

'We don't judge how others grieve,' I said. But, of course, we sometimes did. How could you not when a customer blusters in with haste, dismissive of our sympathy, as if behind the serious facade there was a celebration going on and an eagerness to get to the solicitor.

Richard grunted, contemplated my answer, then said, 'Alright, put this one on the front.' He pointed to the black-and-white headshot of Shirley. Her hair in a beehive, her smile coy. 'And make it big. The other two can go inside. But I want the photos back and please don't bend the corners.' He ran a hand over the photographs, as if smoothing out the grief.

'Of course,' I said. 'She will look as magnificent as she will do in person.'

'When can I see her?'

'Tomorrow. Roger is sprucing her up this afternoon. And if there's anything you'd like to put in with her . . .?'

Richard shrugged.

'There's no obligation.'

'Her personal trainer thinks I should add a small dumb-bell. She loved working out, after all. But then I thought it might add unnecessarily to the weight, for the poor buggers carrying her, and then what about cremation and burning metal . . .?' Richard's voice petered out.

'It's not a bother. We can accommodate any requests. Bring whatever you like tomorrow. Perhaps something lighter, like a sweat towel or some socks? Used or unused, it doesn't matter.'

'Sorry I said you had a shit job. It was out of line.'

I waved the remark away. I didn't mind. People are never themselves when they get to see me.

'Tomorrow then,' said Richard.

I was going to shake his hand but decided to give him a slap on the back instead. He seemed more of a slap-on-the-back kind of a guy.

Generational Pull

The funeral business runs in our family like other families have a history of baldness, a tendency to gout or a predilection to buck teeth. I wouldn't call it a predisposition so much as a predetermination, a foregone conclusion, much like death itself. You need a good heart, not a faint one, and an ability to see humour amidst the darkness.

It all started when my great-grandfather, John Clock, a carpenter, began making coffins and caskets and found a niche for himself in the commercialisation of the funeral business in the mid- to late-nineteenth century. But it was John's son James who looked beyond the hardware and, with his entrepreneurial eye, established Clock & Son Funeral Home in 1939, on the cusp of the Second World War. The fortuitousness of his timing prompted my great-grandfather to say, 'With nous like that, the business is destined for greatness.' Forty-two years later James fell ill with pneumonia and my father took over, and for another twenty-eight years Clock & Son continued to thrive. Then, when my father died twelve years ago, he left me in charge and my mother, Doreen, a financial stake. I have run the business ever since.

The truth is, I once dreamed of being a newspaper reporter. I fantasised about roving the streets looking for neighbourhood news, interviewing eyewitnesses at crime scenes, getting the scoops and reading my byline in print. I decided I was the perfect candidate: I'd seen death, so it wouldn't shock me, and my English teacher said I had a flair for writing. But my destiny had other ideas. Even though I got a newspaper round when I was thirteen, I still had to help out in the business. In the school holidays and sometimes after school, I folded brochures, put out the rubbish, bulk-bought teabags and biscuits, and ate afternoon teas of home-made vanilla slices or, as a treat, a shop-bought cream bun, in the small kitchen out the back. When the time came to leave school, Dad signed me up for a series of funeral courses, beginning with the Certificate in Funeral Operations and ending with embalming training. It was assumed I would start working at Clock & Son straight away.

In many ways I didn't mind. Surrendering to my fate seemed an easier, risk-free option. It was a vocation I was familiar with that came with inbuilt job security and a boss I already knew. My future was laid out for me like surgical instruments on an embalming table and that warmed my belly like a hot toddy with a generous glug of brandy.

So, at nineteen, I became a funeral assistant and found I was inherently equipped for the job. I could ease others' worries better than my own and had astute listening skills from having grown up sibling-free and child-shy. I enjoyed the order of procedure, legal and funereal, and was content to receive instructions, obeying the historical hierarchy within the business whereby my father sat at the top and me at the bottom. My mother, who worked part-time, was somewhere in the middle. Her role, which she embodied as if she had been the business's inheritor instead of her husband, was customer service and the efficient running of the back end, from beautifying reception to staff management. Our Clock family trio ran as one entity, smoothly, professionally and without a hitch, until Dad died suddenly aged sixty-four when I was twenty-seven.

What a bombshell that was. It threw Mum and me into a blender of shock, anguish and grief with the power switch stuck on high. It was a heart attack that claimed him, his voracious appetite for Mum's butter-laden cooking being his undoing – the snacks of jam-filled doughnuts, custard squares and Friday-night fatty battered fish and chips. What made it even more tragic was how his first heart attack hadn't prompted culinary changes in the Clock household which may well have saved him.

When the first one happened, on a Sunday afternoon, I was cleaning my skirting boards with a toothbrush. Mum called me in distress as Dad tensed in his chair, one arm seemingly paralysed and his face contorted as if a just-swallowed peanut had gone down the wrong way.

'Come now, Oliver. Come now,' she ordered over the phone.

'I'm coming,' I said, leaving the toothbrush on the floor and grabbing the car keys.

It was the only time I remember ever seriously exceeding the speed limit and driving dangerously in a suburban setting. Thankfully for Dad that day, the ambulance arrived before me.

When the second one happened it was seven fifteen in the evening. I was nibbling on peanuts – a dangerous snack at the best of times – when Mum phoned, ordering me back to work.

'Your father's coming in,' she said. I thought it was because Dad was going to berate me for something I'd done wrong and waited for her to tell me so. But no. He had died.

I threw the peanuts I was holding into the sink and told her I'd be right there. I felt calm but in shock, as if I had diverted to my role of funeral assistant and was focused only on the procedures that had to be followed.

'The ambulance will be there tout de suite,' she said, such was her penchant for French phrases, hoping they gave her the air of a sophisticate. 'I won't be far behind.'

It was only when we left the parlour later that night that she burst into tears when hit with the realisation that she was unable to take Dad home with her. It was only the second time I'd seen Mum cry. Even Dad I'd seen tearier over the years than Mum – usually after a client had left the building, especially if the circumstances surrounding their loved one's death had been particularly traumatic. Mum might have rubbed his back for a brief moment but then she usually told him to snap out of it. 'We can't be having customers seeing you like this,' she'd say. She was adept at building a doorless igloo around her heart. No one was getting in, least of all herself. Whereas Dad was like a strawberry cream chocolate with a hard exterior and soft inside, Mum was a chocolate toffee – hard all over. But I don't think she was always this way. I'm sure when I was little and she was younger, there was something more gooey caramel about her.

While my father had not been a pillar of health, he had been a god-like pillar of the community, with a gravitas that we – and no doubt others – thought gave him an immunity to the assured side effect of living: death. For neither Mum nor I had ever truly considered the business without him. It took days for me to accept that the last time my father was there was not to order me around in his usual blustery way but to roll in quietly and inconspicuously, lifeless and cold on a gurney, and, unexpectedly, to call up deeply embedded feelings I never knew existed. Grief clobbered me on the head with the full force of a cricket ball and made me flounder, as if treading water in the deep, scared to drown in sadness.

When the tears had dried up and Mum told me to get on with things, I realised what 'getting on with things' actually meant. I hadn't contemplated inheriting the business at twenty-seven. I hadn't wanted to contemplate inheriting it at all. I gulped panic until I got stomach cramps, became anxious at the thought of having to take the lead and make decisions. I had liked hiding behind my father's jacket flaps. It felt safe, secure. But stepping into his trousers was an altogether troubling and unsettling proposition and one which I had no time to prepare myself for. The one consolation was that Mum was given a twenty per cent stake in the business and the option to stay on as an employee for as long as she wanted. She did. What also got me through the rising panic was the belief that, on the basis of history, the business would tick and whir as it had done for the past eighty years without too much extra effort on my part. For that was the beauty of the surety of death.

Yet I also knew – had read about it once in the finance section of the newspaper – that in long-running family businesses it was usually the third generation who cocked it up. They get greedy or overly ambitious. But I wasn't like that. I believed: why change things when you don't need to? It's better keeping things the same than cocking it all up. So that's what I did: I kept everything exactly as it was.

Last Date

I had one more client after Mr Muir – the husband of a local primary school teacher who had once taught me. Mrs Hetherington was revered and loved by both parents and children and I couldn't have been prouder to be honoured with the task of organising her funeral. Before we even got on to the practicalities, I couldn't help but reminisce with Mr Hetherington on my classroom time with her. How, on Monday mornings, she would get everyone to draw a picture of their weekend. It didn't matter what you drew as long as it represented something about how your weekend had been. Or how she would break out into song whenever she wanted the class's attention. Sometimes, it was singing 'Happy Birthday', even if it was no one's birthday, or she would play an animal noise on her tape recorder and the first person to name the animal would get a sweet. The funniest part was learning that she used to do the same thing with Mr Hetherington, which made us laugh far more loudly than was normally associated with the hushed tones of a funeral home. But it gave me an idea, an idea that made Mr Hetherington slap me on the back, harder than I think he intended to, in delight. 'Let's set up an art station,' I suggested, 'so the children who come to the service can draw pictures in honour of her, and why don't we play the song she most liked to sing as the final song?' Mr Hetherington walked out a happy man, leaving me a happy funeral director.

But then it wasn't very busy after Mr Hetherington left. I browsed ties for sale online and tidied the files on my desk until it was time to close up. When I got home, I did what I always did when I walked in the door: I went to the kitchen. I opened the fridge and hitched up my trousers, unable as they were these days to decide whether to sit over or under my stomach. A breeze of icy air brushed my face. I looked at what was on offer. A row of half-empty condiments lined up in height order stared back at me from the top shelf and, from the middle, various opened cheeses, a packet of ham, a tub of rhubarb yoghurt and a jar of olives. An uninspiring yet tasty slice of my life. I shifted the yoghurt to line up symmetrically with its neighbours, grabbed the extra-strong Cheddar and the pickled onions and found a semi-drunk bottle of red wine in the pantry.

I was about to pour myself a glass when an urge came over me. I don't know where it came from but I couldn't help myself. I held the bottle away from me, as if trying to decipher the label without reading glasses, and imagined it was Marie and that this would be our first dance. I sidestepped and circled, my chin high, shoulders swaying. Who knew what dance I was dancing – a hybrid between a waltz and a tango or some such mash-up – but it didn't matter because I was dancing with Marie, spinning her around the kitchen floor as if we were contestants on *Strictly Come Dancing*. She gazed into my eyes and let me take the lead. *Oh, Marie, will you be mine?*

Then the island bench got in my way, slamming into my stomach, and I nearly slid across it, like a penguin skidding, belly down, on an icy slope. The move with no name. My knee hit defrost on the below-bench microwave oven and it occurred to me that I shouldn't be dancing in socks. But I didn't drop Marie. I gripped her waist as if it were my final act of bravery and gently put her down on the bench top.

Time for wine.

The thing was, I had to do it right. Why couldn't Dad have written a Systematic Guide to Courting? Although, who was I kidding? Dad would have been the last person to ask about the rituals of dating as, according to Mum, it was she who had asked Dad out, having tired of wondering whether 'the nice young man' who gave her the eye every Friday night at the local dance hall was going to do so himself. For Dad didn't do romance. Or, at least, not that I ever noticed. He didn't discuss it, mention or reveal it. As a young man I learned to navigate the elusive world of romance without any help from my father.

I took my glass of wine and a plate of cheese, crackers and pickled onions to the kitchen table.

There had to be a way to broach happiness with Marie again.

Could I do it when I next visited her shop? As she stood amongst the buckets of blooms, rich foliage and oversized gnarled branches, a forest-green apron tied at her waist, her face framed by a black bob, her welcoming smile large and generous? I glugged a mouthful of wine. Therein lay the problem. Marie rarely appeared unhappy. She was usually joyful, her default setting smiling. I'd have to catch her when her guard was down. When the effort of facade proved too much.

Or I could give her a flower. Marie liked to joke that if you poked a stick under her and popped her in a tub of water she wouldn't look out of place. She was like a rose, a single, fully bloomed rose. If I gave her one, could I tweak her heart and make her happy?

Or I could buy her a book on the secret to happiness and write a note on the inside cover. Would I begin with 'Dearest Marie' or 'My dear Marie'? And end with 'Lots of love' or 'Love, Oliver'? Were two kisses more genuine or less affectionate than four? Would she even get the message?

More wine.

At least with Marie I didn't have to explain what I did for a living.

Which had helped the last time I had gone on a date nearly two years ago – with Jean's niece, Shelley – and was what made me agree to go on a date with her in the first place. My previous attempts at enlightening my subjects were rarely successful. My quip – 'I make a living from the dead' – was usually met with blank stares and swallowed winces. What's more, you were always on call, day and night. People keep on dying. Few appreciate a dinner date being interrupted by the death of a stranger. 'That'll be a call from the dead,' I'd laugh. They never did.

With Shelley, I thought, she would not need to wince, grimace or turn away. And if she did, it would have nothing to do with my job.

So the date was off to a good start before it had even begun, and to celebrate I bought candles during my lunch break. Red ones, long and tapered. I had to borrow candle holders from Jean, who nudged and winked ridiculously for a woman of her age. I also bought a selection of cheeses – a rotund Stinking Bishop, a mature Cheddar and a mild Stilton – plus crackers, grapes, serviettes – also red – and a Coldplay CD to update my music collection. The plan, I decided, was to meet at the cinema, see a movie, share some popcorn and go back to my place for cheese and wine. Nothing fancy. A perfectly relaxing, casual evening in which, if I found conversation lacking, we could at least discuss the film. I had even decided to fling off my boat shoes on arrival and leave them lying where they landed to show how much of a relaxed, easy-going guy I was.

But I should have watched the movie trailer. Although I enjoyed it, I had underestimated the amount of violence it contained. Sudden limb removals, brain explosions and crazed characters meant quietly spoken Shelley spent a large proportion of the film with her eyes covered. I instigated a swift exit during the credits and apologised profusely as soon as we were hit by the bright lights of the foyer. Shelley, bless her, told me not to worry and even managed to find something positive to say: 'It had a good storyline and was quite well acted. I think.'

My offer of a cosy living room, a bottle of expensive wine and a neatly arranged cheese platter was to be the perfect antidote to highly strung nerves. Although I immediately regretted the purchase of the

Stinking Bishop. Its stench slapped me on the cheeks as soon as I flung open the fridge door. I gave another round of jovial apologies.

'I can assure you, it tastes wonderful,' I called from the kitchen as I took out the prearranged platter from the fridge. 'I'm a sucker for a decent cheese and have been known to linger too long in the specialty shop around the corner.'

'What about the gourmet ice cream place?' Shelley called back. I wondered if it was because of the pungent odour that she had decided to remain in the living room.

'Been there, too,' I replied, finding two cheese knives to add to the assortment and placing them diametrically opposite each other. I checked my hair in the glass oven door and wiped the bench for the second time.

'Their panna cotta gelato is delicious. Maybe we could go some-time?' Shelley's voice spun a web into the kitchen and wove warmth around me. I was sure the movie had been a mere blip in the evening.

Buoyed by the prospect that Shelley hadn't written me off com-pletely and that she shared my love of food, I decided we would eat in the living room, despite my fear of errant cracker crumbs slipping between the sofa cushions. But just as I was lifting the platter the lights went out. The purring of the fridge stopped. An 'Ooh' came from the living room.

'I think we've had a power cut,' I called out. 'No need to be scared.' It seemed rude not to reassure her.

'Do you want some help?' she said. I heard her get up.

'No, it's OK. You stay there. I'll find a torch. I've got one somewhere.'

I riffled around my drawer of miscellany for a torch, then remem-bered the candles and praised the good timing of a power cut. I took them to the living room and lit them on the coffee table, trying not to shine the torch directly into Shelley's eyes. I couldn't help but notice how lovely she looked in the glow of candlelight, yet could not dwell on the moment for fear I appeared about to interrogate her with the torch. I hurried back to the kitchen to get the cheese and wine. Two more trips later – as I had forgotten the serviettes – I finally sat down.

'If it's not one thing, it's another,' I said awkwardly.

'You were a class act under dire circumstances,' she said, raising her glass. Her jumper matched the colour of her eyes, a murky olive that in soft light was rather flattering. We clinked empty tumblers.

'Would you like me to fill your glass?' I laughed. She giggled along with me until I lingered too long in her eyes while attempting to multitask. There was a fumble of arms crossing, glass avoiding glass and a candle teetering in its holder. The flame caught Shelley's fringe. Its speed shocked. I did the first thing that came to mind: flung red wine in her face to douse the fire as she slapped her forehead with a serviette. She squealed and looked at me, stunned. Wine dripped off her nose and the smell of singed hair took over from the Stinking Bishop.

'Oh my God, what's happened to my hair?' Her hands flapped and touched what was left of her fringe.

The hairs on my arm curled, my jaw dropped. I didn't like to say she now resembled Friar Tuck.

'I need a mirror. Where's the bathroom?' She leapt up and felt her way between the sofa and the coffee table and headed down the hallway. I shone the torch to help light her way.

'It's not that bad,' I called out, following.

'Quick, the torch,' she said, beckoning me into the bathroom.

I stood behind her and held the torch below her chin at bench level. It gave off a ghoulish light around her face. With the unflattering shadows and her tear-reddened eyes, one could argue Friar Tuck now more closely resembled Herman Munster from *The Addams Family*. She let out a wail. I put my arm around her.

'It will grow back,' I said. She shrugged me off and started crying again. 'I'm really sorry.'

She nodded and let me take her back to the living room, to her spot on the sofa. I offered her some cheese. She declined. I ate two chunks in quick succession, then the lights came back on and I got the urge to clean. With a warm cloth and knife I prised the quick-drying candle drippings off the coffee table, dabbed at the wine stain on the sofa, vacuumed the grapes from the carpet. Shelley watched, lifted her feet so I could get the nozzle under the sofa. She offered to help and asked for a cloth but I insisted she stay right where she was, I'd be done in a minute and everything would be just as it was. Except it wasn't.

Maybe it was the leaving of a lidless Jif bottle on the coffee table that was my undoing, its lemon-fresh bleach smell mixing unfavourably with the aroma of spilt wine. Or perhaps it was my clumsy dabbing of her jeans too close to her inner thigh that put her off. I didn't want her looking like she'd been in a food fight. Either way, I knew I was at the bottom of the slippery slope of date death. No amount of apologising was going to change anything. She sat on the edge of the sofa. I tried to make conversation and drank more wine in a short space of time than I should have. But it was no good. We both knew the evening was over. When she muttered an excuse about 'an early start in the morning', I would have hugged her from relief if it hadn't been inappropriate. I called a taxi and it couldn't come quick enough.

I haven't been on a date since Shelley. The experience drained my confidence, rattled my nerves. I was scared of having another date collapse and being unable to revive it. But with Marie being unhappy, could my luck be changing?

The Dance

I still couldn't get Marie out of my head. Or more precisely, the thought
of asking her out. It was unlike me. I normally talked myself out of
things, telling myself that something was not possible, that I wasn't up
to it. In this instance I had at least two reasons to answer back to my
mental dialogue: Marie was still married and I didn't wish to have an
affair. Anyway, I decided, Marie wasn't unhappy enough to leave her
husband for me, nor was she interested in me in the way I was her.
Just because I wasn't a fan of Henry didn't mean she couldn't be married to him. The fact that he seemed to spend incredibly long hours at
work and then forget dinner dates (which he did only a few months
ago) peeved me even more than it seemed to upset Marie, who was
either resigned to it or adept at covering up her discontent. I also had
to consider the possibility that my lack of admiration for Henry was
based on pure jealousy and nothing else. For I couldn't ignore the fact
that he was an exceedingly good-looking man with the biceps of a gym
attendee, who lavished Marie with jewellery I doubted I would have
been able to afford. I'm not sure all of that justified the arrogance he
exuded but, then, who was I to judge? I told myself these things as I
arrived at the local church, where we were meeting to set up the funeral
of a well-known art dealer who had unexpectedly and controversially
passed away. It was the first time I had seen Marie since my reawakened

desire to be with her took hold. But I had to remain professional. We would not be alone. This was a business matter, after all.

As soon as I walked in the smell hit me. Although 'aroma' was probably a better word, as 'smell' assumed at best something neutral, neither particularly aromatic nor dislikeable, like just-washed, unfragranced skin or milk. It was an aroma that mingled oak-scented pews with lilies, stocks, hydrangeas, roses, fern and eucalyptus leaves. Zesty and new mixed with woody and old. It was Marie, the whole of Marie, if I had to condense her into a smell, which was quite a thought and not the sort I wished to have as I greeted her inside the church. All I could think about was Marie being bottled as a scent and me wearing it as a cologne. What an idea! Me, wearing Marie as a cologne, dabbed on my neck, sloshed on my wrists. Me, smelling like Marie, taking her with me wherever I went, leaving a fragrant trail of wondrousness. Was this what it felt like to swoon?

I reached for a pew to steady myself. Drew in a few deep breaths. Then Marie saw me. She walked down the aisle and welcomed me with outstretched arms and a large smile, as she always did, seemingly unaware of how giddy I was with emotion. I mustered an aura of professionalism and put on my public face, the one that didn't show how desperate I was to go on a date with her, the one that didn't reveal my thoughts of her as a tailor-made perfume. I jiggled my tie knot and tugged at my suit lapels to heighten my air of impeccable manners. I gave her a quick peck on the cheek before her arms could envelop me and decided to stay there forever, then I said hello to Marie's assistant, Sarah, and the organist, who had arrived to practise his pieces.

I still couldn't look her in the eye. I couldn't let myself be swallowed whole into a world in which I was not allowed. I pulled out my running sheet and spoke to the minister about the next day's proceedings. There was a frisson of tension in the air, as we were all aware that this was no ordinary funeral. It was high profile and would be under the beady eye of the media and a family whose name reeked of money and infamy.

For half an hour we worked diligently as the sonorous chords of the organ resonated around us and rose up to the stained-glass windows as if about to shatter them.

When Peter, the organist, finished, we all clapped and Marie called out, 'Can I request a song?'

I nearly died when she took my hands in hers. We were close enough to kiss again. I was close enough to smell whatever perfume she was wearing, even though I felt so adrift I couldn't smell a thing.

'Come on, Oliver, let's dance.'

All I could think about was the half-drunk bottle of red wine I'd waltzed so beautifully with the other night, spinning and sidestepping like a pro. It would be our second dance. As Peter pumped out the cheery church tune 'All Things Bright and Beautiful', our hands locked, Sarah sang and Marie led me on a fast, rather out-of-step waltz before the pulpit. I could feel her breath, feel her deltoids. I could have nibbled her ear if I'd wanted to. I forced myself to focus on everything but her very nibbleable ear: the wooden pews, the steps to the vestry, the collection box, the aisle. When that song ended, another one started – 'Be Thou My Vision', a title which couldn't have been more apt, but with a tune that turned our pseudo-waltz into a static sway. Marie smiled at me. I had locked eyes with her without meaning to. I smiled back. Wondered about my wonderings.

'This is fun, isn't it?' She smiled. 'Work should never be too serious, don't you think?'

'I couldn't agree more,' I said, fixing my gaze on her fringe.

'Life is serious enough as it is.'

We jerked side to side like a metronome. I wondered what she meant by life being serious enough. But instead of asking, I said, 'Sorry, I'm not a great dancer,' and laughed.

'You're better than Henry. At least you're happy to give it a go.'

'He might feel awkward dancing,' I said, trying to make her, and by default her husband, feel better.

'Or he might not,' she muttered.

Another sentence left dangling in the air like fog waiting to dissipate. Then the song finished and she released her grip and applauded Peter. We all clapped and the moment was lost. The moment I didn't know how to tackle. The moment in which I could have found out more but didn't. My best friend Andy, whom I've known since high school and flat-shared with in our twenties, would have known what to do. He was the libertine to my bashfulness, his approach to women the opposite to mine. He was one of those guys who had the knack of attracting girls without even realising it. Or maybe he did and was calling their bluff, which seemed an all too complicated strategy to me. Whatever his tactics, he was brilliant at exuding charm and feigning indifference at the same time. Nonchalance was his middle name.

Once, in a bid to understand Andy's inherent yet absent-minded charisma and what kind of pheromones oozed from his pores, I decided to conduct an experiment. Every day for a month I secretly sprayed myself with his cologne, always on the days or nights I thought I might be in the company of eligible girls. It was ironic that the day I met my last serious girlfriend, Claire, was the one day I had forgotten to spray.

The Power Walk

The art dealer's funeral was a success, as they should always be. An unsuccessful funeral is when mourners don't cry, the funeral director doesn't get complimented and flowers fall from the arrangements. Marie ensures no flowers fall, ever.

Marie again. She was still at the forefront of my mind. So much so that, a couple of days later, I did something I'd never done before. I climbed into a coffin. It was resolution number one, which had been preying on my mind – *Thou shalt not grow too large to fit comfortably into a standard-size coffin* – in which I must start exercising. I could slim down for Marie, I thought. I would wait to ask her out until I had lost some of my podge, the excess around my belly that had accumulated from pre-dinner cheese and crackers, after-dinner mints and the occasional serving of cheesecake mid-afternoon, as well as the wine, the port, the creamy pastas and beef stews . . . the list could go on. It would give me time to properly assess Marie's situation, work out how to get myself into tip-top shape, and practise the best way to ask her out. I had never been so motivated to get fit.

And so, when no one else was around – Roger had gone for a lunch break and Jean was at the bank – I got a chair and placed it next to one of our mahogany display coffins perched on a fabric-covered trestle. The lid was already open, revealing the shiny folds of white silk lining. There would be no harm in jumping in to check the ease with which I could slide into its cavern and feel the tightness of its fit. Who needed tape measures when you had standard-size coffins with which to assess your measurements? Before I did, I nipped back to reception, then into the kitchenette and the hallway, to ensure I was still flying solo. When I had given myself the all-clear, I scuttled back to the display room, slipped off my shoes and jacket, climbed on to the chair and stepped into the coffin. Taking care not to damage the silk with my feet, I slid into it and stared at the ceiling. My hips were snug against the sides and my arms wedged next to them. I was about to wiggle and move my limbs to assess the fit when a voice called my name. The shock of hearing another human in close range made me sit up with a start or, at least, attempt to sit up with a start. I could only lift my head, which inadvertently gave me the answer to my question. I needed to lose weight.

'Oliver?' It was Mum. Where had she come from? I wasn't expecting her until later. 'What are you doing?' She sounded worried.

'Hi,' I said, trying to pretend everything was normal and that I hadn't just abandoned all the cheese in my fridge, the salted peanuts in the pantry and that Mum hadn't caught me happily lying in a coffin . . . oh, it didn't bear thinking about.

'You're in a coffin.' Her hands were on her hips, a cotton cardigan across her shoulders and a belt trying to find her waist.

'A customer came in asking how comfortable they were and I wanted to be sure I had been honest with her. You know the importance we place on customer service.'

'You need to get out.'

'Yes, Mum,' I said. 'Do you mind giving me a hand?'

Afterwards, Mum said I was 'unprofessional'.

'Imagine if you'd been eating a chocolate bar,' she said. 'It would have gone everywhere. That's why I never liked you eating chocolate anywhere other than the kitchen.'

When I was a child, Mum would have made me eat chocolate, and anything else sticky, gooey or messy, in the bath, if it had been deemed respectable and acceptable. But right then, it made little difference to her that I'd not been eating chocolate and that I had taken off my shoes and hadn't damaged the inside of the coffin. She should have been pleased that I'd left no sign of my presence when I dislodged myself and that I had resolved to lose weight. Instead, she bemoaned who would eat her chocolate oat slices if I wasn't going to. I told her to stop making them. She wasn't happy. After dusting and distributing boxes of tissues around our rooms, she left and I googled 'exercise for beginners'.

Yoga tickled my fancy. It required slow movement as opposed to high cardio exertion, employed stretching as the main activity and balance had always been one of my fortes. Wasn't there a yoga studio nearby? I was sure I had seen a sign recently for one in the neighbourhood. And there it was. A lovely website with images of lithe brown bodies contorting into shapes I didn't know were possible. I checked the timetable. There was a beginners' class at lunchtime – soon – and a discount offer if you pre-bought ten classes. I imagined a sea of clothed bottoms mooning me in my discreet spot at the back of the class. I imagined my own bottom adorned in sweat-absorbing sports shorts the likes of which I'd not worn since high school. I decided to go for a stroll instead.

It took every ounce of self-discipline to avoid the kitchen when I walked in the door at half past six. To not think about the dribble of wine in the bottle in the pantry, the dips in the fridge and the cheese straws in a tin. I walked with determination to my bedroom and changed into an old T-shirt and long board shorts I'd not worn for at least two years. They were the only vaguely appropriate exercise attire I owned. I drank water from the tap in the bathroom – as thirsty as I was, I couldn't risk entering the kitchen at any cost – and left the house, heading in the direction of a nearby park.

The heat of the day hadn't dissipated and there was no wind. Only very occasionally did I wish I lived by the beach, and now was one of those times, which was ironic, considering I was wearing board shorts. But instead of a fresh sea breeze wafting inland I had to contend with still air thick with car exhaust, gusts of grime, Chinese takeaway fumes clawing at the footpath and tightly knit, paint-peeling buildings gasping skyward.

I should have gone the back way. Nevertheless, I pushed on, swinging my arms towards greenery and open space. I weaved my way through commuters just disembarked from a bus, dodged a large dog turd and avoided tripping on uneven pavements. Glancing down a laneway, I felt a pang of envy seeing tattooed teenagers kissing. It wasn't their youth or their tattoos I particularly cared about. It was how long it had been since I had kissed. It didn't bear thinking about. And yet here I was thinking about it. The barrenness of my lips, their lack of romantic attention, my mouth that was good only for consoling others, which was fine for everyone else, just not for me. It was a selfish thought, I know, but that's what happens with envy. The only thing these thoughts were useful for was making me speed up, hurry away from the kissing teenagers and get my lungs working, my forehead sweating.

By the time I arrived at the park, I was so out of breath I sauntered in at a slower pace and found a bench to sit on. A girl who looked too young to be a mother pushed a baby on a swing while texting. A crisp packet flapped around in the sand at her feet. A light breeze had picked up and tickled the trees but did little to cool me down. I got up. I shouldn't be sitting. I had weight to lose for Marie. I power-walked around the park's perimeter and I thought back to what I could give her, having dismissed my previous ideas of a rose or a book.

What about jewellery?

I bought Claire a bracelet once. But that had been easy because she had pointed it out to me in a shop in the city and I went back to buy it for her without her knowing. It was a surprise of sorts. Then I bought

Jean a brooch for her fifty-second birthday thirteen years ago. I spent hours googling brooches, unable to decide between an antique jewel-encrusted piece or something more modern. In the end, I gave up and went to the shops, taking Claire with me for support, even though she was as befuddled as I was.

'I don't like the pressure of having to choose,' she said. 'You've known her longer.'

'Yes, but you're a woman. You wear jewellery,' I said.

'Not brooches. No one wears brooches.'

'That's not the point. Jean loves them and wears one every day. She must have dozens.'

'No one could ever accuse you of being thoughtless, Oliver,' she said. 'It's admirable, you know.'

I remembered her words exactly, word for word. I looked at her then and felt saturated in warmth, as if I'd gone from standing in an air-conditioned cheese room to having my head in a heated pizza oven. That's when I pictured us buying a ring together – Claire peering eagerly into the sparkling glass cabinets and me holding her hand, not bothered which one she liked, just that she was eager for one. It was a careless assumption, as it turned out, for I was to discover later that in Claire's world you could be too thoughtful. When our relationship hung together by a thread like a coat button about to fall off, she said more words I remembered equally as accurately but wished I didn't: 'I like that you think of me, Oliver, but sometimes you care too much. Don't take this the wrong way, but I feel suffocated by your niceness.'

That was the start of the end. There was no reneging on the nicety. That's just who I was. Anyway, how could you complain about someone being nice? As Andy said, I was better off without her if she couldn't handle niceness. Yet her comments had hurt, as any sort of criticism, warranted or unwarranted, does. Once it's out in the world and seeded in your head, it's hard to remove, like cooking oil stains on your favourite shirt. In hindsight, the whole affair really affected me and I retreated, sheepishly, from the world of relationships at age twenty-seven. Then, with Dad dying and my new business responsibilities, I had enough on my plate as it was.

Once before all of that, during Marie's four-month dating hiatus during her beginnings at Clock & Son, I very nearly asked her out. It took me the first three of those months to realise I fancied her – that the sweaty palms and heart palpitations I was getting in her company were not indicative of some serious illness but a crush. I spent the next month concocting ways to ask her out. But it was my over-diligence in trying to come up with a sound dating opportunity as well as procrastination that made me miss out. Because not long afterwards she announced she'd met a guy – Henry – who appeared to be everything I didn't think I was: spontaneous, charming, charismatic, good-looking, and she had fallen for him like a religious devotee falls to their knees in blind adulation. Those four months of in-between-ness was a lost opportunity I only realised in retrospect. It was a banging-your-head-on-a-wall moment. But only hypothetically. I met Claire a few months later and, even though I threw myself into that relationship with as much enthusiasm as I could muster, those feelings for Marie never entirely went away.

I was in a good rhythm now, my arms pumping and my legs at full stride. I clocked in at the swings twice and on my third circuit the girl with the baby had gone. I was the only one there. I continued for a fourth round, which sounded impressive and I was impressing myself, but in reality it was a small park and even the word 'park' was too inflated a word to use. It was more of a green space tucked between terraces like the hyphen between two words. I picked up my pace for a final walking sprint to the finishing seat, where I collapsed for a minute's breather.

I got up from the seat as the day's light was dimming and the street lights were turning on. A fresh wind made the loose bark on the trunk of a gum tree flap, as if applauding me for a day well done. I made my way back home wondering if I could justify eating last night's chicken Parmigiana on the basis that it would be wasteful to throw it in the bin, and if I would ever decide what to do about Marie.

As it happened, I didn't have to choose. Marie decided for me. A few days later she called.

Something to Say

I was eating a ricotta, tomato and lettuce sandwich on multigrain bread when Marie phoned. She wanted a catch-up. Naturally I said yes, but felt my waistband and wondered if there was any noticeable change. It was doubtful. I hadn't been dieting for long, after all. I put the sandwich down, thinking I'd only eat half.

'Is there a problem?' I asked, wondering if the arrangements for a local councillor's funeral were proving tricky, given his wife's mahogany taste on a plywood budget. 'You haven't run out of flowers or anything?' I laughed.

'No, not at all,' she said, but she didn't laugh along with me or allude to anything further. 'Five o'clock this evening?' She was uncharacteristically brusque.

'Sure,' I said.

Marie was definitely sad, I decided. Perhaps things really were bad on the home front. *Maybe she does want my 'ear' this time, and all the advice and soothing words of consolation I can give her. I will be her devoted ear, the one who listens as she wants to be listened to, the one who can stroke her hand and help her in a time of need.*

'Will I stay or should I leave?' she'll ask, and I'll tell her that she must act upon her heart.

'If you're dreadfully unhappy, then you mustn't stay,' I'll tell her. 'It's not like you have children to think about, only yourself, and you must be true to yourself.'

I'll tell her I'll be there for her every step of the way. I'll offer to take her to the movies and out for dinner to take her mind off the demise of her marriage and make her feel better. I will not kiss her or ask her on a date. None of that. Not yet. It will all be platonic, all above board. I will be the perfect gentleman friend. Until she is ready.

I was so pleased that not only had I resolved what to do but had made an honourable decision in line with the man I liked to think I was that I gobbled up both halves of the sandwich in delight. There was not a wilted leaf of lettuce spare. It didn't matter. My decision afforded me more dieting time so I could transform myself from chubby friend into chiselled beau. Well, chiselled may have been pushing it, but there was no harm in fantasising.

I urged time to speed up, but we had no new customers and no last-minute call-outs. The afternoon dragged. I forced myself to do paperwork. Mum reorganised files. Jean paid bills. Roger left early after polishing the embalming instruments.

Finally, it was four thirty. I combed my hair and redid my tie for no other reason than I wanted to look as good as possible. At four forty-five I drove to the café-bar where we often met to discuss work. Unlike other meetings, this time I was nervous.

I saw Marie sitting at a table by the window. I waved from the footpath. She raised a hand. I had to compose myself and finger-comb my hair before walking over to her.

'I've ordered some wine. Hope you don't mind,' she said.

'You know I don't mind,' I said. 'So, how are the flower arrangements going?' I asked, but before she had time to answer I found myself continuing to natter about how Mrs Dalgleish, the councillor's wife, could be tricky, or rather pernickety, about the finer details, how dry the weather had been and how I hoped it wasn't affecting flower quality, and whether or not I should be worried that this week was proving to be one of the slowest weeks in the industry that I could remember. It was simply nerves. Thankfully, Marie interrupted me.

'Oliver . . .' she said.

'Yes?' I felt a fool for going on.

'I didn't really want to talk shop,' she said.

Of course she didn't.

'You see, I have something to tell you,' she started, but then the waiter came with the wine. She turned to look out the window, her chin resting on a hand, her jaw stiffening. The waiter placed two glasses of wine on the table, reached for the water bottle and poured two glasses. The liquid sloshed in slow motion then settled to a gentle surface spin. He asked if we'd like anything else and I said to Marie, 'How about some olives?' but she didn't respond so I ordered olives for us, pleased with my self-restraint at not requesting nuts as well. When the waiter left, she faced me again.

I smiled then clinked my wine glass against hers. The olives arrived. I passed them to her but she declined. She still hadn't taken a sip of her wine and I'd already had two large gulps. I felt I had to say something, as she seemed reluctant to begin, but I wanted her to know that I didn't mind, that I was her friend and that anything she told me would be in strict confidence.

'I don't know how to say this,' she said.

I instinctively took her hand and gave her a napkin. 'It's OK,' I said. 'Take your time.'

When she had regained her composure, she began again. 'The thing is, I can't quite cope with all this talk of other people's funerals when I'm going to have to discuss my own.' She emitted a laugh – well, in retrospect, it was more of a sardonic snigger – and chewed a trembling lip.

I stared at her. This was not going to plan. She couldn't make jokes about her own funeral.

'I'm sick, Oliver. Really sick. Like, they can't do anything about it sick.'

The words coming from her mouth were confounding. This wasn't going to plan at all.

'What do you mean, you're sick?' I said.

'It's what everyone gets these days. I can't even say it.'

That's when I noticed. How had I not seen before? The dark rings around her eyes, her sunken cheekbones, the hollowness around her clavicles. Make-up couldn't cover it all. I clenched her hand and took a napkin for myself. I said every possible phrase of consolation I knew but the words sounded vacuous and wanting.

'I am so sorry, Marie, so, so sorry.'

'I know,' she said, squeezing my hand.

'You'll be getting treatment, though, won't you?' I said.

She shook her head, shrugged. 'It's too late.'

'Too late?' I choked.

She shook her head and shrugged again.

'No treatment at all? I can't believe that.'

'Palliative only.'

I nearly regurgitated the olives.

'I'm sorry, I think I'm going to cry again,' she said. 'I thought telling you in a public place . . .'

She gripped both my hands and we held ourselves together as the air around us thickened and solidified. Sounds eddied. Smells dulled. There was only me and Marie.

If only we could have stayed like that for ever.

The Ellipsis of Life

Of course, we couldn't stay like that for ever. We couldn't even stay like that for longer than a few seconds. Or it may have been a minute or two, I really couldn't be sure. Just like I couldn't be sure how I got through the next couple of months. You see, if I had to break down life as if it were a sentence, so much of my world existed at the full-stop end of life. Or more precisely, the space after the full stop. And I was happy with that. I had been around the dead so often that it was natural to me. I knew how to handle a dead person – how to slide a body, not lift it, how to insert eye caps under the eyelids to prevent sinkage, how to massage rigor mortis from limbs to help with the embalming process. These things may sound gruesome but, to those in the industry, they're not. We understand that this is a person who is no longer themselves, that the person who was once there has gone. That what is left needs tending to, like we would a shell found on the beach whose inhabitant has moved house, which we want to keep, cleaned and washed. This is the part of life I am used to: the finale, the denouement, the punchline.

What I had little experience in was the ellipsis of life. The bit before the end that no one wants to know about, the part where words are hard to find, stumbled over or not said at all, when the act of doing is only the biding of time. When the living are preparing to die. I blundered my way through Marie's final three months and her death like some stuttered, unfinished question, as if I were a sentence comprised of half-words, half-ellipses and multiple question marks. A terrible sentence that was meaningless, pointless. Nothing I did could make her better; nothing I said could change the future. If only I could have stopped time.

Initially Marie carried on working, but it didn't take long for fatigue to take over, then the pain, loss of appetite and increasing ennui. 'Oh, Oliver, it's hideous. I feel as if I've been taken over by alien forces.'

I gripped her hand and could do nothing but agree and empathise. Even when she stopped working, she still wanted to feel a part of the business. She loved what she did and never wanted to stop. The shop was her life. Sarah and I would conduct meetings at her house. I would show her photos of the arrangements Alchemy Flowers made for us and get her advice for future bouquets. 'Remember to mix things up,' she'd say. 'Don't do the obvious. You could put daisies with red wattles or baby's breath with hot-pink gerberas and palm leaves. And whatever you do, don't confuse the smells. For instance, delphiniums can't go with lemon-scented gum foliage; stocks can't go with calla lilies.' I'm sure Sarah knew all of this, but it was like I was getting a weekly crash course in floristry. I'd get Sarah to make her a mini bouquet of every one we did so she could feel part of it all. She loved it so much I made sure it came with a safety pin so she could wear it like a corsage.

Even though we mainly talked work at her house, it felt the closest I had ever been to Marie. Not only was I in her home, I was heating soup I'd brought over on *her* stove, I was making cups of tea in *her* kitchen, even putting *her* clothes in the washing machine or dryer, if needed, as Henry seemed less attentive to household duties than I would have been if I were her husband. She said she didn't want me to fuss or to think I had to become her domestic help but I sensed she liked the attention. Or maybe it was just having someone else around to talk to and making the house less quiet than it would have been, had she been alone. It wasn't always about work, though. I occasionally dropped by on the pretence of talking shop when really I just wanted a chat with her myself – to whinge about Mum or tell her about a movie I'd seen at the weekend, or even just to drop in some artisanal chocolates I had discovered at the new deli down the road. The fact that I sat on the end of her bed – *her* bed, with *her* white linen covers – made me feel so much closer to her than I ever had been. Yet it didn't feel wrong; it felt so very, very comfortable. One time I joked that the cover could have done with an iron and did she want me to bring over my portable garment steamer next time? I wasn't trying to be funny but she laughed so hard she had to have a rest afterwards and I realised with sadness how there was a fine line between having fun and overdoing it when you've got a terminal illness. I made a note to try not to make her laugh so much next time. Better to have more little laughs for longer than bigger ones for shorter.

Henry was always an enigmatic figure in the background. He was usually at work when we did home visits or, if not, appeared keen to make himself scarce. I sensed he had little interest in talking to me, which I put down to the nature of my job. I suppose he put me in the box of 'wife's work colleague' and the fact that I dealt with death twenty-four-seven made me an even less appealing friend proposition than I might otherwise have been. He would mutter, 'Oh, you again,' if he saw me arrive and then make a joke about how he'd left a sink full of dishes for me to wash up. I'd always thank him in a jovial way, as if I too thought his attempt at humour was funny, even if I didn't, and felt put out at how lowly he thought of me. Yet if I'm honest, it was a situation that suited me fine as I enjoyed having Marie to myself and wanted to feel as if, for a brief moment, that I always had her to myself and always would. Then, in Marie's last week, when she chose to move into palliative care and I visited her every day, I still barely saw Henry. We were shadows passing in the corridor. I tried a few times to engage him but he seemed even more withdrawn from the world, sombre and morose, which, of course, were perfectly reasonable emotions for a man in his ghastly situation.

Even then, Marie still wanted to stay abreast of the funerals.

'Come and sit here,' she'd say, patting the edge of the bed so that I would pull the chair up close and sit next to her. 'Tell me everything.'

Even if she was too tired to keep her eyes open, she wanted to listen, to imagine, I suppose, that she was still involved in it all and to take her mind away from her new reality. She'd ask me to bring her roses, so I'd take in a sprig or a bunch, whatever I could get. Her favourites were Fragrant Plum, an opulent, sweet-smelling rose whose petals were a light lavender colour with smoky purple edges. She breathed in the scent of every rose I took her, holding on, I suspected, to all it signified. I tried to keep things lively, making her laugh at customer foibles or Mum's fixation with buying decorative tissue-box holders. And she did laugh. She laughed as well as she could right up until the end.

And then the end came: Marie died.

I do not wish to dwell on that day, suffice to say that I managed to keep it together for her funeral. While Clock & Son was tasked with the job, Mum ensured I was relieved of all duties. She knew how closely I worked with Marie (just not how close I wanted to be with her). I hovered, pretending the funeral was for someone else, and clung to the church rafters, present but not present, unable to concentrate, unable to remember.

Coming home later that day, I had never felt more alone. No one knew my feelings for Marie and, most likely, they never would. And now there was no point in them ever knowing anyway. I had to grieve on my own in private and hide the full extent of my grief in public. For unrequited love and grief make awkward bedfellows.

And it was to bed, that Friday afternoon in May, that I wanted to go; to curl up under the covers and mourn my loss. I couldn't get out of my suit quickly enough. It was like flinging off the day, the funeral, the depths of my sadness and discarding it all on to the floor. In my haste, a button flew off the shirt, ricocheted against the window and plopped near the skirting board. I stared at it for a long time. It was like staring at myself: the lone fellow in the corner. I ignored it and went to bed.

Then I woke to my first weekend without Marie, which turned out to be pretty much the same as every other weekend, except there was a hollowness that followed me around. I hadn't realised how much she had been with me in my head, how focused I had been on asking her out, how the past few months had been dominated by her sickness and working out when I could spend time with her. With the few friends I had now otherwise occupied with babies, new wives or businesses they were getting off the ground, my weekends were most often spent alone. I may have made small talk with the barista at my local café when getting my Saturday morning coffee and croissant, nodded at someone in the street who was keen to forget they knew me because I was a dreadful reminder of their loss, or, conversely, accepted an embrace by a virtual stranger who appreciated what Clock & Son had done for them, but these were superficial encounters with people I barely knew. And always, I went home alone. I read the newspaper alone, tidied alone, cooked alone, researched holidays I would never take alone, spent more time than I knew was necessary hunting out the best jam to serve with my croissant alone, went to call-outs alone. The list could go on.

Worse, the button that lay lacklustre on the carpet fluff seemed a symbol of my life. In normal circumstances I would have sewn it back on, if not immediately, as soon as I could. Yet I realised in despair that weekend how this simple act was, in fact, the perfect – read horrible – metaphor for my life. My daily routines were done as systematically and rhythmically as a needle going in, out, in, out. A single needle with a single thread through a single button, over and over and over. That was me, the single man, with the single life, doing the same things, over and over. And all of it, alone.

At work I had to pretend I had it all under control. That my expressions of grief were appropriate for my status as Marie's colleague-friend, not her colleague-paramour. 'Grin and bear it' didn't even come close.

I was teeth-clenching grinning and not even bearing it. Worse, I was grieving a lost opportunity. Sure, it may not have been an opportunity I was allowed, but I had been in love with Marie and had been unable to fully enjoy the benefits that being in love brings, even if from afar. Perhaps that was what pained my heart. That I felt cheated and filled with so much regret. If only I had put myself on the line and asked about her marriage, then we may have had a chance. But now I will never know. My dreams of us being together were, and would now always be, mere fantasy. They could never again bring me comfort or hope, and that made me feel even more alone than ever before.

Then I took my eye off the casket where Clock & Son was concerned. I took my eye off everything, to be honest.

Maltesers

A month later sleeting rain sluiced the sky and brought with it an unseasonal chill. The summer had been the driest on record and now we were 'in for a wet one', according to weather reports. I woke up that first day of the rains and decided the change in weather was a good excuse to stop shaving. Well, that wasn't the real reason I ended up with a beard. It was because I couldn't be bothered to shave. Instead of doing it every day, I skipped a day, then another, until I found the fuzz on my chin had thickened and spread.

Andy said I looked like an explorer, which I took as a compliment, and I fantasised about the places I'd like to travel to, like the romantic streets of Paris and the wild English countryside. Then he joked that the only thing I had ever explored was the insides of bodies, which normally would have made me laugh. It made me think of all the places I'd talked about visiting but hadn't, how far removed I was from being a true explorer – I didn't even own a fashion backpack, let alone a hiker's one with hydration kit and compass pocket – and how difficult it was to take time out of the business to attempt any sort of exploring at all. I explained to Mum, who had taken a dislike to my facial hair, that it helped keep me warm. So I trimmed it. But only when I could be bothered.

I relaxed my weight-loss programme, too. There was no need to punish myself any more than I had to, I reasoned. Change had to be sustainable and I was pretty pleased I'd sustainably incorporated more greens and fewer salted peanuts into my diet. I just had a problem with my sweet tooth. It couldn't be helped. Sugar had always been a panacea and Mum and Jean were no help with their afternoon sweet treats, a consistently full tin of sympathy biscuits and the new addition of a large jar of jelly beans in reception – Jean's idea, made on the basis that 'a burst of colour and a sugar hit does wonders for one's mood'. For every one a customer took, I popped two. Anyway, what was the point of dieting now that Marie was no longer around? What was the point of any of my recent resolutions when I didn't have her to unwittingly spur me on? While I went to work with my belly full, I felt hollow. I was a tyre with a puncture, a Mars bar wrapper without the Mars bar, the toast without the marmalade. I used to joke how working with the dead made you feel more alive. Yet this time it had the reverse effect. Like I was alive but not living. It was the strangest of feelings and it rattled me. I would be turning forty in a few months and had never envisaged reaching that milestone dispirited and loveless, and exhibiting signs of dishevelment. Whoever coined the phrase 'life begins at forty' got it very wrong.

Feeling sorry for myself, I lost all sense of caring. I don't know if it was because I was trying, in a bizarre way, to cheer myself up or whether I momentarily became delusional from the grieving, but I decided to show customers that funerals needn't be gloomy. Jean's jelly beans were just the start.

On the morning following the last day of the rain an older couple came in. I assumed they were married. My first mistake.

'Hello, Mr and Mrs . . .?' I said.

'We're not together,' the woman said. 'I'm Judith and this is my brother, Brian.'

'Apologies. Nice to meet you,' I said, offering my hand. 'Please come in.'

Her French-bulldog eyes were slathered in light blue eye shadow, a look we'd passed over for our female clients around the late 1980s, and her brother had dark rings under his eyes, a sign of either insomnia or sinusitis.

'We're here about our mother,' she said.

'I'm very sorry for your loss,' I said. My second mistake. Judith lacked the usual, expected sadness for when a parent dies.

'Don't be. She hung in there for longer than was necessary, didn't she, Brian?'

Brian wiped an eye but didn't answer. I detected sibling tension.

'So, Jude,' I said, trying to lighten the tone. 'May I call you Jude?' My third mistake.

'It's "ith",' she said pronouncedly. 'Jude-ith.'

I apologised. Brian shrugged. I ploughed on, metaphorically flipping open Dad's Folder and asking them the standard questions. It was when Judith mentioned their mother's penchant for sweets and chocolate that my ears pricked up.

'Let's sprinkle Maltesers around her body,' I suggested.

'Excuse me?' Judith's nose was upturned.

'It doesn't have to be Maltesers. We could use Smarties or after-dinner mints, Roses chocolates or Lindt balls.'

'Don't be ridiculous.'

That's where I should have stopped, cut my losses and realised that the idea of adding extras to the coffin to honour their mother was not being well received.

'We can throw in all sorts of things. It's a wonderful way to person-alise the experience.'

'Who for?'

'You.'

'She had a tooth abscess when she died.'

'I'm sorry.'

'You'd have had one, too, if you ate the amount of sweets she did.'

'For goodness' sake, Judith, the man's only trying to help.'

I'd almost forgotten Brian was there. His chin jutted forward, his eyebrows a semi-permanent arch, as if life perplexed him, or maybe it was just his sister. He seemed open to the chocolates idea.

'I like bananas, but I don't want them rotting next to me when I'm gone,' she said.

'What's the harm? It's what Mum loved.'

Judith looked at Brian as if she were going to slap his cheek.

'How about another idea?' I said, to remind her she had an audience. 'We could have a bowl of sweets at the church entrance, something for guests to munch on while they wait for the service to start?'

'This isn't a children's birthday party, Mr Clock.'

'Mum loved birthdays,' Brian said dreamily, as if remembering a particularly poignant birthday moment.

'That's exactly it,' I said. 'It's all about remembering what they loved, bringing those things into the service and maybe, even, back into your life. Memories are what sustain you when a person has passed. They're very powerful.'

'So is my backhand,' Judith said, standing up.

I couldn't believe she'd said that. Brian couldn't believe it either. He looked at her in horror and slumped into the seat, as if hoping the chair offered time travel.

'I've decided not to use your services after all,' she said. 'I'll make arrangements for Mother to be moved elsewhere. Come on, Brian.'

'Please don't go,' I said, although I suspected my pleas were in vain. 'They were only suggestions. We don't have to do anything you don't want to do. We could have a beautiful bouquet of antique cream roses instead – the Iceberg variety comes to mind – that would perfectly match her blouse,' I added, quickly trying to emulate something Marie might have suggested.

'Too late. I already have an image of Lindt balls I do not wish to have, and they were one of my favourites. Goodbye, Mr Clock.'

I watched Judith and Brian leave. I watched business walk out the door and did little to stop it. I still believed Mrs Cummings senior would have loved having a selection of chocolates dotted about her body and wondered if I hadn't sold the idea as well as I could have. Regrets were accumulating like bills yet to be paid.

Then there was the customer to whom I revealed too much. People may say they support recycling and upcycling but that doesn't mean they want to know that their relative's hip and knee implants can be melted down and made into road signs and car parts. I misjudged a woman called Tessa who had the look of someone supportive of sustainability with her loose harem-style pants in an elephant print and hair down to her fourth rib.

'You've got to be joking,' she said, when I told her that her father's double hip replacement had benefits way beyond improving her dad's dodgy joints.

'It would be helping the broader community,' I said. 'No one wants to die in vain.'

'He didn't die in vain. He was eighty-four and had a good life.' The woman was sitting at the edge of her seat now, twiddling a ring.

'No, of course not, but there has to be more to dying than just vanishing, poof, into thin air.' I don't know why I said that. Words were coming out of my mouth without my brain being able to stop them. I kept thinking of Marie and how I felt that she had died in vain, even though she hadn't been fighting a cause and had no means to fight her cancer. It was the seeming pointlessness of it all.

'Look, I haven't come here to philosophise and I don't care about a bloody road sign.' Tessa was becoming agitated.

'I understand.' I nodded. I was truly sympathetic, but maybe she didn't think so. Perhaps I wasn't giving off the right empathetic vibe. 'I'm very sorry for your loss,' I added, telling myself to immediately revert to the Folder. *Do not under any circumstances deviate again from its system, Oliver Clock.*

'Anyway, how do I know that you won't surreptitiously dismantle Dad's hips when I'm not looking?'

I was horrified and reassured her that we were never surreptitious. 'We don't do anything you don't ask for,' I said.

'But how can I be sure?'

'I won't tick the box.'

'What box?'

'This box here,' I said, pointing to the checklist on page two before me.

The woman stared at me as if her face had frozen momentarily then burst into tears. I reached for the tissues, but she stood up and walked out. I rushed after her with the tissues, flapping the box like a peace offering, rapidly trying to summon up a thoughtful Marie suggestion but, in this instance, I couldn't think of anything quickly enough.

'Tessa . . . Ms Ritchie . . . Please,' I called after her. She didn't turn around but left, letting the open sign clank against the door as it shut.

'Oliver? What's going on?' Mum came out of the cupboard behind reception.

'Nothing, Mum, it's fine. She's upset about her father.'

'Those tears were not ones of someone grieving. I've been around here long enough to know one tear from another. I hope you didn't say something out of turn.'

'Of course not. She just needs time.' I grabbed a handful of jelly beans and headed back to my office, with the sneaky suspicion Tessa's father would be leaving our premises sooner rather than later.

Nails in the Coffin

I used to joke that the only reason my parents wanted me working in the business was so they didn't have to change its name. I was the only child and the only son. Except, technically, I wasn't an only child, I just grew up as one. I had a little sister, Lily, who died aged two when I was four years old. She was struck by lightning on our back lawn, which sounds like an unbelievable thing to have happened and the sort of story an only child with a vivid imagination would make up to get attention and sympathy for their siblingless status.

It was a tragedy of no one's fault but Mother Nature's. It was raining, large heavy drops from large heavy clouds that hung low in the sky. Lily wanted to dance in it – to jiggle and giggle as she did whenever there was music playing. Yet that day in the storm she jiggled and giggled in the wrong corner of the garden at the wrong time. Seconds either side and she would still be dancing now. As I was never given a proper explanation for what had happened, I spent the weeks following looking for her around the house – in the wardrobe, behind doors, in the playhouse outside. The places where we used to play hide and seek together. My parents refused to join in, which I thought was strange and uncaring. Usually they encouraged my love of playing hide and seek. I badgered them for a while but it only made them angry and me more confused. Where was she and why wasn't she coming back? 'She's gone, and that's that,' was all I'd get, and the subject was closed, which was uncharacteristically blunt of Mum at the time. She had always been the type of mother to explain things fully, as if she were an employee of *Encyclopaedia Britannica*. After that, it was like Lily had never existed, and I grew up as an only child who had never had a sibling.

I'm not sure how long it was after Lily's death – it could have been six days, six weeks or even six months – when Mum began gathering together all the reminders of the daughter she had lost. I caught her one day in Lily's bedroom with a neatly folded pile of clothes, soft toys and linen stacked on the floor. What I remember most was the pink, so much pink, the same colour as the baby pink layer in a liquorice allsorts square.

'What are you doing?' I asked her. I began looking through the toys for no other reason that I can remember than nosiness.

'Stop that, Oliver,' she said. 'We don't need them any more.'

'Why?'

'You know why. Go and play with your Lego.' When she turned and stuck her head back in the chest of drawers, I eyed a grey elephant, which stood out amidst the pink, shoved it under my top and ran out, not to play with the Lego but to hide the elephant behind the row of toys on a shelf above my bed. For years to come, the happiness I got from that elephant was disproportionate to what a child should usually get from a soft toy. It wasn't so much childish glee at deceiving Mum – although I felt a little of that as well – so much as joy at safeguarding a little piece of Lily within the family.

Now, it seemed, I was back to deceiving Mum. For, a few weeks after Tessa Ritchie walked out, I lied to her again. I didn't like lying, but I didn't want her to worry. I told the same lie to Jean, too, who queried why we were losing customers rather than gaining them. I couldn't bear to tell them that some of our new clients were unfairly taking exception to some of my suggestions – suggestions I felt were perfectly reasonable, if not wonderfully imaginative, which meant we were not only losing business but money. Why couldn't these people embrace out-of-the-box thinking? One particular gentleman, with whom I thought I was get-ting on amicably, became affronted when I asked, after learning that he imported fireworks, whether he'd like his wife shot into the sky in a rocket. It was a marketer's dream scenario.

'It's new into the country,' I said. 'A handheld ash-scattering gun. They're from – no surprise – America. But hear me out,' I said, when his face distorted into an expression of disgust. 'It will shoot your loved one's ashes over twenty-one metres into the sky – or wherever you wish to project them. Just not at someone else or into an oncoming wind, of course. You can even add confetti.' I smiled. You'd think I was the sales rep. 'I can put you in touch with the company, if you like? My friend recently did a photo shoot for their promotional catalogue. He said they were "bloody awesome" – excuse my language.'

It was Andy who told me about them. He had bought two to keep hidden in the attic for when the time came. One for him and one for his new wife, Lucy.

The man looked at me; his skin had turned as grey as his wife's. 'Just because I deal with fireworks does not mean I want a whatever-it's-called,' he said.

'You have to admit, it is appropriate.' I winked. I can't believe I winked. What was wrong with me?

He didn't wink back. Instead, he left and took his wife with him.

Then I had an idea of my own. One which I thought I should patent or, at least, see if it was viable or not from a manufacturing per-spective. Snow globes. Everyone loves a snow globe, don't they? Even adults at Christmastime. A little shake and snow falls over a Christmas scene, taking you back to your childhood, romanticising the festive season. Who cared if it was summer? Snow globes were still popular. Well, imagine an 'ash globe' with a photo of a deceased loved one sur-rounded by things that represent them. You give it a little shake and their ashes flutter around them. It'd be like scattering someone's ashes over and over, whenever you felt like it. *There's something in that idea*, I thought. *Something very saleable.*

The problem was, no one else thought so.

Especially Mum, who overheard me mentioning it to another customer. I was hoping for third time lucky, three times over. You know, like three squared, because third time lucky the first time didn't work.

'Oliver, what are these ash globes you're talking about?' Mum asked.

'It's a new invention, Mum.'

'I've never heard of them.'

'They don't exist yet. I thought I could do one of Marie as a trial run.'

'Don't be ridiculous.'

'I'm not,' I said. 'I think we need better ways to remember people by, better ways in which to celebrate lives once lived.'

'It's insensitive, crass.'

I rubbed my bearded chin, which helped me think, and regretted having not been able to do so in the past when my chin was hair-free. 'That's pretty disparaging, Mum.'

'Well, I don't know what's got into you, Oliver, but you haven't been yourself lately and I don't think it's a coincidence that the business is suffering.'

'The business is fine. We've lost some customers, that's all.'

'Why don't you take a break? Jean, Roger and I will manage.'

'I can't do that.'

'Why not?'

'I've never taken a break before.'

But I was tempted. I went home that night and thought about Mum's suggestion. I could try and be an explorer for a week. Go somewhere I'd never been before, which wouldn't be hard, as there weren't many places that I had been. I fantasised about Russia in winter. Reread an article from the weekend newspaper magazine on Peru. Imagined a boat trip down the Rhine. But then, who would I go with? Did I want to travel on my own, and was one week enough in which to become an explorer? I scratched my beard. Wondered if I should shave it off. Yet I still couldn't be bothered doing that and thought of all the reasons not to take a break. There would be too many things I'd have to organise in advance, and then I'd worry about the business. It was too risky and reeked of the unknown. I might have been lonely at home but at least I had the comfort of an established routine to look forward to at the weekends, call-outs notwithstanding. In the end, the decision was taken away from me. Roger called in sick that afternoon.

'I've had a bad bout of salmonella,' he told me over the phone, his normally authoritative voice weak and drained. 'Sorry, Oliver, it's bad. I can't hold anything down. The doctor says I need a week off work. I'm extremely dehydrated and losing weight as I speak.'

'I'm so sorry to hear that, Rog,' I said. 'Don't worry about work. Just get yourself better.'

I got off the phone, secretly pleased the decision had been made for me. Reason prevailed. My fantasies needed filing away, as usual.

Except when the time came for me to undertake a full embalming, I wasn't sure whether to thank my father for making me learn the procedure, which meant I wouldn't have to find a temporary replacement, or curse him for ruining my chance to have a holiday, just when I was coming around to the idea. In the end, I cursed both of them. Having done little body preparation or embalming of late, I had underestimated the benefits of Roger's anosmia. The strength of my stomach was tested, my nose pushed to its limits, my fat fingers working to capacity. After the first one, I resolved to change my modus operandi. The best way to reduce my presence in the embalming room, I decided, was to employ the art of dissuasion, telling clients who asked about them that full-body embalmings were less popular these days, much more costly and bad for the environment. I also enlisted Jean's help with the dressing and make-up application for those happy to take the option of temporary preservation.

Three weeks later, Roger still hadn't reappeared. I was tiring of plugging noses and mouths as if I were patching up a draughty house and removing bodily fluids as if siphoning fuel from a car. Even Jean's enthusiasm was beginning to wane and she, by her own admission, loved colour-coordinating lipsticks with nail polish and blow-drying hair. But she'd rather be doing it on herself than a dead person she didn't know. Mum spent two days pressuring me into calling Roger, but I didn't want to hassle a sick man – a man who was thin enough already without a stomach bug to help him lose weight.

In the end, Roger called. I was relieved at how much brighter he sounded.

'You're all better, then, Roger? That's great news,' I said.

'Actually, I had to get worse to get better.'

'What do you mean?'

'I was starting to come right when I had a fall. I was in the kitchen in my slippers, and slipped on a dribble of water. Clonked the back of my head on the edge of the bench and got knocked out like a light. Great thumping lump on my noggin when I woke. Christine was going crazy, as you can imagine. She thought I would never open my eyes again. She didn't think to check my pulse, I might add, but that's by the by. What happened next is the best bit.' He paused for effect. 'My sense of smell has come back.'

My ideal embalmer was not so suited to the job any more.

'It sounds extraordinary, I know,' he continued, 'but the doctor says this can happen sometimes. They've yet to fully understand it, but who cares? I can smell again, and I can't tell you how wonderful it is. I thought I didn't mind not smelling, but it's a helluva lot better than I remembered. I'm just loving it. Christine's cooking is a dream and now I understand what you thought of those vegetable juices I drank. They're rank, really rank. I think it's the beetroot.'

Roger didn't stop. I had never known him to be so chatty. On and on and on he went about all the different things he had been smelling and tasting and how he had already put on weight, can you believe it?

'That's great, Roger,' I said. 'It's amazing, a miracle you could say.'

'Yes, Oliver, it's a miracle.'

'So . . .' I started, wondering how enthusiastic he was about coming back, since it sounded as if he had spent the last week enjoying his new-found ability.

'So . . .' he repeated, 'that's the thing – I don't think I can do my job any more. Well, I could but, quite frankly, I don't want to.'

I made agreeable noises, even though my senses filled with the sullied sweet aroma of formaldehyde.

'Let's face it, I've given it a pretty good dash. Twenty-five years. It's time to do something else.'

My heart sank, dropped straight to the bottom of my belly. 'Of course it is. I completely understand.'

'I'm really sorry, Oliver. I don't want to let you down, but now that my smell is back my heart's not in it any more. You don't mind, do you?'

'Not at all. You deserve to make the most of your reborn sense.'

'Ha!' He laughed. 'Yes, you could say the "nose" have it.'

I held the phone away from my ear as Roger's guffaws pummelled my eardrums.

'I won't leave you in the lurch. I'll tidy up loose ends and all that. Although, just quietly, I'm looking forward to a trip to Italy where I can inhale pizza through my nose.' He laughed again.

I laughed with him. I was happy for Roger yet I couldn't help but feel a twinge of envy at his newly appointed embalming-free status and had an awful feeling that his departure was another nail in the coffin of my slowly dying business.

The Competition

Still grieving for Marie, I was now mourning the loss of my embalmer and spent the next few days praying that no one wanted embalming – prayers no funeral director should ever make. I even secretly typed up a job description for the ideal Clock & Son embalmer, despite Mum having decided we didn't need to hire anyone new just yet, praising me for being 'perfectly adequate' and rejoicing in the money we would save. But I didn't send it off, knowing it would be one deception Mum would find out about and that I didn't want to be party to her reaction when she did. Writing it behind Mum's back was naughty enough and elevated my blood pressure to a most unsatisfactory level, which required an immediate consumption of chocolate. Having run out of Mars bars, I had to make do with a Kit Kat finger.

It was when I was dusting my acrylic stationery holder and rearranging the paper clips so they lined up perfectly that she burst into my office like an exploding jack-in-the-box.

'A new funeral home has opened!' she cried. 'A new funeral home on our turf!' Exclamation marks flew off her like cartoon expletives.

I tried to calm her down and Jean rushed in with a biscuit, as if that were a cure-all for any crisis, but she wasn't interested.

'*And* it's promoting a bargain deal,' Mum said, slapping a flyer on my desk. Her chest rose and fell erratically, her eyebrows arched worryingly.

I picked up the flyer. *Plan now before it's too late. Get the funeral you so desire and save*, it said.

'They're undercutting us, Oliver. We won't survive if this carries on. I've done our books, too. We're losing money, and now this!' She picked up one of my pens and began stabbing the desk.

'Oh dear,' Jean said, leaning over my shoulder to read the flyer. 'Do you think they're bulk-buying coffins?'

'If you ask me,' said Mum, 'it's a one-size-fits-all funeral service designed to push people through at breakneck speed. They're probably not even using coffins but doing some sort of bulk-burn bargain-basement deal.' She gasped at the horror of this possibility.

'Surely not,' I said. It was too outrageous to even contemplate. Didn't Mum realise I had enough on my mind, without something else to worry about?

'Dreadful,' Jean said. 'It makes me want to swear.'

'Swear all you like, Jean. Oliver and I are going to check them out. Come on, Oliver.' Mum flapped a hand at me to hurry up. 'I'll show you where they are. It's not far in the car.'

I really didn't want to have to get up and take a trip in her car but felt I had little choice. Telling her I was still sad and very possibly depressed about Marie would have opened myself up to an interrogation I didn't wish to have. So I gave Jean the flyer and followed Mum out of the door.

Mum had left her car – a small second-hand Nissan hatchback in red ('So others can't miss me,' she said after its purchase) – in the middle of the small car park behind our building, leaving no one else the ability to either leave or arrive. I would have driven myself if I'd had the foresight to take charge. But before I knew it Mum had ushered me into the passenger seat, shut the door and jogged as best as a seventy-seven-year-old could to the driver's side. Fumbling with the keys, brake and foot pedal as if she couldn't remember the order in which to do things, she speedily – too speedily – lurched out of the car park.

'Slow down, Mum,' I said.

'It's alright. I've taken my blood pressure pills,' she said.

'Have you got some with you?' I asked, lifting up the compartment between us behind the handbrake.

'You're not having any.'

'I'll need them if you keep driving like this.'

'Oh, for goodness' sake, stop thinking of yourself and focus. There is a competitor on our patch. We need to decide on a plan of action.'

I looked out of the passenger window and watched pedestrians and shop fronts fly past, their clothes and street signage blurring and the colours blending and bleeding into each other, as if rain washing down the car window had turned everything into one big splodge. It was the perfect imagery for the way my life was turning out, and now, it seemed, the business. Having a competitor nearby just meant yet another thing to have to worry about. Mum's fingers gripped the steering wheel, her knuckles whitening, and she leaned into the wheel as if trying to get a closer view of the streetscape. She eased off the accelerator as we turned off the main road and into a quieter, semi-industrial street, with a row of original terraced houses on one side.

'I know this street,' I said.

'Yes, your grandparents lived at number forty-three.'

Before my bike accident, when I was allowed, I'd ridden my bike along these flat pavements, riding to what was once a corner store, to buy caramel chews for Grandma. Mum would watch me from the front gate through Grandad's binoculars all the way there and all the way back, never taking her eyes off me.

'There it is,' I said as we drove past the wine-coloured terrace with its rusting balcony railings and parched pot plant at the front door.

'Forget your grandparents' house,' Mum said. 'Your focus should be down there.'

I looked to where Mum was pointing. At the end of the street, where once there was a derelict building, shone a brand-new one, like a beacon of the future. I recognised the name – Green Light Funerals – as one of a chain of funeral homes with several offices in our city and around the country. Perched on top was a billboard the same size as the floor space of our entire reception, featuring a grinning middle-aged couple looking far too pleased with their alabaster teeth. Above them bold copy offered a supersized service of *24/7 caring for you and your loved one over and above anything else*, and below it the words, *Send off the dearly departed with a Green Light Funeral.* It looked a slick little joint with its shiny mirrored glass frontage sparkling in the sun, poetically reflecting the sky and clouds above. The McDonald's of the funeral world had landed on our territory, imposing itself on our independent family-run funeral home, which had been serving the community perfectly well for eighty years, thank you very much. I nearly dry-retched. We had never had to worry about others taking our business before; we had the market nailed, or so I had thought. How would we be able to compete with them? Was this it, then? Was this the beginning of the end? Was Clock & Son dying? Would there be no more comforting chats with cadavers to help me through?

'Oh, Mum,' I said.

'Yes, Oliver,' she said. 'It's not good.'

Maybe it was time to close down. Forget cost-cutting and having to do more embalming; we would all retire. Mum and Jean were of that age, after all. If only I had Marie to talk to and commiserate with. She would know what to do and, perhaps just as importantly, what to say to make me feel better. It was at times like these that I realised just how much Marie had been part of my life. She had been a true ally. I just hoped I had been the same to her.

'Can we go back now?' I said.

'I think we should go inside, do some snooping,' Mum said.

'I'm not snooping. I've seen enough.'

'Oliver! What's got into you?'

'I have to get back. I've got an appointment,' I lied.

'Well, alright then, but we need to decide what to do about these people,' she said, reluctantly starting the car up again. 'We need an action plan. We have to do something or we'll be left behind.'

We drove back in silence and Mum, thankfully, let me mull over this discovery without imposing an action plan of her own. She knew I needed time to digest the new and unexpected, that I'd missed out on the Clock quick-thinking and spontaneity genes. She dropped me off on the high street with a pat on the knee and told me to, 'Have a think and we'll reconvene when you've done so.'

I got out of the car and waited at the lights to cross the road. I had never properly looked at our building from this perspective before. Usually my focus was on the pavement, watching for other feet, potholes and dog poo to avoid, my mind on other things entirely. I surveyed the building as if I were an impartial bystander and didn't like what I saw. Compared to the new funeral home, Clock & Son had the facade of a weary old man, with its chipped corners and faded frontage. You could tell the building had once blushed with the virgin grandeur befitting its standing in the high street, but now it suffered from nearly one hundred years of ageing and, I had to admit, a dose of neglect. Some of its ilk could get away with a dash of dilapidation and still exude handsome heritage, but the Clock & Son building had simply seen better days. I couldn't remember when it was last painted or the street signage updated. Even though my father had died and I had no son, I kept the business's original name for ease of continuity. Since taking it over, I had changed nothing. I hadn't thought I'd needed to.

But now I realised Clock & Son was one giant vacuum cleaner that hadn't been emptied in decades. Perhaps I should never have taken it over in the first place. It wasn't like I'd wanted it. 'The Business' had been forced on me against my will, which may sound histrionic, but it was true. And now I was proving the statistics correct. I, the third generation, was failing it. By the time I turned forty I could be an out-of-work, loveless, still-grieving funeral director who had been unable to keep the family business afloat.

What a dreadfully unsettling thought.

When the lights changed, I crossed the road and headed straight for the jelly bean jar in reception for an instant fix of sugary comfort, neglecting to notice a visitor sitting against the freshly plumped sofa cushions.

Candles

From the corner of my eye, I saw a woman stand up and reach out her hand. I stopped, turned.

'Hi, I'm Edie,' she said. 'I hope you don't mind me dropping in without an appointment.' She had a heart-shaped face, strawberry-blonde hair that bounced when she moved and a smile so large it stretched from cheek to cheek, as if trying to spread happiness further than her face would allow. What could I say? That, actually, I did mind? That I wasn't in the mood to sweep the grieving off their feet with heart-warming words of consolation because I was grieving myself? That my business was doomed and her solitary funeral would do little to perk it back up again? Perhaps I paused too long before answering because Jean got in first.

'It's not a bother at all. Tea?'

'Thank you, that would be lovely,' Edie said.

'Jelly bean?' I offered, showing her the jar.

'No, thanks.'

'Don't mind if I do. It's been a long day.' I shook the jar to muddle the colours around and picked out two black jelly beans that had risen to the top. My favourite. I popped them into my mouth. 'Come through to my office.' I placed the jar back on the reception table and gestured for Edie to follow me.

'How can I help?' I asked, hoping I could turn this unplanned appointment into something swift and profitable. I promised myself I would say nothing to scare her away.

'This is kind of unconventional,' she said, as I brought up our funeral checklist on the computer. 'You see, I'm just starting out and I won't know if it's got legs until I actually do it and I need someone willing to support me.'

I was about to ask what she was talking about when she continued.

'I'll explain. I'm a trained perfumer. When I say trained, I mean I have a diploma in aromatherapy and did an artisan perfume workshop up the coast. I've done a lot of fragrance mixing, too. I'm an expert mixer.'

I looked at her animated face and the smile I was not in the mood for and realised I should have turned her away in reception.

'You mean no one has died?' I asked.

'Oh, no, sorry. I'm not here to organise a funeral.'

My lips stuck to my gums as I considered a response. I was unused to appointments without relation to a deceased. And right then, I didn't feel like an appointment with anyone, let alone someone who was not offering a potential glimmer of business.

'I'm a pharmacist by trade,' Edie continued. 'I work not far from here, at Kingsmith Pharmacy – you may know it? I've been there about five years. But my passion is smells. Beautiful smells. I thought how wonderful it would be to create them, then I had this idea and was intrigued.'

I opened my mouth to stop her but she was too quick for me.

'I thought, what if you could recreate the smell of a loved one who had died so it felt as if they were still with you, as if they were really there in the room with you?'

'Look, sorry to interrupt but . . .'

'Please, hear me out. I'll talk quickly, then it won't take long,' she said, so earnestly I couldn't say no. 'The more I thought about the idea, the more I wondered if it could be done. I decided the best way to embody a scent and have it truly around you is to put it in a candle. So I learned to make candles.'

'Candles?' I repeated.

'Yes, that's right, candles, and because the only person I know who has died and whose smell I can remember is my grandmother, I created a candle for her. She was all washed linen and roses and an oversweet perfume Mum knew the name of. So I mixed and blended and *voilà*, La Lumière d'Edna.' Edie reached into her bag and produced a rotund candle with the name embossed on a white label and a black sketch of an angel wafting gaily above. 'I am proactively harnessing the power of scent in the most sense-intense way possible. Here, have a smell.'

She lifted the lid. I tentatively sniffed, sceptical as to how you could bottle a grandma and what she might smell like when lit. A potent whiff of something I could only describe as a blend of talcum powder and cheap cologne overwhelmed my nostrils and tugged at my throat. I stifled a sneeze.

'I know you didn't know her, but that's not the point. Mum says it's her exactly. The stupid thing is, we don't want to light it because then she'll disappear.' Edie sighed and replaced the lid.

I smiled. It was definitely time for Edie to go. 'Thank you for introducing yourself . . .'

'What do you think of it?'

'It's . . . intriguing.' I looked at my watch.

'It is?'

'You said so yourself.'

'I did?'

'But it's not right for us, I'm afraid. We need to stick to our core business.'

'I'll tell you what, I'll leave you my card. I'm happy to do a trial. Probably best we do, to test the market, see whether customers like the idea.' She rummaged in her handbag. 'Oh, here it is.' She placed a creased business card on my desk. 'I haven't totally decided on the name yet. I was thinking "Memory Candles" or "Angel Candles", but I do like "La Lumière de so-and-so".'

She bit a nail. I forced myself to look interested as I stood up. She rose, too, took one last gulp of her tea and asked me to think about it. 'I mean, what else have we got left in the end but memories?' she said as she left.

Not long ago, I would have jumped at such a scheme, especially one that was already thought out and ready to trial. But I'd lost interest in new schemes to razzle-dazzle customers, as they only seemed to scare them away. I'd experienced entrepreneurial disappointment and, with everything else going on, I wasn't up to contemplating Edie's candles, let alone trialling them.

Henry

I sat back at my desk and rested my head in my hands. What a day. What a terrible, upended day, which no amount of drawer tidying could possibly alleviate.

'A new funeral to organise?' Jean said, coming into my office.

'Unfortunately not.'

'Oh dear. And what about your visit?'

I shook my head. 'It's not good, Jean.'

'Oh dear,' she repeated.

'How about we go home early today? What do you think?'

Jean opened her mouth to speak just as a man called out from reception, 'Anyone here?'

'This could be business,' Jean whispered, her face lighting up.

I perked up for a minute, too, until I discovered it was Marie's husband, Henry, whose flaring nostrils did not bode well.

'There you are, you little . . .' he said. The last time I had seen him was at the funeral, when, outwardly, he had appeared composed and was dressed as dapperly as he always was. But now his face was ruddy and blotchy, his eyes bloodshot and his hair below his ears. His shirt was undone to the sternum and the buttons wrongly matched their holes.

'Everything alright?' I said, going over to him, even though it was clear things weren't alright. Had he come to complain about the funeral or our services, even though it had been nearly three months ago? He had seemed fine at the funeral, had been convivial, even. Maybe he'd bottled up his complaints and only now felt he could air them? We had worked so hard to make Marie's send-off the best we could. Sarah, her assistant, had worked through the night on the flowers, Jean had changed caterers – going up a notch with the food spread, ditching single-layer one-flavour sandwiches for quadruple-layer multiple-flavour clubs, mini home-made pastry pies and handmade sweetmeats. I offered Henry significant discounts on the costs – even though I knew he could afford them – as I wanted to ensure Marie had the coffin she wanted, a top-of-the-line eco-friendly number with the most beautiful floral bouquets spilling over the top. If Henry hadn't been happy with what we had done, then that was it. That really would be the end of Clock & Son. We had lost our touch. If I couldn't get it right for Marie, then I couldn't get it right for anyone.

'Sit down, you twerp,' Henry growled, surlier than I had ever seen him. He pushed me on to the sofa with a finger. Annoyingly, I went down as easily as a knocked matchstick tower.

'Henry, I'm sorry if you're dissatisfied with our services . . .' I stammered.

'I know what you've done.' I detected daytime drinking, the cloying, stale smell of alcohol leaching from his skin.

'We will refund you, won't we, Jean?' I suggested. 'And we'd be happy to talk through your grievances to ensure we won't make the same mistakes again. Believe me, customer happiness and compassionate service is very important to us. Would you like to come through to my office . . .?'

I got up, but Henry grabbed my tie and pulled me towards him. I nearly fainted from the fumes. Jean gasped. Our bellies touched and I couldn't help but notice that his was distended, like mine, only it was taut, like a balloon about to pop. I wondered if he was so distraught with grief that nothing we could have done would have been good enough. That's when I remembered Dad's adage that one of the problems with being a funeral director is that you see the dead at their best and the living at their most wretched. Marie's husband was a case in point.

'Henry, please, can you let go of my tie? It's my favourite.' I laughed nervously, hoping to dampen his anger by lightening the mood. Instead, his lip curled in distaste rather than jocularity. I changed tack and went for empathy instead. 'I understand you've gone through some tough times. You must miss Marie and I'm truly sorry about her passing.'

'Oh, I know you are,' he said accusatorially. 'And I thought you were a decent guy.' He ran a tongue over his teeth and blinked in slow motion. 'Albeit a bit of softie.' He yanked the tie with one hand so that I was close enough to count his pores. He swayed. I wondered if he needed the tie for support. But then he raised his other hand and said, 'You've made me very angry, Oliver Clock.'

He wasn't going to . . .? Was he? I closed my eyes so I didn't have to look and braced myself for the full force of his fist.

'What are you doing? You can't do that.' Jean's voice was unusually high-pitched and flaky. 'I'll call the police. I'm going to call the police. Help!' she called out, as if there were anyone else within earshot.

Henry relaxed his grip and lowered his arm. I opened my eyes. Henry stared back. Jean pulled an expression I had never seen her make before. If I wasn't so shaken, I would have laughed. Jean couldn't look intimidating if she tried.

Henry rolled his shoulders back and stuck his chest out. 'No need,' he said. 'The man knows what he's done. And I know what he's done.' He released the tie and pressed it against my chest so forcefully I lost my balance and landed on the sofa again, bouncing like a tennis ball – or maybe it was more like a basketball losing air.

'That's it, I *am* calling the police,' Jean said. 'This is a funeral home and we don't tolerate violence.'

'Calm down. I'm leaving,' he said, and turned to go.

'But wait,' I said. 'What have I done? I don't understand. I thought this was about the funeral.' I didn't like resorting to pleading; it only reinforced my inferior position of ignorance.

He didn't answer but walked out before I could find out any more, leaving behind the stench of animosity and fear.

'Good grief,' Jean said. 'What was that all about?' She fluttered a hand to her chest as if mimicking a speedy heart.

'I don't know, Jean, I really don't know.' I was no more enlightened than she was.

Pub Talk

As soon as Henry left, I locked the door and told Jean we were definitely going home early. She didn't protest. I even told her to have the day off tomorrow if she wanted it and considered giving myself the day off, too, considering the stress of recent events and lack of any business. Jean nodded. She still looked pale and I felt bad she'd had to witness such an encounter with Henry. I was shaken by Henry's wrath but equally perplexed as to what I had done to deserve it. It was most troubling to think we had disappointed Marie's husband so much. If only – ironically – Marie had been around to ask. She would have been embarrassed by her husband's behaviour, of that I was certain, but she may well have also said, 'Oh, don't worry about him, he's been a little cranky of late' or 'He's been having a stressful time at work lately.' Or maybe not. Not even a beetroot dip and sesame-seed breadsticks walk-in-the-door snack could appease my disquiet. With little else to eat and unable to settle my fretfulness, I decided to call Andy to see if he'd be up for a drink at the pub.

'Sure,' he said. 'I can meet you there at five on my way home.'

Brilliant. Andy could distract me from my business woes, as he loved being a problem solver, and I wouldn't have to eat toast for dinner. I hadn't intended to unload my concerns on to him as soon as we sat down, but I didn't think Andy would mind. He was a good friend, a true mate. My best mate, if I thought about it, the one I had spent the most time with over the years, from school to flat-sharing and now living only a suburb away. He was the person I'd go to first in a crisis and I believed I was the same for him. We'd helped each other through the good times and the bad; we'd been each other's confidants. Like the time his mother ended up in a coma and they thought she wouldn't make it – I was the first person Andy called. Or when he met Lucy and after date three told me she was the one he was going to marry. Or when he asked me to help him try and dress more smartly (a pointless exercise, as we both knew 'charmingly bedraggled' was part of Andy's DNA). And we were the last two bachelors that we knew. That is, until Andy got married last year and I was his best man. I couldn't deny I felt a little envious of him then, and worried that my role as confidant had been bumped to second place. We may have been total opposites, yet somehow it worked – or maybe it helped make our friendship flourish.

So when he said, 'Did you have a good day at the morgue?' I told him how bad things really were at Clock & Son – no embalmer, minimal business, a new competitor, money worries and then Henry's unexpected and unsettling visit.

'Wow,' he said. 'That's heavy. What are you going to do?'

I shrugged, felt the weight of despair on my scapulas. 'I don't know, Andy. The easiest thing would be to retire, to close Clock & Son before we go under.' I stared into the depths of my beer bottle.

'What? And throw the family business away? You can't do that. Anyway, what would you do?'

I sighed. It all seemed too hard.

'What does your mum think?'

'She wants to snoop.'

'Ha! Then again, knowledge is power, as they say.'

'True, but ignorance is also bliss,' I said.

'But don't you want to know more about the new funeral home and what Henry's gripe is all about?'

'Well, yes . . .'

'So maybe some snooping is good idea. And why don't you text Henry? You've got his number, haven't you?' Andy's eyes lit up.

I shrugged, finished the beer and thought about ordering a burger for dinner.

'Let's do it now.' Andy picked up my phone, which I'd left on the table in hopeful expectation of a call-out, and passed it to me. 'Tell him you're sorry he's upset and that you want to rectify his grievances. You'll feel better when it's resolved.'

I wondered if this could be my way of checking in on Henry on Marie's behalf. It was the sort of thing she would have done for me, I'm sure, if the situation had been reversed. 'OK,' I said, and started typing. But then I got cold feet and couldn't finish it. Henry's flaring nostrils in my offices had indicated an angry man, and alarmed me. The thought of them made me anxious. 'Perhaps it's better to pretend it didn't happen,' I said. 'I don't want to upset him even more.' I held my thumb on the delete button.

'Stop being Mr Nice Guy. I think you should find out. Come on, I'll do it.' Andy took the phone from me and rewrote the text. Then it was gone. Sent into the ether before I had a chance to read it.

What I didn't expect was a swift reply, let alone the reply I got: *I've read her diary. I know what was going on.*

I let the phone fall on the table. Was I mentioned in Marie's diary? Surely it was only in a professional sense.

'What? Has he replied?' Andy picked up the phone. 'Mate . . .' he said, his chin hingeing open and eyes widening.

'I thought he was dissatisfied with our services.'

'What was going on between you and Marie?'

'Nothing was going on between us.'

'Are you sure?'

'Of course I'm sure.' But I felt myself blushing and Andy's raised eyebrows made me realise that sometimes you can't keep things secret for ever.

'Do you have time for another beer?' I asked.

Even if he didn't, Andy stayed, and I told him how I was in love with Marie. The relief I felt after I had done so was immense. It was as if I'd passed the baton of a burdensome secret on to Andy so he could share the load and ease the strain. It's how I imagine a criminal might feel when they finally admit to a crime. It might mean jail time but at least they don't have to lie or hide any more. I guess that's what's called being honest. Opening up and taking ownership of your wounds. What's more, in a weird way, revealing my secret actually made it seem less bad. But then, as I said to Andy, 'Nothing happened between us; I never told her how I felt.'

'Well, aren't you a dark horse? Now you *have* to find out what's in the diary. I think you should pay Henry a visit.'

The thought of turning up on Henry's doorstep filled me with panic, much like how I felt the first time I stood at the precipice of a diving board during a group swimming lesson when I was nine. First, I saw my toes, ten small white digits gripping the board. Then I saw the blue water undulate around me, the same colour as the single layer of tiles that cut the white wall in our bathroom in half. For a second I thought the board was on top of the water like a surfboard and I was standing, hovering on top, a surfer yet to make his moves. Until I realised, in a panic, the incalculable distance between me and the pool. One minute it was so close I could touch it with my hand, the next it was a six-storey department store below, an oceanic abyss ready to engulf me and not bring me back to the surface. Agreeing to visit Henry was like thinking about diving into an abyss, where I had no idea how to do it and what would happen if I did.

The Visit

That night I didn't sleep. All I could think about was the diary. What had Marie written? Why had it upset Henry? Had she felt something for me? Had she thought about me as I had her? It was an outrageous idea, one I couldn't get out of my head, and was the only reason I agreed to Andy picking me up mid-morning the next day and taking me to Henry's.

I went through my wardrobe and took out three shirts, three pairs of cufflinks, four ties and two suits and laid them on the bed. Which to wear? Which would best demonstrate that I meant business, that I would not be rattled by Henry's threats? I got out my portable garment steamer and ran it over each item, even the ties. While it was still on I did the pillowcases. I would have gone around the flat if I'd had more time but Andy was arriving in ten minutes. I refocused and chose the blue suit, white shirt, red tie and the silver O and C cufflinks Mum gave me for my thirtieth birthday.

Andy turned up in jeans and a T-shirt.

'Wow, look at you,' he said. 'Smart, as always.'

I got the steamer and fired it up.

'Get that thing away from me.' Andy flapped a hand.

'You could at least be wrinkle-free,' I said.

'Very funny. Let's go.'

He didn't realise I would have steamed him all over if he had let me.

In the car, my confidence rapidly dwindled. In the state Henry seemed to be in, he probably wouldn't care if I turned up in Speedos. Thank goodness for Andy. He would know what to say. I could let him do the talking, knowing how dreadfully I suffered from 'after wit' when put on the spot – or, as Mum liked to say in her poorly pronounced French, 'l'esprit d'escalier'.

When we arrived, I let Andy go ahead, unlatch the picket-fence gate and walk up to the house, while I lagged behind, trying to hide. The box hedge lining the path, usually clipped, was frayed and patchy and the pockets of lawn either side sprouted weeds. What dishevelment! Marie would not have been happy. Henry couldn't even keep the garden tidy. I let the gate swing closed and bang shut.

'What if he's not in?' I whispered.

'We come back tomorrow.'

I wasn't sure about that idea. I wasn't sure about any of it now. I ran to the side of the house and flattened myself to the wall, like they do in the movies.

'What are you doing?' Andy followed me with a look of bemusement.

'Shh.'

'You're being ridiculous.'

'You don't know what Henry's like.'

'It'll be fine.'

We heard the front door open. 'Hello?'

'I'm not talking to him.' I shook my head to reiterate my point.

'Yes you are. Come on.' Andy pulled me away from the wall and pushed me towards the front of the house. Henry held on to the front door, scowling. The door swayed as he swayed.

'What the . . .?' Henry said. He wore an out-of-shape polo shirt and ill-fitting jeans. He looked as if he'd just got out of bed. Looked as if he'd turned himself against the world. Poor bugger.

Still, my toes curled. I was standing at the edge of the diving board. Andy put a hand on my shoulder. 'Don't worry,' he whispered in my ear, and walked towards Henry.

'Hello,' he said. 'I'm Andy, a friend of Oliver's.'

'Are you now?' Henry slurred. The gap in the door narrowed. Henry's head began to disappear.

'Don't close the door,' Andy interrupted. 'We're not here to cause trouble. We just want to chat.'

'What about?'

Andy looked at me. 'The diary,' he said.

'Go away.'

'No.'

'You can't threaten Oliver without an explanation.'

'Are you his lawyer?' Henry laughed.

'No.'

'I don't want to talk about it.'

'Oliver has the right to know.'

'Has he lost his voice?'

Andy elbowed me and gestured for me to speak.

I raised a hand and kept it raised, as if I were a robot whose elbow mechanism had jammed. 'Hi,' I said.

Henry stared at me, his eyes bloodshot and swollen.

'If you explain the diary, we'll go and forget any of this happened,' Andy said.

'It's your fault I read it in the first place.' Henry threw a drunken finger at me. 'I was going to stick it in the coffin until you suggested keeping it as a nice reminder of her. Fat load of use that was. I wouldn't have unlocked the bloody thing then.'

Henry's accusations of my guilt hurt. I felt like a shrivelled-up nothing, a dried-up truffle mushroom good only for chopping and cooking.

'Just go away,' Henry said, closing the door. Andy put a foot in it.

'Come on, Henry, just tell us what this is all about.' Andy plastered a grin on his face and pushed his leg into the door.

'You're persistent little buggers, aren't you?'

I didn't want to be a persistent little bugger. I touched Andy's arm to get his attention but Andy wasn't budging.

'We're not leaving,' Andy said. 'We'll stay here all night until you tell us.' Andy clearly *was* a persistent little bugger. He put a hand out to keep the door open, which made Henry stumble.

'Hey!' Henry said.

'Well . . .?'

'What's in it for me?'

'A discount on your next funeral.' Andy smiled at me. I couldn't return the gesture, was unable to fabricate a smile. I admired Andy's chutzpah but was unable to emulate it, having spent my life shamefully chutzpah-less.

'You've got to be kidding?' Henry said.

'No, Oliver's a very accommodating man. Anyway, why should he give you anything when you're the one who barged into his funeral home and threatened him?'

Henry rolled his eyes and sighed a raspy, rattly sigh. 'Alright, alright.' He let go of the door and let us inside.

'You can sit in there.' He pointed to a reading room to the right of the front door. I followed Andy in and we perched on the edge of a velvet-covered chaise longue. I wanted to lounge on the chaise longue instead of teetering on the edge as if I were about to jump out of a plane. Henry disappeared down the hallway. Heavy drapes hung on the window opposite and books framed an original fireplace. A large ceramic vase sat noticeably empty in front of the hearth.

My right leg jiggled uncontrollably. Andy put a hand on it. 'Relax,' he said.

'You haven't seen him in action,' I said.

'You haven't seen *me* in action.'

'I don't want to.'

'He's had a few, so he won't be hard to topple.' Andy chuckled.

'Here,' Henry said, returning. He had a whisky in one hand and a leather-bound journal in the other, its lock damaged and dangling. He handed it to me. A delicate whiff of roses and a hint of leather floated up from the diary. I wanted to put my nose against the cover and breathe her in.

'Don't stare at it. Open it.'

Stupidly, I didn't think I could open it now that I was holding it. I felt torn between an urge to read the pages as if ravenously scoffing food and reluctant ethical duty. I didn't believe it was mine to read and I wasn't one to pry. Yet it felt as if everything about my past was sealed inside the journal. That opening it would somehow change the present and impact my future. Andy nodded at me. *Go on*, he was saying. *Go on, just do it.* My fingers readied at the bottom corner. *Come on, turn the cover. Turn it.* Oh, the curiosity of wanting to know what lay inside. The urge . . .

But no. I couldn't.

'Stop looking at the damn thing and read,' Henry ordered. He drank what was left in his glass and steadied himself against a standing lamp.

I was frozen. As much as I wanted to know what Marie had written, I wanted to leave her and Henry in peace without causing any more aggravation. Henry may have acted inappropriately at Clock & Son the other day, but he had been drinking. He was probably ashamed at his behaviour and had overreacted to whatever he had read. The man needed more time to grieve, more time to accept.

'For goodness' sake, give me that.' Henry snatched the diary off me. His sudden aggression made me twitch. I may have felt sorry for him but he still made me nervous. The diary pages cracked as Henry flicked through them. 'Here, this is the bit.' He waggled the diary in front of me.

'I can't,' I said.

Andy nudged me.

'You *can't*, can't you?' Henry shouted each word, the 'c's catching in his throat like phlegm. 'You stupid prick.'

'Look, mate,' Andy said, 'why don't you just tell us?'

Henry's gaze moved from his glass to somewhere else entirely. His mouth drooped. His shoulders sagged.

'I had no idea.' Henry spoke again, this time more subdued, more measured. He shook his head slowly. 'No. Bloody. Idea.' He paused and gestured with the glass. 'No bloody idea,' he shouted drunkenly, and flung the journal at the fireplace.

'Because I thought she loved me. I thought all this time . . . Maybe I wasn't the best husband. Maybe . . . I don't know. But I did love her, I did.' He paused. 'Except, you see, she didn't love me.' His face crumpled like paper; his bottom lip pouted like a petulant child's. 'No, she didn't love *me*. She loved *you*.'

A strange noise came from the back of my throat. I think it was from me. It could have been Henry. White noise jammed my ears.

'Close your mouth, you silly little man,' Henry sneered. He pointed his glass at me, closed one eye and pretended to pull the trigger on a gun, sound effects and all.

I jumped. Even Andy jerked.

'Alright, you can go now. Show's over,' Henry said. Sweat pooled in his armpits.

But wait! What did he mean, she loved me? Was it really a heartfelt non-platonic love and not merely the love of a meaningful friendship? How did Henry know this for sure? What had Marie written exactly? I eyed the diary lying by the hearth, battered and bruised. Andy was doing the same. I should lunge for it. Or, at least, Andy should. Andy had fast-twitch muscle fibres. Or so Andy said. *Go on, Andy, get it. Get it!*

He didn't. He stared at it, then said, 'I'm sure Oliver would like to read the diary now.'

'Too late. Get up and get out.' Henry grabbed Andy's shirt, pulled him off the chaise longue and shoved him towards the door.

I was next. Henry yanked me to my feet before I could do anything, say anything. 'Go, and don't bother me again.'

'Well, that goes for you, too, you know,' Andy called back. But it was a feeble response which held no sway with Henry. The door clattered shut behind us, l'esprit d'escalier following closely on our heels.

Andy fumbled with the ignition, swearing as he did so. 'That was crazy,' he said.

I took off my jacket. Wiped my brow. I was speechless. Was it true that Marie had loved me? One minute I was loveless, the next I was full to the brim. I looked out at Marie's house. It now seemed changed. Its white shutters were whiter, the sandstone frontage more textured, the potted colours brighter, the grass and weeds greener.

'She loved me, Andy, she loved me.' I must have sounded like a fool, but I didn't care.

Andy lifted a hand off the steering wheel and placed it on my shoulder. 'Are you alright?'

'It's like I've been flipped and landed on my head.'

We turned down a side street. I strained my neck to keep the house in view, until it disappeared completely. I felt like I'd left a piece of me behind and wondered if I'd ever get it back again or whether it was best left there for weeds to grow over.

'I wish I'd got the diary,' Andy continued. 'I wanted to grab it, but I'll be honest, Henry spooked me.'

Was I stupid not to have read the page Henry offered me? I could easily have indulged my inquisitiveness and satisfied my desire to find out what Marie had penned about me. Did it actually contain words of love, phrases of romance dipped in regret? Did she really say she loved me? My gut ached at the thought of our reciprocal love for each other.

How had I not known? I rested an elbow on the door and my head in a hand. I closed my eyes and thought of Marie. How she liked to surprise me by dropping a Lindt ball into my jacket pocket without me noticing. How her sweet tooth rivalled mine. How thoughtful she was, how quietly confident and overflowing with kindness. How tactile she could be and the wondrous feeling I got when she'd touch my arm unthinkingly. How much her words of professional advice and guidance meant to me. I wiped a tear from my cheek. Darling Marie, oh, darling Marie.

'Hey, mate, don't be sad,' Andy said. 'This is good, right? She loved you, too!'

'Yes, Andy, she loved me.' I nodded, and then, unable to help myself. I shouted, 'She *loved* me! She loved *me*! *She* loved *me*!' I put emphasis on different words, each meaning as equally important as the other, and ended with a whoop to try and scare off my melancholy.

'That's the way,' Andy said. 'Be happy at this news. Now you know that Henry's anger had nothing to do with your business.'

'Well, yes, that's good news, too.' I felt a burst of joy rise up.

Then it went and popped when it reached my throat and I started sobbing. My chance at true, mutual love was gone. Gone! And here I had been, thinking my love had been one-sided. That I had been loveless, or worse, unlovable. But no, it wasn't true. I had been loved. I was lovable!

One minute I was up, the next down, swinging like old-fashioned balancing scales. I didn't feel I could take any more news – good or bad. So many things had happened recently to upset my status quo that I didn't think my nerves could take it any more.

'Oh, mate,' Andy said. 'Hang on, I'll pull over.'

'I'm OK,' I said.

Andy stopped the car and patted my leg. 'It's a lot to take in and you're allowed to feel sad.' He pulled a serviette from the compartment in his door and gave it to me. It smelled like a stale muffin.

I blew into it and dried my eyes but they only started welling up again and tears dribbled in a constant trickle down my face. I needed another serviette, but Andy didn't have one.

'Sorry, Andy,' I blubbered.

He patted my leg again. 'It's OK. It'll be OK. I know, why don't we make a toast to Marie? That'll help cheer you up.'

It sounded like a good place to start so I agreed and Andy started up the car again and drove to the pub. I wiped my face on my suit sleeve and thought about the dual properties of hot chips and beer – comforting and celebratory treats at the same time. But I knew now that nothing could beat the endorphin-induced euphoria of discovering you were loved by the woman you had been secretly in love with. The instant gratification of salty fried food didn't even come close.

Seeing Blue

When Andy dropped me home, all I wanted was to wallow in the warmth of love. To hold that feeling of joy, as if I had overcome my fear of jumping off the diving board and was freeze-framed in a forward dive in the tuck position, hovering mid-air, suspended in a ball of happiness – blue sky around me, blue water below me. Where I was sitting in a bubble of mutual adoration that no one could pop and where nothing else mattered but Marie's love for me and my love for her. I flopped into an armchair and wallowed. I was a bee with a flower bed all to myself. I was a sommelier in a barrel of Penfolds Grange. I was a chocoholic in a lake of melted Mars bars.

Until I opened my eyes and realised I was once again alone in my one-bedroom flat with no one to keep me company, not even a goldfish. An overwhelming feeling of loneliness and despair came over me. What was the point of finding out Marie loved me when she was no longer around to share it with me? When our love for each other was going nowhere but down a dead-end street? I should have taken my own advice and stayed in the blissful state of being ignorant. I remained in this befuddled and despondent mood for at least half an hour, doing nothing but feeling sorry for myself. A pathetic, lonely Oliver Clock.

Eventually I got up. If for nothing else but to change, to get out of my work clothes and into something more comfortable. Then I pootled around the flat, aimlessly tweaking the minutiae. Ensuring the remote controls sat parallel in a row on the coffee table, the spices were aligned in the spice rack, labels facing out, and the pictures on the wall weren't crooked. These tasks usually gave me comfort; they were small rituals around which I could retain a feeling of order and control. But today I felt more discombobulated than I had ever been and no amount of symmetry seemed to ease it. I had basked in a momentary high and then, bam, it was over and I felt flatter than a flat-pack IKEA table. I was soon to turn forty and what did I have? A business that was dying and a life that was lifeless. I was a funeral director burdened with an inheritance I hadn't asked for and an overbearing mother. I was a man with no sweetheart to cherish his love handles, no siblings to confer with and no children to foster into the future. I was a man knocking on the door of middle age with no hobbies, a minimal social life and an unbearable love in his heart for a woman who had passed away. A man who could have spoken up about his love before she died, and maybe, just maybe, they could have had a few precious months together, yet I'd let the moment slip away and now it was too late.

This called for more drastic action. I turned my attentions to the bookshelf, whose lack of order of any kind – height, alphabetical or otherwise – I found most upsetting. How had I not noticed before? I decided colour-coding the spines of the books would be the most aesthetically pleasing configuration and threw myself into the task of taking apart and reordering the bookshelf with the fervour of a dog digging sand. Anything to try and make myself feel better. Then I found my notebook of resolutions in a colour that didn't match the rest. That stopped me in my tracks. Not its pale lemon colour so much as what lay inside – my vows to change, to ask Marie out; the determination I had exhibited but never followed through on. I flicked through the notebook. There were pages and pages of lists here.

Earlier resolutions were broad and loose, like *Thou shalt go on an overseas holiday*; *Thou shalt go on an adventure* (although what sort I hadn't specified); *Thou shalt learn a language* – Italian perhaps, but not

French because that was Mum's foreign language of choice; *Thou shalt stop eating cheese and lose weight*. Then they got more specific, like *Thou shalt buy an abs Kruncher machine as seen on TV*; *Thou shalt watch less television*; and *Thou shalt get a pet*.

I had achieved none of them. Most, I hadn't even tried. They were fanciful notions of a chubby man fixed to his sofa. A man who was turning forty, when? I did a quick finger count. Soon, very soon – three months soon – and what did I have to show for it? I had spent years thinking up resolutions and jotting them down. The time and mental energy I had wasted. It was all for nothing!

This realisation abruptly ended my colour-coding. I dropped the notebook, rested my wine glass next to a thriller by Jeffrey Archer and held on to the corner of the bookshelf to steady myself. Then the bloody thing started shaking, threatening to spill the first books I had arranged with spines of a red hue. I should have had that custom built-in made after all. It was like I was in the middle of an earthquake. An earthquake to ruin my tidying! I collapsed into the armchair, buried my head in my hands and let the earthquake of emotion do its thing as tears spluttered down my cheeks and my body shook with the full force of Mother Nature. I was a burst water mains of grief, expunging my sorrow for Marie, pity for myself, my unrequited love and the loss of my dreams – however fantastical they might have been.

I was crying so much that tears came out of my nose and I had no box of tissues at the ready, or even a nicely ironed handkerchief to pull from a jacket breast pocket. My right sleeve would have to do. Then the left. Then the bottom of my shirt, which had half come out of my trousers. When finally I emerged, puffy-eyed and clothing-dampened, the earthquake over, I felt exhausted, drained like a corpse of its blood. I couldn't even remember having rearranged the bookshelf and couldn't be bothered putting it back together again. I splashed water on my face and changed into my pyjamas. I opened the fridge to tempt myself to eat but couldn't even do that. I lay on the sofa in front of the television, hugging a cushion. When I woke, it was nearly time for bed. I don't remember cleaning my teeth, turning out the lights or even putting my clothes away. All I wanted was to forget who I was.

I slipped under the covers and dreamed of what a life with Marie could have been like. Days spent holding her floral-scented hands, kissing her cherry lips, planning a future together in which we worked and lived as one. I dreamed of resurrecting Clock & Son's standing in the community: a funeral home that flourished, one I would be proud to pass on to the next generation. I dreamed of a future Clock & Son where there was a new son or daughter to pass it on to. I dreamed of eating all the cheese I wanted without putting on weight. I dreamed of travelling with a companion to wine regions in France. I dreamed of not being alone, lonely, with a business that was doomed and a future that was empty. I dreamed of the next decade of my life that included a woman who loved me and my quirks, and I her and her quirks, with two children by our sides, living in a house, not a flat, the contents of which I had neatly ordered and arranged. A life that was perfectly symmetrical in every way. I dreamed of everything I wanted but didn't have. I don't know if they were proper dreams or awake dreams. The two merged into one, with me drifting in and out of a sleep that was far from restful.

Advice from the Grave

I'm not sure what's worse: being in the middle of a breakdown or coming out the other end, exhausted and empty. When I woke, not only did I feel physically and mentally spent, as if flushed of all my innards, but the flat felt eerily hollow as well. I padded around it aimlessly, every move I made echoing miserably; my slippered footsteps seemed loud, my own sneeze made me jump, my jaw creaked audibly with every chew of a Mars bar. How utterly soul-destroying.

It made me realise how terribly alone I now was. That my dreams of Marie joining me in the apartment would never be. That my flat was not to be a home for the two of us but would remain as it always had been: a one-bedroom dwelling for a single man. Even the term 'bachelor pad' was too lofty a nom de plume for it. For that implied a place of carefree fun for a man who enjoyed the single life, revelled in it, even. I was not that man. I had nothing to revel in.

All I had was a tired old double bed whose mattress dipped on one side only – not because of any amount of over-exertion but because of my own dead weight lying in the same spot by myself, night after night. I may have had a kitchen that was big enough for two to cook in and a family of four to dine in, a living room that could comfortably seat six and a courtyard just big enough for a small drinks party (if you didn't mind touching your neighbour and not attempting to mingle) and yet I was always there alone, microwaving meals for one, sitting in the same middle section of the sofa in front of the TV as I always did or perching on an outdoor chair staring at my attempts at potted decor as if waiting for Marie or other guests to arrive.

For a long time I had been dreaming of Marie arriving and never leaving, imagining what it would be like to know that every day she would wake up next to me and join me in the flat after work in the evenings. If I got home before her, I would open the place up, start preparing dinner and have her favourite drink ready for when she walked in the door. She would burst in like a bright bunch of peonies, kick off her shoes, and we would kiss – passionately, of course – then talk about our day. The flat would hum with the chatter of two people connecting, two lovers uniting. Oh, how romantic it all was. Oh, how romantic it could have been. How real it had once seemed – even if it was only in my imagination. Now, the flat was like an abandoned bomb shelter with me the sole survivor. The only shoes being kicked off were mine, the only kissing to be had was on the TV, the only chatter came from my thoughts clattering in my head. And outside seemed a scary place that was undesirable to be in.

So, what did I do? Well, I didn't know what to do with myself. I didn't want to leave the flat, encounter other people, go to work and pretend everything was just fine. I wanted to be alone and yet, ironically, I didn't want to be alone! Oh, the torment of loneliness, the anguish of grief. It wasn't like it was a weekend, when I had my usual routine. These few days were unlike any day off I'd ever had. It was a never-ending time of nothingness in which I had no purpose and no meaning; and nothing was achieved. I would go to make a cup of tea and then forget I'd put the kettle on. I'd turn on both the radio and the television for company until the ingratiating voices of presenters and soap opera actors irritated me and I turned them off. In the shower, I would stand under the hot water, staring into space, and forget to wash. I would start to dress but only get as far as undies and track pants. Is it possible to *look* homeless when you have a home? Is it possible to *feel* homeless when you have a home?

I can tell you that it is.

Then, when I was rummaging in a kitchen drawer looking for my toothbrush, which I was starting to absent-mindedly leave in odd places, I found an old key ring of Dad's – one he had designed himself. I'd forgotten it was there. It may have been his pride and joy but it hadn't been a hit with customers. The design of a coffin-shaped key ring in brown-coloured stainless steel with a silver rim and the Clock & Son name in the middle was never going to take off. Who wants a coffin dangling on the end of your keychain? Only Dad did, and so he was the only one that we knew of who used it, until the link broke. Then he died and I inherited it – another little memento I shoved in a drawer. The thought of it made me sad. Not that I'd left it in a drawer never to be fixed, but that I never got to spend more time with Dad. I ran a finger over the shiny coffin. Dad used to say, 'Coffins are not the end, they're merely a new beginning.' It was not how everyone saw it, but you could rely on Dad for the one-liners. Like the corny pun he once coined, to be said in jest after costs were discussed, which always got a giggle from me but no one else: 'And if you don't cough up, you might be cough-in.' Mum quickly put an end to that one-liner and made sure it never entered The Folder of Systematic Funeral Protocol – that gem of a document filled with Dad's sage advice. I had a copy of it in the flat, for Dad had insisted we all take one home with us, just in case we needed to dip into it after hours or, in my and the embalmer's case, if we got a call-out in the middle of the night and needed to refresh our words of consolation. I went to the bottom drawer at the end of the kitchen bench, found the Folder, took it out and flipped it open to the introduction.

Grief takes many forms. It's like the sky: one minute rolling with angry thunderclouds and rain, the next lightly sprinkled with cumulonimbus . . .

Dad actually said that to people, and most were too overcome with sadness to register what he was talking about or to ask what 'cumulonimbus' meant. I took it upon myself to explain if they were looking quizzical. I'd quietly whisper, 'A thick fluffy cloud,' as Dad continued on with his analogy. When I took over from him, I discounted the intro as too meteorologically jargonistic but now I realised how true his words were. Right then I felt blanketed in stratus, a low-lying grey cloud that hung heavy over me.

. . . But eventually, I promise, the clouds will lift and then dissipate to reveal a freshly washed blue sky.

At that moment it was like Dad was talking to me and me alone. It hadn't occurred to me to use the Folder for my own purposes and I bet Dad never thought his son would get solace from it either. It had only ever been meant for others, as if we were immune to the effects of grieving.

I took the Folder to the kitchen table, sat down and listened to what Dad had to say. *You've got to accept all the different cloud formations that come and go and may do so for some time yet. They're all part of the process, Oliver. Do not berate yourself for the clouds, do not worry if they hang around, do not fret if they bring storms; let them. Let them wash you, cleanse you, refresh you.* It was like he was talking to me from whatever cloud type was, at that moment, lingering over my flat. Dear old Dad. His at times gruff exterior belied his ability to help us as purveyors of funeral management to sensitively handle the grieving, even if it was in the form of a geography lesson with a sermon-like tone to it.

A tear bubble burst from the corner of my eye. It didn't feel the same as those from the day before; it was more of a sentimental tear, from knowing that Dad was still with me and that, perhaps, in death, he was giving me more emotional support than he ever had when he was alive. How strange but, also, how immensely comforting.

I don't know how long I sat there reading his cloud-inspired introduction over and over until I wasn't really reading the words so much as clutching on to Dad's voice, but eventually I mentally returned to my seat at the table. I glanced at the wall clock; it was two in the afternoon. I suddenly felt hungry. There was a tub of strawberry yoghurt all on its own on the second shelf. It would be breakfast and lunch rolled into one. I took it out, gave the fridge shelf a quick wipe down while I was there then slurped the yoghurt with a spoon as I leaned against the kitchen bench. There wasn't much other food to tempt me but it didn't matter; my appetite had not properly returned. Yet already I could tell something had shifted. I wouldn't say I felt better, more that a little of the cloud had thinned. While I didn't resume normal activity for the rest of that day and couldn't face it the next day either, I did a pretty good job of not fighting the cloud. And I had Dad to thank for that.

Rescued

After two days, several unlistened phone messages and a few door knocks, Andy turned up. His head appeared at the living room window, like that of a newly acquired giant gnome.

'Mate,' he called out, tapping on the glass. 'Mate.'

I opened the window. 'What are you doing?' I said, even though it was perfectly clear: Mum had sent him over.

'Everything OK?' he asked.

'I needed a few days off, that's all.'

'Do you want to talk about it?'

'There's nothing to talk about.'

'OK, but since I'm here, do you want to let me in? Or we could chat like this, me in the garden, you inside with your untamed beard and old track pants I've never seen you wear before. What is going on?' Andy looked horrified.

I touched my chin. It had never felt so hirsute. I feared a resemblance to an overused cat scratching post.

'I jest,' Andy laughed. 'I'm jealous. You know I can't even grow a goatee and am already half bald at thirty-eight.'

I looked at him and pondered the idea of an Andy gnome. Perhaps if he'd had more of a paunch . . .

'So are you going to let me in?' He looked at me, waiting expectantly for an answer. Of course I was going to let him in. I left the window and went to the front door.

'Jeez, what happened in here?' he said, gesturing to the gross untidiness of my flat. It did look pretty bad, now that he pointed it out. 'This is not like you, mate, not like you at all.'

'Tea? Beer?' I said.

'Whatever you're having.' He pushed some books to one side with his foot so he could get to the sofa.

I handed him a beer and we sat in silence for a few seconds.

'Is this about Marie?' Andy asked.

I shrugged.

'It's OK, mate, you know you can talk to me.' Then he let the silence do the talking, urging me to speak.

'It's everything, Andy. Marie, the business, my life . . . I'm nearly forty, and what do I have to show for it? Nothing, Andy, nothing. I may not even have a job by the time I turn forty.'

Andy looked at me thoughtfully. 'You know,' he said, 'I've always been envious of you. Your tidy, ordered life, the safety and satisfaction of an inherited vocation.'

I couldn't believe Andy was saying this. I was the one who had been envious of him, with his dad who was always travelling to exotic places, his artistic mother who let the kids do whatever they wanted so long as it was legal, and four sisters who were encouraged to follow their hearts. They'd all ended up in a creative job of some sort and Andy had become a photographer. He was a man who could live in the moment and enjoy the moment without worrying about what came next. And he had an uncanny ability to counsel, acquired I suspected from being surrounded by women and girls as a child.

'You've always had it together, you know,' he continued. 'You're composed and annoyingly sensible *and* you can work around death every day. I sure as hell couldn't.'

'I don't know how to do anything else.'

'But why would you want to? You've got a job for life. People aren't going to stop dying, are they?'

'They may be dying but they're taking their business elsewhere.' I looked away. Felt my eyes well up again. I didn't want to cry in front of Andy when he'd just told me how much he admired my composure. Lightning lit up the living room, highlighting for a few seconds the dust on my coffee table.

'What you've got to remember,' he said, 'is that you're number one. If you don't care enough about yourself, who will? You need to believe in yourself. Believe that you have the power to turn things around, fix your business and your love life.'

I took in Andy's words. I'd never thought of myself as having power, the option to make change rather than have change forced upon me. The thought of it gave me the shivers, as did the second flash of lightning, which was like a whip across my neck. Around us rain intensified into one thunderous applause.

'Jeez, you still don't like thunderstorms, do you? Remember that time, years ago, when I'd persuaded you to try golf and we saw a storm approach? I've never seen you run so fast back to the clubhouse.'

'My sister, remember?'

'Oh yeah.'

We didn't speak for a few minutes but listened to the thunder grumble under the weight of clouds and the rain easing to a polite clap, until it sounded as if it wasn't clapping at all. Andy looked at me thoughtfully, then said gently, 'Look, I think you need to move on from the past and try something new. It doesn't matter what. Go on a date, change things up at work . . .'

I got what he was saying but it was hard to get Marie's diary out of my head and to stop wondering exactly what she had written, imagining the words, *her* words about *me*. I probably didn't look as enthused about Andy's suggestions as he'd have hoped because he then read my mind and said, 'Are you still thinking about the diary?'

I nodded.

'I know it was great to find out about Marie's feelings for you, but the thing is,' he whispered, as if scared someone else might hear, 'she's no longer with us.'

I nodded again but couldn't speak. I was on the verge of choking up once more. I couldn't admit to Andy just how much I loved her, how I had wanted her to be my girlfriend, my wife, my forever woman. It would have sounded pathetic. Feeble. As if I were a loser who couldn't even fall in love with someone who was single and still living. For I was scared – scared about the future without Marie in it. I had become so consumed by the reason for her unhappiness and whether I could ask her out that I hadn't contemplated a future without her, which may sound fanciful, possibly even preposterous, yet that was the sum of it. And now I was left bereft, lost, future-less. All sense of purpose gone, *poof* . . . I sighed, unable to give any sort of response that would have been acceptable to Andy in that moment.

'Look, I'm sorry it didn't work out how you would have liked,' Andy continued. 'But now it's time to move forward. We've got to rethink your future, get you out of this funk.' I loved the way Andy included himself in my problems. He didn't need to do that, but it meant a lot. I nodded to show him how much I appreciated his words of advice, even if it all seemed too hard. It was like I was wedged between two rocks and couldn't get out. I knew I wanted to get out but not how I would do it – only that I wanted Marie alongside me at all times, which, sadly, didn't appear to be part of Andy's future for me.

'What I think,' Andy advised, 'is that you should be over the moon to find out how Marie felt about you but accept it's time to move on. And if you don't want the business to go under, do something about it. Try something new. That goes for your life, too. Sometimes change requires getting out of your comfort zone.'

I pondered Andy's words, which I knew were intended to be wonderfully inspiring, then clinked my empty beer bottle against his. 'Thanks, Andy,' I said.

'You'll be right, mate, I know you will.'

I felt better after Andy left. He may not have solved anything but a tiny weight had been lifted; more of the cloud had dissipated. I found my yellow notebook and skimmed previous pages. It was alarming how many times I had written *Thou shalt ask Marie out* – not that I'd repeatedly penned the phrase but that I had never done it. The words were hollow, whimsical notions of an apathetic daydreamer. Somehow I had to turn from fantasiser to doer; I had to banish the clouds and find the blue sky. I edged across the sofa so that I was no longer sitting in my usual spot in the middle. The seat cushion was firmer, less sunken closer to the end. I could still watch the television, even if it meant a slightly angled view, but it wasn't the end of the world. Plus, there was the sofa arm to lean into if I wanted and more room to stretch my legs without having the coffee table immediately in front. I sat there for a minute enjoying my new position, then did the only thing I knew how to do. I found my notebook of resolutions, turned to a fresh page and wrote a new list. But, this time, I felt more determination than I ever had before; my pen strokes were more defined, the lines etched deeper, the resolutions formed with stronger resolve.

Thou shalt enjoy the feeling of knowing you were loved and not let it get you down.

Thou shalt try something new.

Thou shalt get out of your comfort zone, maybe even take a risk.

Thou shalt not let Clock & Son go under.

I read them over one more time and smiled to myself. Marie would have been proud.

PART TWO

I must stop pretending I have a busy social life.
I must stop buying so many ties, especially ones featuring galaxies.
I must stand up for myself.
I must get a life.
Can you 'get a life' or does life find you?

The Invitation

The next day I woke up drained but reinvigorated. This time I was determined to try my new resolutions, and number one was the easiest place to start. Marie had loved me and I loved her and that joyous feeling was going to help get me through the challenge of the other resolutions. I returned to work as if I had never been away and brushed off Jean's words of concern and Mum's questioning looks. I even rejoiced in doing an embalming because it was our first death in two weeks and so cause for celebration. At home, I restored my books to the bookshelf in colour-coded groups and my notebook of resolutions to the drawer in my bedside table. I didn't even mind when Edie returned with another candle sample. My mood had lifted and I was happy to humour her.

'This is La Lumière de Monty,' Edie said. She lifted the lid and waved the candle under my nose. She really did have a lovely face, warm and welcoming, and was wearing a striking black dress with flowers, a print like glossy, fashionable wallpaper. 'What do you think?'

I leaned forward to sniff. A pungent smell of something unbearably sweet evaporated up my nostrils. 'And who is this?' I asked.

'It's my cat.'

'Meow,' I said, which I hadn't intended to; it just came out.

'It's an unusual fragrance, I know,' she said. 'It's my secret concoction. The point is, I can make pretty much any scent you like. Obviously, recreating the aroma of cat is tricky and I wouldn't normally do animals, but when you get it right, you really feel as if your pet or relative is with you when you burn it.' She smiled, as though this were a totally normal thing to say.

'Well, it's certainly unique,' I said, wondering how to let her down gently. 'You're like my florist, who was very creative. She could turn any idea into a bouquet.'

'For me, making candles is a welcome change from the very uncreative pharmaceutical world in which I work.' She laughed. 'Look, I know you've already heard my sales pitch, but I would love the opportunity to make these for your clients. You see, smell is so powerful. When you become aware of your sense of smell and the smells around you, everything comes alive. Life comes alive. Most people aren't aware, and they're the ones not living. Things become more nuanced – that's what a famous perfumer once said, "more nuanced". When you want to remember someone fondly, all you want is the sense that they're still with you, the sense that the nuances of them are still alive.'

Then Jean walked in. 'Ah, Jean,' I said. 'This is Edie, the candlemaker I was telling you about.'

'What do you think of this one?' Edie said, shoving the candle under Jean's quivering nose.

Jean tilted her head skywards as if trying to decipher the source of the scent. 'Potent, but nice,' she said.

'It's my old cat. She was a grumpy old thing by the end, but loyal and surprisingly affectionate.'

'Isn't that lovely?' Jean said, before turning to me and tapping her watch. 'You have a client shortly, Oliver.'

It was a cunning ploy, but I was happy for her to define an endpoint to the meeting. Yet after Edie had left I couldn't help but think about what she had said. About keeping alive the memories of someone who had gone. About the nuances of smell. About the promise of being remembered for ever – or as long as a candle's burn time lasted. I may have been basking in Marie's love, but how long was that going to last and when would my memories of her begin to fade? Already she was becoming blurred at the edges, her voice muffled by the sound of my voice trying to find her. It was happening too quickly and I wasn't prepared for her to dim (as if I would ever be). I didn't even have a photo of her. The only one I'd ever had was a newspaper clipping from when she won a floral award several years ago, but that got thrown out when Mum was on one of her spring cleans. I'd had a phone message from her that I'd listened to repeatedly until it got wiped by mistake. It may have only been, 'Hi, Oliver, can you call me when you get a minute?' but, still, it was her voice and it was comforting to hear. And that was it. All I had were fuzzy memories.

But what if there was another way to capture her? Could Edie actually be on to something?

I grabbed a pen and paper and indulged in a moment's fantasy. If Marie were a candle, what would it smell like? Which scents would I pick for her?

The first one that came to mind was sweet peas. If I had to pick a smell that represented Marie, it was sweet peas with their candy-like scent of summer. What else? Freshly cut leaves, slightly damp, crisp and new. Her hand moisturiser, with its subtle nose of honey and lanolin. I drummed my fingers. Ah, yes, rosé wine. She loved a glass over our lunchtime meetings, twisting my arm (not very hard) for me to join her. And what was the fragrance I smelled when I leaned in to kiss her on the cheek? She never wore perfume, claiming it reacted with her skin, so it must have been some sort of cosmetic. Powder, perhaps, or face cream? Edie was right: now that I was thinking about it, it's all about the nuances. And I couldn't forget zest of mandarin. It was her favourite fruit.

I sat back in the chair and let the front legs lift off the floor as if I were a kid at a school desk. How glorious to be remembering Marie in this way. How wonderful to think there was a way to keep Marie alive. It was an outlandish notion but one I couldn't get out of my head.

Could a candle of her be just what I needed to prove I was achieving resolution number one? I could light it on my fortieth birthday. It would be the only candle I'd need.

As I envisioned La Lumière de Marie, tinged a pale lavender colour, like that of a ruffled sweet pea blossom, my phone lit up with a text.

Are you free next Saturday night? Andy wrote.

I replied in the affirmative and wondered if I still had Edie's business card. It wasn't in my letter holder or under the notepad.

Good. We need to get you back into the real world, Andy wrote.

There it was, wedged between Roger's resignation letter, behind the pencil holder.

Dinner party at ours, 7.30.

Trust Andy to still be looking out for me. A dinner party at his may not come under any of the other resolutions I had written, but it would counteract the old one of trying to stop watching infomercials. Plus, it would give me a wonderful reason to enjoy a night away from my flat and maybe even allow me, if the occasion arose – or even if it didn't! – to refer to where I lived as a bachelor pad. I sent him two emojis (a champagne bottle and a party hat) and returned to the list of scents I had created for Marie. I needed another indulgent moment remembering. I closed my eyes and inhaled. But all I got were the faint remnants of Jean's perfume and a whiff of cold coffee from the mug by my computer. What if Edie really could make a candle of Marie? I could have her surrounding me wherever I cared to put her. At work on my desk or in the viewing room, at home by my bed or on the coffee table, as a reminder of our love for each other. Was there any harm in finding out? No one else needed to know. And if the candle was not reminiscent of her, I could give it to someone as a present or donate it to charity. I reached for Edie's business card in the letter holder and ran my fingers over the embossed wording. This called for action, not procrastination. Perhaps this was resolution numbers two and three both at once! Who cared if it contradicted Andy's advice; he didn't understand how much

Marie was helping me move on. Would I have entertained Edie's business idea if not for Marie? I don't think so.

In a rare moment of decisiveness, I dialled Edie's number and, before I had time to change my mind, I was discussing candles that smell of the dead – or, more precisely, of the woman I loved. The adrenaline rush I got from making such a rash decision without consulting anyone, overanalysing or delaying, required an immediate lie-down. When no one was looking I attempted a mindfulness moment on an empty embalming table.

The Dinner Party

By Saturday I was tripping the light fantastic, to quote the song 'The Sidewalks of New York', whose tune I only recently discovered at the funeral of a hundred-and-one-year-old tap-dancing hobbyist. A dinner party in itself wouldn't normally induce such a reaction in me, rather it was the realisation that I was about to attend a social occasion the likes of which I had not enjoyed for months. Months! I did not put going to the pub after work with Andy or having dinner at Mum's in the same category. Hadn't Andy said I should be looking after number one? I felt so buoyed by the idea that I went to the barber's to get my beard taken off. I flossed my teeth and decided to indulge in a celebratory steaming of my underwear. Marie would have been proud.

That evening I stood in my freshly steamed white Jockey Y-fronts and striped socks, wondering what to wear. It wasn't like I had to impress anyone. Andy's wife, Lucy, was as relaxed on the clothing front as Andy, embodying what I'd call a polished gypsy look, and their other friends who were coming, Simon and Sue, whom I had met several times before, dressed on the casual side as well. They were creatives, after all. No, tonight I was dressing for myself, the man I wanted to be outside of the business. A man who could move on from wearing track pants after hours. A man who was tripping the light fantastic in the warm glow of reciprocal love.

I pulled out two shirts from the wardrobe and stood before the mirror. My stomach waved a cheery hello. I sucked it in, but it wouldn't disappear. Maybe I should try dieting again. I could decline dessert or the cheese platter if I could show some self-restraint. My arms and shoulders definitely had the unfortunate padding of a man too used to snacking on leftover barbecue sausage. I stood up straighter, wondering if I would ever see muscle again. I angled sideways, but my profile reminded me of an egg with legs. Sure, the socks didn't help and maybe my underwear could be updated, but would there ever be a time when I looked as if I had stepped out of a Calvin Klein ad? Was there any point in even trying? The best I could probably hope for was an affiliation with Old Spice.

Time to dress, to cover up the egg. I picked a light blue linen shirt whose sleeves I could fold back for a more smart-casual look and a pair of dark denim jeans, my latest purchase, bought when I was fantasising about asking Marie out. This would be their first outing.

Andy and Lucy lived in a narrow terrace with a brick facade and wrought-iron railings. On the street-front veranda huddled a herd of pot plants, two cane chairs with faded cushions and a low-dangling wind chime. Lucy may have been tidier than Andy but she was no minimalist. Her love of bohemian and vintage items en masse meant there was never just one of anything. Inside, rows of books lined the hallway, plants filled corners, Turkish rugs covered the floorboards and an array of mismatched mugs hung on hooks in the kitchen. There may have been clutter, but it was organised, clean and welcoming. Dodging the hanging macramé pot-plant holder, I pressed the doorbell.

'Hey, Oliver, great you could come,' Andy said, slapping me on the back. 'How are you feeling?'

'A bit better, thanks, Andy.'

'Excellent.'

I followed his flapping shirt tail down the hallway. A fug of spiciness cloyed the air – possibly Moroccan. Already I was looking forward to Lucy and Andy's wonderful cooking and selection of wine. Lucy welcomed me with a big kiss, her dangling earrings hitting my cheek.

'You remember Sue and Simon, don't you?' Andy said.

We exchanged greetings. Simon was a fellow photographer and Sue a watercolour artist.

'And this is Sue's sister, Caroline.'

'Hello, Oliver,' Caroline said. 'Nice to meet you.'

I looked around for a partner. There didn't appear to be one and no one else was mentioned. I glanced at her ring finger. Empty. It was a pleasant change to not be the only single person amidst a room full of couples. We shook hands rather formally, but her warm smile helped soften the formality. It was so engaging that I think I lingered longer on the handshake than was socially acceptable. I then turned my attention to her other physical features: mid-length brown hair, well-plucked eyebrows, tanned skin – possibly recently exfoliated – and half a thumb length of visible cleavage. I sensed Caroline was doing the same to me, which is why long handshakes are usually inadvisable.

As Andy handed out drinks and Lucy passed around blinis, Caroline sidled up to me and started chatting.

'Are you divorced, too?' she said. 'I'm glad to be shot of mine but it's a drag being single.'

'No, not divorced,' I said, and put a whole blini in my mouth to avoid disclosing any more detail.

'You're a funeral director, aren't you?'

I nodded.

'Intriguing,' she said, touching my arm in a way that suggested she was either brushing off dog hair (heaven forbid) or smoothing out a crease (highly unlikely). 'So what's it like, really, to be around the dead all the time?'

'It's very quiet,' I said, deadpan.

She laughed, louder than I was expecting. I didn't feel the need to explain that most of my work was spent around the living. It would have ruined the moment. I waited for the next question. Because there's always more than one.

'You must get some strange requests. Do you? Go on, tell me. I'm not squeamish.' She elbowed me in delight.

When I started working in the funeral industry, I thought it would be fun to make up answers to such questions, as if my work revolved around making B-grade horror movies, until I realised I didn't have to fabricate. Humanity did it all for me.

'Well, yes, I do,' I said, reaching for another blini as Lucy passed.

'And?'

'Once, we had a woman who bequeathed her four gold teeth to her four grandchildren.'

'Really? What an inheritance!'

'Then there was the time a man requested the return of his wife's breast implants. I didn't like to ask if he had someone else in mind for them.'

I hadn't noticed Caroline's eyes during the long handshake but, now that they were popping out in shock, I noted how striking they were.

'Is Oliver regaling you with tales from the dark side?' Andy said, joining us.

We all laughed, even though I don't think Caroline had believed anything I'd said, and the talk turned to Andy's latest photographic gig and the difficulty of capturing the full beauty of a hamburger in one shot.

Over dinner, Caroline and I were seated next to each other, with Andy opposite me, Simon opposite Caroline and Sue opposite Lucy. I raised my glass to Andy as a personal thanks for the invite and the fine food. He winked at me in return, which I thought was a strange response to a toast, but I winked back nonetheless, which made him chuckle. I hadn't intended to drink at speed yet found myself enjoying the evening so much that I was guzzling wine like a three-litre four-wheel drive going through petrol, which made me laugh more loudly at comments that were only mildly funny. Thankfully, Caroline didn't mind and seemed more than happy to join in with me, which just added to the overall mood of conviviality. As I savoured the last mouthful of dessert, unwilling – unable – to contribute to the current conversation on everyone's next holidays, I felt a hand on my knee.

'It's good, isn't it?' Caroline said.

'Lucy is an excellent cook,' I agreed. I kept my hands on the table, one gripping the spoon, the other the bowl, too scared to let them disappear under the table and acknowledge a stranger's hand still on my knee. I couldn't remember if a woman with whom I was not in a relationship had ever left a hand on my leg, as if it were a discarded sock that had been mislaid. On discovering a discarded sock, the normal course of proceedings would be to find its partner, ball them together and put them in their rightful place – ideally in colour-coordinated sections in your sock drawer. Yet if I so much as touched the hand, let alone tried to lead it to its partner, Caroline might get the wrong idea. If I left it there, I would appear compliant. If I flicked it off, it would be rudely dismissive. I looked at Caroline, who hadn't stopped talking, and tried not to think of her hand as one half of a lost pair of socks.

'My attempts at making desserts,' she was saying, 'are like metaphors for my marriage. They either collapse, are undercooked or don't set.' She let out a laugh and licked her spoon.

She seemed oblivious to where her hand was. We were both acting as if it was perfectly socially acceptable for her hand to have wandered and found my thigh, which was possibly, at this very minute, tensing unnaturally.

'More dessert wine?' Andy asked, and started pouring before I had time to answer.

The sticky liquid wrapped itself around my tongue and clung to my teeth. What I needed, rather than more wine, was the bathroom. When Caroline engaged in a conversation with Lucy about the benefits or otherwise of pet insurance – Caroline having a cat and Andy and Lucy having lost their dog a few months ago because of an inoperable tumour – I eased myself off the chair, letting her hand slide away. Blood rushed to my knees. I teetered, then lurched to the bathroom. After I had splashed my face with water and gulped a few mouthfuls to help sober me up, I checked myself out in the mirror, fixed my hair and re-rolled my shirtsleeves.

'I think the night's going well, don't you, Marie?' I said quietly to my dear friend. I was pleased with my choice of shirt, whose buttons hadn't popped post-dessert, as well as my newly de-fuzzed chin and wine-boosted repartee, which seemed to have been well received. Yet, now that I was away from the table, I felt the draining effects of all the socialising and lashings of wine; suddenly I was overcome with tiredness. I hadn't been out this late in a long time, middle-of-the-night call-outs notwithstanding. As I exited the bathroom, burbles of chatter and laughter tumbled down the hallway. Needing a minute or two longer by myself, I turned in the opposite direction and headed for the back door for a moment's quiet reprieve.

I stood in the back porch, looking out at the dimly lit brick court-yard with its handmade vertical garden and terracotta pots. Moths fluttered frantically around the bare light overhead and invisible tree frogs croaked, as if something were lodged in their throats. The air was filled with a pungent plant perfume I couldn't identify.

'You don't have a cigarette, do you?' I hadn't heard Caroline sidle up to me on the step.

Perhaps she needed a bit of fresh air, too.

'Sorry, I don't smoke,' I said.

'Me neither.' She laughed. 'I told myself I wouldn't smoke at all this year but it didn't last long. Resolutions never do. I'm not addicted or anything, but I do like a puff on a night like tonight. Particularly under the stars.'

If I shielded my eyes from the porch light I could make out a smattering of stars like luminescent pinpricks. They made me feel very small and completely insignificant.

'I reckon,' she said, eyeing me up, 'that you could tell me what the stars are. You seem like a man who might own a telescope.'

Where did she get that idea from? 'Sorry to disappoint but I don't own a telescope. I don't even own binoculars. I do have a magnifying glass somewhere but that's only good for reading the ingredients on packets of food.'

She chuckled. 'You're a funny man, Oliver Clock.'

As I contemplated how funny I really was, she edged closer to me. I wondered if the bigness of the night made her feel small and insignificant as well. Her arm brushed mine. If we both turned our heads to face each other in a synchronised-swimming kind of a way, we would have been close enough to kiss, give or take a centimetre or two. I don't know why I thought that. The only woman in recent years I had been this close to in order to kiss had been Marie and it was immensely disappointing that we hadn't been able to. I had to take a step back to regain my personal space. But then it seemed as if Caroline was going move forward again, which would have meant me taking another step backwards and us inadvertently dancing the two-step. Thankfully, she didn't, and two cats hissing in a neighbouring property snapped me out of my two-step-dancing thoughts.

'We should be getting back,' I said.

'Yes, come on,' Caroline agreed.

'I was just telling Oliver,' she said as we rejoined the guests, 'how I've signed up for salsa dance lessons.'

I don't know why she said that, when we hadn't been discussing dancing at all. Had she read my thoughts on the two-step or was she wondering what the others thought we'd been doing together? Heaven forbid!

'Have you?' said Sue. 'I never knew you wanted to learn to dance.'

'That's what happens when you divorce.'

'Who are you doing it with?'

'Oh, no one. You don't have to bring a partner.'

'Oliver will go, won't you, Oliver?'

I swivelled my head in Andy's direction.

'Will you?' Caroline said, turning to me.

In front of everyone, I was being committed to Latin American dancing lessons. My toes curled, my thighs tensed, the tiramisu cha-cha-ed in my belly. Help!

'It sounds like fun,' I said, as jovially as I could. 'But it's hard for me to commit to things like that in my line of work. A hazard of the job.'

'It's tough being on call most of the time, isn't it?' Lucy said.

For once, I was happy for the talk to return to the funeral industry. Dancing wasn't mentioned again. I could go home, relieved that salsa moves had only been a light conversation starter.

The Day After

The following morning I shuffled around my flat like a slow-moving wombat with a headache. I couldn't even bend down to pick up the clothes I'd stepped out of the night before. I was suffering from day-after regret: the chunks of Camembert and alcohol-laced tiramisu that were still wedged in my belly, Andy's generous servings of wine lounging in my frontal lobe. I also woke up with a great big question mark over Caroline. For it suddenly occurred to me in the annoyingly bright light of the day that she may have been flirting with me. Had that lone hand on my thigh been put there on purpose? Had her closeness on the porch been predetermined? And if so, was it the one-off flirtation of a tipsy, single dinner-party guest to another tipsy, single dinner-party guest or was there an expectation of possible future encounters? Or did it mean nothing at all? It was an unexpected conundrum that made a sore head even sorer. But whatever the case, it didn't really matter, for my heart was with Marie, and whether she was living or not was, at that time, irrelevant. So I told myself to relax about the whole thing and be happy that a very small section of the resolution box labelled 'get a life' had been ticked.

When my stomach had settled, I made a late breakfast of toast liberally spread with marmalade, and a mug of tea. I don't know why, but I ate as if I weren't still full from the night before; it was basically just an excuse to eat marmalade. Then all I could do was lie on the sofa and stare at the ceiling. A tiny spider crawled across the paintwork bubbling in one corner. My head throbbed, my mouth was furry. The spider scuttled back in the other direction. I detected a thin line of web. If I had been feeling more energetic, I would have got up and swiped it with a broom.

When the phone rang early that afternoon, I was still on the sofa. I must have fallen asleep. My eyes were heavy and my mouth was growing mould. The spider had gone. Another body was heading to the mortuary. I hauled myself up, changed into a suit, splashed my face with water and ran a hand through my hair. I took a moment to stroke my chin and appreciate its new-found silkiness and remember how good I had felt about myself last night compared with how guilt-ridden I now felt. My tripping the light fantastic had turned into a marvellous stumbling in the dark.

It was a slow drive to Clock & Son as rain sluiced the windscreen and shot water bullets at the car. Even at full speed the windscreen wipers did little to clear my vision. I met the transfer driver at the back entrance and was soon in the dry, preparing the mortuary room. Nursing-home bridge champion Juliet Brown had the figure of a ballet dancer and the pink hair of a 1980s Cyndi Lauper. Lightning lit up the metal table and surgical instruments. I groaned at the sight of them and another body to be preserved. Just because I could embalm didn't mean I wanted to. But right then I had no other choice but to get on with the job. The only consolation was thinking of Marie and letting her beautiful voice suggesting suitable flowers for Mrs Brown be a pleasant distraction from the formaldehyde fumes. I reckon she would have picked something like hot-pink gerberas to coordinate with Mrs Brown's hair. 'Yes, Oliver,' I could hear her say, 'we must find a flower that's exactly the same colour. It's the attention to detail that matters.'

Then my phone vibrated against my leg. I paused with the suture and pulled it from my pocket. It was a text from Caroline. Had *she* been listening to me instead?

I really enjoyed last night. Are you still up for salsa dancing? I hope it wasn't presumptuous of me but I've booked you in with me. It starts Tuesday evening.

What? I stepped back from Mrs Brown. I couldn't have her suffer from a mediocre job because I was in shock. Surely this was a joke. Caroline didn't even know me.

I assume salsa dancing is a euphemism for going for a drink? I typed, in the hope that a humorous response would get me out of it.

Funny, but I was being serious. I've signed up for beginner lessons. I know I said you didn't have to bring a partner but I think it would be more fun if I did and you seemed keen.

Oh.

Plus, she continued, *I want to get fit.*

Ah.

'What do you think, Juliet? Do I go out with this woman?' I asked, in an effort to decide. 'I mean, I've only just met her.' But Juliet wasn't giving anything away. Unless I did a superlative job on suturing her lips, she was only ever going to look sad for me. What would Marie have thought about it all? I wondered. She loved dancing and may well have encouraged me to get more instruction in case I ever needed to be a dance partner.

A torrent of rain waterfalled, thunder cracked. I put the phone on the table and recommenced on Juliet Brown, trying to remember Jean's tips on teasing hair – the deceased's family having specified that her coiffure resembled her favourite style: as if electrocuted. But the comb got stuck. I stepped away from my mess and reread the texts. *I want to get fit too*, I replied, *but not sure if dancing is my thing.* It was better to be honest.

Come on, it will be fun, I promise.

I admired my handiwork on Juliet Brown. How glamorous and content she now looked. As if her new appearance had given her the confidence to take on the next stage of her life with courage and spunk, and a whole lot of crimson lipstick. I read Caroline's text again. What had I written about going out of my comfort zone and taking a risk? I may have regretted not asking Marie out but that didn't mean my next encounter with the opposite sex had to end in missed opportunities and regret. What's more, it was another great excuse to avoid spending an entire evening alone in my flat. When things had ended badly with Shelley, Marie had told me to keep my chin up; that things would only get better. Was this things getting better?

OK, I texted. *But I'm no great shakes (pun intended).*

I slid the phone back into my pocket and, as I did so, a peculiar sensation slithered through me. I had just been asked out on a date! A living woman was interested in me and offering solace from lonely singledom. 'Yay,' I said to Juliet Brown, who definitely looked happier for me now. After I said my goodbyes to Mrs Brown and tidied up, I retreated to the kitchenette. Shadows walked past the window; the rain had not let up. Then something crashed to the ground. A pedestrian squealed. I rushed outside to find the large Clock & Son sign that had swung under the awning for my entire life lying on the pavement, the wood cracked between the 'S' and the 'o'. I looked around to see if anyone was hurt, but whoever had been close to its fall had hurried on. The sign was long and heavy, but I managed to half lift, half push it out of the way and lean it against the building. Water drizzled down its paintwork and on to the pavement. The pounding in my head worsened. The dregs of a hangover mixed with a dollop of panic and a serving of the doldrums. I went back inside, locked up and drove home, aware that resolution number four about reviving Clock & Son still lay inert and lifeless in my notebook.

Snooping

Whenever it rained, I'd go outside and dance like Lily had, to see if I could go to the same place Lily had gone, but I was always rushed inside and the only place I ever went to was my bedroom. After Lily died, the world became a risky place to live in, a place in which many things were deemed 'too dangerous' and my mother's language became sprinkled with 'don't's, the way my father used salt. I found it easier to do as she said because I was that kind of a child: compliant, malleable. Then somehow my mother's 'don't's settled into my mental vernacular. *No*, they'd say. *No, Oliver, don't. Hold on. Hold back.* And because of this fear I struggled to make decisions – well, not make them so much as enact them. I could make a decision in my head and even write it down in my notebook, but doing it was a different matter. I would think of all the things that could go wrong, the risks that might be involved, the possibility of failure. I feared the unknown as others are scared to eat food past its use-by date. The 'don't's won over from the 'do's time and time again, until it seemed the natural way to be.

Whether my parents talked about Lily in hushed voices, alone together at night, I do not know, but they never spoke about her with me after she died or about her in my presence. It was as if she had never been born and the picture I had of her lying on the lawn wasn't real or had been confused with an image I had of us both lying in the back garden looking at the summer sky, feeling the prickly grass beneath our limbs and giggling for no other reason than to laugh at things that weren't funny.

I did try talking to Mum about Lily once. It was after Dad had died, and I'd not long been running Clock & Son. She was polishing the display coffins and I was heat-steaming the coffin linings. It came up because I'd just told her how Andy's attempts at getting me to play golf had been thwarted that weekend by a thunderstorm. She wasn't impressed – not because we weren't able to play but because we had thought to go out at all when bad weather was forecast. A typical Doreen response.

Instead of changing the subject as I should have, I blurted out, 'Do you miss Lily?'

I knew immediately it was the wrong thing to say, for the polishing cloth paused. You could virtually hear Mum's teeth grinding. Nevertheless, I kept going, which was made all the easier because we were not sitting opposite one another making eye contact. All I wanted was the chance to talk about my sister.

'It must have been so hard for you and Dad,' I said. '*I* miss her and I didn't really know her.'

The cloth made its way to the door. 'Haven't you got an appointment soon?' she said, and walked out, buffing the door handle as she left.

And just like that, I never mentioned her again.

Waking to a storm-free, freshly scrubbed sky, I decided if I could say yes to a dance class, I could find a way to broach Lily with Mum again. There had to be a way. I just hadn't found it yet. And, I thought, as I shaved for the first time in weeks, it was time to focus on resolution number four: saving the business. Mum was right, we had to find out more about the competition and so I would follow her suggestion and snoop.

I searched my wardrobe; I would go undercover. I would be like an anonymous food critic pretending to be someone else in order to critique a restaurant. I couldn't risk the possibility of being spotted. How did I know that Green Light Funerals hadn't already checked us out? What if that woman who came in three weeks ago had in fact been faking displeasure at our services and her dramatic postulations of grief were all a ruse? That she was not upset at the death of her husband but gleeful at finding out how bland and fusty Clock & Son was? What an outrage if that were true!

My blood pressure rose sufficiently for me to disregard the mess I was beginning to make, flinging any item of clothing I thought could successfully disguise me on to the floor. Do I wear the plaid golf shorts Andy once gave me? What about the painting overalls I bought five years ago when I'd thought of repainting the flat? Or should I just wear a suit with a two-pound-shop moustache and sunglasses? The character options were endless. But I had to remember I wasn't going to a fancy-dress party. This was serious. This was the future of my business.

I settled on a baseball cap, sunglasses, ancient jeans that bagged around my bottom and an oversized American football top an old school-friend once brought me back from the States as a joke. I would refrain from ironing any of it. No one would think it was me. I flipped the cap backwards. Even better. Not only did I not look like a funeral director on his day off, I resembled a middle-aged rapper. I re-dressed in my suit, carefully folded my disguise into a bag and took them to work. Operation 'Snoop Clock' was about to commence.

I found Jean on the footpath, staring at the broken business sign. The sun was out but the wood was still damp. Pedestrians moved around us as if we were invisible. The homeless sign was ignored.

'The storm last night,' I said.

'Not just that,' she said, and pointed.

Overnight, someone had graffitied the sign as it lay prone and vul-nerable on the path. The 'l' of Clock & Son had been scribbled out, the crude nom de plume now something that could be used to describe various other businesses, but none a funeral home.

'You're kidding?' I said.

Jean rubbed my back. 'It had been there a very long time.'

'I know, but did someone have to deface it?'

'Look at it as a chance to freshen things up.'

We stood in silence for a moment, as if paying the sign our respects for a life well lived, decades of hard service.

'We can't keep it here,' Jean said, rubbing my back again. 'Doreen is coming in later. We can talk about it with her.'

We heaved and fussed with the sign before I realised it would be easier if it was in two pieces rather than one. I bashed the crack with a foot and raised a hand to passers-by in apology for them having to witness a man in a suit attacking a sign. Three stomps and it split. We took both pieces out the back into the car park and left them resting by the bins, turned inwards to avoid offending. Inside, I showed Jean the contents of my bag.

'I thought I'd visit the new funeral home and pretend to be a customer, find out what they're doing.'

'In those?' Jean said at my choice of disguise.

'I don't want to look like me.'

She started laughing. 'Well, you certainly won't. Have you told Doreen? She'll want to come with you, you know.'

'I know, but I think it's better she doesn't.' She could be a liability; who knew what she'd say?

Jean nodded. 'Another thing, Oliver. I've been meaning to ask – are you alright after Henry's visit? Did you sort out what his complaint was about?'

I couldn't possibly tell Jean the truth. Or, more accurately, I wasn't prepared to tell Jean the truth, so I told her it was fine and that Henry wasn't coping well. She gave me a quizzical look. She, like me, knew that grief and violence towards a funeral director were an uncommon combination, but she let my comments pass as if they were a perfectly reasonable explanation for Henry nearly ruining my favourite tie.

'Alright then, I'll leave you to change,' she said.

Even from the end of the street, the neon Green Light Funeral sign shone like it was advertising an American diner. It was a brand-new yellow BMW next to my dusty old silver Astra. Even worse, its billboard signage made it look as if they were a dental practice spruiking teeth-whitening services. The fake happiness made me queasy. Funerals may be celebrations of life but you had to go easy on the joy and there was nothing worse than a smug funeral director. I pulled over and parked on the street, adjusted the cap and put on my sunglasses. As I walked up to the front door, I tried to summon the confidence of a man used to lying.

I kept my head high, wondering if I should swagger. I looked straight at the reception desk as I walked in and was so mesmerised by the young man with an unnatural-looking tan, telephonist headphones and enviable gnashers that I tripped up the white-tiled entrance steps, stubbing the big toe of my right foot. The sunglasses shot off my face and the cap frisbeed behind me. My disguise thwarted!

'May I help you?' the man said, peering over the countertop as if I were an inconvenience to his day.

I shoved the cap back on the right way round and affected nonchalance and a saunter but feared I was only limping.

'I need to organise a funeral.' I leaned on the smooth marble reception top – was it even real? It was a slick joint with plush velvet seating, gold table lamps and gold-rimmed glass side tables. The curtains shimmered like ice. Windows gleamed. It's how I imagined Las Vegas to be.

'I can make an appointment for you with one of our funeral directors,' the man said, his hair stiff with greasy product, his skin taut and glossy.

'It's OK. I just had a few questions about the deal you have on,' I said.

The man slapped a brochure – the one Jean had shown me – on to the counter and looked very pleased that I had asked about the deal. 'This month, it's two for one. Buy two coffins for the price of one.'

'This month only?'

'Next month there will be another deal.'

'I see,' I said, appearing interested. 'But I only need one.'

'You could buy one for yourself . . .'

Huh?

'Or maybe the person who needs it now has a partner who might need one later.'

What?

The phone rang. The man took the call, his tone ingratiating, his words well practised, then returned his attentions to me. 'All our coffins are flat-pack reinforced cardboard. They store neatly and can be recycled. Unless you want a cremation, of course. They burn beautifully. Our newest range is the do-it-yourself coffin, which you can decorate. They're really popular.'

'Decorate with what?'

'Anything you like. Photos, drawings, poems. Then there's the trimmings.'

'Trimmings?' I found myself moving away from the counter, away from the man and his smarminess.

'The added extras,' he said. 'For that wow factor. Everyone wants to impress, don't they? Why should funerals be any different?'

Call me ignorant, but I hadn't considered one-upmanship to be a factor in funerals. It was all too much to take in. I admired their coffin options but disliked the focus on the facade. Forget the wow factor, where was the care factor? I stopped by the table and chairs at the glass window frontage, where a large vase of peonies sat, full, fat, majestic-looking. *I could get Jean on to these*, I thought. They would be a welcome change to her current obsession with Australian natives. They looked so lovely, luscious even, that I couldn't help but touch one of the petals. I gasped. They weren't even real. I retracted my hand and shoved it into the pocket with my sunglasses.

'Aren't they great?' the receptionist said. 'We have bouquets of life-like artificial flowers that can be rented. They're much cheaper than real ones and it means we can use them again. If you're really on a budget, we've got the Plastic Flora range, or if you're prepared to spend a bit more, the Silk range. It's not real silk but looks like the real deal. Like those peonies there. You can see all our bouquets in this folder.'

I didn't want to. I'd seen enough. Marie would have been appalled. 'What a choice,' was all I could think of to say but, really, I was horrified. Not once had he asked me about the funeral I was organising, if I needed ice for my big toe, or shown any concern as to whether I might be grieving. And there wasn't a single box of tissues in reception. The place was fake, glittering with flashy appearances of little substance, done on the cheap.

'I can throw in a discount on the flowers, too, just for you.' The man bared his teeth again, which brought to mind the face of a grinning chimpanzee. Lots of gum.

'I'll have a think about it,' I said.

'Let me see if a funeral director can meet with you now.'

'Don't worry, I've got to go. Anyway, my friend isn't dead yet.' I turned to leave. I couldn't wait to get out.

'Would you like to leave your name and number? Please, take a brochure.'

'It's OK, thanks,' I said, and muttered something about being late.

I stepped out of the fluorescence of Green Light Funerals' reception into the soft light of the day and air fresh with the smells of reality. In the car, I whipped off the cap and rested my head on the back of the seat.

Sometimes I wondered what it would have been like if Lily had grown up and inherited the business with me. We could have dropped the 'Son' and been The Clock Family Funeral Home or just Clocks' Funeral Home. Maybe Lily would have been good with the books or the admin and could have taken over from Mum. Or maybe she'd have been more interested in embalming and could have become Clocks' chief embalmer, a younger face than Roger and a female, no less. There weren't enough of them in this industry. How different it might have been. Then again, maybe she'd have had no interest at all and could have had an easy escape being the second child and not a son. And I'd have been left in the same predicament as I now was, slumped in my car in bad clothes bemoaning how the competition had sprung up in the same street as my grandparents, as if they couldn't leave either side of my family alone.

I may well have wallowed there for quite some time, had it not occurred to me. Wasn't the whole point of Clock & Son that it was, and always had been, a family-run business? That what makes it is its history, its spirit, its tradition? Not only that, but hadn't I made my mark, just like my father and his father before him? I had stamped sincerity and care all over the place – arguably more so than Dad, whose strict rule-following had been of a past era, and Mum, whose greatest asset was in practicalities and organisation. Yes, I had! And didn't I have the bedside manner to rival any good doctor, with the soothing voice of a night-time radio presenter? And hadn't I once been told that my ties brought unexpected cheer to an otherwise sombre encounter? Why hadn't I realised this before?

'That's it,' I said, hitting the steering wheel with a hand. 'I'm taking them down.'

I clicked the seatbelt over me and started the car. Fuelled with a new optimism, I drove with haste out of the street and back to Clock & Son and made a mental note to add this new decision to my notebook of resolutions.

The Diary

It's all very well saying you're going to 'take someone down' – which was a statement better suited to the villain of an action film than a pacifist like me – but it's another thing entirely knowing how to do it. I burst into reception as if I really were a movie villain with a crafty plan but, really, I had no idea what that plan was, which was just as well, because my mission was delayed as soon as I walked in the door.

'What are you doing in those clothes?' Mum said, looking up from the dusting. 'It's not very professional. Oh, and by the way, Marie's husband paid us a visit. He bought you a present. Isn't that nice?'

I stopped dead, looked at Jean. She shrugged.

'He was going to post it until he found out the cost,' Mum continued. 'It's over there.' She pointed the feather duster in the direction of a package wrapped in brown paper on the reception desk.

My stomach did a back flip. Mum followed me to where Jean sat.

'Well, aren't you going to open it?' She fluttered the feather duster over the parcel. Jean sneezed. Mum apologised.

I picked up the package and tucked it under my arm. 'I'll open it later,' I lied.

'I think you should open it now,' Mum said, following me into my office. 'Perhaps it's a belated thank-you present for our services.'

She twirled the duster, exposing a hand dappled with sun spots. The package was burning a hole in my armpit.

'Who knows?' I said, even though I knew exactly what I was holding.

I sat at my desk and turned on the computer. 'Sorry, Mum, I've got a lot to catch up on.'

'I can't imagine what. It's been as quiet as a fully booked morgue.'

I typed an email to no one in particular as Mum watched, her thickened ankles rooted to the spot.

'You still haven't told me why you're in those clothes?'

'I will, don't worry,' I said, continuing to type gobbledegook.

Mum tsked and turned to go. I resisted the urge to leap up and shut the door behind her, which would only have aroused her curiosity even more. Instead, I reached for the scissors and, with the parcel on my lap under the desk, gently cut open one end. The diary slid out from between a layer of bubble wrap. A letter dropped to the floor. I wondered at a man who bothered to use bubble wrap on something he didn't want. I picked up the note.

> *You may as well have this, now that I've been unfortunate enough to read it. I'm trying to turn my life around and have joined Alcoholics Anonymous. As part of the programme, we're supposed to make amends to those whom we've wronged and do something symbolic to put the past behind us. I could argue that you should be doing the same to me but, as that wouldn't be in the spirit of things, I won't. I didn't mean to wrong Marie and I didn't mean to wrong you (although you deserved it). My symbolic act is to give you her diary. Right now, I don't want it hanging around. Henry.*

I ran my hand over the soft, worn leather. Pressed the diary to my nose, breathed in Marie. Buttery, earthy, raw.

'I can't hear much typing,' Mum called out.

I shoved the journal on to my lap and started typing again, letting my fingers run over the keys as if I were a speed typist, but all I could think of was the diary. When I heard Mum and Jean engage in conversation, I pulled it out and opened it, not at the beginning, but at a random spot towards the end.

Tuesday

He's drinking again.

Friday

I surprised a client with an arrangement I've never done before with poppies and gumnuts. They really loved it, so I think I'll do it again, and maybe experiment with other combinations of Australian natives and traditional English flowers.

Saturday

I didn't go into work today. Sarah covered for me as I didn't feel well. I still don't, really. It's probably just fatigue. As usual, Henry isn't much use.

I flicked through some more pages.

Sunday

Henry was on better form today. He said he wasn't going to drink any more and I want to believe him, I really do. For the whole day I pretended it was true and we had a great time, just like the old days. We went for a long walk, had lunch by the beach, saw a movie. It was perfect.

Tuesday

Well, that didn't last long! Am I surprised? Henry is back to his usual self, but worse. I don't know how much he'd drunk, but he was staggering around the house like a new-born giraffe trying to stand up, walking into walls and knocking over the living-room lamp. We started laughing. Well, he did, and I joined in nervously, as if it was something to laugh about.

Wednesday

I met up with Oliver today. What a sweetheart he is. We have a lot of funerals on at the moment yet he's so incredibly calm and generous at letting me be creative with the flowers. Sometimes I get carried away, but he's happy to convince customers they should go with my ideas. He's always patient and attentive with the poor souls who are grieving. It takes a special person to do his line of work.

Friday

I was with Oliver again today. We were discussing the long-lasting attributes of gladioli, of all things, when I nearly told him how much I loved him. That, in fact, I have been truly in love with him for the last ten years. I can't believe it! It was the caring way he listened and made a joke about whether

Dame Edna was as knowledgeable about her favourite flower as I was. Thank goodness I stopped myself. I mean, I'm married. I don't really know why I'm thinking these things. I'm like a teenager all over again. Maybe I'm having a mid-life crisis.

I took a deep breath, had to look away. Was this what childbirth was like? Painful, joyous torture? Yet, like the process of a baby being born, there was no turning back; I had to keep on reading. But the next line stopped me once again.

The funny thing is, I think Oliver feels the same.

She knew? How could she?
My past life flooded through me, as if I'd swallowed a bucket of water and spat it out again. And all this time . . .

Thursday

Henry forgot to pick me up after work again. Is he losing his memory because of the drinking? Whatever it is, he's becoming more and more forgetful and I'm going to have to talk to him properly about it. But the truth is, I've fallen out of love with him.

Friday

Henry says he's giving up. Even though the bottle in the garage is gone, I've asked him to go to AA. I don't think he can do it on his own, even though he says he can.

Saturday

We had a 'date' tonight. It was Henry's idea and he organised it. To be fair, it was a lovely restaurant and we talked about old times, which helped me forget about the new times. He kept professing undying love, as if we were young lovers. I suppose I should be grateful, but I didn't feel the desire to reciprocate. He's still off the drink, and he's been great, really. But he's lost my trust and he's not the man I once loved. I don't have any love left for him any more. I've tried to get it back, to find it again. But it's gone. I'm empty. Even now that he's been off the drink, it's not there. And I thought I loved him sober.

Wednesday

I can't live with Henry any more. I'm thinking of leaving.

What?

I want to be with Oliver.

Sherbet fizzed, confetti burst, rockets fired off around me. I had to read that line over and over and over until I knew it by heart, which shouldn't have been difficult, but in the state I was in I was incapable of doing anything – standing upright, walking in a straight line, reciting the five times table. I read each word slowly as if each were profound in its own right. *I. Want. To. Be. With. Oliver.* She wanted to be with me.

It's probably a stupid presumption to make – that Oliver would want to be with me – but I feel we have a connection. If I wasn't with Henry, then I could test the waters with

Oliver. Oh gosh, did I write that? Does that mean I must leave him?

The diary slipped from my grip and fell on to the keyboard. The computer made pinging noises and the cursor zipped along the screen on a trail of its own. Was this what it felt like to do the hair-raiser ride at an amusement park? Anticipation followed by excitement, ending with projectile vomiting? I jumped a few more pages and continued reading.

Friday

It's scary to think of leaving Henry or, rather, having to tell him I want to leave.

One month later: Thursday

I hate you, life. I hate you. I went to the doctor today and now I hate him, too. Not really, of course, as he is a kind, gentle man, but I hated what he had to tell me. I hated trying to keep my composure when, inside, I wanted to scream. I hated the receptionist smiling at me when I walked out. I hate the world. I hate everything. Except Oliver. There's no point in leaving Henry now. Even if I do live longer than they say, I'm still dying. No one would want me. Not even Oliver. Why burden anyone with my desires? And who knows how Henry would react. I've got enough to deal with now, as it is. A dying person gains regrets and loses dreams. Life's shit.

I rested my head in my hand. If only I'd have known.

Sunday

This dying business sucks. I don't even feel like I'm dying. What's dying supposed to feel like? If dying means endless crying, then I've died. I'm gone. Kaput.

Friday

I hope Oliver finds his soulmate. He deserves to love and be loved. He deserves a family. He'd be a great dad. Maybe if I'd been with him, I'd have been able to have children. But why torture myself with that idea! Henry was good for nothing in that regard. He didn't even want to consider adoption.

So it was true: Marie loved me as I loved her. We were soulmates without even realising it. We had successfully hidden our feelings from one another, endured one-sided loving that caused us nothing but heartache. Oh, how could we have not known? How could Marie have not told me, and I her? And yet how close had I been to revealing my feelings to her? So close, so terribly close. But I'd been a fool and hadn't. A tear droplet dampened the entry, smudged and blurred it. Then another and another. My eyes filled with so much water I couldn't even see the words clearly any more.

'Oliver?'

How long had Mum been standing there? Multiple lines of the letter 'd' filled my computer screen. I took my hand off the keyboard and wiped my eyes.

'You're crying? Is it to do with the parcel?'

I shrugged and closed the diary.

'Is it about Marie? I know you were fond of her.'

I nodded but couldn't bring myself to explain my lost romantic opportunity, how my love for a married woman – colleague, even – was an unrequited love turned requited posthumously. I couldn't even tell Mum I had commissioned a candle of Marie. Or that my version of a sensible slice of cake was very different to hers. Or that I couldn't stand the way she bought tissue holders, as if covering them in gauche floral boxes would disguise what they really were – snot receptacles for the grieving.

She came around to my side of the desk and rubbed my shoulders. I appreciated her trying hard to offer me comfort. Demonstrative hugs and affection didn't come as naturally to her as did protecting me from the world and telling me what *not* to do, rather than what *to* do.

'If you want to talk, I'll listen,' she said.

'Thanks, Mum,' I said, but still, I couldn't.

She let her hands rest peacefully on my shoulders and said, 'You know, Oliver, sometimes life has a strange way of showing us it cares. And the act of accepting this can be the hardest thing to do.'

That was profound. It was like Mum knew what had been going on all along. Or did she have some sixth sense that only she could tap into? Or was it just that she knew her son? I had no bloody idea. What I did know was the regret I was filling up with. Marie's, mine. It was a regret far worse than eating a whole pizza when half would do or confessing to a deceased client that you fancied their daughter. Despite Mum's words, life was unfair. No matter how many axioms or glib phrases of consolation she spouted, life sucked.

La Lumière de Marie

After Mum quietly dusted her way out, I must have sat there for a good twenty minutes doing nothing. Just staring, feeling sorry for myself and blubbering intermittently like an old tap spluttering into action.

Then I heard the clink of Jean's nifty new spectacles chain. My life may have turned upside down but everything else was carrying on just as it had been. I wiped my eyes, slapped a cheek and pretended to be doing costings on the calculator.

'Knock, knock,' Jean said softly. 'Can I come in?'

I nodded. From the way she spoke and then tentatively came in, I suspected Mum had enlightened her on the parcel as much as she was able to.

'Are you alright, Oliver?'

I nodded again, put the calculator back in the drawer.

'I'm sorry to bother you but you have a visitor. It's that girl. She's back peddling her candles. I can send her away if you like?'

My heart skipped a beat, as it does when you're about to see the one you love reincarnated as a candle, the one whose lost love you were now grieving. For a minute, I couldn't speak, fearing another outburst of waterworks.

'Why don't I say you're busy?' Jean suggested.

And yet, Edie had Marie's candle. What if it brought Marie back, if only for a brief, aromatic moment? What if it was our love reincarnated? 'No, Jean, it's OK. I'll see her.'

I wiped my eyes again, put the diary in a drawer and waited for Jean to bring Edie in.

'Oh hi, Oliver, I almost didn't recognise you,' she said.

The disguise! 'Yes, sorry, not my usual attire.' I ruffled my hat-flattened hair and brushed down the top, which had a tendency to resemble an expanding parachute. 'Please, have a seat.'

'I hope I'm not interrupting anything,' she said, 'but I wanted to bring you your friend's candle. It's all done.'

You could argue that Edie's arrival could not have been more timely, given my distress at reading Marie's diary. Then again, there was a case for it being very bad timing indeed. For now it felt as if everything rested on this candle. I yearned for Marie so much that it had to be her. It had to conjure memories of her in a way that other things couldn't. I needed Marie with me and this was the best I was going to get. Edie reached into her handbag and took out a candle wrapped in tissue paper. I closed my eyes and willed the tears to stay away. My stomach was a cluster of moths trapped in a light. She placed the candle on my desk.

But wait, I wasn't ready!

'My apologies,' I said, as calmly as I could. 'I didn't offer you a drink. Tea? Coffee? Water?' I stood up to get her a drink in order to stall the lifting of the lid.

'I'm fine, thank you,' she said.

I stared at the candle with its creamy wax, shiny silver cap and label with a flowery font and floating angel. 'So, here she is, then.'

'I think you'll like it. I hope you'll like it. I spent quite a bit of time preparing the scent, adjusting the fragrances so it was a subtle combination of the smells you suggested.'

What would I do if it wasn't Marie? If it smelt like something else entirely, something unpleasant, like saccharine talcum powder, or the cloying scent of a two-pound shop? It didn't bear thinking about. I picked it up. It had a reassuring weightiness to it, as if it were solid, dependable. Then I had to remind myself that it wasn't Marie at all: it was just a candle. A candle that hopefully smelt of something nice, like one of Marie's favourite flowers, if nothing else. But who was I kidding? I didn't want that. Was Edie aware how much I didn't want that?

I smiled at her. She smiled back.

'This is it,' I said, as if a dollop of lightness would hide my trepidation. Edie chewed her lip, waited. She was probably urging me to hurry up. *Hurry up, you fool, because if you don't like it, I'll flog it elsewhere.*

With an exaggerated gesture of a pantomime actor, I removed the lid. A burst of something zesty and citrussy with a hint of roses and a sweetness I couldn't name hit my nose and carried me out of my office and into the local church where Marie was creating exquisite, no-expense-spared flowers for the service of a well-known personality who had unexpectedly and controversially passed away. Fusty, oak-scented pews were overrun with lilies, stocks, hydrangeas, roses, fern and eucalyptus leaves. Sarah was also there, helping Marie, and the organist arrived at the same time to practise his pieces. There was a frisson of tension in the air as we all knew our contributions had to amount to something spectacular. For this was no ordinary funeral: it was high profile, under the beady eye of the media, and a family name that reeked of money and infamy.

I picked up some of the sprigs and smelled them. So fresh and invigorating was the pine scent of eucalyptus and the heady smell of the lilies and stocks that together they created another aroma entirely. I surreptitiously dropped a fallen leaf into my jacket pocket and chatted to Sarah about how long it would take them to finish. It was when Marie cheekily called out a song request and the organist obliged that we all relaxed. Sarah started singing. Marie locked arms with me and we fast-waltzed stupidly by the pulpit, which ended in a spray of laughter and enthusiastic clapping by the minister. What I took home with me that day was not just an abundance of joy in my heart but, on my hands, a delicate bouquet of flora and foliage and the subtle residue of Marie herself.

I inhaled again, just to be sure. Why, yes, Edie had nailed it. There she was, darling Marie, escaping like a genie in a bottle. I put the lid back on to keep her in. My head swooned. I thought I might pass out. It wasn't a good look for a funeral director who's seen all manner of passings to faint from the smell of a candle. I steadied myself with the desk against the subtle spin of my office swivel chair.

'It's incredible,' I said. 'I think you've got her.'

'Have I?'

I half lifted the lid and stuck my nose in for a third time. 'Yes. Yes, it is Marie.'

'I'm so pleased,' Edie said, visibly relieved. 'Please, take it home and light it. Make sure it smells as good when it's lit.'

'Why don't I do it now? Wait there, I'll find a lighter.' I rushed out to the kitchenette to get one. 'Here we go.' I ran back, holding the lighter aloft, and lit the candle.

I closed my eyes and breathed her in.

'She was a florist, you know,' I said. 'Whenever I went into her shop, depending on what time of the year it was, I'd be overcome by the most spectacular of smells.' I was wandering, physically in my office and mentally back to the past. I couldn't help myself. The candle was having the most peculiar effect on me. 'Her shop was like a degustation menu at Botticelli's down the road, a feast for the senses. Even the water she sprayed over the plants to keep them fresh added scents to the air. An aroma of a rainforest, freshwater rivers and rain after a sun shower.'

Then I remembered where I was, who I was with. I hadn't meant to babble on about Marie like I had. I hadn't even told Andy how much I loved Marie's shop. My face reddened. 'Sorry, I didn't mean to go on.'

'It's OK,' Edie said, touching my arm. 'Take a moment to remember your friend.'

Her hand stayed on my arm as I took a moment, as she suggested. Neither of us spoke and I thought I would actually cry once more. But, thankfully, after a long minute where I recovered myself, Edie started talking again, with impeccable timing.

'Smell is more powerful than people realise,' she said gently. 'Its memory never fades. When you smell something once, it stays with you for the rest of your life. That's why I started the candles. I wanted a way to remember my father, who's in the last stages of Parkinson's. I thought how amazing it would be to have something for Mum and me to remember him by other than photos or memory. Something that triggered a sensory message.'

'I'm sorry about your father,' I said, remembering Dad's folder of appropriate phrases.

'Thanks, but the stupid thing is, I can't seem to get him right. Mum said I was wasting my time, but when I made Grandma Edna and Monty she changed her mind. She liked them so much, she thinks they could work.'

I nodded. Thought about the kookiness of the idea and yet how evocative the candles could be, how powerful it was to have the person you missed embodied in a scent. Then I did something I have never done before. I made a decision on the spot, an act of spontaneous impulsion spurred on by the pure joy Edie had given me. By how she had made Marie come alive again. I couldn't believe the rush of decisiveness that came over me. I'd reached the dizzying heights of spontaneity, all thanks to Edie.

'Alright, let's do it. Let's make candles that smell of the dead. Let's give others the gift you have given me.'

Edie leapt out of her seat and clapped her hands. I thought she was going to hug me, which would have been very awkward indeed, considering we were about to embark on a business transaction. Resisting the urge to get back into character and do a hip-hop hand gesture in jest, I pretended I was in the suit I should have been in and offered her a hand to shake and tea and biscuits instead.

'Oh, Oliver, thank you. I'd love to stay and talk about it more but I need to get back to work,' she said, looking at her watch. 'I wasn't expecting such a quick decision.'

'Neither was I.' I laughed.

'Let's set another time. And please, use the candle to think of nice things about your friend. It's meant to give light, not darkness. You don't need to be sad.'

'Thank you, Edie, I will.'

After Edie left, I disappeared into the morgue on the pretence of checking up on a client so I could contemplate in peace what I had just agreed to. I pulled up a stool next to seventy-six-year-old Mr Johnson, whose family was still debating whether he should wear the wetsuit he liked to surf in or the suit he had bought for his daughter's wedding, which needed another outing to justify the cost, and told him about the candles.

'I reckon they could be our signature offering,' I said, leaning on the coffin. 'They would set us apart from the others, don't you think? Yes, Clock & Son would not just be the place you went to leave this Earth, it would be where you went to be remembered. It would be the start of your new beginning. We would become a funereal candle conglomerate like there has never been before. What do you think, Mr Johnson?'

Feeling Mr Johnson's silent approval, I got off the stool and returned to my office. The delicate fumes of Marie greeted me at my desk. They curled through the air as if beckoning me to the light that Edie was talking about. Now, not only did I have Marie's diary and her words of love, I had a candle to bring her back to life, which I think Marie would have been pretty delighted about, too.

Salsa Dancing

It was this that helped me turn up to my first date with Caroline. I put Marie in a mental box called 'Love that will not get me down', Caroline in one called 'Getting out of my comfort zone', and the salsa dance class into a box called 'Trying something new without making a fool of myself'. Anyway, just because I was in love with Marie didn't mean I couldn't socialise with Caroline. Categorising these aspects of my life helped compartmentalise them emotionally and keep me focused on my resolutions. Not that it stopped me fearing the experience of learning to dance with a woman I didn't know. Normally it would have sent me running for cover into the mortuary, making up an excuse about having a last-minute call-out or a stubbed big toe that needed resting. But this time I resisted. I wanted to impress Marie with my new dance moves.

Caroline met me at the entrance. 'This is going to be fun,' she said. She was dressed in what appeared to be a tennis outfit – a short white pleated skirt, pink polo shirt and black salsa dance shoes. I looked less sporty in my suit trousers and short-sleeved shirt, as I was hoping to emulate the dress of a male ballroom dancer.

Inside, the Latino Danza Studio hummed with a motley bunch of salsa virgins and the catchy rhythm of Latin-American music. Caroline let her body move with the beat. I tried tapping a foot.

'Have you danced before?' she said.

I thought of the waltz Marie and I had shared in the church. 'Not officially,' I said.

'Me neither, apart from some ballet as a child. But don't worry, it's a beginners' class.' She closed her eyes, her body undulated, the skirt flicked.

I tentatively gyrated. Tried to loosen my hips. I toe-tapped, finger-snapped. But already I could feel myself getting out of sync, continually a click behind the beat. I feared my body would go into shock and my idea of dancing the night away would result in a frozen shoulder or a pulled hamstring. Yet, here I was. I had turned up. I was going to give it a go.

'Ooh, here's Ricardo,' Caroline cooed. 'He's the teacher. Come on.' She grabbed my hand and led me away from the wall as Ricardo's rolled 'r's and lithe hips seduced us into thinking we'd be dancing like him in no time.

For the next hour I was pushed and pulled as if being made to shuffle dust around the dance floor like a vacuum cleaner, hip-touched disconcertingly by Ricardo and bossed about by Caroline as if I were a disobedient dog unwilling to be trained, but I gave it my all. I may have twirled after others twirled, my feet one foot behind the others', but I didn't mind. I was doing my version of the shimmy in celebration of being there in the first place. Of my new venture. Of taking charge without Mum knowing.

When the class was over, Caroline squealed – it was the only way to describe her delight. Then she brought up my bow-legged shuffle with a chuckle, which I didn't think was necessary, but I laughed with her in the interests of conviviality and tried not to be offended. I could have made a joke about how she resembled a rabbit in heels, all fluff and plumpness, yet I wasn't that kind of a guy. Nor, in fact, did I mind. I had to admit I found her beguiling. What's more, I was in full admiration of her apparent ability to not worry about what others might think of her, a trait that made me secretly envious.

I leaned against the wall to get my breath back. Caroline practised a solo move, enjoying the swirl of her skirt, then slipped off her dancing shoes and replaced them with white trainers. 'I must have easily burned off the birthday cake we had at work today,' she said.

'The stress of merely thinking about doing it worked for me,' I said.

She laughed. 'Well, I appreciate you coming with me. Shall we get something to eat?'

Never one to turn down the offer of food, I said yes. Outside, the sky glowed bright blue in the half-sun, half-moonlight, midway between day and night. A bus hurtled past, teenage girls squawked and a pair of flying foxes jetted across the skyline. The smell of sizzling garlic from a nearby Italian restaurant spun out on to the road and threaded its way along the footpath, wound around road signs and suffocated a stray cat.

'Hey, listen,' she whispered. 'Don't let Ricardo see, but I bought a packet of ciggies. I know I shouldn't but I couldn't resist. Thought we could have one as a treat?' She glanced around furtively and reached into her handbag as if pulling out a bag of illicit drugs.

'Not for me,' I said.

'Oh, come on. One won't hurt.'

'Sorry, it's not really my thing.'

She shrugged. 'Don't mind if I do.'

As she opened the packet and set a cigarette alight, I pulled out my phone.

'Miss anything?' Caroline said.

'Dead quiet.'

She chuckled. 'It must be weird, you know, being around death all the time.'

'You get used to it. At least the dead are more predictable than the living.'

She pulled a face.

'Sorry.'

'Stop apologising.' She blew smoke into the sky.

I almost apologised again. I think it was nerves. Was I nervous because I had accepted an extension of the date? Or was I scared about what I had started today, for what the future may hold?

'OK, what do you feel like?' she said. 'We could get one of those gourmet burgers down the road? I love their sweet-potato fries, don't you?'

What a question! Of course I had a penchant for sweet-potato fries, and food always calmed my nerves. She took my hand again and, if my muscles hadn't been filling with lactic acid, I would have skipped with her down the road, a man on a first date, having achieved a new resolution and delighted to no longer be dancing.

More Spontaneity

The next day I had a swing in my step only dancing – awkward or otherwise – could induce. I had gone out of my comfort zone again! Caroline was proving excellent practice in this regard and, if there were to be similar encounters, I resolved to make the most of her availability. I was also pleased that, since she had suggested a post-dance meal, she hadn't been greatly put off by either my inability to master salsa footwork or my dodgy dance clothes. The closeness of the dancing reminded me what it was like to connect with a living woman, even if it was tinged with sadness that I couldn't have learned salsa dancing with Marie. With a sashay of laissez-faire in my loins, I arrived at work and surprised Jean with a takeaway coffee and an apricot pastry.

'You're very chipper,' she said, tearing open the bag at her desk. Today's brooch was a silver flower with sapphires in its centre, a fortieth-wedding present from her husband.

'Oh, you know . . .'

'I don't know if I do.'

'I went dancing last night.'

'Dancing? Not on your own, I presume?' She looked at me over her glasses. The raised eyebrows were either a sign of her incredulity at my hip-swinging adventures or at having a mysterious dance partner. Most likely both.

'No,' I replied.

'Really?'

I smiled.

'Is she nice?'

I smiled again. I didn't wish to disappoint Jean by divulging that my interest in Caroline had nothing to do with romance, so I said nothing.

'Keep me updated, won't you?' She took a bite of pastry. Her mauve shoulders sighed, then she said, 'You never told me how your visit to our competitor went.'

I looked at Jean. She was tickling retirement age now. Having started working at Clock & Son when my grandfather was still around – part-time when her children were young and then full-time when they got older – she was as much a part of the family and the business as any of us. Although, unlike my real mother, she was someone I felt comfortable talking to about things that might be troubling me. She was more open to chatting, better attuned to her emotions. Yet now, I realised, I hadn't told Jean anything about recent events.

'I'll be honest, Jean, I didn't like sleuthing and didn't like what I found,' I said, and told her about the faux flowers, glitzy decor and compassionless receptionist. 'I know we have to accept the competition is here to stay but I'm not sure what to do about it.'

'Have you talked to Doreen?'

'Not yet.'

'You know, Oliver, I do believe that you, as the next generation, can carry it on. The business may have been around longer than both of us put together – even longer if you include your great-grandfather's coffin-making expertise. But sometimes change is necessary and I think now is your time to shine. Your mother will come around to any ideas, I'm sure she will.'

'Thanks, Jean.' I gave her shoulder a squeeze and she patted my arm.

'Why don't we do a survey?' she suggested.

'Survey of who?'

'The general public.'

'People out there?' I pointed in the direction of the street.

'Yes, why don't I type up some questions?' Jean seemed chuffed with her idea and went back to reception. I was glad to have her support, even if I wasn't sure how a survey could help us. What would we ask, and would anyone really want to talk about funerals?

Pleased to know Jean was on my side, I celebrated by cleaning my desk. I wiped away dust from the computer screen, flicked off a large crumb from yesterday's sandwich that was wedged between the numbers eight and nine on the keyboard, and tipped out other blobs of indiscriminate bits and bobs. I thought about how I hadn't told Mum about the candles or my sleuthing. I was trying out something new and actually quite liking it. When a veterinary practice rang asking if we offered funeral services for pets, I was reminded of the embalming job ad I had written. To be honest, to enact resolution number four – save the business and let me focus on what I did best, what we needed was an embalmer, not a survey. I found the job description and reread it. Then it occurred to me: in all my years as a funeral director I'd never had to recruit anyone before. All our employees had been hired by Dad, myself included. And it made me wonder whether what I had penned was acceptable and how, when the time came, I would conduct the interview. What questions should I ask? Quick, Dad's Folder of Systematic Funeral Protocol! Wasn't there a section on staff recruitment? Indeed, there was. I thanked Dad for his attention to detail and foresight and amended the job description in light of his instruction. Then, without giving myself a chance to reconsider, I emailed it to the Institute of Embalming and a recruitment agency. More spontaneity!

Then Jean called out, 'I've sent you some survey questions. I'm just popping out now.'

Jean's questions were extensive. *What do you imagine when you think of a funeral home? Do you prefer wood panelling or mock marble; fake flowers or real ones? How important do you think music is? Have you thought*

about your own funeral? Have you heard of Clock & Son Funeral Home?
Would you follow us on Facebook if we were on there? What do you think of
our building – what's your first impression? It made me nervous to think
what some of the answers might be. What if fake flowers won hands
down? Would we have to offer them, too? I would have to tell Jean
when she came back that a survey may not be a good idea.

I cleaned some more. Time drifted and Jean still wasn't back yet.
What was she doing? Her mobile was on the desk so I went outside to
try and find her. I scanned the pavement. No sign. I walked to the kerb
and looked across the road. There she was, a clipboard in one hand,
the other reaching out to passers-by like a granny evangelist recruiting
members. Every so often she caught someone's attention and, as they
politely stopped and listened, she scribbled on the clipboard.

I called her name. Waved an arm. Everyone else heard but her. I
jogged to the pedestrian crossing, my tie trying to catch Jean's attention,
pushed the buzzer and waited, all the while watching Jean approach
strangers, arms gesticulating, the brooch glinting whenever she turned
and a ladder creeping stealthily up the back of a stockinged leg. Cars
ambled, nose-to-tailed. Pedestrians accumulated. They nose-to-tailed,
too. Finally the traffic stopped. I strode ahead of the crowd and got to
her, out of breath.

'Jean! What are you doing?'

'Hello, Oliver,' she said. 'What a response I'm getting! Except there
are too many questions. People lose interest around question number
ten.' She looked as pleased as Mr Johnson had when I'd finished prep-
ping him.

'Good grief,' was all I could muster.

She lurched towards a man coming in the opposite direction.
'Excuse me, sir, would you mind if I took a moment of your time? I'm
from Clock & Son Funeral Home across the road there.' She pointed
in the direction of our building. 'I know death is a dreadful business
but we want to make the transition as easy and welcoming for everyone

involved. Would you have a minute to answer some questions in the interests of customer service?'

I looked away, pretended I wasn't with her. People parted around me.

When she finished with one, she started on another. I looked at my watch. I shouldn't have left the place unattended and I hadn't brought my phone.

'You go.' Jean nudged me. 'I'll do a few more. It's quite fun! Back soon.'

'But I wasn't sure . . .' My words were left hanging as she walked off. Jauntily. With purpose. The clipboard swinging. Next target: a girl guzzling a milkshake. I couldn't help but admire Jean's spunk yet feared she was rushing in without proper planning. Not only had we not discussed the survey but she had neglected to do due diligence on whom she was targeting. Her eagerness verged on overpowering, especially to young girls in knee-high socks who probably thought rigor mortis was the name of a rock band.

When I returned Mum was at reception riffling around the papers on Jean's desk. 'Goodness me, Oliver, where were you? I thought you'd all died.'

'Very funny.'

'Where's Jean?' Mum relocated from the desk to the side table and peered into the vase. 'The flowers need more water.'

'Busy,' I said.

'You can't both go out and leave the door unlocked. There should be someone here at all times. It's a shambles.' She adjusted the lilies, twisting and turning them to sit just so. 'I do like lilies. Such sweetness.' Her face clouded momentarily, then she turned the vase as if its angle displeased her.

'Sorry.'

'You know anxiety is not good for my health, Oliver, and I'm on blood pressure pills. I was about to call a search party. I even called beforehand, but no one answered. What's going on?'

'Sorry, Mum.'

General Improvements

When Jean finally returned, Mum was still loitering, bemoaning the lack of clientele. I suggested we congregate in my office. If I didn't tell Mum about the survey, Jean would, so I decided there would be no delay; we may as well do it together. I pulled out the two apricot-coloured guest chairs for them to sit on. They had been top of the line in their day, the fabric a quality linen, the squareness of the style 'on trend', but now they reeked of the early 1990s, neither fashionably retro nor dismally tattered. The curtains were a similar shade and my dark wood desk large and imposing – a hangover of a twenty-five-year-old Doreen makeover.

'What do you mean, a survey?' Mum asked.

'Jean?' I said, as I needed enlightening as well.

'I've had such a great time talking to the locals,' she gushed, and having seen her at work, I knew she wasn't exaggerating.

'Really, Jean.' Mum sounded displeased, as if our standing in the community meant we were above talking to people in the street. 'Alright, go on, what did they say?'

'The general consensus is that people look for professionalism, experience and trustworthiness in a funeral home. But first impressions count and at the moment we're not doing so well. We're perceived as outdated and stuck in the past.'

'*Mon Dieu!* Have these people stepped inside?'

'I doubt their views would change, Mum,' I muttered, looking at the has-been decor and drab furnishings in my office.

'I think that's being unfair.'

'The idea of a funeral home using social media was met with nervous laughter.'

'Social media?' Mum said. 'Who would want to see pictures of someone's embalmed uncle?'

I was impressed Jean had thought to include social media and wondered how it would work. 'If it was done the right way, maybe?' I suggested. 'We could post inspirational quotes, links to stories about how to help someone grieve, or images of unusual sarcophaguses, like the beautiful cast-glass one recently made for the Danish queen . . .'

'That's absurd,' Mum said. 'What we need is a new sign so people know we're here. Not a Facebook account to lower the tone of the industry.'

'Yes, we do need a new sign,' I said. 'But maybe a Clock & Son makeover wouldn't be a bad thing.'

'Just because the new place has marble . . .'

'I don't mean with marble. Perhaps a paint job, new carpet?'

'But we did a renovation in 1998,' Mum said. 'Your father upgraded the embalming tables and we painted the inside "egg white".'

'That was years ago. The egg white is now egg yolk.'

'You can't get rid of the wood panelling.'

'Maybe we could stain it a lighter colour?' Jean suggested.

'The chandelier in the viewing room is definitely staying,' Mum insisted. 'It's been there since Clock & Son was first established.'

I may not have loved the chandelier with its crookedly sitting mock-candle lights and the clusters of crystal drops in regular need of dusting, but I had to agree with Mum that it was impossible to imagine the room without it. It represented Clock & Son's history and brought a little sparkle to an otherwise sombre room.

'And the table and vase in reception. They were your grandmother's. You can't come through with a rubbish truck. Jean and I regularly replace the flowers and I think Jean is in agreement that we need to mix up the varieties and arrangements more often, aren't you, Jean?' Mum was on a roll and didn't give Jean a chance to respond. 'If you really want change, I'll move the furniture around.'

'I'm not suggesting we start today. It's something to think about, that's all.'

'And it will all cost, you know.'

'I think what we have to do,' Jean said with characteristic diplomacy, 'is be proud of what has already been established but not dismiss the voice of the people. They're the ones who'll help guide us into the future.'

'Well, thank you, Jean,' Mum said, and announced she was going to disinfect the surgical instruments, as if, sitting unused, they were festering with the bacteria of the living.

I may have been unsure about the survey and a renovation but it was good to have broached the subject of change with Mum, even if she was resistant to it. It did make me wonder how on earth I was going to tell her about the candles and the embalmer ad, let alone try and talk to her about Lily again. All of which, I decided, required a dose of fresh air and a serving of something sweet. I asked around if Jean or Mum wished for an afternoon treat and headed down the road to our favourite patisserie. To my pleasant surprise a text from Caroline greeted me when I arrived.

Do you fancy a visit to the beach on Sunday? It's meant to be a scorcher.

I was as fond of the beach as I was of corked wine. Going as a child wasn't encouraged. Mum had an aversion to the sand and Dad got heat rash. It didn't help that we lived in the inner city. Rather like Dad, my fair skin was prone to sunburn and I disliked seagulls swarming over me when I ate. Once, when I went with friends as a teenager, a gull pinched a crumbed prawn that was halfway between my fingers and my mouth.

Then there was the time when I got caught in a rip and was taken out to sea. I knew not to fight the surf but feared how far the ocean would take me. As I was about to raise an arm to alert the lifeguards, before my fear turned to panic I was picked up by a surfer. He paddled me back to shore as I rested, face down, on the surfboard, as if I were his catch of the day. I felt less inclined to go to the beach after that. Yet here I was being invited to the beach with a woman who seemed to want to keep seeing me. It was the offer of another date and surely I couldn't argue with that?

Sure, I replied, and immediately chose the medium-sized lemon meringue pie sitting on the middle shelf of the front counter, two cakes in from the left.

When I returned to work, Mum was still there. She cornered me in the kitchenette.

'Oliver?'

'Yes, Mum?' I said, slicing the pie.

'I know you've been sad recently . . .'

She did? I scooped pie residue from the knife just to check it was as good as it looked.

'And I wanted to give you this.' She handed me a long, thin, black weathered box.

I frowned. Mum only gave gifts at gift-requiring occasions: birthdays, christenings and Christmas. She looked sheepish, as if she knew she was acting out of character and wasn't entirely sure how to behave. 'I probably should have given this to you before.' She looked at me expectantly. 'Well, go on . . . open it.'

I lifted the lid, releasing an aged, oaky smell like that of an antique shop. Inside, lying in pleated royal blue satin, were a silver shoe horn, a button hook and a clothes brush.

'They were your grandfather's – Grandpa James – and then your father's. Silly to have them sitting unused in a drawer, given your love of immaculate dressing,' Mum said.

I ran a hand over the pieces. They shone as if they had been recently polished. 'They're beautiful,' I said.

'I hope you'll use them.'

'Of course I will,' I said, and reached out to give her a squeeze. 'Thanks, Mum.'

She leaned into me awkwardly for a few seconds, or it could have been a minute, but certainly no more, before removing herself from my touch. 'Well, there's no point waiting until I'm gone for you to have them, is there?'

That evening, as I heated up a beef pie, I told Marie about my day. How chuffed I was at Mum's present, having already tried out the clothes brush on my jacket, but how nervous I was at the idea of a Clock & Son makeover and how desperately I wished she could have given me her thoughts, offered sage advice and a dollop of good taste. I had no experience at renovating and was hesitant to upend the building without some proper thought having gone into it. Choosing paint colours could not be done in one sitting – even though Marie probably could have. As it was, I had to make do with a one-sided conversation with myself and a candle. Then I reread excerpts from her diary, as I had been doing every night since it had been in my possession. I didn't just focus on the bits about me either; reading her words and hearing her voice gave me comfort. Her diary entries started three years ago – I didn't know whether there was another diary before that or whether this was her first. As it began on January 5, I liked to think she was a resolution-maker like myself and had decided to start a journal that New Year's. For she even wrote things like, *I must do more exercise* (February 10) and *I should cut back on the rosé, if for no other reason than for Henry's benefit* (August 24).

I loved her ruminations on flowers at the flower market and the pride she got from creating the ideal bouquet. Then there were the entries where she talked about things we'd done together which I had forgotten about. Like the time we got lost going to visit a client in a nursing home. We were laughing so hard at our navigational ineptitude that, when we arrived, we had to wait a few minutes more in the car to regain a more respectful and sombre countenance. Then there was the time I helped her move her business into larger premises. It was four years into her owning her business and she wanted my help with the layout. She seemed to think the way I dressed was the perfect qualification for advising on flora and fauna placement on a shop floor. I didn't protest, as I knew my attributes were less suited to that than they were to heavy lifting, which was what she got Henry and her nephew to help her with.

Of course, I couldn't help but lean towards any entry in which I was mentioned and it wasn't just learning that she thought me kind and gentle but other things, too. Like how she noticed every time I bought a new tie and how she thought I was such a good listener. I was only listening how I always listened – two ears on full alert, eyes attentive and mind focused. It pained me to think that Henry may have lacked such conversational skills with his wife or, worse, just wasn't interested enough in what she had to say. I held on to Marie's compliments the same way I liked to savour every mouthful of a Mars bar. It was a joy to sleep with the diary under my pillow and her candle by my bed.

Death by Toaster

Finally, later that night, someone died. I met the daughter of the deceased, Vicky, at the mortuary. Although Hugh Simmons's death was sudden, it was far from painless. The cruel forces of dementia made him shove a fork in his toaster to remove the crust he had forgotten to retrieve for breakfast three days earlier, when he was toasting a fresher slice of bread. Electricity initially jolted him lucid and sharp and then it killed him.

'He was an accident waiting to happen, I'm afraid,' Vicky said. 'He spent his life like that, to be honest. He'd successfully climb mountains in the middle of nowhere, then come home, trip on a door jamb and break his foot. It was ridiculous that he insisted on living at home. But he had a carer and I visited most days. It's such a shame he thought it was time for breakfast.'

'Many would envy such a full life,' I said.

'It was very full and surprisingly long, although latterly he was eating several breakfasts at various times of the day. I'm glad it was over quickly.' She stroked her father's hand, his fingers now resembling roasted purple potatoes, the skin waxy, the fingernails white. 'Sorry to call you late, but Dad had funeral plans and, given that he didn't want to be embalmed, I felt I needed to organise things straight away.'

Hooray! No embalming. I almost broke out into my version of a tap dance. 'No problem,' I said. 'It's all part of the job. We can conduct the funeral as soon as you like, as early as tomorrow afternoon, even. But I'm sure you'll want some time with your father.'

'The thing is,' she whispered, leaning towards me, 'he's got an unusual request.'

'We're open to anything.'

'He may not want to be embalmed but he does want a viewing.' She leaned in closer, as if she might be overheard, though we were all alone. 'But . . .' She looked around. 'He asked to be placed face down. Can you do that?'

'We can do whatever you wish,' I said.

If Mr Simmons got comfort from the thought of his body lying face down in a casket when he was alive, then I was happy to accommodate his request in death. And if this made his daughter happy, then it might, even in a small way, pluck away some of the pins of sadness. Then my sleep-deprived mind wandered and I wondered, could this be our new tagline? 'We'll place you in the coffin any which way you like?'

'Thank you,' Vicky said, stepping away. Then she came in close again and whispered, 'You see, he wants to be face down so that everyone he didn't like could come and . . . you know . . . kiss his . . .' She raised her eyebrows and pointed to her bottom. 'Arse!' she cried out, with such force it startled me. 'Oh my goodness, I can't believe I even said that word. It's my father I'm talking about.'

'You could say gluteus maximus?' I suggested.

She thought for a minute. 'But it doesn't have quite the same ring to it, does it?' She laughed.

Driving home with the cool night air blowing in through the open car window, I thought about the man's request. You would think, the length of time I had been in this game (twenty-six years, if you included my unpaid hours as a teenager), that I'd have heard it all. But this one topped the lot. What gumption! And what a sense of humour that kept on chuckling after he had gone. I imagined Marie and me having a laugh over the idea of including a tall, thin columnar cacti amongst his funeral flora – an in-joke to Mr Simmons giving his finger to the world. For even in death, the man was doing what he pleased. He hadn't let life choose how he lived and he wasn't going to let it dictate how he'd be buried. I might use that as an example to others, I decided. I could add it to the page of True Stories – Tales to Inspire, Uplift and Motivate in Dad's Folder of Systematic Funeral Protocol. Or we could put it on Facebook, if we ever set it up.

Or, maybe, I would write it as a resolution in my notebook: *Thou shalt not let life choose how you live.* Which could have been a euphemism for *Thou shalt not let embalming or your mother rule your life.*

When, by the end of the week, I had received three applications for the embalming job in my inbox, I decided, spurred on by my interpretation of Mr Simmons's motto, to get two of them in for interviews and not to tell Mum. The first was a man similar in age to me with enough years behind him and also in front of him to make him a possible contender, and the second a woman who, while younger, still demonstrated the sort of experience I was looking for and, if I wasn't mistaken, I could just make out the start of a tattoo running down one arm in her profile photograph. Maybe *she* could be the new face of Clock & Son.

Talking Candles that Smell of the Dead

I had never expected to become a man of clandestine activity, yet Friday proved to be a very secretive day. I not only contacted the embalmer applicants but organised for Edie to come in to discuss the candles when Mum would not be around. I was also pleased that this time I could present to Edie the more professional Oliver Clock dressed in a suit. Weirdly, my choice of tie coordinated with Jean's brooch, which was a vintage silver star with crystals. My tie was more of a galaxy star theme, a nod to the bigger universe and how small our place in it is. I was quite pleased when I found it; it would be a new style to add to my collection. I immediately bought four in different colourways in case they were a discontinued line.

'Edie, how lovely to see you,' I said. 'Please come in.'

At a guess, I would say Edie was five foot six and would easily fit into one of our slimline coffins, allowing plenty of room for added extras if so desired. I quite liked the emerald-green dress she was wearing in a style reminiscent of the 1950s. It really brought out her eyes.

'Thanks, Oliver, and thank you for supporting my candles. I've got some ideas on how we can get them off the ground.'

'Excellent.' I pulled out a chair for her and moved the plate of eight biscuits (I liked to appear generous and to use an even number), which I had arranged in a concentric circle, closer to her. I offered her something to drink and, once the refreshments were taken care of, I sat down and we began.

'Firstly,' Edie said, 'I think we need a selection of samples to show people and a checklist of questions to ask interested clients about the deceased.'

'I know all about lists,' I said, thinking of my notebook and the bullet-pointed resolutions inside.

'Good.' She nodded. 'The key is finding out what made the person tick, what was their essence. That's what the scent becomes. We can ask things like: what were their hobbies? What foods did they like?'

'Should I be writing this down?'

'I've done it already,' she said, pulling out a piece of paper from her leather document holder. 'You might want to add some more. To be honest, it doesn't matter how many we have so long as we can help people identify their ideal scents. With the samples, I was thinking I could make candles of people you know – that way you can be genuine when you're selling them. I could do one of your cousin, a colleague or your father, for instance.'

But the mention of my father suddenly jarred my vision of a candle conglomerate. The smell of Dad started overpowering Edie's voice. Everything about my father came flooding back. It was as if he were sitting next to me and we were having a beer together in the old days. The weekday Dad with spicy aftershave and peppermint mouthwash, mingled with the weekend Dad and the heady smell of cut grass, slightly damp and earthy, spring-like. Soil. Weeds. Dried blood from hedge cuts. Sweat. Sunday mornings with eggs, fried and buttery. Lukewarm tea. Six o'clock beer. I missed those relaxed times with Dad. I missed him in the business as well, if I was honest. But Andrew Clock as a candle?

'Oliver?'

'Yes?'

'The samples?'

'Ah, yes. Let's not do one of Dad,' I said. 'Maybe Mum? She's still here, so that would be a real test. Although I warn you, she won't be easy to win over. Unless she thought of the idea, she'll resolutely dismiss it,' I said. The better scenario would be if Edie successfully made a candle of her but we told Mum nothing about it.

'OK. Go,' Edie said.

'What?'

'Brainstorm scents for your mother. Don't think too hard, just fire off smells.'

Except my brain stumbled, fumbled, as if grappling for the light switch in the dark. Battle-axe Doreen seemed to be someone to whom no smell was immediately associated. I thought hard and then tried not to think hard, but the more I thought, the more I overthought. *Come on, Marie, help me out here.*

'Say the first thing that comes into your head.'

'Castor oil and moth balls?'

'Mmm, interesting,' she said, rather diplomatically. 'My mum tends to have a lavender drawer-liner whiff about her' – she laughed – 'which is an easier smell to work with. Does your mother wear a particular perfume?'

'Eau d'Overbearing.'

She laughed again and touched my forearm as I was bringing a shortbread to my mouth. A frisson of something shot up my limb. Biscuit crumbs sprinkled. Did she feel it, too? 'I know it can be hard,' she said. 'We don't usually analyse how people smell, do we? So what about food? What does she like to cook?'

I thought about the meals she cooked me when I was a child and how I'd dreamed of never eating them again. 'Corned beef and parsley sauce,' I said. 'And overcooked pumpkin. I guess that's not much help either.'

'Some people are harder than others. Maybe you're too close to her. I know I am with my mum. Sometimes it comes down to a memory you have or something you did with her as a child . . .'

It was strange how Edie was trying to draw out fond memories of Mum when I'd never really thought of her in that way before. Many of my memories may have featured Mum but not necessarily in an affectionate way. She was just there, a strong and quietly supportive presence, as if she were an extra thigh I never knew I needed.

'We could always make them up?' I suggested, still unable to come up with a Doreen signature scent.

'Fragrances of the pretend dead?' she said. 'That might work. We could keep it simple. Do a floral one for a gardener – scents of jasmine, gardenia, violets. Maybe a coffee one. Yes, I've always wanted to try that. We'll need the best coffee beans.' She had a cute way of crinkling her freckled nose up in concentration and squinting seconds before coming up with a new thought. Her enthusiasm was charming. Her love of brainstorming rather infectious.

Then I had an idea. 'Let's ask Jean. I'll warn you, she's sceptical, too, but I need her on board with this.'

Edie nodded. 'She would be perfect. I've already noted her honey and butter undertones.'

'You have?' It seemed to me that the pharmaceutical world was not making enough of Edie's gifts.

'I have a sensitive nose. I think she would make a fantastic candle.'

I don't think Edie realised how she was sounding, like it was perfectly normal to scrutinise how people smelt and then bottle them up as if collecting samples of their blood. It was really quite endearing to be with someone so passionate about their work. And it was this that made me like her and her idea even more. Although I didn't dare ask what she thought I'd be if turned into a candle. Some unpleasant combination like embalming fluid, soft cheese, red wine and cologne, no doubt. It didn't bear thinking about, so I got up to find Jean.

Jean's response was as I predicted: less than enthusiastic. 'I can't believe you're doing this,' she whispered, as if someone might hear, although there was no one in reception. 'I thought you hated the idea.'

I explained about Marie's candle. How it really was her. How the candles could be Clock & Son's exclusive product. 'They might not make us rich but they'll help us stand out. Look, I want to give them a go but we need examples of what they could be like, how they might smell. We want to do one of you.'

'Have you gone funny in the head?' she asked.

'No, honestly, Jean,' I said. 'Come and meet Edie properly. She's lovely and definitely not funny in the head either.'

'Well, alright.'

I formally introduced them to each other and let Edie tell Jean more about the candle concept. Jean still looked unsure, then Edie touched her arm and reassured her that no one else needed to know about it and that if she didn't like the candle she could throw it in the bin. But I think what got Jean over the line was her story about her father and how she was determined to capture his true scent for ever. 'You'll be surprised at the effect smells have, their power to evoke, remember, tug at one's emotions.'

Jean nodded. 'I have to say that was a lovely sales pitch – and I do like your dress,' she added.

'Thank you. It's from my sister's vintage clothing store.' Edie let Jean touch her skirt and they had a moment admiring the fabric, which unexpectedly made me jealous. I could appreciate quality material as well as anyone.

'I still think it's a crazy notion,' Jean continued, 'but you've got me intrigued. I can't imagine what I might smell like.'

'Brilliant,' Edie said. She got her pen poised. 'All you have to do is tell us what you like.'

'Pastries,' I blurted, and winked at Jean.

'I don't always eat pastries.' Jean fiddled with her brooch.

'Yes, that's what I thought: a buttery undertone with the sweetness of honey. Perhaps notes of vanilla and a hint of figs? Do you like figs?'

'I do. I also like chocolate. Seventy per cent dark,' Jean said. 'I won't settle for anything less than delicious, you know, and if I'm happy with the candle, I'd like to keep it once you've finished parading me around.'

'Of course, thank you. You're a star!' Edie leapt up and gave her a hug.

Jean accepted the informal acknowledgement of thanks and even patted Edie's back, which must have meant she had made an impression. 'On that note, I'm leaving for the day. Lovely to meet you, Edie. I look forward to your creation.'

'Thanks, Jean,' I said. 'Can you swing the door sign to "Closed" on your way out?'

We listened to the front door click shut and it seemed as if, for a minute at least, my office was now scented with figs and honey.

'How lovely is she?' Edie said.

'Jean's amazing; she's been with us for years,' I said. 'If you can get her candle right, she'll be singing your praises.'

'No pressure, then?' Edie laughed.

'Well, if it's anything like Marie's . . . You captured her perfectly. Another biscuit?' I offered her the plate.

'I'd better not. I do a lot of baking and should really cut down my consumption.'

'Baking?' I said, my interest piqued.

'Do you bake?' she asked.

'No, I'm better at eating it.' I laughed. 'What do you like to make?'

Edie pulled out her phone and showed me a photo. 'This is a favourite. It's a three-layer hazelnut meringue with berries and mascarpone cream. I've made it a few times for friends for special occasions.'

Edie was rapidly going up in my estimation: a woman with the nose of a sommelier and an expert baker. What an excellent business partner she was becoming. 'Are you sure you're in the right vocation?' I laughed again. 'It looks better than half the things at the patisserie down the road, and I should know, as I'm a valued customer.'

'Pharmaceuticals pays the bills,' she explained. 'But I do prefer being creative.'

'Let's continue being creative, then,' I said. 'What do we do next?'

'I thought we could have some brochures made, then go door-knocking at nursing homes and florists'. Take the samples. Try and sell them.'

'I know just the person to photograph them,' I suggested, telling her about Andy.

'Great,' she agreed, 'and I've written some copy.' She handed me a typed sheet.

Send your senses down memory lane. Our Lumières by Edie Jones are bespoke soy candles handmade in memory of your dearly departed. The scent is made to your exact specifications in honour of the person who has passed away. The candle will embody scents of your beloved and be a beautiful reminder of everything they represented to you. The essence of your loved one will become a special candle with a burn time of 48 hours. We'll keep your bespoke scents on file so the candles can be refilled as you wish. What better way to remember that special person who has passed than with Les Lumières by Edie Jones?

'Excellent! This is what you needed to give me when you first came in. I might have signed up straight away.'

She laughed. 'Sometimes it's easier writing things down.'

'I know what you mean,' I said, thinking of Dad's very useful Folder.

'Then I thought, down the track, if people are liking them, we could create a website, do PR . . .'

'Morning television?' I said, putting a hand to my heart. What suit would I wear?

'That might be jumping the gun.'

'Of course.' I nodded, coming back down to earth. But it did sound gloriously enterprising. No one would want to die without having a candle made of them. I'd show the other crowd how to run a funeral home from the heart; how to be sincere not saccharine; how to be traditional with a twist. 'And what about costs – margins and pricing? I can't really buy them off you wholesale when they're made to order, can I?'

'I was thinking the best way would be for me to calculate the cost of production – which I have done, based on what I've made already – we agree on a retail price and then split the profit fifty-fifty.'

'That sounds a very good plan,' I agreed, the symmetry of her numbers proving most amenable. 'I'm not familiar with bespoke candle prices so I'll let you guide me.'

'Well, we don't want to make them too expensive or too cheap. I'll email you a spreadsheet of the pricing I've done so far and you can let me know what you think.'

I smiled and glowed from the inside, as if I had been lit myself. I had never thought of myself as an entrepreneur. Or should I be called a funereal-preneur? The thought made me laugh out loud, which was disconcerting for Edie. More so when I slapped the table in glee, juddering the teacups on their saucers.

'Oops, sorry,' I said, apologising for my enthusiasm, which sounded like an odd thing to do in retrospect. But thankfully my excitement only added to hers and we must have looked a right pair, high-fiving each other over the desktop when really we should have formally shaken hands.

I just hoped the idea took off.

The Beach

There's nothing like starting a new business venture to end the week. Or, I noted, shake up one's year. Over the years I had thought about trying something new. Once, I was going to learn French cooking so I could impress Mum with the French theme or woo a girl I hadn't yet met. But then I had visions of getting a call-out in the middle of whisking a roux sauce and the thought of congealed lumps forming as I was forced to abandon it made me never take it up in the first place. It's there somewhere in my notebook from about two years ago, which is where it has remained in written form ever since.

But now, thanks to Edie, I *was* starting something new and doing something for the business, and I hadn't even written it down. It called for a spontaneous celebration with someone at the pub. But Andy was having a date night with Lucy, and my other friends who were reliable last-minute pub-goers, Terry and Simon, were tied up with babysitting (Terry) and a fortieth-birthday party (Simon). I didn't feel I knew Caroline well enough to ask her for an unexpected Friday night drink, and anyway, I was seeing her on Sunday. I went home and decided to celebrate with Marie.

What I also secretly wanted was Marie's approval of Caroline. Not so much what she thought of her but to know that she didn't mind me going out with her. After pouring myself a beer and lighting Marie's candle, I broached the subject.

'So, I've been asked out by Caroline again,' I began. 'It seems she still wants to see me – ha! The thing is, I don't want you to be upset about it. It doesn't change how I feel about you but Caroline seems good fun and it would be a shame to say no to a date when it's being offered, don't you think? That's what I've been telling myself anyway.' I drank some beer, enjoyed the scent of the candle. 'You know I've always valued your opinion and it would be most reassuring if I knew you approved.' I paused to gauge Marie's response. It was always hard to tell but, as I was used to talking to cadavers, I wasn't anticipating an obvious response. Eventually, the flame flickered and I took that as a yes. 'Thank you, Marie,' I whispered.

Happy that Marie had given me her blessing, I decided to clean the fridge.

On Sunday, I met Caroline at our agreed meeting spot on the board-walk by the third tree at the beach. The sounds of the sporadic squeals of children in the shallows and the sea licking the sand came to us in waves of warm air. Heat steamed the pavement and scorched our skin.

'How great is this?' Caroline said. 'Look at it, what a view.' She gestured to the vista and I thought she was about to break out into a dance twirl.

It was a spectacular sight. Everything sparkled as if sprayed with glitter. I salivated at the thought of an ice cream.

'How about a swim?' Caroline said.

I looked longingly elsewhere and then spotted an ice cream shop across the road. 'Maybe an ice cream first?' I suggested.

'OK.' She shrugged and hooked an arm in mine, and we strolled to the shop. I kept our strolling to a lazy pace to string out the length of time it took to buy a cone, eat it and let the food settle before swim-ming was mentioned again. Caroline smelled of coconut and sun cream and the shop of hot waffles. It was all far more enticing than what lay behind us.

Once we had bought our cones, we walked back, linking arms again. I repeated the lazy stroll until a bench seat came into view. I veered us in its direction.

'Where are you going?' Caroline said.

'I find it's more comfortable looking at the beach than sitting on it, particularly when eating ice cream. All that sand, you know?'

'You're too funny,' Caroline said. 'But that's what you do when you're at the beach. You sit on the sand. Come on!' she cried, and pulled me away.

I lurched forward against her tug and watched in slow motion as my scoop of raspberry ice cream toppled from its beautiful perch on the delicately spun waffle cone on to the concrete before me. It splattered and dispersed, resembling, I noted with disconcerting accuracy, a freshly transplanted heart.

'Oh, no,' Caroline said. 'Here, you can share mine.' She shoved her choc-mint ice cream under my nose.

I gave it a lick but it wasn't the same. 'It's OK,' I said. 'I've still got the cone.'

'I insist we share,' Caroline said. 'Come on, let's find a spot on the sand. We can sit on our towels.'

I took a bite of my cone and reluctantly joined Caroline on the sand.

As soon as her cone was gone, Caroline leapt up, as if the sugar had just hit her bloodstream. She threw off her dress and announced, 'Time for a swim,' with the enthusiasm of someone who loves swimming far more than their companion does. I watched her run down to the water, calling for me to join her. I swallowed a gulp of dismay. It's not that I thought we wouldn't go into the water, it was more that I had underestimated her love for it and my residual fear. Yet I didn't want our Sunday ruined because I stayed stuck in the sand. Wasn't I on an outing with a woman who was keen for me to accompany her in everything she did? I wasn't spending my Sunday alone and lonely, but with a vivacious woman who was throwing herself into the experience. So I joined her at the water's edge. Little waves splashed my ankles and chilled my broiled feet.

'This is bliss,' she said, raising her face to the sun.

I made a non-committal noise, not wishing to let on that I was more of a stroll-along-the-promenade kind of a guy, despite the dangers of runners, cyclists, skateboarders and power-striders with pedometers attached to their arms jostling for space on the pavement. You couldn't be too careful.

'It's swimming I love the most,' she said. 'Not that I swim-swim. It's more floating around like a bloated starfish. I could probably do with swimming properly. I mean, I did tell myself I needed to get fit.' She looked as if she was taking a moment to seriously consider the idea before shaking it off as if shooing away flies. 'OK, let's do it.'

Then she was in, jogging until she was in up to her knees then diving. She emerged as if being spat out of a drain, water spraying as hair flew around her head and stuck to her face. She peeled it off. I waded in a little further. My knees didn't object. She wallowed on her back, toes pointing to the sky.

'You've got to get in quickly.' She laughed.

I edged in some more. A part of me really did want to dive in like she had but I couldn't make myself do it. The depths unnerved me. You just don't know what goes on under all that water. Things lurked. Invisible rips tugged and pulled and the surf ricocheted you around like a pinball in a slot machine. Then there's the marine life.

'Come on,' she called.

I waved. I didn't want to be ungrateful for her encouragement yet I couldn't help but think that Marie wouldn't have been so bossy.

'You've still got your T-shirt on.'

I closed my eyes, breathed in deeply. It was now or never. I took off my T-shirt, felt the sting of the sun against the pastiness of my stomach, flung it back to the sand away from the sea and walked in. I should have made a running start, like Caroline had, but I disliked running more than I did swimming. An ice-cold tickle at my waist made me start.

'It's harder going in slowly,' Caroline said.

I bent my knees and slunk into the water, letting the sea sway around me, pushing and pulling, lifting me off my toes. For a second I forgot where I was, who I was with and what I was supposed to be doing. Or was that the point – that I was supposed to be enjoying the moment rather than worrying about what might happen next? I lay on my back, letting sunlight stick to my skin, salt settle in the creases of my lips and the sea gel my eyelashes together.

'Yay, you're in!'

I gave her a thumbs-up.

'Come and join me. You don't need to stay in the shallows.'

'It's OK, I'm fine here.' I was just happy that I was in the water with Caroline, together, even if there was a distance between us.

'It's more fun when you can't touch the bottom.'

I wished she wasn't so persistent.

'I'm not touching the bottom.'

'Suit yourself. I'm going to swim out. It's quite flat today but I want to try some body surfing.'

I waved her off and splayed my arms and legs like a starfish to stay afloat. Closing my eyes, I enjoyed the heat of the sun on my face and the sensation of weightlessness. The tide tugged at my body, slowly coaxing me out of my depth. I let it. I tried to stay calm because I knew I could put my feet down at any moment. For a few minutes it was just me and the sea and the sky. Then a hand yanked at my swimming shorts from under the water. I swallowed a handful of sea and floundered. My arms flapped uselessly. I emerged as Caroline did, spurting water skyward like a dolphin.

'It's OK, I've got you,' Caroline said.

I couldn't speak. I treaded water frantically and feared I resembled a heaving puffer fish.

'Sorry, I didn't mean to give you a fright.'

It's impossible to shrug when you're breathless beneath water. My feet flapped next to hers. Our chests touched, legs knocked. It couldn't be helped. The sea was doing what I knew the sea could do best – taking control and manipulating us like puppets. Just as I got my breath back, Caroline planted a kiss on my lips. It was so quick and spontaneous that for a minute it was hard to believe it had happened and when my mind caught up it wasn't sure what to think of it. Was it purely done for buoyancy or was it out of genuine romance? Or maybe both at the same time? Or was it merely the result of having been close – *again* – and Caroline couldn't help herself and was now regretting such a forward, spur-of-the-moment decision? Right then, in the undulating sea, I felt unattractive and undeserving of her attentions whatever the reason for them and, even if I had wanted to reciprocate the kiss, her lips were now no longer where they had been, the distance between us having moved with the motion of the tide and our treadmill legs. My slow-to-respond, lingering pucker was captured by the salty air and blown away by the breeze. She smiled.

'Shall we get out?' I suggested, unsure how to respond when all I could think about was the ache in my frantically treading legs.

'Oh, come on, stay,' she said.

'I think I'll head back.' All I wanted was terra firma under my feet. The surety of damp, compacted sand under my soles and the dependability of gravity.

'OK, I won't be long.'

I watched Caroline bob out to a breaker, then wave to me before I attempted a half-hearted breaststroke towards the beach. Finally, I had my feet on the sand, my body on the towel. I was spent. I flicked water off my face and squeezed the sea from the hem of my swimmers, then nestled into a dip in the sand and rested on my elbows and wondered, now that I could think more clearly, what to make of the kiss. Caroline emerged from the shallows, having taken a wave all the way to shore. She grinned at me and headed back out. How she loved it. How I didn't love it. It was draining trying to love things that didn't love me back. It suited me to keep my adrenal glands on energy save and my blood pressure simmering on low just as much as body surfing suited Caroline. Did it matter that we enjoyed different things? Didn't opposites attract? Did the kiss mean anything?

I was snoring when Caroline came back. I knew I was because I heard a snort erupt when she poked my shoulder.

She laughed. 'You'll get sunstroke.'

That was all I needed.

We agreed to call it a day once Caroline was dry.

But when a woman says she's going to bus home and you've come by car, the only courteous thing to do is offer her a lift. Perhaps she'd been hoping for this all along, as Caroline didn't hesitate to invite me back to hers for a drink. Buoyed by this unexpected date extension, I said yes. It was either that or going home to an empty apartment, soothing sunburn on my own, making tea for one and watching the six o'clock news by myself again.

Caroline's flat was all white – the walls, the floors, the sofa, the kitchen – glaring white with touches of pale pink and dove grey. On first glance it looked immaculate, until I spotted the papers shoved under the sofa, a basket jumbled with 'stuff' by the coffee table, magazines in a pile in one corner, a collection of used candles on the mantel. The smell of hours-old coconut suntan lotion still lingered in the air, along with the whiff of kitty litter.

'What would you like?' Caroline called from the kitchen. 'It's not too early for wine, is it?'

I sat on the sofa and checked the time, then decided I didn't care what the time was. Desire was punching holes in my timidity. Or maybe it was the sunstroke.

'Not at all,' I said. I slipped off my shoes and flicked through a coffee-table book of photographs of Australia full of red dirt and scorched skies, indigenous grins and dehydrated gum trees.

'Here you go,' Caroline said, returning from the kitchen.

She handed me a glass of wine and placed a bowl of mixed nuts on the table. I put the book to one side. We talked about our work and I sidestepped the realistic aspects of my job in favour of a Hollywood-style version to keep Caroline's imagination taint-free. She edged closer, offered me nuts. I felt saltier than they were and in need of a shower. But I ate the nuts instead, sipped the wine and enjoyed how enamoured she seemed to be by what I was saying. 'That's so great,' she repeated, 'I don't know how you do it.'

'Well, you know,' I said, as if it all came easy and Clock & Son weren't teetering on the edge of collapse and that the dead weren't moving down the road and around the corner.

By now, Caroline was so close I could feel the squishy bits of her hips warming mine and count the sand granules in her hair. The next thing I knew her glass was empty, her legs were over mine and a hand was squeezing flesh. Then she kissed me again. This time there was no doubting the reason. For this was no quick peck and buoyancy issues could not be to blame. She kissed me and giggled in alternate motions, as if unsure which to settle on. She was unlike any other woman I had been with – assertive and adventurous – and it was at once alluring and disconcerting. My first kiss had been with a girl named Karen, whose hair was so curly you couldn't easily slide your pinky finger into one of the ringlets. I knew this because I tried – it was a dare my classmate

Darren made up when we were eleven. Anyone who succeeded was named King for the Day. No one did, but plenty got close. I got so close I was able to peck her lips, which made her giggle. Except, when I tried to remove my finger it got stuck, entwined in frizz. She squealed so loudly it alerted the teachers. I never ran my hand through a girl's hair again.

Caroline's kissing was taking me on an adventure over which I felt I had no control. It was energetic, seductive, bewitching – three things I felt unaccustomed to being and feeling and . . . oh, my goodness, I then started thinking of Marie and how this could have been Marie's kiss, Marie's mouth, Marie's taste. *You fool, you must not think of Marie. Not now, not with a real, live woman kissing you on her sofa and with you, yes you, kissing her back! Focus, Oliver, focus. Or should I put an end to this carry-on before it gets out of hand?* But Caroline was certainly focused on me, her hand fondling places that hadn't been fondled in ages, as if she were rummaging in an attic that needed airing. I couldn't help but nestle my lips between her ear and her hairline. She sighed. I tried touching her leg as she had touched mine. She kissed with gusto. I followed suit then found her breasts. Glorious. Yes, OK, I couldn't deny it: it was glorious. She found my belly and soon my T-shirt was off, and her dress. How had we come this far without having showered?

I closed my eyes and let her find the fluff between my folds, her hand warm, her breath sweet. It was all going so fast and yet, and yet . . . I told myself to run with it. That I was now fully ticking two resolution boxes: getting a life and going out of my comfort zone. Caroline let me know what she liked and what she didn't, offering an intermittent running commentary that was unsettling, but I wanted to please. My foot knocked the book off the coffee table, which made her giggle and throw two cushions on to the floor. I resisted the urge to pick them up as she pressed her lovely body on to me. How long it lasted I couldn't be sure but eventually we reappeared in the present, cheeks rouged, out of breath again.

'Thirsty?' she said, bouncing up and disappearing into the kitchen, unconcerned that her bikini and dress were scattered around the sofa. I wanted to gather them up and fold them. Instead, I put on my shorts and picked up the photographic book, fixed a bent page and put it back on the shelf under the coffee table. I felt flustered but exhilarated. Caroline returned with two glasses of water. 'Don't worry about tidying up. I prefer a bit of mess. Neatness makes me nervous. I tidied up earlier just in case you came in, as I wanted to make a good impression.' She laughed. 'Don't expect this all the time.'

Caroline snuggled into me, all flesh and goosebumps, and rubbed my belly. I felt another burst of spontaneity come over me, or was it Caroline's? What was going on? Swimming and sex in the same day? Caroline was proving to be a wondrously unexpected addition to my life. Then my phone sang from the beach bag crumpled on the rug.

'Don't get it,' Caroline said, so forcefully I thought she might slap my thigh.

'It might be work,' I explained, reaching for it.

But it wasn't. It was a text from Andy. *We're pregnant!*

'Wow,' I muttered.

'Pardon?'

'Andy's having a baby.'

'Oh, how wonderful.'

Well done, I replied, *I knew it would happen.*

'They've been trying for a while.'

Caroline sighed. 'I'd love a baby.' Then, with renewed energy, 'I think we should celebrate. Come on, let's go again.'

'Yes, let's celebrate,' I agreed, not being able to believe my luck. Andy should get pregnant more often.

She nibbled my ear. Then my shorts were flung off for a second time and left dangling on the table light like an upcycled lampshade.

'I love celebrations,' she whispered, or was it a coo? I couldn't tell. I didn't really care.

It wasn't until I was in the kitchen helping prepare dinner – more spontaneity! How extraordinary to find myself, unplanned, in another woman's kitchen, chopping tomatoes! – that I suddenly thought of Marie again. I didn't intend to think of her then but she popped into my mind as if she'd suddenly got jealous of Caroline and changed her mind about giving me her blessing. Or maybe she was telling me to slow down; I'd done enough for one day. Whatever it was, I couldn't believe how disconcerting it was to have the ghost of someone you loved in the room with someone with whom you've just made love to. It was as off-putting as having sex in the same room as someone's pet. That happened to me once with Claire, until I told her that under no circumstances could I have her Jack Russell staring at me from its bed by her bed. She took it as me saying, 'It's me or the dog,' when I wasn't. Although it may as well have been, given what happened with the relationship. The dog won.

I tried to focus on the salad but felt discombobulated and distracted. Was it possible to fully engage with a living woman when your love for a deceased woman continued to feel real? It was as if, in Caroline's kitchen, I suddenly, unexpectedly, had an existential crisis and I had no one to talk about it with – least of all the two women at its heart. I pushed on through dinner but had lost my verve or nerve or something and was keen to go when it finished. Caroline had other ideas.

'Stay,' she said.

'Thank you, but . . .'

'I mean it, stay the night.'

I couldn't tell her my dead paramour was giving me grief, that I felt the tug of a tide pushing and pulling me between my past desires and the future, never fully out of one and into the other. What's more, I had no spare clothes, no toothbrush or cologne.

'I can't,' I said, wishing ironically that I had a dog to feed. Instead, I blamed work. It was an easy out and I felt guilty for lying, but I had pushed the boundaries of spontaneity as much as I could for one day.

She nodded but I detected a hint of dejection.

'I had a great day and a great evening,' I said, to make her feel better. I leaned over and kissed her on the lips, a soft, lengthy kiss to make her realise I meant it. And I did mean it. I think I'd just overstayed. Caroline had yet to understand that there were only so many new things I could do in a day – in the past, it had barely even been one! I knew it may prove detrimental to the relationship if I tried explaining this to her, so I didn't. It was much better to end on a good note than have disaster strike when all you were doing was trying to please. Plus, I knew full well the effects of having too much of a good thing, particularly where Mars bars were concerned.

In bed later that night, I couldn't sleep. So much had happened in such a short space of time. Andy would be jumping around, slapping me on the back for the kiss and all the rest, but its unexpectedness had thrown me off guard, as had the ease with which I succumbed to it. Yet I couldn't deny that I felt something. It was pleasurable and it ticked a resolution. However, as stupid as it sounded, I felt as if I had gone behind Marie's back, that I had cheated on her. If I was being honest, what I really wanted was for the tryst to have been with Marie. When Caroline kissed me and we untidied her living room, I did, for a second, imagine it had been. Oh, the gut-wrenching reality of what it really was. How conflicted I felt. I wiped my mouth to rid it of any remnants. It made no difference. Perhaps I should be banned from swimming out of my depth ever again. On top of all that, my skin still burned from the heat of the day and I couldn't get thoughts of Andy and Lucy's announcement out of my head. They were having a baby! I hadn't realised it at the time, but the excitement I had felt for them was overshadowed by envy at their happy family life. A life I didn't have.

Embalmers

A new week began and I pushed aside my feelings to focus on work. I was back being undercover, meeting two embalmer candidates I had high hopes for. It was a buoyancy also fuelled by the knowledge that my time as sole embalmer was coming to an end. That I could turn forty and rule out the fumes of formaldehyde as one of my signature scents.

But applicant number one, James 'Jimmy' Miller, was fifteen minutes late, which gave him a black mark straight away, and I felt like saying, 'Decomposition will wait for no one.' But I didn't. Instead I ushered him into my office and shut the door. He sauntered in and sat in the chair as if he owned it, with his chin jutting out, his knees spread and his elbows resting on the chair arms with the confidence of a car salesman. I had to remind myself he had an impressive curriculum vitae, having worked in the industry for more than twenty years, and I was keen to hear how he answered my questions. I started off with the usual, such as 'What qualities do you think you bring to the job?' to which he replied, 'Steady hands and a fascination for body parts.' I didn't like to ask, 'Any body part in particular?' as I knew of a mortician whose obsession with ears – making plaster casts of them in the name of art – cost him his job. Instead, I gave a tick to answer one and put a question mark over the second. It was his choice of words more than anything else. Then I threw in some curly ones.

'How's your stomach?' I said.

He looked down at his belly, which was tucked in quite nicely behind his shirt. He had a slim waistline from what I could see, with little bulge, which I tried not to get jealous about.

'I mean, do you have a strong one?' I continued. He didn't get my double entendre straight away, which was another black mark, but at least he lightened up eventually.

'Oh, I get it,' he said, nodding. 'Nice one. Yeah, I've got a strong stomach. Stronger than anyone I know, to be honest. And I work out. I've pretty much got a six-pack. I can handle anything, don't you worry.'

That's when he pointed a finger at me. Well, it was a finger and thumb gesture, as if mimicking a gun. He meant it in a good way, I'm sure, but with me it had the opposite effect. It was like he'd jabbed me in the chest. Or shot me, if it really had been a gun. Then he started telling me about his expertise in 'fixing' unusual cases, rattling off anatomical Latin names, biochemistry waffle and surgical techniques as if I knew nothing about embalming and he thought it would impress. His *pièce de résistance* was comparing his work to one of the city's top plastic surgeons and telling me how adept he was at turning the ghoulish into palatable viewing.

That did it for me. James 'Jimmy' Miller got one big cross. I escorted him out courteously and promised to get back to him within a few days – long enough to make him think I had spent some time deliberating, agonising even, over whether he was a suitable candidate.

By contrast, Cora Mulligan's multifaceted bodily adornments belied her endearingly sweet and humble nature. I counted six studs forming a scythe on her left ear and something that resembled a charcoal nail poking out from her right lobe. She had short peroxide-blonde hair with black roots and wore a smart black-and-white patterned shirt which on second glance I realised featured tiny white skulls, and not flowers, as I had at first thought. A vine-like tattoo crept up the side of her neck and a skull was stamped on the inside of one wrist, which I only noticed because of her prolific hand gestures. As distracting as the details of her etchings and the shine of the metal was, she came highly regarded from a funeral home up north, having, they said, a 'dignified approach to the work and extensive creative flair'. I just hoped her creativity didn't extend to recreating the make-up she currently wore. Purple eyeshadow, black winged eyeliner that dripped vertically under her eyes and blood-red lipstick of the Gothic variety suited few, especially not the elderly.

Her liberal attire aside, I was impressed by how she shook my hand with gusto and bounced into my office paying compliments where they weren't even necessary, and was keen to ask me questions as much as I was her.

'I like to think of myself as a caretaker of the dead,' she said in response to the same set of questions I'd asked Mr Miller. 'I try to care for them as if they were still alive. I also like caring for those who are left behind. We can't take away the sadness but I like to think we can help ease the pain.'

Good answer.

And when I asked about her stomach, she merely chuckled and said how it was currently full up with a smoothie. I laughed and was delighted that not only could we spend a few minutes debating the merits or otherwise of 'green' smoothies but that her preference, like mine, was for a good old-fashioned milkshake.

I was keen to give her the job.

'Really?' she said.

I must have said it out loud. My second impulsive decision of the month! The Marie effect was proving to be pleasantly long-lasting.

'Well, why not?' I said. 'I'm impressed.'

'Thank you.'

'If you're keen, we'll do a three-month trial period,' I said. 'Why don't you have twenty-four hours to think about it and come back to me if you have any further questions? I would like to reiterate that I am keen to fill the position as soon as possible.'

She looked as pleased as I was with the whole idea, which I took as a very positive sign that my embalming days were numbered. I shook her skull-embellished hand and walked her to reception. It was unfortunate timing that Mum walked in at the same time and that I had omitted – hadn't thought it necessary – to tell Cora that the other half of Clock & Son was unaware I was hiring.

Mum's eyes widened, her eyebrows rose – a sure sign the tattoos had shocked. I hoped that was as far as her reaction would go but no, she also decided to speak.

'Hello, dear. I hope Oliver has been looking after you well.'

It all went downhill from there.

'Cora, meet my mother, Doreen Clock,' I said. I couldn't not introduce them, after all.

'Oh, you're a Clock?' Cora laughed. 'I'm here for the embalmer job.'

She turned to me as she said, 'The embalmer job, dear?' then visibly squirmed, as if her knickers had ridden up too high when she saw the decoration on Cora's outstretched hand.

'Yes, it must be tough running a funeral home without one,' Cora said.

'Oliver is doing a fine job, I must say.' And with that, Mum shut the conversation down.

I let out a nervy laugh and led Cora to the door. When she had gone, Mum didn't hold back.

'So, Oliver, you seem to be on a trajectory of subterfuge. Going behind my back yet again.'

'Well . . .'

'I thought we had agreed that you would do the embalmings to save money.'

'I . . .'

'And even if we were to hire an embalmer, we're not getting someone with tattoos. Did you see the state of her? Dreadful, Oliver, dreadful.'

'It's no big deal, Mum. Tattoos and piercings are de rigueur, as you like to say.'

'I don't care. So were mullets in your day and I didn't let you have one. Please don't tell me you've hired her.'

I said nothing but looked down at my tie to discover a crusty egg-yolk stain I hadn't realised was there.

'Oh, Oliver!'

Then, in less than the time it had taken me to do the two interviews, Cora was unhired – Mum calling her before I had the chance to let her down gently – and Mum was admiring the CV of James 'Jimmy' Miller, whom she thought 'infinitely more respectable'.

'He's not so young, for starters, and if he doesn't have any tattoos or other nonsense, like you say, then if we have to hire someone, I *might* acquiesce to trialling him,' she said.

I looked out the window behind her. Blurred legs fanned past. A constant throng of pedestrians, many of whom were, according to Jean's survey, unaware we even existed. Mum's interference made me feel as invisible as Clock & Son's presence seemed to be. Why bother trying to make a decision when it was shot down? Mum may have thought she was being collaborative but the way she overrode me was, quite frankly, belittling. Yet I was desperate for another embalmer and for Mum to even use the word 'acquiesce' in a sentence meant I would have to compromise to get one.

'Yes, Mum, we need an embalmer.'

She pointed a finger at me. 'A trial is all I'm agreeing to. One month.'

'Yes, Mum.'

Half an hour later I watched Mum walk to her car from my office window. She twirled the car keys, like I sometimes did when I felt good about the world. The crystal key ring caught the light, bounced lightning streaks across the cars. She spotted me and waved. I smiled and waved back but wished she hadn't turned up today, taking over and undermining my decisions. But really, what was she doing still working? Shouldn't she be spending her time lunching with friends, doing aquacise for her arthritis or volunteering at a charity? She got into her car and accelerated jerkily in reverse, braked suddenly then drove slowly – very slowly – out of the car park. She couldn't have been going more than fifteen kilometres an hour. She took up the whole entrance and kept another car waiting. She should have caught the bus. I wondered if I should go and help but I didn't want her telling me off. *I'll buy her a travel card instead.* She couldn't argue with a present. *I'll throw in some flowers, too.* She liked having flowers in her house. The truth was, I admired her resilience and drive but resented her constant involvement. It niggled like a pinched nerve.

Later that evening, Andy called as I was ironing my underwear, celebrating Mum's acquiescence to getting an embalmer.

'Hey, mate, have I caught you at a bad time?'

'Not at all,' I said, putting the phone on speaker and continuing to de-crease a crotch.

'Good, good. Look, I know it's last minute but I was wondering what you were doing Saturday week? We're having a gathering to celebrate.'

'More news? I can't keep up.'

'No news. Just a celebration of life and the baby,' Andy said. 'It's an excuse to have a party, really.'

Unless you were otherwise engaged and couldn't change the date, you never turned down one of Andy and Lucy's parties. They knew how to socialise with generosity of spirit, food and music. 'Obviously, Caroline, too,' he added.

'Obviously.'

'Excellent,' Andy said. 'Any time from seven thirty.'

Bath Time

After my last rendezvous with Caroline, it became apparent that our relationship – or whatever you wanted to call it – was turning into an extended practice run for me getting a life and out of my comfort zone. She wanted to keep seeing me and, I'll be honest, I didn't *not* want to see her. Yet I wrestled constantly with the Marie dilemma. I kept trying to tell her – Marie – that I didn't feel the same way about Caroline as I did her. I had to compartmentalise the two. At home I had Marie and her diary, and outside of home I met with Caroline. But I couldn't ignore the slow, creeping-up feelings of guilt that I was in some way cheating on Marie. The rational part of me knew that, physically, I wasn't, but the irrational, emotional side felt that I was.

Still, Caroline and I went on a few more dates – two dinners and one movie. Neither quite so remarkable as going to the beach or salsa dancing (I used my left foot as an excuse for getting out of the next class – a pretend injury, not a metaphor for my dancing ineptitude). Two dinner dates and a movie warmed my heart even more, if I'm honest. I didn't need adrenaline to appreciate a pleasant encounter with a gregarious woman. What's more, she was proving a welcome distraction from all that was happening in the business – both the good and the bad. I didn't want to burden her with my business worries or have to explain the candles just yet until we'd had some success, nor did I care to bring up Marie so Caroline knew the back story. I was happy for conversation to revolve around anything other than death and the other woman in my life. But then, over dinner, she started pressing me about 'us'.

'So, Oliver, I was wondering,' she began, toying coyly with the spaghetti on her fork, 'do you think that you and I . . .?'

'You and I?' I repeated. As she hadn't finished the sentence, I was unsure exactly where she was going. I shoved a piece of steak into my mouth.

'Yes, you know, us. Are we officially a couple? I was just wondering because I like to know where I stand and don't like it being all airy-fairy.'

Thankfully, the steak mouthful I had cut was larger than ideal and required extra chewing so I could process what she had said and work out how to answer. I realised I had been perfectly happy with 'airy-fairy', taking each date as it came without dwelling on the future. Going out with Caroline had been like an experiment for me, on so many levels. Of course, it was advantageous that I was enjoying her company but I hadn't entertained the thought of us as an 'us', joined as one like a comedy duo unable to perform without the other. But it didn't help that we were more like a trio, the third party unbeknownst to Caroline. I finally swallowed, except the meat took a while to go down; Caroline's commitment question seemed to have given me indigestion.

'Are you alright?' she asked.

'Yes, I'll be fine,' I said, wincing with chest pain.

'Have some water,' she said, pushing a water glass towards me.

'Thanks,' I muttered, and took some sips, appreciating the delay in having to reply.

Then Caroline started up again. 'You see, the older I get, the surer I am about what I want and have no desire to waste time drifting aimlessly if there is no future. You must feel the same?'

I nodded.

'Andy and Lucy's baby news hasn't helped either.' She sighed.

I nodded again, remembering how Andy and Lucy's engagement announcement had made me feel. She looked at me and waited.

'So?' she said.

I really wanted to answer in the way she wanted me to in order to be agreeable and make her happy but, considering that meant committing fiercely to an 'us' in a future I hadn't previously contemplated, I couldn't do it. And yet, I still wanted to see her again . . .

'Well,' I said, 'I don't want us to break up so does that mean we are a thing?' I said it light-heartedly, hoping it would cover up the fact I was unable to bring myself to say 'couple' or 'official' either separately or together in the same sentence. She looked a bit taken aback so I added, 'I want to keep seeing you, Caroline, and if you do me, then . . . yes . . . I guess . . .'

She smiled and nodded and I squeezed her hand across the table, pleased she seemed happy with my committal of sorts. Thank goodness the waiter appeared then so the conversation moved to whether we wanted desserts or cheese and wasn't brought up again.

At the end of the night, I waited with her for a taxi and watched her drive off. She wound down the window, blew me a kiss and waved her right arm furiously. I began to panic, and started running after her.

'Put your arm in!' I shouted, waving my arm as well. But she paid no attention. 'Your arm, Caroline, your arm, get it in!'

The car got smaller and smaller as I became more and more out of breath. I stopped running, pulled out my phone and wrote her a text.

Please stop waving at me. It's very nice of you but it's also illegal to extend a limb from the window of a moving vehicle.

I pushed send. Phew. At least now she knew.

I was simultaneously looking forward to and dreading Jimmy Miller's start. I wanted a new embalmer, of course, just not him. It didn't help that he arrived late, again. Only by ten minutes but, still, I wished I hadn't noticed his tardiness, as I wanted him to work out. I tried to put aside my doubts about the suitability of his fit with us and his penchant for lax timekeeping. I'm sure Marie wouldn't have been impressed either and would have preferred Cora. Mum, however, was enamoured.

'I like the shine of his shoes,' she said when we'd left him to become familiar with our embalming room.

'Literally or figuratively, Mum?'

'Both, dear. He makes your shoes look quite dull.'

I looked down at my shoes. I know I shouldn't have. I should have walked away and not let her dig get to me. I didn't like to think that I or my shoes needed a polish, so I went to the jelly bean jar. Except Mum was on a roll and told me off as she placed a fresh bunch of pink lilies in Grandmother's crystal vase by the frosted window. She said I was eating more than the customers, which was probably true, but then, as I told her, that wasn't difficult, as we'd not had that many. The day had barely started and already I was keen for it to end. I went to my office and shut the door. Inspired by my bookshelf at home, I decided to rearrange my work books in a more pleasing manner. I couldn't extend to colour-coordination, as most books on the funeral industry, grieving and counselling tended to be rather dour in colour, so I settled for ordering them by height.

That night, I decided to follow Andy's orders and look after number one. I would soak in a hot bath and stay there as long as I wanted. As soon as I got home I changed into my dressing gown, leaving my clothes draped on a chair in the bedroom. I could put them away later, I thought, trying to emulate a carefree mindset. I lit Marie, took her into the bathroom and ran a bath. Remembering I had some fragrant additions in the vanity, I got out a packet of muscle-soak bath salts scented with eucalyptus and peppermint oils, which I'm sure Edie would have approved of, and a large yellow bath bomb decorated with purple cornflowers designed to 'wash my cares away and brighten my mood'. I picked up the salt packet and dumped the whole lot in. Next went the bath bomb. Instantly the water went yellow and fizzed like sherbet. Purple cornflower petals swirled like tea leaves. Steam aromatic with an oily fragrance curled up from the bath. What was I getting myself into? Next: easy-listening music. A relaxing ambience was not complete without a few synthesised underwater instrumentals or Spanish guitar riffs. I set them to play on my phone with the volume on medium, starting with the healing sound of dolphins and waves, the perfect music with which to reach a state of mindfulness, or so I'd heard. Better than the deathly silence that envelops you when lying on the embalming table. When the bath was three-quarters full – a giant glass of effervescent multivitamins – I turned off the tap. I felt quite pleased with myself at this point. It was all going swimmingly. The stage was set for my relaxation.

Until the doorbell rang. I didn't want to answer the door. I could pretend I wasn't home. It rang again. And again. It was too hard to ignore. I tiptoed to the door and peered into the peephole. A magnified eye looked back. A voice called my name. I looked into the peephole again. Caroline looked like a mushroom. Or a magnified sperm.

I opened the door.

'Hi, Caroline.' I cursed myself for sounding so pleased to see her.

'Look at you in your robe.' She said it like I was a handbag dog in a tartan coat, then rubbed my arm as if the terry towelling had aphrodisiac properties. 'Am I interrupting anything?' She strained to see into the living room.

'No, not at all.'

'Oh, good, can I come in?'

'I was about to have a bath.' I felt a sudden rising panic. Help! Marie was flickering in the bathroom and the diary . . . where was the diary?

'Oh, Oliver . . .' She sighed a decadent, indulgent sigh, as if in anticipation of more sighs yet to come.

That's when I should have suggested we catch up at a later time. I really wanted to try and focus on my 'me time' alone, with number one not a number two as well, and I certainly didn't want her encroaching on Marie's terrain. But I didn't. I was too busy panicking about Marie when she invited herself in. Except the last thing I expected was for Caroline to want to join me in the bath. I wasn't anticipating so much enthusiasm. As soon as she'd walked in and shut the door, she started disrobing, unbuttoning her shirt and whipping off her belt with such vigour I didn't feel I could stop her. And all the while, she was heading to the bathroom with me trailing behind, as if I really were a stupid dog in a tartan dog coat, and wishing I could have downed some of Mum's blood pressure pills. *Sorry, Marie, I'm really sorry about all this*, I repeated over and over, and made a quick detour to my bedroom to hide the diary in my sock drawer, carefully laying it over my selection of navy socks. I met Caroline back in the bathroom, hoping I had also successfully hidden my feelings of anxiety, and then blew out the candle.

'Oh, I thought that smelt quite nice,' Caroline said.

'It can be a bit overwhelming,' I muttered, and shoved the candle in the vanity cupboard.

'Shame it looks like someone's peed in the bathwater,' she added.

'It's a bath bomb.'

'I know, silly.' She laughed then angled her head to listen to the music, as if I had high-tech speakers set in the ceiling piping music of my choice to select rooms of the house.

'Dolphins,' I said.

The downward trail of her mouth suggested I fast-forward to the next track. I didn't hesitate, as I liked to please. Then she was fully naked and submerged in lemon liquid, two cornflowers stuck to a nipple.

'Come on,' she said, tapping a hand on top of the water, as if she were patting the seat next to her.

There seemed no turning back and . . . well . . . I had always wondered if my bath was big enough for two. And, at least, in the bath,

Marie's diary was safe from discovery. I took off the dressing gown and folded it neatly next to my clothes, stepped over haphazardly thrown underwear and sized up my spot. Thankfully, Caroline hugged her knees to her chest so I could ease in, then she unravelled and we entwined legs to maximise space. It was tight, granted, but we fitted.

'This is a nice surprise,' she said. 'I didn't mean to turn up unannounced but I was missing you. Just because we've both been busy doesn't mean we should neglect each other, does it?' I wasn't quick enough to come up with an answer but then she didn't seem to want one, as she started up again. 'I saw Lucy tonight and felt the baby.' She sighed. 'I didn't feel anything but I knew it was there, floating in amniotic fluid.'

Baby talk already! I looked down and splashed water on my face to cover a look of more panic I didn't think I could hide.

'She looked so happy . . .' More sighing. 'It was probably kicking away. Sucking its thumb.'

I smiled. Peeled cornflowers off my cheeks. Was she teetering around the edges of a discussion about us? About her babies? *Our* babies? I had to say something before she pressed me to comment.

'I didn't think it had a thumb yet?' It was all I could think of.

'Maybe not, but it's nice to imagine.'

Quick, change the subject. 'How was work?'

'The usual. Except for a client who wants to dress two women as boobs to advertise his bras. I think he has a problem, to be honest. All he talks about is breasts.'

'I guess you would if you were selling women's underwear,' I said, and laughed stupidly.

I was just relieved the conversation was now on more comfortable territory. I was hardly relaxed – my cares were still floating in the bathwater and the energetic guitar strumming coming from my phone far from meditative – but with Caroline so happily ensconced I started to wonder whether I should have dimmed the lights and lit a different candle, added a slug of bubble bath for a froth of discretion. As it was, the downlights were highlighting with glaring unsubtlety every fold and freckle on our bodies, the bruise on Caroline's thigh and the paunch I was unable to fully shake, not dissimilar to a half-deflated balloon. I sucked it in.

'He's fixated,' Caroline continued. 'He once told me how he'd pulled a prank at the tennis club he belongs to. Took down the flag they had flying and replaced it with a bra. Can you believe it? He raised a bra on a flagpole.' She shook her head.

'That's daring,' I said. 'And kind of funny.'

'The tennis club manager didn't think so.'

'No, of course not.' I didn't want her to think I didn't agree with her. I was now distracted by the soap, the shrunken slab sitting on a dish next to me. What to do? If I offered it to her first, would she think I thought she was in need of a clean? But then, I didn't want her wondering whether I was going to wash. What was bath-time etiquette for a virgin bath-sharing couple?

The water was now more tepid than hot and, with my head next to the tap, I couldn't risk a scalded scalp by adding more hot water. I grabbed the soap and rubbed it over my body, then attempted a casual underwater soap-pass to Caroline, as if I didn't care whether she took it or not. Her eyelids fluttered. She reached for the soap. A tingle tickled my loins. She lathered herself with gusto, which would have been the perfect prelude to segueing to the bedroom, had she not leaned forward for a kiss. Her bottom, slimy with soapy residue, slid backwards. She nose-dived my belly and I clonked the back of my head on the tap, which made me yell just as Caroline reappeared, spurting bathwater in my face. Some I swallowed, some slapped my forehead and dripped into my eyes. She stared at me. I wasn't sure if it was a look of shock, disappointment or regret.

'Baths are renowned for being unreliable.' I blurted out a laugh to lighten the mood.

'I'm sorry,' she said, wiping spray off my face.

'Time to get out?'

She nodded.

'Let me go first so I can get you a towel.'

I found her a clean one in the cupboard under the bathroom cabinet and gave it to her as if it were a coat I was helping her to put on. But I was still unsure of the protocol of unexpected bathing. As I dried between each toe, I tried to gauge if the kiss was still on offer. If I forgot about Marie, I decided, I should be able to fully embrace the moment. But it was hard to tell Caroline's thoughts, as she appeared more focused on drying herself – under her breasts, around her scapulas, behind her knees and around her hairline. As much as I yearned to be the one to let my hair down and instigate another smooch, I didn't dare. What if she'd lost interest and turned me down? What if the bath face-plant had changed her mind about bathtime romance with me? Or, in fact, any romance with me at all. It wasn't worth the risk. We finished drying in silence. Then, after I'd wrapped the towel around my waist, deciding whether to put the dressing gown back on or to get dressed properly, the towel was whipped off and Caroline had me pressed up against the basin, a tap yet again poking me from behind. I forgot about the tap. And the bright lights. And the water dribbling down my back. And Marie's candle in the cupboard. Ah, Caroline . . . you've answered my question.

She rested her head on my shoulder. I stroked her hair. I had managed to divert Caroline from the bedroom to the living room, in an effort to separate Marie and her. I couldn't deny that in the throes of passion my worries dissipated, but now I had to try really hard to focus on compartmentalising them.

'That was nice,' she whispered, twiddling one of my few chest hairs.

'Yes,' I replied.

'So now that you've seen me again, do you want to keep seeing me?' she asked with a cheeky smile that I sensed belied a certain earnestness. Here she was, pressing me again about my intentions. Why couldn't we go on as we had been, having a bit of fun without the pressure of future commitment or the dissection of what it all meant? When I left it a second too long to respond, she added, 'I'm not trying to scare you, Oliver. I know what I want but I'm still unclear about you.'

'Of course I want to see you again,' I said.

'And again and again and again?' she asked.

I laughed and kissed the top of her head but left her last sentence dangling in the air as if pegged on a washing line waiting to be taken down, and changed the subject.

'Have you eaten?' I said. 'Would you like to stay for some home-made frittata and reality television?' I couldn't not ask her. She was already in my flat and I owed her one, as it was.

A flash of vexation passed across her face – presumably because I hadn't fully engaged with her question – but she let it pass. 'Of course I would,' she said, with a squeeze of my arm and a peck on my pec – or what would be my pec if I went to the gym.

I squeezed and kissed her back and wondered what she'd smell like if she were a candle. Hairspray, coconut oil, lemon verbena. Cat.

With Caroline buying me time to think, I managed to shovel her cluckiness in a cupboard and focus on appreciating her company. We were sharing an evening at home, cooking dinner together, me whipping eggs and her chopping herbs, watching television snuggled on the sofa, an arm gently resting across her shoulders and her hand occasionally slapping my thigh in merry response to the TV programme. How lovely, the joys of partnership. Yet how sickening the guilty feeling of having cheated.

The Samples

A few days later, the candles samples were ready. This was very good news. Edie was proving reliable, efficient and, as it turned out, punctual. She was already at the café in which we had decided to meet – so as to avoid an unnecessary encounter with Mum – when I arrived eight minutes early. She apologised for being early and I apologised for making her wait, which made us both chuckle, as the clock was still to land on our agreed time. The meeting was off to a good start.

'They're all here,' she said, grinning and pointing to a large bag by her feet. 'Shall we order first?'

'In normal circumstances I would have said yes but, as this is no ordinary circumstance and I can't wait to smell them, let's save lunch for after,' I said.

She smiled and, for the first time, I appreciated the straightness of her teeth. In fact, everything about her smile was really rather appealing. Her lipstick was one of the best reds I'd seen in a long time and I wondered whether we should add it to our collection of body-viewing lipsticks and if I could ask Edie for its name. What a thought, me talking lipstick brands with Edie!

She reached into the bag and placed each candle gently on the table. 'Which one shall we start with? I've made two for pretend people – a gardener and a barbecue-lover – and three for Jean.'

'You choose.'

'OK. Close your eyes.'

I closed my eyes. There was a clink of a lid lifting, then a diffusion of sweetness: scents of jasmine, gardenia, freesia. Nearly Marie, but not quite. A garden she may have grown and flowers she may have tended. A botanical wonderland.

'The gardener?' I suggested. She nodded. 'I like it.'

'Next one,' she said.

A smoky, spiced tang twitched my nostril hairs and teased my taste buds. It took me to the butcher's not far from the parlour. Their wild-boar sausages with chipotle chilli. My mouth salivated. I thought about buying some on my way home from work.

'This better not be Jean.' I laughed.

'Poor her, if it is,' she said. We laughed some more and I sniffed again.

'I tell you what, it's making me hungry.'

'That's good, isn't it?' she said.

'Well, yes, but isn't it meant to be a memory of a person, not a sausage?'

'I thought I should show my versatility. It's the sort of candle I'd make for my nephew if he let me. Josh likes to think he's a barbecue-sausage connoisseur. Except the idea of the candles "creeps him out" – his words – so I've let him off the hook. He's only eleven.'

'He might take to the idea when he's older.'

'True, and it is tricky making a candle of someone who can smell themselves. For Jean, I made three, as I wanted to get her right. I mean, when you smell yourself, it needs to be spot on.'

'But does anyone really know what they smell like, except when it's bad?' I thought about festering breath, fusty feet, the pong of sweaty skin and unwashed clothes.

Edie laughed. 'I guess not, but we all hope we smell nice, don't we? We all have "good" smells, the natural, unperfumed scents we carry around with us every day. The ones we're unaware of that make an impression,' she said. 'You know, there's a woman who's made her career as an olfactory scientist, a guru of smell. Sissel Tolaas studies smells and recreates them. She has seven thousand smells bottled in a lab in Berlin. She's been making cityscapes, capturing the scents of cities.'

'Sounds a bit bonkers.'

'Do you think people will think we're bonkers doing this?' she said. 'I mean, you didn't like the idea to begin with.'

'Yes, but you sold me with Marie. You're not having doubts, are you?' Edie pulling out would be the final nail in the coffin.

'No, but it means we really have to get the samples right and, even more so, Jean. If Jean likes it, she'll be the drawcard.'

The thought of customers sniffing Jean at her desk gave me a turn. Heaven forbid. I couldn't have Clock & Son turning into a freak show. Worse, a jaded, old-fashioned freak show, as we'd still not agreed on the refurbishments.

Edie touched my hand. There it was again, the frisson, the caring touch of a quietly confident woman. 'I know what you're thinking,' she said, as if she were also telepathic. 'But don't worry, Jean doesn't have to be on sniffer parade. I just thought that if she liked it, she could vouch for its authenticity. Remember, I'm doing this for the same reason you're doing your job. To help people during the tough times. To turn pain into something positive. To offer precious moments with loved ones in a way no one has done before. I may dispense drugs for a living, but there are plenty of other ways to treat malaise.'

Edie's words were touching and insightful, her skin soft and luminous like a full moon.

I nodded. 'I couldn't have put it better myself.'

'So are you ready for Jean?'

She wafted each candle twice under my nose, paused and did it again. My nose twitched, my head went fuzzy. 'Can you do it again?'

'I used base notes of vanilla and cocoa with top notes of honey and amaretto. A little bit of sweetness, but not too much. I didn't want it to be overpowering. It's important to get the balance right.'

I moved my nose over the three candles again and took a moment to think. 'Number three,' I said. 'I think number three is Jean at her best.' Jean's morning pastry treat. Her home-made almond slice. The buttery smell of her jumpers after a weekend of baking.

'Great,' Edie said. 'Let's hope Jean thinks so, too.' She held up two crossed fingers.

'I know,' I said. 'Why don't you come by after work and we'll find out?'

Jean was refilling the tea bag tin and I was counting Post-it notes for something to do when Edie arrived. The first thing she did was compliment Jean on her brooch – a wooden cat with a painted face – and then adjusted it for her, as it was sitting on an angle. Edie may well have liked it, but what brilliant timing and tact. If you'd asked me, I wouldn't have thought Edie was a brooch-wearing woman, more of a necklace-wearer. Like the cake-slice pendant necklace she had on that sat just below her neck, where the clavicles met her sternum. She pulled out a business card of her sister's vintage clothing shop and told Jean how she always stocked a selection of jewellery and brooches. 'You should visit,' Edie said. 'Tell her you know me. You never know, she might give you a discount.'

'That's very kind of you,' Jean replied, taking the card.

'Well, now, I've got your candle here,' Edie added, patting her bag.

'Goodness me,' Jean said. 'I know you were going to make a candle of me but now I'm not so sure about it. I don't see how the idea will catch on. Isn't it detracting from our core business? I have all these unanswered questions.'

I took Jean's hand. 'It's OK, Jean. Edie and I have discussed everything and we have a plan in place. Why don't you smell your candle first, then we can tell you about it?'

'I'm not sure whether I should be excited or repulsed.'

'We're aiming for excited,' Edie said. 'I know it may be hard to feel emotional and have memories prompted when you're smelling yourself, but feel free to give it a go.' She laughed.

'Well, that's an interesting concept, isn't it?' Jean agreed. 'I'll do my best.'

Edie took out the five candles she had made and lined them up, evenly spaced in a row on the reception desk. 'Three are you and two are pretend people, for sample purposes. You need to open your mind to the idea and close your eyes in order to smell.' Edie mimicked the ideal candle-smelling action, over-exaggerating the lifting of the lid, the breathing in, and sniffing enthusiastically. Then she picked up a candle and lifted its lid. 'Your turn. This is Oliver's favourite.'

Jean looked at me, then at Edie. 'Here we go.' She leaned over the jar and smelt, albeit less exuberantly than Edie. A scent trail of honeyed vanilla and cocoa beans snaked through the air like invisible mist and plucked at Jean's nose. She closed her eyes and inhaled again, thinking intently about the delicate pong of herself. 'Well,' she said, straightening up and twirling her glasses.

'What do you think?'

'Can I smell the others?'

One by one, the three of Jean and then the rest, Jean smelled and sniffed and nosed out the subtle variances in scent. It was like watching a drug sniffer dog moving between luggage on an airport carousel.

'I must say, they're all quite nice,' she said. 'But I think Oliver may be right. This one could well be me. May I take myself home?'

The thought of Jean taking herself home bottled as a scented candle was a bit nutty. Sweet Jean with an amaretto honey fragrance! But, hopefully, it was nutty in a good way. I phoned Andy that night, excited to be giving him a job.

'It's not a big one, but I'd love it if you could do it for us,' I said.

'I'm not photographing a dead person,' he said.

'Don't worry, it's nothing like that.'

'Or a coffin. Sorry, they creep me out, whether there's someone in them or not.'

'Andy, don't panic. It's candles.'

'Candles?'

So I told him all about them and how I had suggested to Edie that we get some professional photographs done. I waited for his response. It was as if I could hear his brain ticking over, which was disconcerting, as Andy was usually a quick thinker – even his mind had fast-twitch muscle fibres.

'Geez, I don't know what to say,' he said. 'Candles of the dead – don't they sound appealing?'

For someone with Andy's creativity, you'd think he would have a better imagination. 'Trust me, Andy. I wasn't sure at first either but when Edie made one of Marie . . .'

'Ah, Marie . . .' I could tell he was nodding, which offended, if I'm being honest. It was as if I wasn't still allowed to have feelings for her.

'Yes, Marie,' I said defiantly. 'It's her. She really is in the candle.'

'Do you know how that sounds?'

'I know, it's amazing! Look, don't you always like to say, "You won't know until you try"? Well, I want to try this, Andy, I really do. They might not be my ticket to early retirement but they will set us apart from everyone else. If we do it right, there is no reason why we can't turn a little profit and, more importantly, attract customers to Clock & Son and deflect them from the competition.'

'OK, then.' Andy let out a big sigh. I thought he would have been appreciative of getting some photography work, even if it was only going to be a half-day job.

The Misunderstanding

The day of Andy's party shone crisp and clean like a sun-dried business shirt and I decided to invite Caroline over beforehand for drinks and nibbles, even suggesting that we get ready together, which she took as a euphemism for sex, which I wasn't opposed to. I felt confident, having already had Caroline over and successfully compartmentalising her and Marie, that I could continue to do so even in my own flat, provided we avoided the bedroom. Even though I was on call and couldn't have any alcohol, I really wanted to let my hair down and enjoy Caroline's company. I had all the ingredients to make my favourite sparkling cranberry and lime, and gin and tonic for Caroline. When she arrived I cracked a joke about how we could practise our salsa moves at Andy's, show everyone what dancing was all about. I mixed the drinks and lit some newly bought vanilla-scented candles. In the living room, I lowered the blinds and spun her around half undressed and made her laugh. I loved it when she was happy and not tripping over moods or being bossy and demanding. Just simply happy. I kept going with the body twirls until we ended up on the sofa, then dismantling the cushions. It would have been easy to stay there for longer but we had a schedule to keep. 'Perhaps a shower?' I suggested, to keep the evening moving along. 'You go first. I'll get you a towel.'

Then it was my turn. I was so happy I sang in the shower and didn't mind that Caroline could hear the notes I didn't reach and my dud tone.

I'd just stepped out when I heard a shriek coming from the bedroom and thought for a second that she was adding the staccato to my alto when in fact she was genuinely crying out about something. Wrapping the towel around me, I ran in.

'Spider?' I said.

'No!' She shrieked again. My worst fear, which on a scale of one to ten had risen to an eleven – higher than my fear of being seen in public in unironed clothes – eventuated. Caroline held Marie's diary in one hand, opened on a well-thumbed page scuffed from my repeated readings. 'What's this?' she said, jabbing the page with a finger.

Oh, how I wished there had been a spider crawling along the bed. 'What are you doing?' I asked, when really I was thinking: *What are you doing in my bedroom and how did you find the diary?* Had I left it out on the bedside table by mistake or had Caroline found it in its new hiding place inside a drawer in the bedside table? *Oh, Marie, I'm so sorry.*

'Oliver?' she said.

'It's a friend's diary,' I said. 'Actually, do you mind?'

'What do you mean, a friend?' She moved her arm so I couldn't get it.

'You know, a friend.'

'Is she a lover?'

'What?' I was so taken aback by her question that I blushed, which had the unfortunate effect of making me look guilty.

'I thought so.'

'No, she isn't. Wasn't. You see—' I was about to explain but she interrupted.

'I've read it, Oliver. Don't lie.'

'I'm not lying.'

'Is she the reason you don't want to commit to me?'

'No,' I said, even though it hit a nerve. She flung the journal on the bed covers, scrambled off the bed and gathered her clothes off the floor. 'Caroline, please . . .'

I went back around to her side of the bed. I wanted to calm her down, rub her back and make her see sense.

'Don't touch me.'

'But there's nothing for you to worry about.'

'That's what they all say,' she said, pulling on her skirt.

'Who?'

'Every cheater.' She wriggled into her top.

'I'm not—' But I still couldn't get a word in.

'You think you can have your bit on the side while preying on other people's feelings?'

'What? No.'

'I'm not going to put up with it.' On went the shoes.

'You don't have to because it's not true,' I said. 'You see, she was my florist—'

'Oh, please. I don't want to hear it.' She grabbed her bag and pushed past me into the hallway. I followed. A trail of water accompanied us.

'Please, you must understand. She's no longer around . . .' I should have said 'dead' but, ever since Marie had died, I'd gone off that word. It's so brutal and final and not the sort of word you want to use in relation to someone you've only recently discovered you had been in love with and they you.

Caroline stopped, then turned to me. 'You mean . . .?'

'Yes.' I nodded. 'So now will you let me explain?'

She rummaged in her handbag for a cigarette and shoved it in her mouth.

'I thought you'd given up.'

'Yes, well, you're making me want one again,' she said, which didn't explain why she had a packet in her bag, but I let it ride, as I was more concerned about clearing up the misunderstanding.

'Let's go outside, then,' I suggested as she was about to light up.

She followed me out to the courtyard and leaned against the railing. I thought about sitting but didn't like the metaphorical implications of her standing over me, so I stood, too.

'Well, go on, you've got my attention for as long as this cigarette lasts.' She lit it and took a puff.

I kept the story simple, telling her how I first met Marie, how we worked together, how I had no idea of her feelings for me, about Henry and the diary. She remained silent throughout, resisting I'm sure the desire to interrupt, ask a question or give an opinion.

'At least that puts the diary in context,' she said when I finished. No apologies for her accusations, I noted, or for reading the diary in the first place. 'Why didn't you tell me this before?' she added.

'I tried, back in the bedroom.'

'I mean before-before. I've told you about my cheating ex-husband who I was madly in love with, about falling out with my brother, how I embarrassed myself at a work Christmas party, about guys I've dated and wished I hadn't. I've opened up to you about all sorts of things. Yet you've told me so little about yourself. So little that's really true.'

I scuffed leaves off the paving stones. She had a point. I hadn't opened up to her like she had to me. 'It wasn't intentional,' I said, and apologised again.

She took one last puff of her cigarette and stubbed it out in the nearest planter. For a few seconds we gazed at the moon, a thin sliver of curved silver like one of Jean's brooches.

'So do you think this is fate at work? Us standing outside looking at the stars, like we did the night we first met?' she said.

Where was she going with that?

I shrugged. 'I don't know, but are we friends again at least?'

'At least?' she said, turning to me. 'Oh my God, Oliver, you know how I feel. I want to be with you. Not just as friends but properly, as a couple. I want to know that you're committed to me, to us, to the future. Maybe to a family of our own, one day.' Her eyes started watering and I wished I had a freshly ironed handkerchief to give her. 'And I'm scared, Oliver. I'm scared of being alone.' She wiped her eyes with the back of a hand.

'Me, too,' I said, and I meant it. I didn't fancy a return to the loneliness of singledom either. The man I wanted to be – the one I had written about in my notebook of resolutions – was not one who was single and alone. He was not cooking meals for one, fantasising about going on solo holidays or talking to dead people as if they were his confidantes.

Yet if I were being even more truthful to myself, I didn't like the speed at which our relationship was progressing – or, more to the point, the pace Caroline was enforcing. I wanted to like Caroline and was trying really, really hard to make it work. Just like I'd imagined how wonderful it could have been if Marie and I had worked out. But it was all going so fast. The impulsiveness at which I had agreed to sell candles that smell like the dead and suggested our outdoor talk when I was still wrapped only in a towel was as much acceleration as I could handle.

And yet . . . and yet . . . Caroline wanted *me*. You couldn't help but be a little flattered by that, could you? She seemed so sure about us that maybe there was something in it. Perhaps I was wrong to doubt and avoid committal. Perhaps I should try and let Marie go and throw myself wholeheartedly into being an official couple with Caroline. For at that moment – despite her grip on my arm – I'd rather have been with Caroline, officially or unofficially. Ideally, not in my bedroom, with the diary, of course. At that moment, I wanted everything to be convivial between us, with no animosity. Whatever the future held, right then I wanted us to be like the complementary matching of cream cheese and smoked salmon, or perhaps a Riesling with a spicy Asian dish, or even imperial stout with dark chocolate truffles – an unusual pairing, you might think, but they really do work together.

I took Caroline's hand and squeezed it. She smiled and nodded. The truth was we were both feeling the same; we just had different ways of dealing with it.

'Let's not argue any more,' I said.

'I promise,' she agreed.

'So, shall we get ready to party?'

'Only if you change out of your towel.' She laughed.

The nursing home call-out was unfortunate timing – we'd only just finished getting ready! I had been so relieved that our dispute was over that I was keen to enjoy the party together. It didn't help that Caroline pouted when I told her I had to go. 'I'm on call. It's the nature of the job, I'm afraid,' I said, quickly changing into a suit.

'Have I told you your job sucks?' I'm sure she meant it in a more jovial way than it came out but I really could have done with some empathy right then. I didn't want to go as much as she didn't want me to, now that we'd made up. 'Go on, off to your little morgue. Don't worry about me.'

'Maybe we can catch up at the weekend?' I said, trying to ignore her petulance.

'I know,' she said, her eyes widening. 'Take me with you.'

'What?'

'Show me what you do. I'll stay out of your way. You won't even know I'm there. Oh, yes, that would be fun.'

'I can't do that, I'm sorry. There are privacy issues, for starters.'

I thought she'd have left it at that, but no, she didn't let up.

'I'll be quiet, I promise. Anyway, the person who's died won't care, will they?' She started laughing raucously and found it difficult to stop.

'Sorry,' I said again.

'Alright, Mr Humourless. But I'm being serious, you know. You can pretend I'm your helper, a trainee or something. No one will know.'

I looked at what she was wearing. There was so much cleavage it could very well wake the dead, and then everyone would know. Not that I told her that. I didn't mind her cleavage. It just wasn't appropriate in either a nursing home or a morgue, where it might lead to all sorts of inappropriate awakenings.

'I'm sorry, Caroline,' I said, squeezing her hand.

'Fine, I'll go to the party on my own.'

I opened my mouth to speak but the bedroom door slammed. It was a door-slamming-in-your-face moment like the ones you watch in television sitcoms that you think don't actually happen in real life. Well, it happened to me then and I was left swallowing a whoosh of air and a giant gulp of bewilderment.

I rushed after her but she had already left, leaving the front door wide open. I stood on the threshold, listening to the echo of my voice calling her name. Perhaps I was also hoping she would rush back full of apologies, telling me how sorry she was I had to work and how she couldn't wait to see me again. When it was clear that wasn't going to happen, I grabbed my car keys and headed to the call-out.

Spermatozoa

I slept in late and woke wondering if the events of the previous evening had really happened. Life seemed to be galloping ahead in the most unexpected and emotional of ways, over which I felt I had no control. I didn't like upsetting Caroline or her thinking badly of me. Then again, she needn't have been so petulant about the nature of my work, which she didn't seem to understand, as others did – Edie being a case in point. What's more, I was angry. How dare she read the diary in the first place! It wasn't hers to pick up and open on a whim. It was private property. *My* private property. Well, and also Marie's. I pulled it out from under my pillow, where I slept with it last night, kissed its cover and held it to my chest. What a disagreeable state of affairs. As I held the diary close, I swallowed an uncomfortable thought. If the diary could cost me my relationship with Caroline, would I somehow have to try and live without it? Could I actually do that? If I let go of Marie, could I then find true love with Caroline? A flutter of panic tickled my ribcage. *Oh, my goodness, Marie, is this what I have to do? Perhaps if I hide you out of sight – properly hide you this time so that neither I nor anyone else can easily see you or find you, then maybe I could give it go. It's not like I'm throwing you away nor dismissing what we have, is it? We could do a trial run. It could be an experimental resolution.*

Without bothering to get my notebook and write it down (it was an experiment, after all), I went in search of a suitable hiding place and decided upon the jumper drawer in the wardrobe at the bottom of all my drawers. As it was not yet winter, I would have no need to delve into it for a few months and, if anyone bothered to open that particular drawer, it would only serve to highlight how paranoid and nosey they were. In between five neatly folded jumpers and my favourite button-up forest-green cardigan, I carefully placed the diary. There. Done. It was completely covered, completely hidden in wool. Goodbye, Marie.

I spent the rest of the morning telling myself that no matter how discomfiting and potentially rash-inducing trying to live without Marie might be, I should be proud of myself for having taken action.

Go, Oliver.

When I realised that all there was for lunch was the same as what I'd had for breakfast, I got dressed and headed out the door to buy some provisions. When I returned there was a gift on my doorstep, soon followed by a text from Caroline.

Sorry I missed you. Probably should have called first! I hope you didn't have to work too late last night. I've left a peace offering at your front door to say I'm sorry.

A peace offering to lift my spirits? How lovely of her. She had clearly realised the error of her presumption and was ready to make up. A red rose and a package wrapped in red paper sat on the doormat. My heart swelled like the liver of a fattened goose destined for foie gras. I picked them up and took them inside.

The rose didn't smell but was a beautiful shade of blood red. I put it in an empty chutney jar with some water – my vase collection consisting of only one large cylindrical number Mum gave me when I moved into my first flat – and unwrapped the gift. The paper sprang open to reveal a box of Lindt chocolate balls and a Blackmores vitamin jar from their

Conceive Well men's range. The sight of it gave me a start. I stepped back from the bench. It wasn't exactly the sort of peace offering I was expecting.

I stared at the jar and its contents. It was like a cadaver had come to life and I needed a moment to process the shock of this new reality. It only took a couple of seconds, but then I was out of the kitchen and into the living room as quickly as I could, if only to get the offending vitamins out of my line of sight. I rested an arm on the back of a chair and let my head loll. I had come over queasy all of a sudden. But instead of regurgitating the mango smoothie I'd just bought, which would have been most upsetting and such a waste, I started to think. To take stock, properly, of what was happening. My sperm was being hijacked without my consent by the woman with whom I was trying to be in a relationship. Of course, it was flattering that Caroline wanted my sperm to be in optimum condition – what man didn't want sprightly spermatozoa? But it was also terrifying. And it was terrifying because I wasn't ready. It was too much, too soon. I thought hard. It may have hurt my head, as had the ice-cold smoothie I'd drunk too quickly, but I had to work out what to do and when. It was especially hard not having Marie or Andy or a cadaver to talk to. I knew they would all have been encouraging me not to commit to something I didn't want to, yet also telling me that it wasn't fair to keep Caroline dangling. And so, the conclusion I eventually came to was the resolution I had made a while back: to stand up for myself and, I realised, this was precisely the type of situation which required you to stand up for yourself. *Go on, Oliver, stand up for yourself.*

I resolved to talk to Caroline.

No, not sometime in the future. It had to be now.

I fetched my phone and started dialling.

No, hang on; these things needed to be done in person.

I picked up the phone again and texted her: *Are you home? Can I come over?*

Yes, she replied, so quickly it was as if her fingers had been poised and waiting.

Coming now, I texted back.

Caroline answered the door in a fetching dusty-pink dress and matching lipstick. She looked far too glamorous for a Sunday afternoon.

'You look lovely,' I said.

'Thank you,' she replied, letting me in.

She offered refreshments, which I accepted on the basis that it would give me more time to pluck up the courage to stand up for myself. I had made the visit; now I had to follow through with my resolve. Once we were settled on her sofa, Caroline sitting closer to me than was ideal for someone about to stand up for themselves, she asked if I had got her present, which annoyed me, as I should have brought it up myself if I was to have the upper hand. But at that point, any hand I could get would be much appreciated.

'I did get your present, thank you,' I said. 'It was very kind of you. That's sort of why I'm here.'

'Do you like it?' she said. 'I know how much you love chocolate . . .' A strong whiff of amorousness overpowered her living room; an arm flung itself around me.

'You know me too well,' I replied, which was not the reply I should have made, given the other half of the present was something I did not want at all. She was looking at me far more passionately than was desirable, given what I was trying to do. *For goodness' sake, Oliver, hurry up and stand up for yourself.* 'The thing is, Caroline . . .' I began.

'Yes . . .?' She looked at me semi-concerned, semi-expectant. I wondered what she thought I might say.

'The thing is,' I repeated, 'I'm not ready for babies just yet.'

Caroline put a hand to her chest. 'Oh, wow, Oliver, for a minute there . . .' She sighed, then started laughing. 'It's OK. I understand. Well, I'm *trying* to understand. But there's no harm in taking the vitamins, is there? It's all good preparation for when you are ready.'

'Well, yes, I suppose it is,' I agreed.

'Take one tablet a day and it should keep everything ticking over healthily,' she said. 'I bought vitamins for myself as well. It takes two to tango, if you get my drift.' She laughed.

I didn't laugh with her.

'Oh, Oliver, don't look so worried. I'm just being frank with you. I'd love a baby and I've realised I really want one with you. You're a calm, compassionate funeral director and . . . well . . . think of the children we could have.'

She looked as if about to swoon or perhaps collapse into my chest in a lovingly pleading sort of a way. I got ready to catch her but all she did was look up and flutter her eyelashes.

'I suppose you could say I'm with you in spirit,' I said. My experimental resolution with Marie was, I think, working and so there was no reason not to go along with Caroline's desires, if not practically, at least metaphorically.

'Oh, thank you, Oliver. I don't want to rush you but it means a lot to me that we're on the same page. You know,' she continued, 'I don't know if I should tell you this but before I met you I was looking into sperm donors. I found one that loved swimming . . .' She paused, as if thinking wistfully about what could have been. 'But I don't want to go down that path, not if I can help it.'

I stroked her leg, the one exposed through the slit in her dress. I was both relieved and pleased that not only had I stood up for myself but that I hadn't scared Caroline off. She appeared open to waiting, which made me feel calmer, and I decided to view the vitamins – should I wish to take them – as healthy preparation for something that may or may not happen in the future. Caroline smiled at me and I smiled back. I almost started thanking Marie in my head for helping me find the courage to stick up for myself but quickly put an end to that. Instead, I pushed her aside and let Caroline gently kiss my lips.

Waxing Lyrical

At work the next morning, Jean came straight into my office, humming. The pearly-blue opal on her brooch caught the light streaking in from the blinds. She looked like someone who had eaten all the pastries in the cake shop.

'Bill lit me last night,' she said.

'Really?' I said.

'He loved it. I loved it, too.' She clapped her hands. 'If that's my aroma, then I do smell jolly nice. Oh dear, it's too funny.' She put a hand to her chest and hummed again. 'I tried not to think it was me, though, considering the premise of the candle venture. It's still a little unnerving.'

'So do you approve?'

'Well, I like Edie very much. She appears knowledgeable and is clearly doing this from a good place in her heart. And I can't deny that she did an excellent job with my candle. So will you be telling Doreen about them now?'

'Not yet. You know how she is with new ideas,' I said. 'Plus, I want to get some sales first, to prove to her that we're on to something.' What I really wanted to prove was that I could do it on my own. Edie and the candles would stay my little secret and, for some strange reason, I was liking it that way.

After that Clock & Son went deathly quiet. Even the phone was dead. I chewed my nails and waited two hours for something more to happen than a window cleaner touting for business. I didn't like turning him away, so I told him he could try again in a couple of months. It's nice to give people hope or, as I do in my line of business, a little comfort from the pain. I called Caroline, even though she was also at work. We had a brief but, dare I say it, flirtatious conversation full of innuendo which did my Marie-less ego proud and which I hoped went over Jean's head, had she overheard. Caroline said I should come over to hers sometime that week, which I thought a marvellous idea; the more we stayed away from my place during the early days of the experiment, the better. Eventually we got a walk-in. A man with stringy hair and a prominent nose whose mother had died. I wondered if she took after him and would need an extra-long coffin because of his height. I didn't get a chance to find out as all he wanted to talk about was her rather than the practical points of organising a funeral. I set aside my questions and let the man speak.

'She was a trouper, my mum,' the man said, 'a real trouper. She hardly ever got sick either. I couldn't understand it. She never got colds, when there's me, sniffling and snuffling every winter.' He shook his head. I copied him in empathy and was about to bring up the subject of the funeral service when the man started up again.

'Did I tell you she never feared how or when she would die or the actual act of dying? It was the concept of no longer being that scared her the most. Not being able to feel, see, hear . . .'

'Smell?' I added.

'Yes, smell, too.' The man paused, sucked his cheeks, crumpled in the chair. 'I hope she's found somewhere to be again, somewhere to feel, smell, hear. I mean, if she hasn't . . .?'

'I'm sure she has,' I said.

'But you don't know that.'

'Well, no. I don't. But it's nice to think so, isn't it?' I wanted to reassure the man that this was all part of life, the mysteries of what happened next. Then I realised: this was the perfect opportunity, the ideal segue. I couldn't let such an opportunity slip.

'I know a way in which you could keep her memory alive,' I began. Oh yes, what timing, and the confidence that came over me! I could sell this man anything.

'But I'll never forget her.'

'No, I hope you won't . . .'

'What is it, then?'

'A candle,' I said.

'A candle?'

'Yes, we're offering a new service.'

'I don't think Mum wished to be reduced to melted wax.'

That's when the words skated out as if slipping uncontrollably on an iced lake, even though I hadn't practised in front of anyone – dead or alive – what I was going to say. 'Think of it as setting her soul free, letting her back in our world – *your* world – in your memory.'

'Sounds like crap.'

His comment was just the impetus I needed. I rushed into reception and came back with Jean's candle.

'I have one, here, of a very dear friend, La Lumière de Jean,' I said, and placed it before the man, who continued to look at me as if I weren't the man he'd thought I was when he first walked in. 'Our candles are bespoke, made to the fragrance specifications of the customer. You tell us what she loved – it could be absolutely anything – and we'll tailor the fragrance to suit her. It will embody her.'

I gave my jacket lapels a small tug, feeling quite pleased with myself. But the man wasn't yet hooked.

'I don't believe you. You're making it up,' he said, crossing his arms and leaning back in his chair.

'I'm not. Here, smell.' I lifted the lid.

'That doesn't tell me anything except it's a candle that smells nice.' The man folded his arms.

'I tell you what, as we're starting out, we'll make one for you free of charge and there's no obligation to take it if you don't like it.'

'You're crazy.'

I grinned. Was I? *It's all above board*, I wanted to say, *the deceased have nothing to do with it, if you know what I mean.* Then the man started crying, his nose dripping heavily on to his faded jeans. I passed him a box of tissues and listened to the familiar sound of enthusiastic nose-blowing.

'Sorry,' he said, and took more tissues just in case.

'It's OK.'

'Do we have to do all this funeral stuff now?' The man looked spent.

'The only thing is . . . your mother? She can't wait too long . . .' In times like these, euphemisms came in handy.

'I know, yeah, I know. Can I take these?' He picked up the whole tissue box, seemingly unbothered by what needed to happen to his mother.

'Please do.'

'I'll come back tomorrow, then?' The man sniffed and tucked the box under an arm.

'Of course. But can I ask, where's Mum now?'

'She's happy,' he said. 'She's in the kitchen, resting peacefully on my dining table.'

The next day at my desk, glossy with wood polish and a recent Doreen dusting, I typed up what I'd told the man with the dead mother on his dining table, the words I'd used to describe the candles. I phoned Edie and told her I had started selling them and that Andy had agreed to do a photo shoot for us. She gave a squeal of delight and didn't mind at all that I'd offered a customer a candle free of charge as a teaser. Her enthusiasm was infectious.

'Don't you worry,' I said, 'I won't miss a single opportunity. Everyone who walks in our door will get the sales spiel.'

The next person to enter Clock & Son was a woman called Julie who had a white bichon frise called Puddles that sat on her lap and stared at me as if deciding whether to trust me or not. It was tempting to try and outstare it, until it raised a side of its mouth and silently let a small fang appear. I refocused my attention on its owner, who seemed oblivious that she was obsessively stroking a miniature monster, and tried to size her up as a candle buyer. Female, aged around sixty, grey hair in a ponytail, a sickly aroma emanating from her blouse; her sister had passed away. The creds seemed spot on. But it was hard to get a word in.

'I've decided, you see,' she said, still stroking the monster, 'that God is unfair, illogical, oversubscribed and completely overrated. I've had enough of Him.'

I texted Jean to make some tea. It could be a long appointment.

'She wasn't meant to go when she did,' the woman continued. 'We weren't ready. *She* wasn't ready, I know she wasn't.' She sniffed and pulled a handkerchief from beneath her wristband. 'I mean, no one was there at the end. I'd buggered off to hang out her washing. The washing, for goodness' sake! Fat use I was.'

'I'm sure you were a wonderful support,' I said.

'I told my sister God will do what's best, that He always has within our ministry. But she started going on about how she should have paid attention. I said, "God's the only one who needs to be paying proper attention." She said, "Oh, I'm not talking about God; I'm talking about Don. He's been having an affair, right under my cancerous uterus."'

The woman paused, drew breath and began again. Jean slipped in quietly with the tea.

'That's when I realised. All this time I'd been misguided. My whole life down the biblical gurgler. When my sister needed her husband the most he wasn't there. No one was.' She slurped the tea noisily. 'Sorry, I only came to talk about coffins.'

'It's good to get things off your chest,' I said, and thought, *Now would be a good time. Offer the poor woman a bit of hope.* I opened my mouth to speak but she was off again.

'Liz always said, "Why do you put so much faith in Him?" I said it was because He knows best. That's what the ministry says. She said, "That's what I used to say about Don but now I know better." "Yeah," I said. "He's useless, bloody useless."'

She drew breath. Finally. That's when I sprung. I hoped talk of candles would help calm her down, be a welcome change of subject. It wasn't.

'Liz hated candles,' the woman said. 'Far too much pong, she used to say. Overwhelmingly pongy. And I can see her point.'

I nodded and wondered if I'd ever get a positive reaction.

'Did you say you can customise the scent?' she asked.

'I did.'

'Any scent at all?'

'Pretty much.'

'Do you do scent of bastard?'

I choked on my tea. Pretended I had a cough.

'I could get one done of Don,' she said. 'I'd be more than happy to burn him. And I know Liz would approve, wouldn't she, Puddles?'

Jean brought me some water.

'Are you alright?' the woman said. 'I was only joking.'

It took me three more goes for the candle concept to attract genuine interest. The client was a girl with short-cropped brown hair, eyes like an owl's and a jaunty walk. She walked in and stood in the middle of reception. Looked around like someone considering buying the place.

'I've never been inside a funeral parlour before,' she said.

'Hopefully, it's not too unpleasant,' I said. 'We try to make it feel welcoming.'

But the girl didn't appear to be listening. 'Yes, it is how I thought it would be.' She nodded, then announced, 'I'm Fran and I'd like to organise a funeral.'

'You've come to the right place.'

'The funeral is for myself.'

But she was still young? Early thirties, I guessed.

'I'm ill.'

'I'm so sorry.'

'Don't be. I don't want my mother doing it – organising my funeral, that is. She organised my wedding and my birth, booking herself in for a Caesarean after the first trimester on the basis that her work diary was already filling up and she needed a set time.'

'No one likes their mother taking over, do they?' I said it like a joke, even though I wasn't kidding. It made me think about my own funeral. Or, rather, the fact I had never thought about it before; I was too busy organising everyone else's. Was it odd for a funeral director not to have planned his own funeral? Or was I like the many chefs whose favourite meal was a burger?

'I haven't told my husband I'm here either,' Fran said. 'Not that I'm trying to be deceptive. I just want to do it on my own. For now, anyway.'

This time, I made sure we discussed the funeral first before bringing up the candles. What sort of coffin would she prefer? What was her budget? Had she thought about flowers, the programme of proceedings, the music, the food? There were so many things to consider and I didn't want to overwhelm her, as overwhelming as the task was. She considered everything I suggested and scribbled notes in a black leather journal in which she had already written the names of the songs she wished to be played.

When I thought the time was right, I threw in one last question. 'Would you like a candle as well?'

She chuckled. 'I'm glad you didn't say "fries",' she said.

'Ah yes, you can tell my snack of choice.'

'I'd have to say no to fries as I've been banned from eating anything fatty, salty or sugary. All the nice things.' She laughed, and I couldn't believe the bonhomie of this girl who should be sad – sadder than most who come in to organise a funeral. 'But I would consider a candle. What are you offering?'

I did my best to sell them appropriately, choosing words that did not imply anything offensive or ghoulish, all the while wondering if anyone would actually commission a candle of themselves. But she listened attentively, studied me thoughtfully.

'I like the sound of them,' she said eventually.

'You do?' I shouldn't have sounded so surprised. I wanted to call Edie then and there, and tell her: *We've got a customer!* Exclamation mark, exclamation mark.

'How much are they? Perhaps I could order a batch? One for each family member and some for friends. Yes, I like it.'

This was the tricky bit. I didn't want to lose her over price. I explained how they were more expensive than most candles but that was because they were premium, hand-crafted, the scents perfected by the candle-maker. She said she didn't mind and that she was happy to go easy on the flowers or choose a cheaper coffin if the budget blew out. Hooray!

'So, what do you need from me?' she said. 'A sample of DNA? A rubbing from the soles of my feet?' She slapped her thigh. 'You've made my day. Look at the amount of tissues I brought with me,' she said, opening her bag. 'That's what I thought I would need after discussing my funeral in a funeral home with a funeral director. But no! You've given me joy. A bubble of happiness I can pootle around in for the rest of the day.' She shook her head. 'Brilliant. It's absolutely brilliant.'

Gladness rose up from my belly and filled my cheeks like an extra-large serving of raspberry jelly and ice cream. 'Don't worry, we don't need DNA,' I said. 'Just a list of scents you think sums you up. They don't have to be traditional candle smells. They could be anything, anything at all. In fact, we did one recently for a barbecue lover. Who'd have thought?' I was tempted to slap my thigh like she had but thought better of it. I didn't want to appear too pleased with myself.

Less than twenty-four hours later Fran called back with her fragrance request: pineapple, lemon, tequila and daffodils.

'My favourite drink, my favourite flower and my favourite quote: "When life gives you lemons, sell them and buy a pineapple." Can you do fifty?'

For the second time that day I spoke to Edie. The latter may have been through a series of text messages, but it felt like she was sitting next to me and we were having a chat over a slice of apple pie, which was really rather comforting.

I went home that night still full of imaginary raspberry jelly and ice cream. So much so that I fancied buying some from the corner store, except I was five minutes too late and they had closed by the time I got there. Instead, I went home, poured myself a glass of wine, did a little dance in the kitchen, singing, 'We've got an order, we've got an order,' like it was the chorus to a really bad song. Then I lit Marie, watched the wick flicker into life and the wax liquefy around it, the scent of her mingling with the sulphurous smell of the blown-out matchstick. I reckoned Marie would have been happy. Delighted with herself as a candle and pleased with me – as me – or, perhaps as the new entrepreneurial me I was turning into. I carried Marie into every room in my apartment, as if using her to smoke out evil spirits with the fragrance of a flower shop. Until I remembered that I wasn't supposed to be thinking of Marie. I quickly blew the candle out and called Caroline instead but her response wasn't as enthusiastic as I'd have liked. I had to backtrack, of course, as she didn't know about the candles, so I gave her an abridged version, without mentioning Marie, to get her up to speed. She made non-committal noises and, at the end of it all, I wasn't entirely sure if she thought they were a good idea or not.

Mr Lowry

Two days later I got to talk to Edie again. The man with his mother on the dining table came back. He presented me with a new box of tissues, which was a very kind gesture, even though we didn't need it. Mum's continual bulk purchase of tissue boxes meant storage space was often at a premium and places where you wouldn't normally find tissues became suitable receptacles – spare coffins, empty mortuary chambers, the fridge. But Pete didn't need to know this. I graciously took his tissue box gift and was about to instigate a diplomatic conversation on how we really did need to get his mother off the dining table when he announced he had changed his mind about the candles.

'Can you do the scent of a book?' he asked.

It was a conundrum I was only going to answer in the affirmative and hoped like mad that Edie could indeed rustle up a candle that smelled like a book.

'Mum was always reading, you see,' Pete said. 'She read just about anything. Mostly books picked up from second-hand bookstores or charity shops. I kept telling her to go to the library, that it'd be cheaper, you know? But it was the smell she loved. She even made me sniff every book she bought. She'd shove them under my nose, as if I hadn't smelled an old book before. Better than sniffing meth, though, huh?' He jerked into phlegmy laughter. 'So, if you can do it, I think Mum would love it.'

Edie squealed when I told her. 'A book?' she repeated.

'Is it possible?' I asked. 'I told the man it was.'

'I don't know, but I'll give it go. Did he say what sort of book? An old book or a new book? Paperback or hardback? A bookshop or a library?'

'He said his mother loved second-hand books, but that was all. Sorry, I didn't think to ask.'

'Don't worry, I love a challenge, but maybe I should create a couple of samples first so he can decide.'

'Good idea.' I was pleased that the tricky question of whether you could make a candle smelling of a book had been met with a positive attitude. 'I'll happily sniff-test again, if you like?'

'I know, why don't you come over at the weekend and help me make them?'

'Help make them?' I said. The impulsiveness of her offer caught me off guard. I may have called myself a sniff-tester but I hadn't intended that to include candle-maker's assistant. 'I don't want to be in the way.'

'You don't have to do it every time but it might be helpful for you to understand the process so you can sound knowledgeable when you're selling them.'

I considered Edie's point, which was fair and reasonable, and I was a fan of preparation and research, after all. How pleasingly harmonious our professional relationship would be if we continued to agree on such matters. There was something very appealing about an organised, efficacious woman. 'I suppose I could,' I said.

'Perfect. How about Saturday? Do you mind coming to my place? At the moment, I do it all in my kitchen.'

What is it about life that, often, when something good happens, something bad follows? Or was that just how my life seemed to be rolling? For that afternoon we had a viewing of the first full embalming Jimmy had prepared – which should by rights have been a very good thing indeed. With customers thin on the ground, he was getting itchy fingers for some 'proper' work and, although his pretensions were beginning to rankle, at least he was saving me the job. I was excited to see his handiwork and the deceased family eager to see their grandfather before he was put on display at the funeral. At ninety-three years old and with a penchant for the bottle (as attested by his son), he was lucky to have lived as long as he did and I had to admit Jimmy had done an excellent job of covering up his sallow skin and strawberry nose. Even what was left of the man's wispy hair was suitably blow-dried and set in place, and if I wasn't mistaken his lips were sealed in an agreeable half-smile. You would have to say that Mr Lowry looked in a better state than when he had come in. Barely a wrinkle. You'd never even have guessed he was dead.

I ushered in the four members of his family who had come for the pre-viewing and told them how we hoped they would approve of how wonderful Mr Lowry looked. They nodded. It was a solemn moment, as it always is. I had tissues at the ready. Jean was preparing a pot of tea. It was all going swimmingly until the moment we stood before the coffin and I gestured to Mr Lowry. As his family looked down, he looked up, his eyes popping open as if he had just remembered a very important fact he had momentarily forgotten. His daughter screamed. The granddaughter fainted. The son leaned in and shouted, 'Dad?'

I called for Jean. Tried to calm them down.

'What the hell's going on?' the son called out.

Jean rushed in to comfort Mr Lowry's daughter, who was on the floor with the granddaughter. I gently closed the coffin lid and tried to explain what had just happened, but they didn't seem to want to know about any technical malfunction with the plastic caps we insert under the eyelids to stop them from opening. The moment of solemnity was gone. I offered to give them a discount and a repeat pre-viewing once we had fixed the problem. They left still in shock, although seemingly happy with this arrangement. I only hoped they wouldn't whisk

Mr Lowry away and complete his funeral with the new crowd down the road, sinking us further under.

It was a slap in the face for Clock & Son and two slaps for James 'Jimmy' Miller. I should never have let Mum persuade me to hire him.

Even Mum wasn't quick enough to come to Jimmy's defence when I told her. She dropped the large bunch of Asian lilies she was holding on to the reception table in horror.

'This is a serious offence, Oliver,' she said. 'We've never had that happen before. Roger was always a stickler for detail.'

'That's what I said to the poor family but they were in such shock I don't think they heard me.'

'I told you we didn't need to get a new embalmer,' Mum said, 'and now this happens. It's an outrage.'

'Well, I knew he wasn't right for us as soon as we met. There was something about him . . .'

'If only you hadn't thought to advertise for an embalmer in the first place.'

We were both getting tetchy. If only Jean had been there to intervene.

'I can't do two jobs at once, Mum, when will you understand that? Either way, Jimmy can't stay, no matter how much you like him.'

Mum unwrapped the flowers and trimmed the stalks. 'On this point, Oliver, I do agree and, as I said before, think of the money we'll save. Shall I do it or you?'

'Well, if you're offering . . .'

'I suppose I hired him, after all.'

'Thanks, Mum.'

'Now,' she said, shooing me away, 'let me get on with my flower arranging. Sometimes I think I could have been as good as Marie.' She yelped with delight at the vanity of her statement and pulled out the dead waratah and flax leaf arrangement Jean had created and replaced them with her beloved lilies. I slunk back to my desk, disillusioned with Jimmy and disgruntled at the thought of having to do the embalming once again. How I didn't want to wash, flush, disinfect, preserve, sew, dress or refrigerate a body ever again! It was all I could do not to hit something. I formed a fist with my right hand, a smooth-knuckled, clean-fingered fist, and made fist-pumping gestures as if I were going to punch the wall. I curled my lips, put some force behind my shoulder. My knuckles brushed paintwork. But I couldn't do it. A punched office wall was as good to me as a fallen business sign. Only worse. I could hurt myself.

Candle-Making

I didn't tell Caroline that I was going to be spending a good part of Saturday learning how to make candles with Edie. Something told me she would be jealous. When she suggested we go out to lunch I lied and said I had to work. It didn't sit comfortably with me, I admit, so I resolved to make it up to her by promising to take her to a smart restaurant in the city – the Italian one whose crab linguine was legendary. It could be an anniversary of sorts, I decided – for what, I'd work out later.

I got dressed in a suit with one of my favourite ties – navy with tiny croissants, which is more tasteful than it sounds. The croissants are so small that it's only when you look closely at the design that you realise what they are. I even polished my shoes, having been unable to get Mum's words out of my head. This was technically work, after all, not a social occasion. Edie lived only a couple of suburbs away but I did have to drive past the street in which Green Light Funerals resided. I could practically hear them belting out their cheap promotions and garish insincerity from where I was on the main road. It gave me the shivers and reminded me that I could not let them get the better of us. Maybe Edie and I could loiter nearby, handing out candle brochures to those about to walk inside. But did I really want to stoop so low as to steal their customers?

Edie's house was a quaint two-bedroom terrace in a quiet street with a nature strip down one side that residents had converted into a shared herb and vegetable garden. You couldn't miss it; her door was painted bright yellow. Edie greeted me with the energy of someone who liked having a front door painted bright yellow and probably owned other things in the same colour.

'Hi, Oliver, come in!' She gave me a hug before I could enter, which was a little disconcerting, as I didn't feel I knew her well enough for us to be encroaching on each other's personal spaces when neither of us required consoling over a death in the family. I reciprocated the gesture nonetheless, as I couldn't deny that I enjoyed being hugged by Edie (in a purely professional way, of course), and then followed her down the hallway to the kitchen at the back.

I was pleased to discover that I was right about the yellow. The windows above the sink were framed by yellow-and-white gingham curtains and the tea towel hanging over the oven featured a yellow-and-white cockatoo. It was all very cheery and welcoming. It was also very tidy, despite the rows of cake stands displayed on shelves on one wall and a cabinet of what must have been about thirty ceramic salt and pepper shakers in various forms: flora and fauna, vegetables and cartoon characters and other unusual pairings. The bench top was set up with rows of fragrance vials, glassware, labels, wicks, a large bag of wax flakes, a candy thermometer and a stainless-steel pot on the stove.

'Welcome to my lab.' She laughed. 'I've got everything set up, and the first thing we need to do is play with scents to get the fragrances right.' Then she paused and looked at me. I wondered if I had toothpaste on my lapel. 'Just one thing: you do look very smart and I like a man in a suit, but I'd hate for your tie to get dipped in wax.'

I looked down. It hadn't occurred to me that my choice of attire was most impractical for candle-making. Edie was wearing jeans and a T-shirt and had her hair in a ponytail, which was not only more sensible but made her look younger than the age I believed her to be: early thirties. I took off my tie and jacket and draped them over a kitchen chair. Practicality won over from professionalism and I rolled up my shirtsleeves as well and felt pleased I had polished my shoes so that any dripped wax would easily come off.

'That's better,' she said, 'and you still look smart,' she added with a coy smile. 'Now, I thought we could start with Fran's candles. The combination she's chosen of pineapple, lemon, tequila and daffodils is really lovely but it's going to be tricky getting the balance of aromas right. Tequila note from the blue agave plant can be strong, woody and spicy. It's often used for men's fragrances but, paired with sour lemon, the sweetness of pineapple and the delicate fragrance of the daffodil plant, it can be toned down. I think we should aim to capture the essence of springtime and the tropics.'

'That sounds highly technical,' I said. 'It's probably best if I merely observe and let you create your magic.'

She laughed. 'Don't worry, it sounds fancy but really it's chemistry. Not really that dissimilar from being a lab scientist, which is what my mum is. She potters with Petri dishes.'

I didn't like to ask what was in her mother's Petri dishes, preferring instead to watch Edie tinker with fragrance oils, the kitchen becoming heady with scent. She dripped and poured, stirred and sniffed, all the while explaining what she was doing and why.

'Try this,' she said.

I sniffed. 'Definitely tropical.' She smelled it again, decided it was too tropical and adjusted the scent. It was a pleasure to watch her being so focused, so dedicated to getting it right. When she was happy with the final result, it was time to seal the wicks in the glass jars with a glue gun and melt the wax. Around us the air thickened with the smells of a Pacific island cocktail and earnest concentration.

'It's quite a process,' I said.

'But I love it,' she said. 'If I could choose any job in the world, it would be a perfumier. Playing with fragrances and oils, taking individual smells and putting them together to create something new. It's kind of what we're doing here but on a grander scale. It's a real art form,

I think. My real dream would be to go to the Givaudan Perfumery School in Paris, the oldest one in the world,' she sighed. 'That would be amazing. What about you?'

I thought back to my notebook of resolutions, the page in which I once wrote my dream jobs, as if I was ever going to get a chance to try them. Cordon bleu chef had been one fantasy, thriller writer another.

'I wanted to be a journalist once, when I was at school,' I said, 'but I didn't really have a choice. Clock & Son has been going for three generations. When you're born into the funeral industry, you die in the funeral industry.'

'Amazing. And are you the eldest, is that why you're running it now?'

'I'm the only one,' I said. 'I'm the Clock and the Son. Well, Mum still works in the business on a part-time, interfering basis.' I laughed. 'She should have retired ages ago but when Dad died and I took over she seemed to think she had to stay. The problem is that she's resistant to change. So resistant that I'm sorry to say I haven't actually told her about the candles.'

'In that case, we just *must* make a candle for her,' Edie said.

I was non-committal. I feared Mum's reaction to the candles and doubted I'd ever be able to find a scent she would be pleased with.

'Once you think of the fragrances,' Edie continued, 'I promise I'll do it. I'd love to.'

'Please don't worry about a candle for Mum. Aren't you trying to do one for your father?'

'Well, yes, but . . . you know . . .' She looked away.

'If you like, I could help you make one of your dad,' I said, and realised my hand had touched her very attractive and slender wrist. I quickly removed it and shoved it in a trouser pocket.

'Thank you, Oliver,' she said, then her tone brightened and she brought the subject back to Mum. 'But what I really want to know is how you're planning on keeping them a secret from your mother?'

It was a very good question and one which I didn't know the answer to. I was afraid it had the unfortunate effect of tainting my character. 'I know I shouldn't be going behind her back,' I said, 'but it's complicated. There's also the delicate matter of Marie and the candle you made of her. It's a long story, but I was very fond of Marie and Mum doesn't know about that either.'

'I know, relationships are never easy,' Edie said, nodding as if she knew exactly what I was talking about. 'My last boyfriend didn't understand my love of collecting, and that was what broke us up in the end. See the corn-on-the-cob salt and pepper shakers, third row to the right? They're the culprits. When I bought them Jack said I had taken kitsch too far and he couldn't take it any more. He said he didn't want to come second best to miniature china condiment holders, which was just a silly thing to say. He said I was wasting my money and being frivolous. I know I can get a bit obsessive sometimes, but I can't help it, I love the hunt. Of course, you could argue that having twenty-two vintage cake stands would be enough and that the one I bought last weekend was utterly unnecessary, but that would mean being a killjoy, wouldn't it?' She laughed.

From where I was now standing, with the afternoon light coming in the kitchen window and catching the glass, highlighting their curves, they looked rather attractive. What's more, I couldn't see any specks of dust. How I admired an attention to cleanliness; it was a most fetching trait.

'They're very sparkly and clean,' I said, 'which must mean you use them, and so that's not being wasteful at all.'

'Oh yes, I do. They're wonderful for when people come over. I'll put anything on them, not just cakes.'

We were silent for a few seconds. I wondered if we were both thinking about cake and how a slice of something sweet would go down quite nicely around about now.

Except then Edie said, 'Jack was one of those people who takes, you know what I mean? And everything had to be done his way. I realised afterwards that I had been handcuffed and couldn't be myself. I'm much better off without him.' She looked out the window and far away across the fence line to goodness knows where and three seconds later she was back in the kitchen and checking the thermometer in the pot of wax. 'Right, I think we're ready to pour.'

I followed Edie's instructions to keep the wicks vertical as she steadied them with kebab sticks and gently poured the wax. It was a slow, methodical process that I found to have therapeutic properties, and Edie seemed pleased with my attempts at perfection. When Fran's fifty candles, plus two extras we could use as samples, were made, we started on Pete's.

'I'm really excited about these because I discovered fragrance oils that smell of attic and paper,' she said. 'I figure if we add some white tea, we should be able to emulate the smell of a paperback book and an old bookshop.'

'I'll take your word for it,' I said. 'Is there no smell that cannot be replicated?'

'Well, no, not really. You know the olfactory scientist Sissel Tolaas I mentioned the other day? She once recreated the smell of sweat from men having severe phobia attacks. She impregnated them into the pages of a Berlin art magazine, *mono.kultur*, to explore the true power of smell and replace their usual photography with olfactory art.'

'Top marks for originality,' I said, 'but who wants to smell fear? It's bad enough feeling it.' I said it in a light-hearted way, hoping she didn't think I was the fearful sort. 'How did she do it?'

'The men were put in a controlled setting and induced to have panic attacks so she could capture their sweat and synthetically replicate its molecular structure. And you know what else? Fear has a smell. Dogs know it. Horses know it.'

'Like the smell of overcooked Brussels sprouts?'

She laughed.

'Or dead fish lying in the sun?' I suggested.

'What about boiled cabbage?' she said.

'I quite like cabbage.'

'OK, wet dog.'

'Yes,' I agreed, 'and dry dog.'

'Ha! What about mould?'

'Mmm, but I do like a decent blue cheese.'

We both started laughing. 'Oh, that's funny, we could go on for days, couldn't we?' Edie said. 'Come on, let's get these samples finished and then it will be time for a cup of tea.'

When all the candles were made and left to rest for twenty-four hours, Edie put the kettle on and produced a tin of mini saffron buns with currants and pistachios.

'This is my new thing,' she said, 'using saffron in baking. It has a subtle fragrance and taste, an unusual blending of honey and hay, and the colour it produces . . . well, you already know it's one of my favourites.'

She took down one of her smaller cake stands and placed four buns on it. I had thought I should get going, that she probably had better things to do than to keep entertaining me now that the candles were made. Then again, it would be rude not to partake of tea and buns since she had gone to the effort of making them.

We sat outside in her courtyard next to pots of red geraniums and a backdrop of washing on the line. It seemed very unprofessional having to look at Edie's underwear and the clothes she liked to wear hanging upside down and swinging in the breeze. I angled my chair so I could look at Edie instead. We chatted some more about our jobs, how we both disliked exercise but knew it was good for us and how we dreamed of travelling to far-flung places like Iceland and Tanzania but had never actually done so. I found we had a lot in common, which boded well for our candle venture. There would be nothing worse than going into business with someone who didn't appreciate the challenges of making non-chewy macaroons or the difficulty of dropping everything for an extended holiday when you had commitments like a job you were tied to or an ill father and a mother you wished to support. After two cups of tea and a delicious saffron bun, I had definitely overstayed my welcome. I asked if there was anything more I could help her with.

'No, it's fine,' she said. 'We just need to wait for the candles to set.'

'It's been a very informative and interesting afternoon,' I said, getting my tie and jacket.

'Yes, we must meet up again to continue brainstorming bad smells.' She giggled. 'Anyway, I should be thanking you because it's been so much fun doing it with someone else.'

I didn't know what to say to that. I had also thought the afternoon fun but me, enjoying candle-making? It was all too peculiar. 'Well . . .' I said.

'Yes, well . . .' she said.

We looked at each other awkwardly and then she gave me another hug, which I was happy to reciprocate in a more relaxed way. She waved me goodbye from her yellow front door and, as I walked back to my car, I realised I hadn't once thought about the events of the past twenty-four hours or, indeed, Caroline.

Standing Up, Properly

I arrived home feeling unexpectedly joyous from an afternoon of making candles and bounced into my flat as if I had lost a lot more weight than I actually had. I'd not long been home when the doorbell rang. I assumed it was a charity, pulled out a note from my wallet and went to the door. As I was about to hand over the money, I realised it was Caroline on the doorstep.

'Oh, hello,' I said. I probably could have sounded happier to see her but I hadn't anticipated such a spontaneous visit.

'Where have you been?' she asked. A hand was on a hip; there was a tone of aggression in her voice.

'I was at work,' I said, thinking it was better to keep up the lie I had already begun.

As it turned out, it wasn't.

'No you weren't, because I've just been to your work and you weren't there and never had been there. I spoke to your mother, who was polishing the coffins.'

'Ah,' I said, kicking myself for being dishonest. Mum always said lies came to no good. Yet if I told Caroline the truth right then, would that make me look better or worse? Somehow, I suspected worse. How did I tell Caroline I was trying to protect her from her own jealousy? That I was trying to avoid a situation just like the one we were now in. Even though I knew I shouldn't have lied, I didn't like the way Caroline was reacting and I wasn't sure how best to pacify her. 'Were you stalking me?' I asked.

'No,' she said indignantly.

'But you've just been to my work.'

'I was going to surprise you. But all I've done is found you out.'

'Found me out about what?' I said, pointlessly, in retrospect.

'That you've been somewhere else, that you lied, that you're hiding something.'

I sighed. This charade couldn't continue. Caroline was getting herself all worked up like a washing machine on a spin cycle. I had to come clean. 'OK, so I was making candles with Edie, the candle-maker. You know how I was telling you about them?'

'You were doing what?'

'It's true. Here . . .' I said, getting Edie's number up on my phone. 'You can call her, if you like.'

'I'm not going to call her.'

'Please.' I waggled the phone at her.

'You could have spent the afternoon with me.'

'Well, yes,' I agreed, 'but this was business.'

'On a Saturday afternoon?'

'I work odd hours,' I said, but it wasn't good enough.

'Oh, forget it,' she said, and turned around and left.

My wonderful afternoon had plummeted to the depths of horribleness.

I went to the kitchen to make both a cup of tea and pour a glass of wine, unable to decide which would make me feel better, and to work out what to do about what had just happened. I sat at the kitchen table and started with the tea. I kicked myself for having perpetrated the lie in the first place. I shouldn't have done it – didn't even know why I had done it, other than to prevent Caroline getting jealous.

And even that was silly because there was nothing for her to be jealous about. I get that she may have wanted to see me but did she have to go stalking me at work? And why couldn't she be more understanding about the nature of my vocation? I *did* work unconventional hours and had last-minute call-outs at odd times of the day and night. I felt guilty and responsible for making her unhappy and wished neither of us to feel this way. The more I thought and the more tea I drank, the more I realised I felt less inclined to be defensive about my profession yet again, even though it pained me to have Caroline think badly of me. I was trying to make us as an 'us' work, but it seemed constantly fraught. I started on the wine. Marie had been giving me so much, and Caroline, for a time, had too, but now it seemed as if she was taking it all away, making the air between us tainted and strained. Her niggling and prying sat uncomfortably with me and, in turn, were making me do things – i.e. lying – that I didn't like to do. It was as if we were in some domestic drama which at any minute could take a dark twist and become a domestic noir thriller. Dear God, what was happening to my life? I felt so hopeless and helpless all of a sudden; panicked and anxious, nervous and stressed.

Then I started crying. I expelled sobs so loud they would have woken the morgue had I been there and had it been full. I sobbed, gulped, spluttered, couldn't seem to get a grip. I poured more wine, slugged, slurped, sobbed some more. It didn't seem to help. *Get a grip, Oliver, get a grip. You've cried enough already this year, you fool.* This realisation only made me cry more. I was a yacht in a storm, a speeding car veering off the road, cake batter in a mixer. Listing, reeling, weaving, churning. I'd thrown caution to the wind, flung off an inhibition to implement some of my newer resolutions, yet where had it got me? I was nearly forty and my life was being hijacked by a woman whose hazel eyes were actually a terrible shade of bright green. In an effort to get a handle on my life, I'd let it get out of control. *Someone, please, change the forecast, put a foot on the brake, flick the off switch. Someone, please . . . Help!*

I drank more wine and then found myself on the floor, curled in a corner against the cupboards, as if that were a perfectly reasonable place to enjoy a fine wine by yourself on a Saturday afternoon. Why use chairs when you had the floor? The thought made me laugh one of those crazed, waterlogged guffaws. I wiped my eyes and nose with the back of a hand, had some more wine. Thoughts sloshed. Nothing made sense. Had I crashed, overturned, over-mixed?

At some point I must have had a vision of myself from above and realised the pointlessness of being in the foetal position on the kitchen floor, particularly when there was a collection of crumbs lining the skirting board that needed sweeping up. I got up and staggered to the sofa, flopped like a rag doll. I lay there, weak and helpless yet relieved the tears had subsided.

That's when I started thinking – properly thinking, the way I liked to do when trying to work things out, when I was able to mull things over without any distractions. I thought about what Edie had said earlier about feeling handcuffed by her boyfriend. I thought about how Andy told me I should care more for myself. I thought of what Marie had written in her diary about hoping I'd find a soulmate. I thought of Lily and how she didn't even get the chance at life and finding a soulmate. They were thoughts I'd never fully processed before. It was all very well writing lists of resolutions and dreams I wanted to happen but maybe it took a woman like Caroline to make me realise what it was that I *didn't* want. I sat up as a feeling of calmness came over me. Yes, that was it. I had to remember what I *didn't* want as much as what I *did* want. Instead of calling out stupidly, pointlessly, for someone else to help me, I had to help myself. I got up to find my notebook of resolutions and a pen. I would write a new entry: all the things I *didn't* want.

Then it came to me in a burst of lucidity, as if my eyes had just snapped open, as Mr Lowry's had at his pre-viewing viewing. It was a realisation of such clarity that I didn't know how I couldn't have realised it before. I did not want to be officially or unofficially going out with Caroline. Not even to ease the pain of loneliness. Not even to help me try things I didn't think I wanted to do. Not even to rekindle a semblance of romance I so yearned for. Not even to imagine a life of happy families. Being with Caroline may have eased my loneliness and helped me try new things but it was as wrong for me to lead her on as it was to pretend to myself that she was the one. It wasn't as if I hadn't tried, but a soulmate wasn't any old soul who happened to turn up and fill a hole. They were the one you wanted to be with for the rest of your life. And I realised then that I did not want to be with Caroline for the rest of my life.

I dusted myself off, splashed water on my face and ordered a taxi to take me to Caroline's. Who cared if I was tipsy? Who cared if I looked as if a storm had hit and my eyes were red and puffy? Who cared if my clothes, which had been ironed, now looked as if they hadn't? I had to do the right thing.

I knocked on her door.

She opened it ever so slightly. 'I don't want to see you,' she said.

'Please. We need to talk.'

'No.'

'Just give me a minute. Please.'

'One minute? Is that all it's going to take?' I nodded. 'Well?' she said, opening the door ever so slightly more. Her eyes were as red and puffy as mine.

It was a shame I hadn't given myself more time to prepare what I was going to say and how I was going to say it. When I could have rehearsed before a deceased client or at least with myself, talking to the room and summoning up the confidence to stand up for myself. All that came out was, 'This isn't working, is it?'

'I thought you'd come to apologise.'

'It's true, I have.'

'So do it.'

'I'm sorry I lied. I didn't mean to hurt you but . . .'

'But . . .?'

I looked her in the eyes, gulped away my nervousness. 'But I need to be honest with you. I need to be honest with myself.'

'What are you talking about?'

'I'm sorry, Caroline. I don't see a future for us,' I said, as assertively as I could.

'What?' Her face dropped.

'I don't think we're right for each other.' For the second time in the space of a few weeks, I was standing up for myself, and it felt good.

'No, no, no, Oliver. We're *so* right! I can't believe you're saying that.' She flung open the door and wrapped her arms around me as if trying desperately to pretend I hadn't said what I had. I felt so bad for her, and kind of bad for myself, as it would have been great if we had worked out but I had to follow my heart. I had to stick to my resolve. So I didn't reciprocate her hug; I *couldn't* reciprocate her hug.

Then she stepped away and stared at me, her demeanour changed. She put both hands on her hips and looked as if she were at a shoot-out and whoever got their gun out quick enough would win. 'You're being serious, aren't you?' she asked, her voice quieter, sadder.

'I'm sorry.' Then I said something which sounded ridiculous in hindsight. 'It's been fun, Caroline, but here's where it ends.' As if we really were in a Western and I had the last word. The only problem was, I hadn't figured out how the scene would end and, as there was no director to shout, 'Cut!' I had to improvise. 'I do hope you find your soulmate,' I added, taking a cue from Marie. 'You deserve to.'

'Oh my God, I can't believe this is happening,' she said through quivering lips and disbelief in her eyes. Then, it seemed she was unable to look at me any longer. She ran back inside and shut the door with as much speed as five hundred million sperm racing to get to the golden egg first, which was an unfortunate analogy, as the only thing my sperm were doing was retreating with cheer.

'Sorry,' I said again, but this time to the door. As much as it was unpleasant being the bearer of bad news, I couldn't help but feel an enormous amount of relief as I turned to leave. 'Thank you,' I whispered, to whom I did not know. Perhaps I had been thanking myself for finally standing up for what I wanted and having the courage to act. Not just that but making the right bloody decision for once. I had single-handedly rescued myself from a woman who was not for me. I could not – would not – enter my forties chained to the wrong woman.

I raced home and picked up the wine bottle still on the bench. There was enough left for at least two generous glasses. *In fact, who cares about a glass?* I thought, and took a slug straight from the bottle. *Ha!* I took another. I usually deemed it uncouth to drink wine from a bottle, and still did. But on this occasion, I thought I could bloody well do what I wanted.

'Here's to myself,' I said out loud.

Then I threw the rose and the vitamins in the rubbish (but kept the Lindt balls because it would have been wasteful to throw out perfectly good chocolates that could satisfy a craving at a later date), and went to fetch the notebook to finally write that new entry . . .

Thou shalt not let others decide things for you.

Thou shalt not go out with the first woman who shows interest in you.

Thou shalt not sacrifice your own happiness for someone else's.

Thou shalt not drink wine from the bottle ever again.

I was so happy I heated up a leftover slice of pizza in the microwave and thought, *To hell with how many days it's been in the fridge!* It hit the spot quite nicely. After I'd washed my hands several times to get rid of greasy pizza residue, I went to the wardrobe and fossicked in my jumper drawer to find the diary. There it was, exactly where I had left it. I pressed it to my chest and let out a sigh of relief. *Here we are again, Marie, here we are again.* Ah, the comforting effects of cheesy pizza and Marie's words: *I want to be with Oliver.* I couldn't tell you how many times I'd read that entry, but it was one I never tired of.

Sigh.

PART THREE

. . . in which I really *must* nail some of my resolutions.
I must do what's right for me.
I must stand up for myself.
I must FACE MY FEARS.

Paperbacks and Pineapples

I arrived at work on Monday filled to the brim with relief. I decided to put what had happened with Caroline into a box labelled 'The Past'. My time with her could be called a lively experience – a bit of fun mixed with undesirable moments of anxiety. Even so, I found it hard to concentrate at my desk and it didn't help that we'd had no deaths and no one asking about our services. The only consolation was Edie calling to say the candles had set perfectly and smelled amazing.

'I can deliver them whenever you like,' she said.

Thank goodness I had something else to focus on.

'Excellent, Edie,' I said. My only hope was that the customers liked them. I knew I couldn't pin all my hopes on the candles to revive the business but, right then, they were the only things that seemed to be working. 'I'll let the clients know and see if they can come in today. Do you think you should be here, too? We can introduce you as the candle-maker.'

'I'd love to.'

I coordinated a time with both Fran and Pete that also suited Edie and aligned with when Mum wasn't going to be here. I was so filled with nervous anticipation that I tidied my desk and ate an emergency Mars bar I found in the bottom drawer and half a peanut slab that was also there. Edie arrived fifteen minutes before the first appointment with the man whose mother was still in refrigeration waiting patiently to be cremated. I noted how she looked as radiant as a well-polished silver scalpel, as well as her continuous use of excellent time-keeping.

'So,' she said, 'who's coming in first?'

'Pete, the book man.'

She nodded. 'I'm nervous.'

'Me, too. Silly, isn't it?' Who would have thought – me, nervous about candles? I didn't like to tell her that if Pete and Fran disliked their candles, then I would be pulling out of the venture, that I may as well concede defeat against Green Light Funerals and that I wouldn't try anything new ever again. Beautiful, bubbly Edie didn't need to know any of that. 'Do you like books?' I added, for want of something else to say.

'Oh, yes, I've always got a book on the go.'

'Me, too,' I said, thinking of the autobiography on my bedside table which I should probably finish instead of reading Marie's diary every night.

'I read to my dad when I can, too – usually once a week,' Edie said. 'Parkinson's has affected his cognitive ability, which is so sad, as he's always loved to read. At the moment we're into spy novels.'

'If you're looking for more, I've got a couple of Jeffrey Archer thrillers you can borrow.'

'Thanks.' She nodded.

'It's a lovely thing you're doing,' I added.

Edie shrugged. 'He's my dad, you know?'

For a minute, I thought she might cry and, while I was more than happy to console her and was fully stocked with tissues, now was not the time, so I changed the subject. 'How was the rest of your weekend?'

'Lovely, thank you. I caught up with some girlfriends on Saturday night and popped in to see my parents on Sunday with some baking.'

'And your creation?'

'Passionfruit custard squares.'

'Delicious.'

'And you?' she asked.

'Oh, this and that,' I said, with a lightness in my voice that made it sound as if I'd had a perfectly normal weekend that didn't involve breaking up with my girlfriend and reading my dead paramour's diary once again from cover to cover.

'I suppose you have to be on call a lot of the time, don't you?'

'I do, but I try not to let it get in the way of things.'

I was about to ask her if she'd bought any more cake stands when Jean appeared. 'He's here,' she said.

Edie stood up. I waited at the door and Pete loped in. I made the introductions and let Edie discuss the candles.

'We weren't sure whether to focus on the scent of a single paper-back or the aroma of an entire second-hand bookshop,' she said. 'There are subtle differences between the two but the candles are meant to be triggers, not exact replicas. We've done one of each so you can choose.'

Pete looked nervously at the two glass jars filled with wax.

'You know, she was reading Dickens when she died,' he said. '*Great Expectations*. It lay open on her chest. She'd been holding it so tightly I could hardly get it off her.' He shook his head at the memory. I got ready with the tissues. Waited. Then the moment passed. Edie stepped forward and told him which candle was which.

'This one is meant to be an entire second-hand bookshop,' she said. 'Every fusty book and dusty shelf with a hint of incense and notes of nutmeg, clove and sandalwood. And this one, an old paperback that's been read and reread, had tea spilt on it and greasy fingers leafing through it. It's got fragrances of aged paper with vanilla overtones. Are you ready?'

He nodded. She lifted the lid of the first one. He leaned in and inhaled.

'Ah, yes,' he said.

Then the next. Edie's hands were clasped in prayer at her lips and I had a sudden urge to hold them myself. Nerves really were getting the better of me.

'Bloody hell,' Pete said.

'Do you like them?' Edie asked.

'Do I like them? I *love* them.' His words soared to the ceiling in delight. He leaned forward again, tilted the lids and let his nose edge in, as if he were smelling a decent bottle of red wine. 'It's uncanny how realistic they are.'

I couldn't help but grin. I thought my face might crack.

'Which one do you prefer?' Edie said.

'I like them both. Mum would have loved them both.' He shook his head again. Sniffed again. 'If I was a betting man – and I'm not – I reckon the first is the one she'd have picked. Can you do twenty?'

Edie and I couldn't get to his hands quick enough to shake. We almost did a three-handed handshake. And Pete slapped me on the back and said he couldn't wait to give them to his relatives. We couldn't have got off to a better start.

Then Fran arrived, passing Pete on his way out. She had gold sunglasses on the top of her head and wore gold hooped earrings. Her face was drawn and pale but her eyes still twinkled. We repeated the introductions and explanation and Edie placed one of her candles on my desk. Fran picked it up and held it to her nose. She closed her eyes and flared her nostrils. I didn't think the act of smelling one thing could take so long. A tear dampened her lashes and trickled on to her cheek.

Quick, tissues. I pulled one out and waited for her eyes to open.

'Gosh,' she said, fanning her face and placing the candle on the desk. She took the tissue and dabbed her eyes.

Edie rubbed her arm thoughtfully. I sensed that Edie wasn't expecting Fran to be so young.

'Sorry, I didn't mean to cry,' Fran said.

'It's absolutely fine,' I said.

'There's nothing like a good cry to make you feel better,' added Edie, as if she'd skim-read Dad's Folder before the meeting.

'I'm happy,' she said. 'Honestly.'

How strange to have someone cry from happiness in my rooms. It was hard to remember the last time that had happened. It could have been when Jean won a year's worth of unlimited magazine reading. This time, it was even more special. We had touched Fran in a way free magazines could never do, and it moved me. It would have been nice to make this happen more often. 'You can cry for whatever reason you like,' I said.

Then she hugged me and reached for Edie and hugged her, too.

'I've got the rest of your candles in a box in my car,' Edie said.

'Fifty more tears of joy, do you mean?'

'And, you know what? I've got leftover fragrance. I'd love to make you more candles free of charge,' Edie suggested, and then smiled at me. I clapped inside. What a superlative human being and business partner Edie was proving to be.

'Really?' Fran said, and started crying again.

'Oh, I didn't mean to upset you.' Edie grabbed a bunch of tissues from the box I was holding and gave them to Fran.

'I'm fine,' Fran sniffed. 'Thank you. Thank you both so much.'

From my window, I watched Edie give Fran the box of candles from her car in the car park and wave her goodbye. A white balloon rose from behind a row of buildings and took off into the sky.

'Yay,' Edie said, returning, her arms out and palms open, as if keeping afloat the high we were both on. I copied her for no other reason than I didn't know what else to do. Except it made us look as if we were about to break out into song – a duet by Dolly Parton and Kenny Rogers. Edie burst out laughing. Before I could stop myself, I started singing 'Islands in the Stream'. I didn't even like the song and there I was, crooning it off-key.

'Feel free to join in,' I suggested. And she did, which gave her the giggles again and made me laugh. We only managed the chorus until we had to stop, breathless from laughing and singing at the same time.

'That was too funny,' she puffed.

'Apologies for my tuneless singing.'

She waved my words away. 'You don't need to apologise. I'm hardly Dolly Parton.'

I smiled. Not because her singing wasn't much better than mine but because of how relaxed Edie made me. It was rare that I sang in the company of anyone apart from myself and I hadn't even felt self-conscious. With this being the case, our working relationship really was going to be harmonious. Perhaps I could add a new resolution to my list: *Thou shalt spend more time with Edie and maybe even make more candles.* What a hoot!

'Let's celebrate,' I blurted, 'with something more appropriate than out-of-tune singing and cups of tea.'

'Oh, Oliver, I'd love to, but I need to get back to work.'

Of course she did. What was I thinking?

'But perhaps now we can get the brochures done? Is your friend still happy to photograph them?'

'Yes, I think he is. How about I tee up a time?'

'And you know, perhaps now you can tell your mum.' She laughed. 'You shouldn't underestimate her, you know. Keep these samples to show her. You might be surprised at her reaction. Honestly, my mother wasn't a convert straight away. And if you tell her you've just sold seventy, that might win her over.'

I knew I had no excuse not to tell Mum about the candles now. I just needed a way to broach it with her so she didn't dismiss them unfairly. It required careful planning and a considered approach. I would start pondering ways tonight, I thought.

The Right Hook

That evening, when I returned home to my flat, I did something I never thought I would do: I took a moment to appreciate my singledom. Yes, it felt quiet and empty, as it always did when I first got home, but now, after having been with Caroline, I realised that being single and lonely was better than being taken and unhappy. And it confirmed that I was still lovable, which gave me a new-found sense of hope. Just because I was single again didn't mean it would always be the case, and my impending forties needn't be envisaged with a sense of doom. It also helped that I had revived Marie's diary, which I let myself dip into whenever I wished. I lit Marie's candle and decided to spend the evening recalibrating myself by doing some pre-dinner pottering in my court-yard, reorganising the pots into a more aesthetically pleasing arrange-ment, pulling out weeds and sweeping the path at the entrance to my flat. Tending to the outside would be a calming, centring way to end the day – a physical spring clean to mimic my recent personal spring clean. But it was as I was using the broom to rid a corner of the front porch of a particularly large cobweb that I got a tap on the shoulder.

It was Henry. 'I've changed my mind,' he said.

'Pardon?'

'I want the diary back.'

I couldn't believe it. I'd just reclaimed Marie again from out of my jumper drawer and I wasn't about to give her back. I said, 'Pardon?'

again, like someone who doesn't speak English, even though they probably would have said, 'Eh?' or '¿*Qué?*' or scrunched their nose and shoulders at the same time to show they didn't understand.

'I want it back because I don't want you to have it. I should never have given it to you in the first place,' he said, slurring his words, as if putting on a bad Scottish accent.

'Well . . . I . . .' I didn't know what to say. What *do* you say to someone asking for a gift to be returned – one that they had supposedly despised in the first place and one that you wished to keep for yourself?

'Come on, you fool,' he said, his body a metronome swaying to an irregular beat.

'What about your AA promise?' I said.

'To hell with AA.'

'I think we should talk about this when you're sober,' I said, leaning the broom against the wall. I thought that was fair. It would give me time to construct my response and mean not having to say 'no' to his face when he was in a vulnerable and potentially cantankerous mood.

He didn't like that suggestion. 'No,' he said, and lurched into my flat. The next minute he was rummaging under the newspapers on my coffee table and looking behind the cushions on the sofa.

'Hang on,' I said, rushing over to right the papers. 'You can't just mess up my house.' The more he rifled through my things, the more determined I became about keeping the diary. I felt protective of Marie and defensive of my right to have it. Henry didn't realise how important the diary was to me. It meant everything. It was my present and my past, and was helping me into the future. If I let it go, did that mean all of that would go, too? My chest fluttered and I was starting to sweat. I couldn't bear the thought of giving Marie away just like that, in a swift act of what would amount to stealing, the way Henry was carrying on.

'Oh, I see,' he said, nodding as if he did understand me. 'You're going to put up a fight.'

'No, I'm not the fighting sort.'

'I am,' he said, and swung a right hook towards me. Fearful, I ducked, but needn't have because he was at least half a metre too far away and all he punched was the air between us, and kept on punching as his unsteady legs gave way and he face-planted into the seat of an armchair. He swore on impact, the arm flopped and he lay still, his body resting on the seat of the chair, his knees on the carpet.

'Henry?'

He didn't respond.

I repeated his name again, a little louder, a little more assertively. Nothing. Was he asleep or, heaven forbid, dead? I tiptoed over to him, as if miming a burglar for a game of charades, which was utterly pointless if he was either dead or asleep, as I wanted him alive and awake. I clapped my hands, whistled feebly. But it was a whistle not even a dog would respond to, so I poked him. His shoulder muscle was impressively firm and taut, which only reinforced my earlier suspicion that if he had managed to hit me, the outcome wouldn't have been pleasant. He still didn't move. I was about to lean over once again to give him another poke when he roared back to life. I leapt backwards, slipped on a cushion Henry had flung earlier on the floor and hit the corner of the coffee table. Pain shot into a cheekbone and seared an eye.

'What's happening?' Henry slurred.

He's alive! I scrambled to my feet. 'It's been nice seeing you, Henry,' I said, hoping he would get the message and leave, having forgotten what he had come for.

'Was it?' He formed a pained expression of confusion, then parts of his face twitched – the side of his mouth, his eyelids, eyebrows, even his head jerked, then lolled. He looked as if he was perched between two worlds – the living and the dead – and I wondered if he really was going to drift into the afterlife before my eyes.

'I think you'd better go now,' I said. I had to get him out before he remembered what he'd come for.

'Can I get a drink?' he said.

Was he stalling, parched or in need of something stronger to kick him back to life?

'Sure,' I said, and went to the kitchen. I didn't bother asking him what he wanted. The helper in me poured a glass of water from the tap, which is what he needed, and the pleaser in me found a mini bottle of brandy I occasionally used for cooking, usually for one of my favourite desserts – poached pears with brown-sugar brandy reduction. I'd have given Henry anything to make him leave. But when I got back, his head had slumped forward and, this time, he was snoring. I did the only thing I could think of doing. I called Andy.

Fifteen minutes later Andy arrived. I put a finger to my lips to remind him to be quiet. Andy's jaw unhinged at the sight of my face, where a lump was forming and blood dribbled, then stifled a laugh when he saw Henry sleeping soundly, peacefully. He gave me a gesture as if to say, *What's going on?*, with eyes like poached eggs, even though I had summarised the situation over the phone. I beckoned for him to come over to me. He sat on the chair arm and I whispered in his ear.

'We've got to get Henry out of here, but I don't know whether to wait for him to wake, or try and wake him ourselves. Either way, I'm not sure how he'll react. He's been very unpredictable.'

'He could be here for hours if we let him wake on his own.'

We both looked at him, contemplating the options.

'I suggest we use that glass of water,' Andy said.

'What?'

'We throw it on him. He wakes. We're on either side lifting him up and walking him to the front door, where there'll be a pre-booked, prepaid taxi waiting to take him home before he's even registered what's happened.' Andy grinned.

Sometimes I wondered if Andy had visions of working in film rather than photography, his stories and ideas having a distinct cin-ematic ring to them.

'I'm not so sure.'

'Have you got a better idea?'

He knew I didn't. We glanced at Henry again, his mouth open like a slot machine dispensing only drool.

'OK, then,' I said, and punched the taxi number into my phone. Once booked, Andy had another idea.

'Let's open the front door and move him in the armchair as close as possible to it, so we can literally push him out.'

But moving Henry wasn't as easy as it sounded. Andy had to push the chair from behind while I held his legs wrapped in the blanket off the ground and shuffled backwards towards the door. A chest-rattle snore startled me so much it nearly made me drop them. When we got to the door, I gently placed his feet on the ground and tried to remove the blanket. But Henry's somnolent self wanted to keep it. He gripped one end close to his chest. I tugged. He tugged. I feared I'd wake him before we were ready.

'Don't worry about it,' Andy whispered.

But the blanket was one of my favourites and I didn't fancy it becoming collateral damage. I persisted. So did Henry. The taxi arrived and Andy went outside to ask the driver to wait. He crept back inside, got another glass of water from the kitchen and gave me the one from the coffee table. I still hadn't managed to get the rug off Henry.

'Forget the blanket. We've got to get him in the taxi,' Andy said. 'On the count of three. One, two, three . . .'

I couldn't believe Andy's plan had actually worked and I managed to yank off the blanket before Henry got tangled in it as he leapt from the armchair. Our unified water throws doused Henry in a more violent way than I was comfortable with, but it did the trick. So startled was he by the force of the cold water and the two of us standing over him that he shot straight out the front door – conveniently close, thanks to Andy's ingenuity – without us having to heave him up and push him out. His speed didn't last long, though, as in his drunken state he stumbled and nearly headbutted a large plant in a terracotta pot. Andy raced out, with me following, to guide him down the path to the taxi. He protested, as we knew he would, but he was also still in a confused stupor and, thanks again to Andy's forward thinking, was easily placated by the bottle of brandy Andy had tucked into his back pocket prior to the water-dousing. We stood on the pavement watching the taxi disappear down the street. I felt stunned, like I had to replay what had just happened to confirm it had really happened.

'Well, mate, that's one way to spend a Monday evening,' Andy said, slapping me on the back.

The slap snapped me out of my daze and another rush of relief flooded through me. Marie was safe. Soft, off-white clouds undulated across the sky like albino flags. The smell of slow-cooked curry from the neighbour's two doors down permeated the air. I thanked Andy and kept thanking him as we walked back to my flat, so much so that he told me to stop thanking him.

'Of course I'd help you, mate, it's a given,' he said.

Six Weeks and One Day to Go

As I made tea, Andy tidied my living room, putting the other armchair back in its place, wiping up residual water with a tea towel and draping the blanket over the back of the chair to dry. Then we sat down and, as I pressed a bag of frozen peas to my face, I filled Andy in on the salient points of Henry's visit. I told him how I liked dipping into the diary every so often, to read Marie's words, to hear her voice. Once I started, I couldn't stop. I told him about Caroline – how she'd wanted my full commitment, even my babies; how she had found the diary, thought I was having an affair, and how I had broken up with her.

'I thought everything was going great with you guys,' Andy said.

'Yeah, well . . . We just weren't right for each other.'

'I'm sorry it didn't work out, but at least you gave it a go,' he said gently.

'I did give it a go, but I'm pleased I've let her go.'

'So why are you still clinging on to the diary?'

'I'm not clinging on to it.'

He gave me a look of disbelief which was really quite unnecessary. 'You could have given the diary back to Henry if it was part of your break-up with Caroline and saved yourself all the palaver we've just been through.'

I swirled the dregs of tea at the bottom of my mug. 'I don't want to give it back, Andy. Anyway, I'd already cleared up the misunderstanding with Caroline.'

'I know it's nice to have the diary but it seems to be causing you a hell of a lot of unnecessary grief.'

'I like having Marie around.' I know I was sounding defensive but Andy clearly didn't understand. 'Did I show you the candle Edie made of her?' I went to fetch it and waved it under Andy's nose.

He nodded. 'Not bad.' He read the label. 'Fancy.'

'It's nice to be able to light it and feel that she's still with me. Like reading the diary and hearing her words.'

'Are you still reading it?' Andy asked.

'Well . . .' I shrugged. 'It's nice to,' I said. 'There's nothing wrong with that, is there?'

Andy gave me a thoughtful look and put his mug on the floor. 'Oliver. Can I say something?'

'You know you can.'

'I don't want to talk out of line, but are you in love with Marie's love, if you get my drift? Or are you actually in love with Marie and do you think it's easy to love her because you can't have her?'

I shrugged.

'Well, I can see the upside,' he continued. 'You get the perks of feeling in love, albeit one-sided, without the hassles of actually having a girlfriend.' If he was trying to lighten things up, I wasn't in the mood. 'Look, whatever it is, I think you need to give the diary back. You need to move on from Marie. It doesn't mean you can't remember her, but you can't have her. You never could. What does it matter if Henry has the diary back?'

'It's comforting,' I added, which probably sounded pathetic in retrospect, but that was the truth.

'It's holding you back,' Andy said.

I'd never thought of it like that before. I chewed a nail. Earlier in the year I had made a resolution to ask Marie out. It was the one resolution I had written in my notebook that I had been properly serious about, the one I had been minutes away from enacting in real life with a real person. And one that in hindsight I had discovered could very well have been achieved, had I not been thwarted by Marie's announcement. My dream cut in half as abruptly as an apple with one of our sharpened embalming scalpels. Yes, perhaps I was clinging on to the diary, but only because of the hope and love and joy I got from reading her reciprocated love for me. The diary was an emotional life raft that had been keeping me afloat these past few months. Hadn't it helped me say yes to Edie's candles and embark on a new venture I never would have taken on in the past? Hadn't it helped me say goodbye to Caroline? Wasn't it helping me move forward?

'I can see where you're coming from,' Andy said, 'but I think it's time to cut the cord.'

'I don't know, Andy. Give it back to her horrible husband?' The thought of doing so made me feel physically sick.

'He's probably not that horrible. He's got a drinking problem, that's all. Considering he lost Marie's love to you, he's doing pretty well.'

I thought about how fear has a smell, or so Edie had said. Right then, it smelt like damp wool and congealed blood. I feared that by giving the diary back I would somehow lose Marie and jinx everything I had done over the past few weeks. That the candles might fail or Caroline might start doing something scary, like stalking me. I knew it sounded ridiculous, yet I didn't want to risk it. Marie was a comfort blanket I didn't want to give up. I got up to get away from the smell and put the peas back in the freezer before they defrosted completely, thinking I could use them later for a pea and Parmesan risotto. But fear followed me into the kitchen. I tried to ignore it and called out to Andy, 'Is it too early for a beer?'

As I opened the door, an image of my baby sister lying on the grass suddenly seeped into the shelves in the fridge, took over from the hummus, mustard, beer bottles and apples. At a glance, Lily looked as if she was sleeping, except she wasn't. She had seen the rain outside, Mum had said, and wanted to dance among it as if it were water from the sprinkler Dad sometimes set up on the lawn, only better. Mum had been spinning cake batter in the mixer and I'd been too engrossed in building Lego on the floor to notice Lily skip out. She was so swift and nimble that no one knew she had gone until Mum saw her jiggling hips and waving elbows under crystal-beaded curtains of rain and ashen clouds charging. She danced and giggled as if the rain were tickling her until lightning splashed off a tree and got her heart fair and square. That was what the ambulance man had said, with elongated vowels and a voice like grinding metal. Fair and square. All I saw was Mum's flapping apron strings and bouncing hair as she ran out through the swing door from the kitchen into the back garden. And all I heard was her wail. It was a noise unlike anything I'd heard before, apart from Dad's drill, which he wasn't always allowed to use, having not inherited my great-grandfather's carpentry skills.

'Hey, mate, what are you doing in there?' Andy called out.

Remembering where I was, I closed the fridge door and shuffled to the living room.

'Sorry, got distracted.'

'Yeah, you left the beer behind.' He laughed.

I went back to the kitchen. Told myself to pull myself together and hoisted my trousers as a symbolic gesture, even though they really did need pulling up, despite my lack of dieting commitment. Why had that memory come to me then, so crisp and clear, like an old film that had been digitally restored? I'd never wanted to remember so much. Never wanted to remember at all. Over the years, I had been successful at shoving memories of Lily in a drawer, the one labelled 'The Childhood Memories You Wished You Never Had', which could have been turned into a sardonic comedy song performed solo on guitar, if I hadn't wanted to forget them. What happened to Lily had made me fearful of so many things. Like lightning. Like discussing Lily with Mum. Like letting go of Marie. Like standing up for myself and my decisions – especially with Mum – and taking risks. Now I realised it was Mum who feared me taking risks. Her fears had become my fears, which was understandable, I suppose, as the mother of a child who had passed away in such tragic circumstances, but wasn't it time for her to let go, too?

All these thoughts flooded my brain like the endorphin rush you get from overindulging a sweet craving. My head was pinging with one realisation after another, so much so that it was too much to take in. When Andy called out again, telling me the fridge door was beeping and asking had I got the drinks yet, I had to snap myself back to the present. I rejoined Andy with the beers and changed the topic of conversation to when he would be free to do a photoshoot of the candles. Yet I couldn't stop thinking: was now the time to face my fears?

When Andy left, I went to the bedroom and pulled out Marie's diary from under the mattress. I looked at the cover, sniffed it but didn't open it. Even though it still smelt of honey and leather, bound paper and Marie, it seemed different to me now.

'You've been good to me, Marie, more than you will ever know,' I said out loud. 'But you know what? Your diary has been troublesome.' I hugged the cover and lay on the bed. Yes, Andy was right. Marie *was* in the past. The love we had for one another may have felt real, and may once have been real, but it wasn't any more. Clinging on to the diary had hindered my ability to fully engage with another woman and being in the middle of a tit-for-tat competition with Henry over it was undesirable and bothersome. It wasn't right for me to denounce Henry's love for Marie because it was tarnished by an alcoholic temper, and yet, having an unrequited love didn't mean it was mine to keep either. All I had wanted was one read of the diary, one insight into her thoughts, and I'd got that many times over. Was it time to give it back? Was it time to face my fears and truly let go?

I sat up, left the diary on the bed and found my notebook of resolutions and a pen from the bedside table. Turning to a fresh page, I wrote in capitals so it took up the whole piece of paper: *FACE YOUR FEARS*. I didn't even bother to write 'Thou shalt', which seemed inappropriately formal and passive for this particular entry. For this resolution was meant to be an order. I added an exclamation mark to enforce the command and make me show that, this time, I truly meant it.

Then I had the biggest realisation of all. It wasn't just about facing my fears – hadn't Caroline persuaded me to go swimming, after all? – it was about being true to myself and doing the things that were right for me and my business. My fortieth birthday was now only six weeks and one day away and it was time that I started making the right decisions, the ones that honoured me, Oliver Clock. For I knew deep down that returning the diary was the right thing to do; that future-proofing the family business was the right thing to do; that now was the right time to tell Mum about the candles, as I believed in them as much as I did Edie; that I should have stood up for my decision to hire Cora Mulligan, as she was the right embalmer for Clock & Son; that eating cheese and cake made me happy and denying myself them unhappy. I was scribbling so fast I hadn't realised I'd nearly come to the end of the notebook. What a lot of resolutions, and not a lot of time before my birthday: only six weeks and one day. I had to start now!

So I did, beginning with the last one. I would buy cake to celebrate my new beginning. It was a shame I had no candles to put on top. But I reckoned it didn't matter; they could wait until my birthday.

I put on a cap and sunglasses to hide my cheek wound, even though it was now dusk, furtively checked that Henry wasn't flattened next to the wall by the front door or hiding behind my car, and drove to the patisserie. I fancied a slice of white chocolate cheesecake or perhaps hot cherry pie I could slather with vanilla ice cream for dessert. But when the last chocolate ganache cake caught my eye, I thought, *Why buy one slice when you could buy the whole cake?* Back home, I placed Marie's candle in the middle of my round four-seater dining table and cut what Mum would call a 'sensible slice' of the cake. It was so good I had to have another. Two 'sensible' slices.

That's when I thought of Lily again. I was standing on a stool at the kitchen bench with an oversized apron folded over and tied around my waist, smelling of raw butter and flour. Mum was next to me waving a sticky wooden spoon as she taught me how to make a cake. I followed each instruction, waiting for the next one, desperate for the mixing and pouring to be over so I could lick the spoon. We were making a cake for Lily's second birthday and would do the icing and decorations during her afternoon sleep. Mum had it all planned, timed to the minute with rose-pink food colouring, pre-bought fondant daisies and two large white candles ready to be arranged. I nearly weed my pants with excitement as the cake mix burst into life, but didn't dare let on in case I wasn't allowed to stick around for the decorating. The memory made me chuckle. This was what remembering someone should be like. I shouldn't be pushing memories of my sister away but welcoming them with fondness and joy. I didn't want to pretend she never existed. Nor did I want to live my life as if I, too, would be struck by lightning at any moment. I owed it to Lily to do something about it.

I ate the last mouthful and opened the notebook again. On the second-to-last page I wrote: *Thou shalt not live your life as if you might be struck by lightning.*

I would have tucked into a third slice if I hadn't thought of Edie. Why she popped into my head right then I didn't know, but it occurred to me that she deserved a thank-you gift for introducing the candles to me and proving they could be a hit with customers. I could save some cake for her. Yes, I would deliver celebratory cake to her tomorrow – a dose of decadence for her hard work; it was the least I could do. I put the rest of the cake in the fridge, the box sliding easily into the middle section, next to a packet of Weight Watchers bacon and a carton of eggs, which reminded me that I really must stock up on food that wasn't breakfast-related.

And I went to sleep that night eager to present to the world the new Oliver Clock.

Cake

I woke early to the sounds of the rubbish truck, which felt symbolic, as if it were a metaphor for the night before and the truck was taking away the old Oliver. It was an analogy I wasn't unhappy about. I dressed in my favourite blue suit and galaxy tie in maroon, and breakfasted on bacon and eggs before fetching the cake from the fridge and heading out of the door. I would start my new life by giving cake to Edie on my way in to Clock & Son.

Just as I found a place to park outside, I saw Edie walk past on her way to the pharmacy. I wound down the window and called out to her.

'Hi, Oliver,' she said, coming over. 'What are you doing here?'

'I've brought you cake,' I said.

'Cake? What for?'

'To thank you for the success of the candles.'

'That's so sweet of you.'

'I'd love to say I made it, but I didn't.'

I picked up the box and was handing it to her through the car window when she suddenly noticed my face. 'Oh my goodness, what happened to you?'

'Oh, that,' I said, touching my cheek, having forgotten that I resembled half a swede and a sliver of red chilli. 'I had an altercation with the coffee table.'

'Are you sure you're alright?'

'Top of the morning, as my father liked to say.'

She looked at me quizzically, which she needn't have as, apart from my wound, I was perfectly fine and felt even better now that I could give Edie cake. 'Do you want to come in and we'll find something for that cut? It's looking a little angry,' she said.

'I don't want to get in the way of your work.'

'You won't be. You can sit out the back and I'll make some coffee. Diana has already opened up.'

'Well, alright then. I suppose you can't have coffee without cake.' I laughed. Tucking the cake box under one arm, Edie led me to the back room of the pharmacy.

'Have a seat on the stool,' Edie said. 'Now, let's have a look at that injury of yours.' She came very close to my face, which was a little disconcerting, yet I couldn't help but notice that she smelled enticingly of apples that had been delicately stewed with brown sugar and a sprinkling of cinnamon. She dabbed at the cut with a damp cloth and applied antiseptic cream. 'You've got a nice bruise forming,' she said, 'but otherwise it should be fine. Keep the cream – use it a couple of times a day for the next few days. OK, let's get the coffee machine on and check out this cake,' she said.

She flipped the lid and immediately the lingering aroma of antiseptic ointment was drowned out by that of rich chocolate. I took another look inside and immediately felt a fool. I had forgotten quite how much I had eaten the night before.

'Did it have an altercation with the coffee table, too?' Edie laughed.

'I'm sorry, I should have mentioned: I indulged last night.'

She looked at me curiously, then said, 'Do you want to tell me what really happened?'

I had not intended to bore Edie with my woes at nine o'clock on a weekday morning, so I stood up to go. 'It's a long story and not that interesting. Thank you so much for your nursing skills, but I should let you get on with your work.'

'It's much better talking about things than letting them bottle up inside, you know. Anyway, I haven't made the coffee yet.'

The way Edie looked at me then, with such kindness and care, made me sit back down. I felt my guard drop and before I could stop myself I was telling her about Henry and the diary; how Marie was his wife and how it was only natural that Henry was angry with me but that neither of us had known we felt the same about each other. I didn't go into extensive detail; it was an abridged version that gave her just enough information so she could understand the significance of the diary for me and how it was similar to a comfort blanket I liked having around. I hadn't intended to open up to her, had never thought I would tell anyone else about Marie and the diary other than Andy. I didn't with Caroline, hadn't with Mum and, come to think about it, I'd never opened up about much to Marie either. Neither of us had divulged our deepest fears, worries or emotions. Yet with Edie, I had done so without thinking. It just felt right, which was really rather odd.

Edie handed me a coffee and a slice of cake. 'You know, I had something like that once. It was a silver bracelet my grandmother gave me for my twenty-first birthday a few weeks before she died. I wore it every day and, because I wore it every day, it felt wrong when I didn't wear it. Like I was missing something. As if something would go wrong because I wasn't wearing it, which doesn't make any sense, but that's what it felt like. Then one day I lost it. I think the clasp must have caught on something and the bracelet fell off without me knowing. I never found it. But you know what? Nothing bad happened when I couldn't wear it any more,' she said gently. 'Everything carried on just fine.'

My conversation with Andy and all the thoughts I'd had yesterday came back to me in a rush of unnerving clarity. 'It's ridiculous, really. All I have to do is give back the diary.' I scooped some cake on to the spoon and reminded myself, again, of the comforting benefits of chocolate.

'I could help you, if you like?' Edie said. 'Two sets of hands are better than one.' She looked at me expectantly.

'You don't have to do that. I've burdened you enough with my problems, when I shouldn't have.' The joy I felt that she seemed to care enough about me to offer to help return the diary was as good, if not better, than a few mouthfuls of chocolate cake. What kind of business colleague does that?

'Honestly, I don't mind.' Then her eyes lit up. 'Why don't we do it now? I can nip out and do it with you and won't take a lunch break.'

'I only have to put it in a post bag.' I laughed. How silly it all was sounding.

'So? I'll come with you. I'm experienced at post office queues,' she said.

'Well . . .' I started, which she took as a resounding yes.

'Great! You'll feel so much better once it's done.'

She took my hand and led me through the pharmacy to my car.

'You've done enough for me already, Edie, you know that, don't you?' I said, following her. 'And you know we have to go to my place first to pick up the diary? Are you sure you have time?'

'I don't mind.' She smiled. 'Honestly, I really want to help.' Then she blushed and looked away.

I felt a fool for letting her insist on coming with me, and yet having her by my side was not unwanted. How wonderful to have someone care about you so much when they didn't have to at all, when their relationship to you was one of a purely professional nature. Caroline hadn't been like that, and we had been dating.

Letting Go

Back at my flat, Edie waited in the car as I went inside. But I couldn't do a thirty-second grab and run. I had to have a minute to say goodbye. I held the diary to my nose, breathing in its aroma one more time. Velvet roses, softened leather, old paper, musky perfume. I closed my eyes and kissed the cover. Then, it was time.

I went back to the car.

'Are you OK?' Edie asked.

I nodded, said, *Goodbye, Marie*, in my head, so Edie wouldn't hear, and started the car.

I reversed on to the street and drove up to the main road. Even though I knew I was doing the right thing, I couldn't help but feel a little sad, a little subdued and quite a bit daunted. This wasn't just about giving something back to someone, handing it over to a post office employee. It was closing the door on one life to let another one open. This was a significant and symbolic moment and I felt the need to observe a minute's silence. Thankfully, Edie noted the importance of the occasion and remained silent, too. In hindsight, I probably should have made light conversation, asked her how her morning had been, thanked her again for the cream she had given me free of charge. But I was too focused on the task at hand. When we reached the main road you could see the red-and-white post office sign in the distance, even though there were still three sets of lights to get through.

Then, I felt a change happen inside me. Like when I realised I didn't have to be with someone like Caroline, who wasn't right for me. Like when you realise death needn't be grisly, that it's just another stage of life. Or that you're not going to die if you eat raw fish, that it can, in fact, be perfectly tasty. As we sat at the first set of lights, watching a group of long-haired, skinny-jeans-wearing teenage boys slink across the road, their hips cavalier, attitudes blasé, I had another idea. I would deliver the diary my way. I would show Henry that I was not a coward. That *I* was in charge of the situation now.

'Sorry, Edie, I've changed my mind.'

'You can't back out now,' she said. 'Look, we're nearly there.'

'No, no, I'm not backing out. I'm backing in. Metaphorically speaking.'

When the lights changed, I turned in to a side street, made a U-turn and enjoyed the sensation of a high-speed car chase, even though I was driving only moderately fast and being chased by no one. I enjoyed making the tyres squeal from a forced hill acceleration and thought, *To hell with stopping at amber traffic lights*, and kept on driving. Flushed from going over the speed limit and attempting a swerved corner turn, I pulled up outside Henry's house and parked under the shade of a tree.

'Is this where I think it is?' Edie asked.

'It is. Do you mind waiting here a minute? Hopefully he's in.'

'Sure.'

I slipped the diary into my jacket pocket, stepped out of the car, shut the door and eyed up my destination. I adjusted my tie, rolled my shoulders and tugged at the suit lapels. I imagined I was Paul Newman in *Butch Cassidy and the Sundance Kid* and walked up to the gate.

Its latch was sticky on opening. I tried to ignore the state of the garden, which was even more dishevelled than when I had last been there. Plants resembled weeds, and weeds plants. Dropped camellia flowers browned themselves in the sun. I looked down the side of the house, where I had hidden on my previous visit, and didn't even contemplate going there if I had a change of heart. I walked straight up to the front door and knocked. When I got no response, I rang the doorbell and knocked again.

The door opened. I felt the momentousness of the moment, like there should have been cinematic build-up music. A slow zooming in on our faces as Henry looked at me and I looked back. He swayed like a tree stabilising itself in a gust of wind, his eyeballs nimble as marbles. I stood rock solid, the diary not obviously visible in my pocket. The old Oliver Clock was waiting for Henry to speak until he realised that the new Oliver Clock should be the one to talk first.

'Hello, Henry.'

His gaze narrowed to my left side. 'Your face isn't looking too good,' he said.

'Yeah, well, no thanks to you.'

'I didn't do that,' he said indignantly, gripping the door for balance.

'Not exactly, but you did threaten.'

Henry frowned, as if trying to remember. 'You deserved it,' he grumbled. 'Anyway, why are you here?'

'I've got the diary.' I patted my pocket.

'Finally,' he said.

'But I want an apology first.' The new Oliver Clock thought I deserved that at least.

'What?'

'I want an apology for barging into my house and making me trip on the coffee table,' I said.

We had a staring competition for all of three seconds until finally he spoke. 'Alright. I'm sorry.'

'Thanks,' I said, and reached into my pocket.

He took the diary off me greedily and held it to his chest. 'Thank you,' he whispered.

Then he started choking up, which isn't meant to be a euphemism for crying. He did it literally. I thought he was going to choke on his own chest phlegm as well as spew tears over the porch, as if he were an overflowing gutter pipe. I reached out an arm to comfort him, although I wasn't sure where to put it. On his shoulder seemed too personal, yet on his forearm too impersonal. I wasn't expecting such an outpouring of emotion and now felt a little bad that I had withheld what he'd wanted or seemed to need so badly. It was as if he were clinging on to anything that was Marie's in a flurry of remorse, regret and despair.

'It's OK,' I said. 'Do you have someone you can talk to?'

He shrugged and wiped a dripping nose with the back of his hand. He stumbled towards the veranda post for support as his knees began to buckle.

'Why don't you sit for a minute?' I suggested, and helped him to the top step. I sat down next to him. We were like the two characters in *Waiting for Godot*, me sweltering in a suit and Henry in his baggy T-shirt, tracksuit pants and slip-on shoes, waiting for something to happen. Or maybe we were hovering mid-moment, waiting for the dynamics to shift and re-form. We gazed over the unkempt front garden towards the houses on the opposite side of the street, Henry still cosseting the diary at his chest, sniffing.

'You know,' I said, 'a friend told me recently that fear has a smell. But I've decided it's the thought of the smell that is far worse than the reality.'

Henry looked at me, back to the houses, to me again and then at his feet.

'You will get through this,' I said. 'It might seem like your world has collapsed, but grief has an agenda and, unlike our public transport system, it sticks to it, trust me.'

He looked at me again, a long, in-depth look which I couldn't easily read. I don't think he'd necessarily fully forgiven me for being the focus of Marie's secret attentions, but something had changed in him. Perhaps it was the realisation that being angry was hard work and, in his case, pretty futile. Or maybe he'd decided I was a more decent guy than he'd first thought, or, at the very least, someone not worth hating any more. Which, if I thought about it as I was doing then, was what I felt about him. That he probably wasn't that bad a husband. Just a husband Marie had fallen out of love with. A man lost and sad who'd got distracted by booze.

'OK, mate,' I said. The fact I even called him 'mate' meant something had changed in me, too. I wasn't sure I wanted him as a real mate but the sentiment of a truce was there. 'I'd better get back to work.'

He nodded and gripped my knee for a second. 'Thanks,' he said and, this time, I think he meant it.

When I got back to the car, Edie let me get in, loosen my tie and rest my head on the back of the seat before speaking.

'He was home, then?' she asked.

'He certainly was.'

'I was thinking,' she said thoughtfully, 'I could make him a candle of Marie. Do you think he'd like that?'

What an extraordinary idea! 'You know what? I reckon he would. That's a very kind gesture.'

I looked at her then and smiled. It felt like I had my very own living talisman sitting next to me and I suddenly wished I could have kissed her rather than high-fived over the handbrake. What a strange effect Edie was having on me. Very strange indeed.

I'll Do It My Way

I arrived at Clock & Son feeling pretty damn chirpy – or how I often feel after a meal of slow-cooked lamb shanks, sweet-potato mash with a dollop of garlic butter and al dente French beans I'd cooked myself. I may now have been Marie-less but it didn't feel as bad as I'd thought it would. In fact, I felt great. The changes Marie had helped me make were continuing. Even though I had let her go, her effect on me was still proving efficacious. I was turning my life around and acting on my resolutions. I was taking charge and moving on. In reception I took a moment to take in my surroundings, as if I hadn't properly considered them before. On the table by the window sat my grandmother's crystal vase, which was always filled with flowers, and Mum's strategically placed eucalyptus-infused tissues in mock-crackle, non-breakable rose-painted boxes, chosen to cope with sudden grief-ridden handling. On the walls were two paintings I had bought at an inner-city art gallery, which I wouldn't have minded hanging in my living room. The sofa, still buxom despite its age, which cosseted you comfortingly in its grasp, with cushions Jean kept fully plump so as to show no signs of the previous sitter. The rich smell of furniture polish, the scent of dust-free surfaces and the one constant: compassion.

There really was nothing like the integrity of three generations. Elements may be outdated but the building was solid and sturdy and Clock & Son estimable and dependable. It was my baby. The business may have chosen me but, without me, there would be no third genera-tion. For Clock & Son was me, my family, my history, my community. I was the Son, I was the Clock, I was the past, I was the present. I was the middleman between the living and the dead. I felt a surge of pride welling from deep within my belly and overflowing into my veins, as if my skin would burst and my shirt buttons would pop open. I didn't want Clock & Son to die a slow death; I wanted it to live on and now it was time to bring it into the twenty-first century. Today I would put in place one of my new resolutions: *Thou shalt hire the embalmer you want*. I just hoped Cora Mulligan was still looking for a job.

I went straight to my desk and found her number. Firstly, I had to apologise for how Mum had behaved and then explain how the other embalmer hadn't worked out, before I could ask, 'You wouldn't still be interested in the job, would you?'

'Great to hear from you Mr Clock,' Cora said, then paused. 'Hang on, let me go into the mortuary, then I won't have to whisper.' I waited as she changed rooms. 'That's better. Where were we? Oh yes, I was about to speak out of turn.' She chuckled. 'To be honest, your call couldn't come at a better time. I took on a new job, but I'm not happy and would much prefer to work for you guys. I liked the feel of your place, the tradition and personalised service.'

'That's very nice of you to say,' I said. 'Traditional and personal are our core values. We have also started offering an extra, unique and customised service to customers that no one else is doing. I would love to tell you more about it if you were interested in working with us.'

'I would be very keen, thank you. Honestly, this place I'm now at . . . the cost-cutting . . . the lies . . . the flash Harrys . . .' She was whispering again, possibly even looking around furtively. I empathised. I knew what it felt like to be overheard by a cadaver or two. It could be most unnerving. 'Do you know,' she continued, 'only a few days ago we were getting ready for a funeral and a viewing, and someone – I won't name names – pulled out the wrong guy but dressed him in the right guy's clothing. When the time came for the family to see him, his wife hyperventilated and he didn't even apologise. Worse, he told them that's what happens when you die. That sometimes you can start looking like someone else. Can you believe it?'

I couldn't. Then again, if this new place she had started at was Green Light Funerals, then I probably could. But how could I find out without breaching any ethical concerns? I needn't have worried. Cora needed little coercing. 'Really?' was all I needed to say.

'Oh, yes, you've no idea. It's horrendous. I won't name names, but the first word of the company name is a colour.'

So, it *was* them, the dirty scoundrels. As upset as I was for the poor customers who had to experience such poor behaviour, this news made me very happy indeed. It was a validation that working honourably and with dignity was the right way to be and that, sooner or later, the word would spread about Green Light Funerals' despicable practices and Clock & Son would come out the winner, the stayer, ready to live on for a fourth generation, if I were ever to produce one.

'Thank you for your honesty,' I said, trying to remain professional and calm and not like a man who wanted to punch the air in excitement. 'I'm sorry it isn't working out for you, but if you were happy to jump ship, so to speak, you may start with us as soon as you like.'

And so it was that I finally got the embalmer I wanted and unexpectedly discovered that the competition was practically drowning in malpractice. I hung up and started laughing, a tremendous guffaw that would have startled Jean and Mum, had they been with me. As it was, I could fill the air with uncompromised chortling and not cut it short for anyone.

Making Clock & Son Sing

I sat for a minute at my desk, enjoying what it felt like to take charge, to experience the new Oliver Clock emerging. I didn't want the transition to occur without taking a moment to appreciate its significance. Finally, I was being true to myself. Finally, my little yellow notebook was something I could be proud of. Or was it me and my actions that I should feel proud of? I took a slow, deep breath, in and out. I now had to prepare for my next task. The big one. The chat with Mum and Jean. I needed – wanted – them both on side. It was time to tell Mum everything. It was time to show them the new Oliver Clock.

I left my office and found them chatting by the water cooler. Mum had just arrived with some fresh flowers and Jean had returned from buying provisions. 'Can I have a meeting with you both?' I asked.

Mum turned to look me. 'Good grief, what happened to your face?'

I said I'd had an accident vacuuming, tripped and hit the coffee table. I'm not sure she believed me, despite her knowing the enthusiasm with which I usually threw myself into cleaning, which was a shame, because it was only a semi-lie. 'I'm fine. It looks worse than it is.'

'Jean, get ice,' Mum said.

'We don't have any.'

'I'll make tea, then.' Mum's cure-all for everything.

'I don't need tea, Mum.'

'But we can't have customers seeing you like this. I know just what you need,' she said, raising a finger to the ceiling and then disappearing to the back room. She returned with a tube of the gloopy embalming foundation we used to add colour and patina to ghost-like visages and started dabbing it on my face.

'Mum!' I swatted her hand away.

'Sorry, does it hurt?'

'I don't want you putting make-up on me.'

'Nearly done.'

'I'm thirty-nine, Mum.'

'So?'

She looked at me as if to say, *What could possibly be wrong with a seventy-seven-year-old woman putting make-up on her thirty-nine-year-old son?*

But, really, enough was enough. *Thou shalt stand up for yourself in the face of your mother.*

'Please don't put make-up on me. I will be forty in six weeks—'

'Oh, yes,' Mum interrupted, 'I was going to ask what you'd like for your birthday. And would you like me to cook a special dinner?'

'I don't know, Mum. We can talk about it another time. What I'd really like is for you to listen to what I have to say. You see, I want to make a new start. I want to make Clock & Son sing again. I want it to shine like it used to, as it still should.'

'I've not heard you so passionate in a long time – not since that patisserie opened down the road.'

Jean twiddled with her silver crescent-moon brooch as if contemplating moving the crescent into a grin.

'I'll take that as a compliment, but I'm being serious. The thing is, I can't do my job properly if I also have to embalm. So, I've decided to hire a new embalmer.'

Naturally, Mum was horrified, especially when she learned it was 'that tattooed thing'. I had to shut her down before she got carried away. I told her it was a fait accompli, and I'm not sure if it was my use of a

French phrase that appeased her but certainly Cora's revelation about our competitor did.

'This *is* interesting news, Oliver, and does bode very well for Clock & Son's future, don't you think?'

'Which brings me to the next decision I've made,' I announced, and proceeded to tell her about Edie and the candles. 'I know they sound unusual, but we have already sold seventy, to two people. I want the candles to be our signature offering, something that no one else does.'

'They sound appalling. And you've sold some already! Why didn't you think to tell me about them before?' Mum said.

'They're not appalling, Mum. I didn't tell you before because I wanted to prove to you that people liked them, that they could be a drawcard for new customers. And Edie is so . . .' I searched for the right word to describe her, as so many suitable words came to mind.

'Edie is delightful,' Jean said, to help me out.

'You know about this, Jean?' Mum was beginning to sound, understandably, a bit put out. I wasn't surprised; it was going as well as I could have hoped.

Jean nodded.

'So, you've gone behind my back.'

'No . . . well . . . maybe,' I said.

Mum gasped. I had to keep calm and stand my ground.

'Look, I didn't want to upset you. But before you dismiss them, please let me show you the candles and introduce you to Edie.'

'Well, it's the least you could do, under the circumstances,' Mum said.

'If it's any consolation, they won't cost us a cent.'

'Thank heavens for small mercies.' Mum was sounding more sarcastic than was desirable. She put a hand to her chest and looked to the ceiling, as if someone up above were offering a modicum of common sense to appease my announcements. 'But don't think I'm going to sign them off just like that. I'll humour them, if you really want me to. Now, can I go and finish the flowers?'

'Just two more things, Mum. We talked about doing a Clock & Son revamp but haven't done anything about it. I think now it's time. We don't need to do a huge one and blow out the budget, just enough to keep the place traditional yet relevant. It's about investing in the future. And I promise not to ditch the wood panelling or any of the family heirlooms.'

Jean nodded. 'I'm happy to start getting quotes for painting and a new carpet, if you like, so we can make informed decisions?'

'Excellent, Jean, thank you. The first thing we definitely need, though, is a new sign, and that's non-negotiable.'

'Goodness me, Oliver, this is all too much for one meeting,' Mum said. 'We should have had separate meetings for each point. There's a lot to think about.'

'There is, and I didn't mean to overwhelm you but, well, lately . . . Let's just say I want to enter my forties differently to how I did my thirties.'

'Next you'll be telling me you're buying a red sports car.'

'Don't be silly.'

'Good, because I can't see you in a convertible.'

Jean stifled a chuckle. Mum looked about to get up.

'Hang on, there's one more thing,' I said. My last announcement ready to go.

'Yes?'

'I'm giving you both permission to retire.'

Mum gasped.

'I'm not asking you to, as you have both been immensely valuable to the business. I'm giving you the chance to do so, if you wish.'

'*Mon Dieu!*' Mum exclaimed. 'I've never thought about retiring.' She glanced at her lap and the wrinkled hands that lay in it.

'You're seventy-seven,' I said.

'I've never liked bowls or bridge. I like being here. You're my family.'

I went over to her and squeezed her shoulder. She didn't shrug me off. 'And this is still your family,' I told her. 'You can still come here. You could be chairperson and sit on monthly board meetings, or I could buy you out and, with the extra cash, you could go travelling. Visit France, practise your French, or try something new. Haven't you always wanted to learn Japanese flower arranging?'

'Ikebana,' she said wistfully.

'What better time than now, while you're fit and healthy?'

She chewed her lip but didn't looked displeased.

'Look, I'm not making either of you retire. I want you to know that I can run the business on my own, make my own decisions about its future and that it will all be fine. *I* will be fine.'

'Thank you, Oliver.' Jean smiled cheekily, as if she had just been let loose in the brooch section of a jewellery store.

'Have a think about it,' I added, even though I could tell they were both thinking already. The air brewed with the contemplation of a new world bubbling within reach.

'Right, well, if that's it, then, I'm going to put the kettle on,' Mum said.

I couldn't have asked for a better start to my new resolutions. And yet it did get better. Later that day I overheard Jean telling Mum about a cruise she was thinking of going on with her husband.

'It's a boutique cruise around the South Pacific,' Jean said over the rumblings of the kettle. 'Maximum seventy-two passengers. I'm not a fan of too many people but Bill has no qualms whatsoever. He'll probably organise everyone into groups for some on-board sporting competition, even if it is only bingo. I like the thought of having everything done for me. What luxury!'

Mum said it sounded marvellous and asked whether she could join them, with a burst of laughter unlike the sound she normally made. I liked hearing them talk with joy in their voices about something other than the funeral business and it made me wonder whether I needed to start looking for a new administrative assistant as well.

Then, as Mum started fussing over a new bunch of flowers – cerise-coloured Asian lilies – trimming the stalks, angling the blooms, rearranging them so they sat just so, it occurred to me. I don't know how many bouquets of lilies I had seen in Clock & Son over the years – hundreds, if not thousands – and yet I had never realised. How had I not thought of it before? I rushed back to my office to text Edie.

Cold-Calling

There's something about making the right decisions that is very good for your posture. I'm sure my slouch lessened over the next few days and it made me wonder when I next saw Edie whether I was a few centimetres taller than her than I'd first thought. We met a couple of days later at Andy's studio after work to photograph the candles. Edie brought one of the extra candles we had made for Fran that was unlit and in pristine condition for Andy to photograph. I was glad Andy could meet Edie and see that the creator of candles that smell like the dead had neither a wart on her chin nor wielded a weapon. In fact, Edie looked quite delightful in a teal dress that swished to reveal the tops of her knees every so often. We didn't really have to do very much. In fact, we could easily have left Andy to it, as expert as he was at product shots against a white background and flattering lighting. Still, we hovered and took turns taking the candle lid off and angling it in a different manner so we had options to choose from. At one point Edie and I leaned in at the same time and I got a whiff of a perfume or cream I couldn't initially decipher. Ripe nectarines? Lanolin? Meringue? Or was it just the scent of her, the sort of scent she would put in a candle if she were creating one for herself? Then Andy told us to stop fiddling and get out of the shot and the moment of deciphering was lost.

Within an hour, Andy was done. He said he would do some digital tweaking and email us the best shots the next day. As I had already primed Clock & Son's leaflet printer for the job and sent him Edie's copy and design layout, we would be able to get the brochures in a couple of days.

Afterwards, Andy and I went down to the pub. We had not done this for a while and I wanted to shout him a beer for helping us with the photo shoot. The seven o'clock news bounced off the big screen near our table, as if trying to talk over the top of us. We could have changed seats but we had been sitting in this spot for as long as I could remember and I saw no reason to change. I bought Andy's favourite beer and two packets of salt-and-vinegar crisps. As Andy ripped open the first bag, the weather presenter forecasted an impending storm, angry winds and record rainfall over a twenty-four-hour period. As we enjoyed the crisps and beer, Andy updated me on Lucy, who was 'still feeling rotten', and how they'd had a scan and seen the baby put a finger up its nose.

'Do you want to see?' he asked, pulling out a photo from his wallet.

We spent a few silent seconds admiring an unborn child picking its nose, then I announced that I, too, had news and told him how I had returned the diary to Henry and we'd reconciled on the porch.

'Well done, mate,' Andy said. He clinked his beer bottle on mine. 'I'm proud of you, getting out of your comfort zone and all that.'

I delighted in the realisation that I had gone out of my comfort zone and hadn't even experienced vertigo. I had returned the diary and, so far, everything was going just fine. I hadn't fallen off a precipice and nothing bad had happened. In fact, it was quite the reverse.

'Edie's nice, too,' Andy continued. 'The candles seem less weird now that I know more about them. It's like you're on a roll, all these changes you're making. Can you possibly jam in anything more?'

I laughed and asked if he wanted another beer. Rain drummed the roof above us and, through the window near the bar, lightning thrashed the sky as if giving it a flogging and I didn't even flinch.

When the brochures were ready it was time to go cold-calling. We had a list of the top ten retirement villages, nursing homes and florists' we wanted to target and our plan was to visit them all to see how much interest we could garner. If cold-calling proved successful, we would draw up another list for another day, and so on, to spread the word. I didn't like to tell Edie I had already earmarked a rather snazzy tie I was considering purchasing for our stint on morning television – a light blue linen number with an assortment of brightly coloured flowers – and wondered if she had a floral dress to complement it. I would ask when the moment was right, when she no longer thought my public relations fantasy was 'jumping the gun'.

I drove to pick up Edie with the box of brochures in the back seat and made a last-minute decision to buy her a bunch of yellow tulips.

'I thought they matched your front door,' I said, when I got to her house.

She laughed. 'Dulux Dandelion Yellow, to be specific,' she said. 'I can't tell you how many sample pots of yellow paint I tried until I found the one I wanted. The flowers are lovely, thank you.'

'Think of them as an added extra thank you,' I said, which didn't really make much sense, but I had no good reason for why I'd bought them for her, apart from an uncontrollable urge that wouldn't go away.

'We've only sold the candles to two people, you know,' she said. 'We shouldn't get too carried away.'

'I'm not getting carried away,' I said. 'Sometimes I find giving someone something for no reason is the best gift of all.'

Her dress had ridden up her femur and I pretended not to look, even though I was finding it hard not to gaze at the whole of Edie and not just her legs. I gave her a brochure instead.

'Fabulous,' she said. 'They look like we mean business, so let's go and get some.'

The first florist we approached turned us away immediately, on the basis they had too many candles already. She wouldn't even let us explain. The second made encouraging noises and kept a brochure and so it went, little by little, making a bit of progress here, not a lot there. Clareville Retirement Village gave us the best reception of all. A gaggle of intrigued nurses gathered around to learn more and each took a brochure as I handed them around.

'It's a crazy idea, but we love crazy around here,' the manager said.

'I'd like to make one of old Dulcie,' said another.

'She was a character, and didn't she used to smell the greatest? What was that perfume she always used to wear?'

'Poison.'

They all laughed. We laughed with them and they promised to tell everyone about them.

By lunch time we had ticked off six destinations and given away a decent chunk of the brochures. Although we received mixed reviews, we got enough positive comments to want to keep going.

'It's all about the publicity, isn't it, getting them out there?' Edie said. 'Word of mouth is going to be our best bet. We need to get people talking.'

I agreed. As far as I was concerned, Edie could keep talking as long as she wanted.

And I went home that day wondering if you could have such a thing as a retrospective resolution. As soon as I walked in the door, I got the notebook from the bedside table and opened it to the last page. *Why not?* I thought, and began to write: *Thou shalt embark on a new and unexpected venture that will help boost business, in which you must bottle smells of deceased clients and sell them as candles.* It sounded absurd and yet I was doing it and it seemed to be working. I gave it two ticks and a star. I then wondered about what Mum had said a few days earlier about what I'd like to do for my birthday. For the first time, I actually felt ready to consider the proposition and even to celebrate – but not merely with a few supermarket candles stuck on a store-bought cake I shared with Mum. It didn't have to be something extravagant, just something worthy of the man I hoped I was turning into. A proper celebration for having survived a tumultuous year and coming out of it not just alive but rejuvenated.

Immediately, I wanted to do something out of character, like unballing all my socks and matching one half with a different one altogether. Or reordering my pantry items so that they weren't in alphabetical order. Messing up my bed so that it was unmade when I got in it. Ha! I would do them now, I thought, there would be no turning back. How wonderfully carefree it made me feel! It was as if I had gained a sense of freedom I had never felt before. The freedom to be someone new.

The Gift

It was exactly five weeks until my fortieth birthday – Friday at five o'clock – and Mum was to meet Edie. I asked Jean to stay back as well. I didn't say why. I wanted it to be a surprise. I was so full of anticipation that I reordered the items in my stationery drawer for the third time that day.

Jean stayed at her desk, looking up at the door every now and again, and Mum did her end-of-the-day decor tweaks – adjusting paintings that were on a lean, plumping cushions, adding water to the flowers, decreasing crumpled sofa arm covers, fluffing tissues. She did a good job, as always. You'd never have known there had been people in the place at all. An air of expectation hovered like low-hanging fog.

Finally, Edie arrived at a quarter past six, her hair tied in a loose chignon and wearing tiny earrings in the shape of macaroons.

'Mum,' I said, 'I'd like to introduce you to Edie.'

'Hello, Mrs Clock,' Edie said, putting out a hand to shake. 'I'm so glad we could finally meet.'

'Hello, dear,' Mum replied. 'Yes, I've heard about you and your candles of the dead.' She sounded embarrassingly disparaging.

'Well, I'd love to tell you more about them,' Edie said, ignoring Mum's dubiousness. She then did something most daren't do: she took Mum's hand and led her to the sofa. I knew I could trust Edie to soften Mum's scepticism and bring her round. 'You see, Mrs Clock, they're not meant to be macabre. They're meant to be memory prompts. You're in the business of helping people grieve and so you know how important it is to encourage them to find the joy in remembering their loved ones. My candles are designed to do just that, to bring comfort, solace and happiness. For what else have we got left in the end but memories?'

I remembered Edie telling me that the first time I met her. I hadn't appreciated the sentiment at the time and thought I must add it to Dad's Folder. What's more, we could have a whole new section dedicated to the candles.

'Before I show you some samples, Oliver and I have something to give you.'

Mum looked at me querulously. 'Really, Oliver, you know I don't like surprises and, lately, you keep giving them to me.'

'This is meant to be a nice one,' I said.

'I'll be the judge of that.'

'I hope you like it, Mrs Clock.' Edie pulled a candle out of her bag and presented it to her.

'Oh, Doreen!' Jean exclaimed.

'I hope this isn't what I think it is. I can't imagine what I might smell like. It doesn't bear contemplating.' Mum glared at me. 'I'm not even dead yet.'

'It's not a candle of you, Mrs Clock,' Edie explained. 'But it is of someone whose memory you may not wish to forget.'

Mum stared at the candle as if it were going to start ticking. We all watched and waited. Hoping. With slow deliberation, she placed her handbag on a sofa arm, re-crinkling the cover, and found her reading glasses.

'You won't need those, Mum,' I said. 'It's all about the smell.'

'Actually, it's better if you close your eyes,' Edie suggested. 'All you have to do is sniff. Or, even better, let the scent come to you. When you're ready, I'll waft it under your nose.'

'Waft? Isn't it usually bad smells that waft?' Mum looked at me, to Jean and back to Edie again. When no one reacted, she sighed, 'Well, alright then, I'm ready.' She closed her eyes. Edie lifted the lid and circled the candle. Mum's nose twitched.

'Waft again,' she said, her eyes still shut, mouth twitching in concentration. 'And again.'

Edie glanced at me. I shrugged. I couldn't tell if Mum's repeated smelling was a good sign or not. Three more times Edie perambulated the candle in front of my mother's nostrils. We all held our breaths. If you could hear air moving, I heard it, loudly amidst the silence.

Then Mum spoke.

'*Mon Dieu!*' she said, sitting upright. Her eyes opened. 'I wasn't expecting *that*.' Mum's gaze drifted out the door and down the street. For a minute, we lost her. No one dared speak in case she never came back. It was like watching her thoughts tripping and skipping to a new land, away from us. Far, far away. Finally, she returned. She looked at me, then not at me, at somewhere else entirely.

'When I found her,' she said, 'she was like a puppet lying flat and all that was needed was string to pull her up and get her moving again.' She looked dreamy, as if the thought of Lily as a puppet were a reassuring one. 'I tried to resuscitate her, but nothing happened. She was floppy and heavy in my arms. I never wanted to let her go.' Mum's voice faded to an almost inaudible whisper. 'The day it happened, your grandmother gave me a bouquet of lilies. I can still smell the rain around us and the lilies in the living room.' She wiped an eye. 'Dear me . . .'

I sat down next to her and put a hand on hers. 'We didn't want to upset you, Mum.'

'I'm not upset. I've been transported back in time.'

'I thought we needed to bring Lily back,' I said. 'To have her in our lives again.'

'You know, Oliver, I've wanted to do that for years. But your father . . . He didn't want to talk about it. Or maybe he couldn't. So I didn't either. We corked our emotions as if they were model ships in a glass bottle.'

Edie picked up the box of tissues and handed it around like a church collection box. We all took one and blew. A chorus of noses to lighten the mood and make us giggle. Then Mum said, 'Can I keep it?'

'Of course,' Edie said. 'It's a gift.'

I gave Mum a sideways hug. She leaned into my armpit. It was as good a hug as we'd ever had. In that moment, it was like no one else was there. It was just Mum and me, reconnecting, like we should have done long ago.

'Alright, that's enough,' she said, resuming her non-sideways hug position. 'I'd like to read the label now.' She put on her glasses. 'La Lumière de Lily,' she said. 'Anything in French sounds nice, doesn't it?' Then she looked up, peered over her spectacles. 'I don't suppose you have time to make one of your father?'

We watched Mum trundle back to her car, carrying the candle as if it were a crown on a velvet cushion. She was a round shadow in a dimly lit street. A wind whipped itself into a frenzy then eased, as if being sucked away by a vacuum cleaner. Jean patted me on the back and congratulated us.

'You've won over a tricky customer,' she said. 'I think Doreen will be most supportive of your business idea now.'

We watched Jean leave, too, her handbag resting on the crook of an elbow and the fabric belt of her dress waving us goodbye. I shut the door and swung the sign to 'Closed' as reception succumbed to a navy dusk. We breathed in the serenity of a few seconds of silence, contemplating the success of Mum's candle, until Edie spoke.

'I'm sorry about your sister,' she said. 'How she was never spoken about.'

I shrugged. I didn't want to make a big deal of it. 'I didn't even realise myself until recently what silence in the face of tragedy does to people. Most of the people I know don't even realise I had a sister.'

She touched my arm. I stared at her hand. And then it happened again. I entrusted Edie with my deepest feelings and opened up to her about Lily in such a way and in such detail I had never done to anyone before, not even with Andy. I told her how Lily died, how it was never spoken about, how *she* was never spoken about. How I often wondered what sort of person Lily might have been, what sort of sister, and what sort of person I would have been, had I grown up with a sibling. How, if I'd known about Dad, I could have been there for Mum. How we could have talked together, reminisced secretly amongst ourselves, laughed at the toy elephant I stole and comforted each other whenever there was a lightning storm.

Edie squeezed my hand. 'I'm so sorry, but I'm very glad I could help in some way and, you know, I'm always here to listen.'

I turned away, cleared my throat. 'Anyway,' I said, composing myself, 'enough about me. How's your dad? Is he doing OK?'

'He has his good days and his bad days.' She shrugged.

'Have you made any progress on his candle?'

'I've gone through so many iterations, particularly to do with his love of fishing and camping. The fish smoker in the back garden, seaweed, insect repellent, trees and cigars, but nothing has been right.'

'You'll do it,' I said. 'It will hit you when you're least expecting it to.'

'I know, but you know what? I've decided to wait. You're right, I should concentrate on being with him and not worry about memorialising him just yet.' She paused, looked at her feet.

'There's no rush, is there?' I said.

'I have thought about making a candle for you, though,' she said.

'Me?'

'I was conjuring scents of chocolate cake, freshly pressed linen, the cologne you wear and marmalade.' She tilted her head as if to summon the scents into the room with us.

'Marmalade?'

'You seem like a marmalade kind of a guy.'

It was then that I realised the strange effect Edie was having on me. I wasn't solely admiring her ability to transform candles into something so much more, or her easy-going, friendly nature. Or even her femurs. I was falling for her, really falling, as if the speed at which it was happening meant a safety cushion would be needed to protect my landing. It was a terrifying thought. Sweat formed on my temples. I felt a lip twitch coming on. We were going to be working together. You can't mix business with pleasure. It was foolish. Nonsensical. Risky. I wanted to run. To skip out the door and not let her see my fear. Not let her see the effect she was having on me. My heart quickened, my mouth turned desert-dry, tongue sticky-tape sticky.

Then I remembered the new Oliver Clock. The Oliver Clock who could dip out of his comfort zone every now and then and embrace a new zone. The Oliver Clock who could make decisions based on what was right for him, who didn't need his mother to cover his wounds with embalming foundation or talk to cadavers to make sense of the thoughts in his head. The Oliver Clock who could let go and face his fears. I wiped my brow and looked at Edie, her green eyes flecked with yellow like the feathers of a lorikeet. She smiled. I think her lips had moved. Had she said something?

'Oliver?'

'Pardon?'

'Would you like me to make a candle of you?'

As I stood like a shadow in the darkening room I could already feel tomorrow's sun rays beckoning a new future. 'Well, that's very kind,'

I said, 'but I don't think I'm ready to be immortalised into a candle just yet.'

'Not even scented like chocolate ganache cake with cherries on top?' She laughed.

'Not even that,' I said. 'I've got more living to do.'

And the new Oliver Clock came up with a brand-new resolution he vowed to start immediately: *Thou shalt give chase and get the girl.*

ACKNOWLEDGMENTS

Immersing yourself in your imagination is one of the joys of being a writer, but bringing a work of fiction out into the world requires so much more than that. This book could not have emerged alive and kicking without the help, advice and encouragement of the following people: my agent, Ariella Feiner, whose enthusiasm and positivity is infectious and whose keen editorial eye worked wonders, as well as Georgina Le Grice and Molly Jamieson at United Agents, who also championed my book from the beginning. The amazing Sammia Hamer and the team at Lake Union Publishing, as well as the wonderful editorship of Sophie Wilson. The sage creative counsel and rigorous mentoring of the effervescent Kathryn Heyman.

My early readers and unwitting support crew: Sandy Leen, Catriona Ling, Sandra Rigby, Nicola Gates and Jane Liggins. My mum, Joceline Wilson, who encouraged grammatical correctness and a love of books from an early age. My dad, Dennis Wilson, whose ability to invent fantastical bedtime stories and silly limericks knows no bounds and who bequeathed me a very 'Wilson sense of humour'. Simon Tebbutt for introducing me to Paul Tobin, who provided insider knowledge of the funeral world. My daughters, Hannah and Amy Riley, who indulged in my made-up letters from the tooth fairy for longer than was believable.

And, most of all, to Will Riley. His unwavering belief in me from when I first put fingers to keyboard, as well as his honest feedback, not only encouraged me to make real the crazy characters in my head but helped make the birth of my third child possible.

ABOUT THE AUTHOR

Jane Riley began her career in public relations before moving into publishing and later launching an online e-commerce business. She has freelanced as a writer and editor and wrote a design blog interviewing makers and creators. She volunteers as an English language tutor for the Adult Migrant English Program in Sydney. *The Likely Resolutions of Oliver Clock* is her first novel.

You can find her on Twitter @JaneRileyAuthor.